THE RIFT

Frederica Pratter

THE RIFT

iUniverse books may be ordered through booksellers or by contacting:

iUniverse
1663 Liberty Drive
Bloomington, IN 47403
www.iuniverse.com
1-800-Authors (1-800-288-4677)

Because of the dynamic nature of the Internet, any web addresses or links contained in this book may have changed since publication and may no longer be valid. The views expressed in this work are solely those of the author and do not necessarily reflect the views of the publisher, and the publisher hereby disclaims any responsibility for them.

Any people depicted in stock imagery provided by Thinkstock are models, and such images are being used for illustrative purposes only. Certain stock imagery © Thinkstock.

ISBN: 978-1-4502-2698-1 (sc)
ISBN: 978-1-4502-2696-7 (hc)
ISBN: 978-1-4502-2697-4 (e)

Print information available on the last page.

iUniverse rev. date: 11/04/2016

Acknowledgements

Frederica thanks her husband Paul J. Pratter for the sharing of ideas that led to the original concepts of this story, his scientific input and his inspiration and encouragement.

The Earth is in equilibrium with marvelous biochemical systems, which are constantly abused by us as we are abused by our fellow humans.

Enlightened humans should be capable of rational behavior at all times—however, at best, it is to say that they are only capable of rational behavior at certain times.

Why is it we cannot function with respect for the incredible complexity, which keeps us living?

Paul J. Pratter (Ph.D. Organic Chemistry)

Scientific explanations of the world does not exclude the role of God in creation.

Pope Francis.

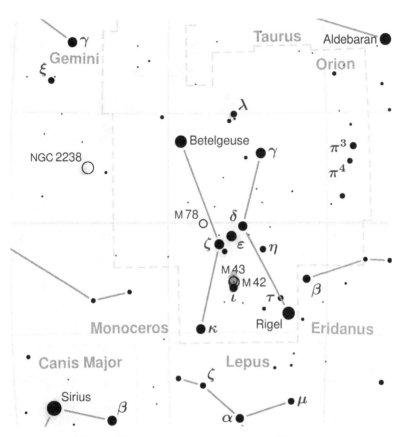

THE CONSTELLATION OF ORION

FOR PAUL

Contents

PROLOGUE

OUT OF AFRICA

Looking from space at the planet Earth one can see the great continent of Africa, which is marked near its eastern shore by a large, long groove that runs along almost the entire length of the continent. This indentation or break in the planet's crust is called the Valley of the Rift. It is not a valley in the common sense. It is an immense deep, scar in the surface of the Earth that in anthropological terms is called a rift. The Valley of the Rift was created by an unprecedented event, happening about two hundred fifty thousand years ago.

In the part of the Rift Valley, today known as Tanzania, lies the ancient Olduvai Gorge, the mysterious cradle of humanity. It is the sole place on this planet that holds the secret of how and why humans exist on Earth. For the local tribes the Olduvai Gorge is a sacred place that has highly inspired their spiritual and ritual imaginations with supernatural wonderment. And, to this day, it has mystified anthropologists from all over the world, who come to dig at the Gorge, where an unimaginable harvest of fossils and bones can be found—some dating back millions of years.

The rush to discover the conundrum of the origin of humanity on Earth and of the planet's past populations has brought anthropologists and scientists of all kind to the Olduvai Gorge, the most fertile fossil ground on the planet. They are all feverishly looking for ancient digs hoping that one day they will find *what* is the Rosetta stone of anthropology, "the missing link".

Ever since Darwin published his theories of evolution, biologists and anthropologists wanted to believe his theory. They were clinging to the hopes that the gaps in the fossil records would eventually be filled in, and "the missing link" in the evolution of humans would be discovered, proving Darwin's theory of human evolution from the ape. However, when it became clear that "the missing link" would never be found because it was not missing, the hopes of the Darwinists were destroyed. There now is scientific evidence that ape-like hominids and Homo sapiens, intelligent humans, are not related. They are two different species.

Ape?—

Human?—

Homo sapiens—homo meaning man and sapiens meaning intelligent or spiritual— are a species that suddenly and inexplicably appeared on Earth around the same time the ape-like hominids disappeared. This is one of the great mysteries in the history of our planet.

Modern DNA research proved what before could only be suspected. There is no consecutive link in the DNA between hominids and Homo sapiens. Hominids evolved for millions of years as Darwin theorized, but then something unexpected happened quite suddenly. A DNA change or a sudden mutation of the chromosomes of hominids created intelligent human beings.

Human intelligence and the human spirit, even though not used fully by most humans, are some of the most puzzling, wondrous things that ever came about. They are a gift from heaven that is more often taken casually and which is considered something that is habitually owned by humans. It is a gift that is misunderstood and abused above all by the followers of the mantras of evil, the followers of Satan.

Where did this intelligent spirit, which makes the difference between ape and human, come from so suddenly?

How? — Why?

EAST AFRICA 250, 000 YEARS AGO.

At the time, this part of Africa was more like the original Garden of Eden. It was a sunny paradise where many species lived in a pecking order that followed the ideal design of natural evolution. It was the finest moment and place in time that would ever arise.

The land was prepared and fertile. It was time the universal spirit should be sown so that it could grow and flourish to fulfill the promise of the beautiful blue planet.

The particular part of the Valley of the Rift, near the Olduvai Gorge, is now arid. Then it was covered with a vast, saline lake with white, sandy beaches and with water as blue and as lovely as the sky. The lake itself was a primeval broth filled with plankton and jellyfish that grew enormous.

A great variety of mammals and birds lived around the lake eating the choice vegetation. Hominids of the species homo erectus were the most developed creatures in the area. They walked upright and stood six feet tall. They were strong, dark-skinned, with some body and facial hair and their sloped foreheads had prominent brow ridges. Their fingered hands enabled them to make stone tools, and they gained coordination in the process. Simultaneously they developed hunting and fishing skills. The hominids also began to understand the concept of gathering and preserving and they learned to build limited homesteads. They were not promiscuous, but usually lived in family clusters.

Scientists today assume that these hominids could experience feelings like love, loss, happiness, and sadness. However, they were not able to express these feelings well. Also, due to the position of their larynx and the lack of a hyoid bone, the hominids did not have the gift of speech. To communicate they used some sort of sign language making sounds with different pitches.

The cataclysmic event that happened in this land like paradise, 250,000 years ago, was a very recent one considering the time frame of the Earth's development. As, in anthropological terms, a few hundred thousand years are just like a puff of wind. However, in spiritual terms, what happened at this point in time, was the most decisive event in the billion year-old history of the planet Earth—the creation of humanity.

Under the wide African sky, dotted with pink and white clouds, lay the shimmering lake. Around the lake, the voices of many animals could be heard. Their harmonies echoed across the clear, blue water.

The sun, hanging low in the sky, had not descended yet when deep shadows were cast over the land and a strong, hot wind began to blow that sucked the moisture from every living thing.

With wrinkled foreheads above deep-set eyes, the worried hominids looked at the sky, sensing an impending disaster. They glanced at each other and then quickly looked away.

The air became hotter and dryer as the wind evaporated leaving cracked skin and parched lips. The animals mewled, howled, and moaned in the surrounding vegetation. Anxious hooves scraped rocks and hard, dry soil. Dry vegetation crackled in the still, ominous air. Looking up through the cloud of dust the hominids shrank from a bright, white orb in the sky. Relentless, the orb moved closer determined to hit its target.

Suddenly all sound ceased. Where were the animals? Why

weren't the leaves rustling? What happened to the birds, the wilder beasts, and the slap of fish breaking the lake's surface for a gulp of air? Silence disturbed the hominids, for their survival depended on their attentiveness to their surroundings. Usually, their environment provided signs and signals guiding them to food, shelter, and safety—usually, but not now. The hominids looked at each other, then back to the sky. Shifting their weight from foot to foot, they shuffled in place, sensing that something extraordinary was going to happen.

Strange sounds filled the air as the temperature rose. The sky darkened and the oxygen was sucked into a black funnel that appeared in the distance like a borer dissecting the wide, blue sky. The funnel approached rapidly. It touched down like a malevolent index finger and drilled a large hole into the ground spewing orange dust into the atmosphere.

A blast of sound, a cacophony, caused the hominids to cover their ears and hunker down on their haunches.

A Cosmic Presence, a gigantic, glowing dodecahedron in the shape of a twelve-pointed, even-sided cross, appeared in the sky above the cluster of the hominids.

The tornado that seemed to be coming out of the Cosmic Presence expanded.

Straight now, erect like a black beam drilling into the ground with enormous power, deeper, wider, the tornado grew and grew sideways. As it absorbed the fractions of the sunlight's spectrum, one by one, it turned into a steady mass. The mass grew—snatching, grabbing, and taking red, green, blue, and yellow elements of the light. Day turned into night. Liquid darkness replaced the day light.

Then, the tornado ceased. The mass was now a black storm cloud lined with red flashes. Consisting of super-magnetic fields, converting liquid gases into plasma energy, the Cosmic Presence above, seemed to react with another element. It emitted searing white flashes that criss-crossed with energetic needles. An ejection of a large, mercury-like bubble followed. The bubble was driven by a brilliant white light. Haloed by laser lights the bubble streamlined as it came down with forceful speed. As it suddenly diffracted sound and color culminated in a crescendo giving way to the vibrations of silence.

In the velvet darkness, myriads of phosphorescent blue-green photon particles floated down like fluorescent rain, illuminating everything. The photon particles adhered to all organic matter, delineating animals, plants and even the translucent jellyfish and giant plankton in the water. Every living thing was outlined in blue-green transparency.

Shaking and pressing together the hominids huddled in fear. It was a futile effort to escape the inevitable. They turned away from the rain of light particles engulfing them and outlining their bodies in translucency. They pushed and pressed into the center of the group, the larger ones forcing the smaller ones out to the edges of the huddle. Grunting, screeching, with desperation rising from their throats, large lips pulled back, exposing sharp incisors. Heads turned back and forth as hairy hands grasped and pulled at the limbs and trunks of those who had claimed interior space. Like surface tension on a drop of water, the group shifted, expanded, and finally shrunk in a futile effort to disappear.

A mesmerizing sound started softly and then trebled in volume as the bubble released an intense light shower, which suddenly covered and immersed the hominids that still were frozen in fear.

The fluorescent particles of the light shower aligned themselves like strings of translucent, glowing pearls, forming the spiraling bands of a double helix that encircled the group of hominids who stood paralyzed.

A breath, a sigh, and then the undulating double helixes

weakened. They were drawn back upward, re-entering the bubble, which was suspended in mid air like a harvest moon reflected in the lake's black mirror surface. The bubble doubled in size. A cosmic blink and the bubble popped, sucking the darkness into its core before it disappeared into the heavens above. It left only daylight, stillness, and the future of humanity in its wake.

Silence surrounded the hominids. One by one, they peeled themselves away from the core of the group. Looking skyward, they saw the ominous Presence above, which was still in the distinct shape of a twelve-pointed even-sided cross.

As the Presence was paling, the hominids looked at each other. They had changed. They felt a paradigm was shifting them that was not obvious at first. They could not figure out if what had happened was a happy or sad event. Pale and drawn, as if their strength was sucked out of them, they looked around. The land around them was unchanged. In their lethargy they did not know what they should do, if anything. The supernatural spirit had called them but without direction or instruction.

They looked up at the sky, where the configuration of the Cosmic Presence was now turning into an intense glowing form of heat. Sensing the heat with increasing terror, the hominids feared they would be burned alive. Trying to escape the heat, some of them ran to seek the cooling waters of the lake. Others ran up the mountainside, seeking shelter in the deep caves above the forest.

Now, the configuration in the sky changed. It transformed itself into a fuzzy, fiery ball, which, as it was sucked upward with enormous speed, became a streamlined comet. As the comet-like Presence left the Earth, an enormous cataclysm happened in the wake of its departure. It left behind a stream of scorching heat, causing fires to flare up in the hills and valleys. Thick black smoke filled the air, turning day into night. A heavy meteor shower came down, battering the creatures unable to escape. It flattened the vegetation, and broke the trees of the forests like straws.

A reverberating thunder came from the center of the Earth, which turned into a roar unlike anything ever heard before. It was followed by the sound of deafening explosions echoing through the land. The ground trembled and shook violently. The lake's water rose upward. A gigantic wave turning into a steamy cloud which was sucked into the atmosphere. The valley, where the lake had been, caved in and broke apart and the churning ground sucked all animal and plant life into a maw.

The quake created a gigantic rift between the valley's west side, which rose to form a mountain chain, and its east side, which rose high and then fell back to the ground forming an arid, barren desert. So great was the cataclysm, it changed the weather in the region.

The super-intelligent entities, inherent in the Cosmic Presence that had visited planet Earth, were content. They were contained in a streamlined comet, traveling through space with such speed it looked like it was standing still. They had some awareness of the scarring disaster the impact of their departure had caused, but this was of no consequence to them. It did not make a difference. According to the laws of time and space, cataclysmic events occurred constantly, continuously shaping and forming the universe. The space bound entities did not care about the great scar in the Earth they had left behind, as long as some of the newly created Homo sapiens survived as the bearers of the universal Spirit. The comet, traveling through space and time, was later seen traversing the Milky Way, where it soon disappeared near the constellation of Sigma Ori in Orion.

The small group of hominids from the lake was now a changed

species. They did not know they had become Homo sapiens. Whatever had happened to them during the visit of the cosmic Presence had weakened them considerably. Their physical strength was transformed into something spiritual which, located in their brains, caused an unstoppable chain reaction. They were infected with a virus of unknown origin, mutating within, causing them to think rather than to react. In the foggy silence of their minds, the piercing ray of thought appeared, immediately conceiving, questioning, and inventing.

Some of them, even though physically weakened, were elated to the core as they felt the surge of the human spirit enter their human minds. Others were fearful not knowing what to make of the new feelings, which fulfilled their human souls.

One of the larger males looked up. He pointed his outstretched arm to the sky and waved his hand. His voice came out warbled. He uttered an expression of wonderment in a language that was not invented yet. The others realized they just had heard the first utterance of a symbolic sound that signified the image of the highest entity—God.

Only the new Homo sapiens who had ascended to the forests of the valley's west side escaped the great disaster. Most of them were able to scramble up the hill, which, at one point had risen under their feet like a wave that carried them upward.

Many of them stayed on and made their new home in the caves of the west valley ridge. Others went on. Their small groups went into the green forest below the far side of the ridge that stretched to the end of their world. As they migrated through the forests and across the valleys and plains, which provided everything they needed, they knew something had happened to them during the visit of the Presence, the fluorescent rain, and the ensuing natural disaster.

Illness had befallen many of them, which in modern times could have been explained as a sort of viral influenza, but at the time was inexplicable and strange, because there had never been such a thing as illness among them. On occasion, they had experienced weakness due to inbreeding, but there was never such a thing as the feverish malaise they now experienced, which was too much for some of the older and weaker ones. They died within a short time. Most of the younger ones, however, recovered from the malaise quickly and became immune to it. During the periods of illness, they lost most of their body hair. The females lost their facial hair, their skin became lighter and more subtle.

The strangest, amazing, and perhaps most frightening thing was the change in the appearance of their heads. Their brow ridges disappeared and their craniums became enlarged. With most of their body hair gone and with their thinning skin and thinning blood, they had to protect themselves from the elements of weather. They began to make frocks and sacks from animal skins and plant matter they used to cover their bodies.

The new Homo sapiens were not aware that, within only one generation, their bodies developed a hyoid bone and a larynx, and that their sign language became enhanced by the utterance of sounds, which soon became words. An actual tongue developed and the Homo sapiens became more and more skilled in using language to communicate.

Another new experience was laughter. It is not known how it began. One day, one of the younger females started laughing. It was a bright and sunny morning. She made a happy purling sound that was contagious and that spread like fire among them. It was the same female who, on another beautiful, easy morning, felt so happy, she imitated the sounds of birds. As she sang a wild, sweet song the rest of the group became so enamored with the sounds she made they fell to their knees and worshipped her like a goddess.

1.

STYNFELDT

CAMBRIDGE, ENGLAND, SEPTEMBER 1940.

Not only was Professor Frederico Stynfeldt one of the most controversial minded professors at Cambridge, but he was also dean of the paleontology department. He was one of many brilliant scholars at Cambridge who always kept an open mind and who constantly searched for the truth despite of the overwhelming traditions and premises that century old colleges, like Cambridge, implied on their researchers.

Stynfeldt had published many papers, and he was writing his first book, which already had found a publisher. But this was before the war had started. Now, it seemed, everything had slowed down and many projects were on the back burner.

Some of the anthropology and paleontology students liked to make a little fun of Stynfeldt's name. Stynfeldt or Steinfeld meant, "stony field." It was very appropriate for someone spending a lot of time out in a stony field digging for fossils. However, Stynfeldt, who was half-Dutch and half-Italian, did not care about their well-meant innuendos. He had not been out digging in years and he was so overwhelmed with work he had no time for anything extra, not even an evening's beer in the local pub at the Eagle Inn.

Marthie and Leo Anderson, the most celebrated paleontologists of the time, were famous for their advanced work in bio-paleontology and archeological finds. They were not only Stynfeldt's colleagues but they were also trusted friends. They had just returned from East Africa to the anthropological laboratories at Cambridge with some highly unusual specimen and twelve extraordinary minerals they had found at the Olduvai Gorge. Professor Frederico Stynfeldt was in charge of aiding, supplying, and supervising the lab. He sometimes worked with the Andersons, helping them with the enormous amount of research that had to be done.

Stynfeldt looked out the window of his second floor office. On the lower part of the building, on the other side of the courtyard, he could see a metal door and two windows with metal rails indicating the lab and office of the Anderson's. He tried to light his pipe but failed. Sucking quietly on the cold pipe, he looked down at the lab's lit up windows. "Too dangerous, a lethal situation," he told himself, knowing in that lab, at this very moment, was kept the most controversial anthropological find of all times. The air coming through the stem of his unlit pipe was reminiscent of his last bowl of tobacco, slightly sweet with the bitter aftertaste of smoke.

He thought of Hitler's recent tirades about race. The Arian race versus the Jewish race, et cetera. Right down there, in the Andersons lab, was proof Hitler's theories of race were pure lunacy.

He nervously thought of putting a guard at the lab door. On the other hand, a guard in front of the Andersons lab would probably draw too much attention.

Looking up he could only see a small patch of the evening

sky beyond the roof of the opposite building. The patch of sky was crimson red.

Stynfeldt, still chewing on his cold pipe, walked down the stone staircase. Stepping out of the building, he first thought of going over to the Andersons lab, knowing they worked at all times of the night regardless of the hour. When he looked at the crimson strip of sky between the buildings he changed his mind. The intensity of the colors in the evening sky gave him an eerie premonition something was going to happen that night. As a scientist, he would never share these feelings with anyone else. Empirical evidence was the only reliable support of natural phenomena, but as he was of a mindset coming from experience, he was forced to acknowledge the wisdom of his gut, his instincts.

The clear September night was unusually mild and rather lovely, no need to put on a coat. He walked through the ancient doorway of the courtyard, outside of the college walls. Darkness had fallen on the fields and grassy parklands. The sky was still lit with the residual light of a spectacular sunset—above a line of turquoise blue, it was filled with a foreboding glow—crimson red.

Stynfeldt was a down to earth man, not a mystic, but looking at the blood-red sky, he sensed somehow that something terrible was going to happen. He heard a dull, steady drone somewhere in the distance. It sounded loud, then louder as it came closer,
— louder and louder—

Squinting, he saw their black silhouettes against the red sky. The flight of the *Walkuere.*

At first, he counted thirty bombers. But they kept coming and coming, filling the sky with their presence and the drone of their engines. He gave up counting. The bombers, followed by hunters, just kept coming. The *Heinkels* and *Junkers* flew in a rather open formation, and then converged right above him. It was clear where they were headed—the city of London. Looking at the planes, coming with incredible certainty, Stynfeldt felt painfully powerless. He waved his fist at them. "Damn you, Hitler! Damn you! Damn you! Damn you to hell!" Biting down on the stem of his pipe still jammed in his mouth, he stared after the planes flying on unstoppable. He knew it would only take minutes until the first bombs would explode in the city.

Turning back to the walls of the college, he struggled to capture his breath and he felt his stomach wrench while tears streamed down his cheeks. Pale faced, a cold sweat breaking on his forehead, he clenched his fist around his cold pipe, yanking it out of his mouth and stuffing it into his trouser pocket as he walked back to his office.

Locking after the labs, where scientific or politically sensitive work was conducted, was the rule. Stynfeldt had the only passkey to the Anderson's lab. He knocked at the iron door three times and then he used his key to open the door.

Marthie and Leo Anderson were so busy working on their discoveries they had no idea of what had just transpired outside.

Stynfeldt came in the door trying a faint smile. He was going to introduce the frightening news, gradually.

Thirty-six years old, Dr. Marthie Anderson, wearing a white lab coat over a subtle floral print dress, was in the back of the lab analyzing tiny bone samples from two skeletons they had found in a shallow grave at the Olduvai Gorge.

Her husband, Dr. Leo Anderson, in his late thirties, handsome with dark hair showing the first silver, wore a white lab coat over his Harris Tweed suit. Deep in thought, he typed with staccato precision on an Underwood typewriter. Hearing the door close behind Stynfeldt he looked up and smiled before continuing his work.

Unaware of the troubled look on Stynfeldt's face, Marthie rushed over to him. "We're close—so very close. Fred, come look!"

Marthie said, pointing at her microscope and apparatus. "It's all here. We can almost prove it—almost, but not quite." She pointed at the skeletons laid out on sheets of thick, soft, brown paper on one of the lab benches. "These humans were created by changing the chromosomes of hominids. Darwin was wrong. Humans did not evolve. They were created. And, if we are lucky, I think we also have found the original male and female—Adam and Eve—the forefathers of all humans on this planet today."

Stynfeldt nodded, containing the complex mixture of his feelings beneath a cool smile. "How could so much chaos be going on outside this bastion of science at the same time the Andersons were about to make history?"

"And, as you know, Professor, these rocks prove it," Marthie continued. "They are made of a crystalline form of carbon, more rare then diamonds. Nothing like this has ever been found at the Gorge. The rocks had to come from an outside source. It seems they were planted in the grave to give us some kind of message."

Stynfeldt looked at the twelve geo-faceted rocks, blood red, diamond-like minerals the size of his fist. He narrowed his eyes to validate what he thought he was seeing in their gleaming interior. "These are incredible. When can we conclude the research phase and publish the paper?"

Marthie looked directly at Stynfeldt. "Only a little bit longer. We are almost there."

Stynfeldt thought how pretty she looked with her dark curly hair, her blue-green eyes, and her pale skin flushed from the excitement of the discovery.

Leo stopped typing. He looked up. They heard distant thumps sounding like explosions.

The glass beakers, test tubes, and Petri dishes rattled slightly with each impact.

"Earthquake?" Leo asked.

"It's not an earthquake," Stynfeldt said. The damn Nazis are here. They are *blitzing* London."

"Oh, no!" Marthie said. She dropped into her chair, grasping her elbows, and pulling her arms into her body, as if protecting her center from the horror happening outside the sanctuary of the college. "Oh, no! Oh, no!" Shaking her head back and forth, she uttered her mantra.

Leo looked at the two of them. As comprehension dawned, his face turned ashen. Pulling himself together, he stood up and went to his wife at her desk. Placing a comforting hand on her shoulder, he looked at Stynfeldt. "Well, it was to be expected—I didn't think they would do it so soon—but it was to be expected. And the RAF is not ready yet, to defend us against the bastards. God help us all!"

Stynfeldt pointed at the fossilized skeletons and the twelve minerals. "We better get this evidence into the bunker."

Knowing what he meant, Marthie began to mentally classify and sort the specimen and samples on the table in front of her. She would pack up everything and send it to the underground vaults and archives, where Cambridge's most valuable scientific evidence was kept during times of jeopardy like this. "We are almost ready. I have about six more hours of work with these. And Leo is almost done with the paper." She pointed at a medium-sized, black and yellow carpetbag. "We brought all our findings from Africa in this bag to England. It should do well for us for now. We are going to wrap everything nice and securely and put it into the carpetbag. Leo will take the bag to the vault."

Stynfeldt nodded. "It's not the most professional way to store or transport evidence of this magnitude, you know that. However, I guess, in an emergency like this it will do. You can always store and preserve everything the right way, after the Nazis are gone."

"Yes, Fred, you are right as always. I also think we should go to London tomorrow, to see if we could help. We are both medical doctors and we could be needed."

"That's right," Leo said.

"I am sorry," Stynfeldt said. "I cannot let you do that. You cannot go to London—too dangerous. Besides, you might be medical doctors as part of your studies, but you are paleontologists in the first place. Your responsibility is not to the individual. You must see the greater picture. All of Cambridge's scientists must stay on and continue their work. And, maybe then, we'll beat that Austrian-boor-son of a bitch."

Somehow, word had gotten around like light-fire. There would be a mid-night gathering and mass at Great St. Mary's Church. A meeting meant to calm the worried souls and to make them part of a community while they were trying to think of what should be done in this harrowing situation.

At midnight, Great Saint Mary's Church, the University church of Cambridge, was not, as usual, shrouded in mist. The Nazis had figured out the weather just perfect. September 7, to September 8, 1940 was a clear night.

The thousand-year-old church overflowed with people. It seemed darkness was everywhere, in the blacked out streets, on Market Square, in front of the church, inside the church lit by a few candles, and in the minds and hearts of the gathering crowds.

When Stynfeldt entered the church, he could barely see them but he felt the angst and desperation of the faculty, staff, scholars, and common people of Cambridge, who filled every nook and cranny of the church spilling out into the square. The great, old organ played at half-treble. A few voices were heard singing, *Dona Nobis Pacem.*

This was almost too much to bear for Stynfeldt. He saw the crowd as the last bastion of the spirit of humanity attacked by technocratic Huns. Stynfeldt's shoulders stooped forward. He took a deep breath of the cathedral air and he sighed deeply.

"Fred, Fred," dimly voiced Marthie and Leo pushed toward him and gave him a hug. Stynfeldt could feel their despair over the bombings and their feelings of helplessness and pain.

They stood in the crowd waiting for the vicar to deliver the sermon, which not only would console and lift their spirits but also give instructions how this war situation was to be handled in Cambridge.

"We finished the project." Marthie whispered to Stynfeldt. "I packed most of everything, including our notes, into the carpetbag."

Stynfeldt tried to see her face in the dark. "Did you take it to the bunker?"

"No, I told you. The vaults are closed until morning. Leo will take it then."

Unfortunately, the next morning was clear again. Stynfeldt always complained about the weather in England. "Fog and rain, rain and fog," he would say. "Where is *o sole mio?*" Yet, this morning the sunshine was not welcome. A little fog would have put off the Nazis from bombing London—maybe.

Stynfeldt woke up late. In his striped pajamas, sucking on his cold pipe, he made himself a cup of tea. He turned on the radio—the news was that the Nazis were still bombing London relentlessly. "They want to break us, but they won't. Because England is older and wiser than any country in Europe, and the RAF will beat the *Luftwaffe* any time," he said to himself. He wanted to believe his own words, but he was not sure he could.

The phone rang. Stynfeldt took the receiver from the wall-mount and put it to his ear. It was Marthie calling from their small house in the quaint town of Burwell, about ten kilometers outside Cambridge.

"Good morning, Fred."

"I'm not sure it is a good morning."

"We turned on the news. The Nazis are unrelenting."

"Yes. Are you good? How is the baby?" (The Andersons four-year old daughter was always referred to as the baby.)

"Oh, we came home very late. The nanny was great. The baby is fine. We are all fine, but tired."

"I can understand that. So am I—very tired—of war and the horrible things Homo sapiens do to each other."

"The reason I am calling, dear Fred, I want to remind you, we didn't have a chance to take the carpetbag to the vault. It is all packed and ready to go. We locked it up in the lab. We need to take care of things here—we won't be in until later—I'm asking, if you could take the carpetbag to the vault?"

"Well, I'd better do that. Don't worry. I'll do it."

"Thanks', dear Fred—and take care of yourself."

"I will. And good luck to you all." Stynfeldt was a little surprised that Marthie called him dear Fred. But, given the circumstances it was understandable that she was emotional.

Stynfeldt was a little nervous about arriving late at his office. A few doctoral students and faculty were in the antechamber waiting to talk to him. He was glad to see that, even after a night of a bombing raid on London only 80 kilometers away, life went on in Cambridge, as it should. He briefly acknowledged the waiting people. "Good morning, I will be right with you." He then quickly went into his inner office.

It was over an hour later, after Stynfeldt had discussions with two scholars, when he suddenly remembered Marthie's phone call. "Dear Fred, take the carpetbag to the vault!"

He got up from his desk and went over to the window. He looked down at the yellow building across the courtyard. It seemed the iron door to the Anderson's lab stood open at a weird angle. Stynfeldt's blood froze. He turned pale. He ran out of the office. "Excuse me, an emergency!" he told the people in the waiting room." Pulling out his latchkey, he ran down the stone staircase and across the courtyard as fast as he could, only finding he did not need the key. A precise round hole had been chiseled out of the door where the lock had been.

The lab was ransacked. Tables and chairs were pushed around and broken glass and papers were strewn all over. It looked like the place had been turned upside down and rummaged through.

The carpetbag was gone, and with it the evidence of the Anderson's findings.

Stynfeldt's first impulse was to use the phone, but he then thought better. He pushed the button of the fire alarm. Within minutes, the shrill sound of the fire alarm brought on two security guards. He knew it was no use, but he yelled, "quick, search the premises! Look for anyone carrying a carpet bag!"

Two more guards appeared at the door.

"And you stay here and make sure no one touches anything!" Stynfeldt yelled at them as he ran out the door, across the courtyard, and back up to his office. He fell into his chair, grabbed the phone on his desk, and dialed the Cambridge operator. "This is Professor Stynfeldt! This is an emergency! Call the local police! Then give me Scotland Yard! And, operator, after that call the Andersons, the number is Burwell 358. I am standing by at my office."

Stynfeldt sat in his chair, trying to think what he should do next. The phone rang.

"Yes, operator."

The operator's voice sounded cool. "Professor, the police should be arriving any minute. I could not get through to Scotland Yard. No one can get through to the city now. They are in a state of disaster. But I will keep trying."

"And the Andersons? Burwell 358?"

"I rang that number twice, but there was no answer. I will keep trying that one too."

The police came and talked to Stynfeldt, who explained everything they wanted to know. They snooped around the Anderson's lab for some time that seemed endless. Then, they secured the iron door and put a seal on it.

Stynfeldt was in a state of exalted nervousness.

The operator was not able to get through to Scotland Yard in London. And, as many times as she tried the number in Burwell, there was no answer.

At around four in the afternoon, Stynfeldt sat at his desk, searching aimlessly through some papers.

The local police supervisor was in uniform. Stynfeldt could hear the clicking of his boots as he walked up the staircase and into the open doors of Stynfeldt's office.

Stynfeldt looked at him. "Sit down, please."

The police man was firm, "thank you, but that's not necessary. I have some news for you."

"Let's hear it."

"There was an accident on the road to Burwell this morning. A black Austin was hit by a milk truck. The milk truck was speeding down an agricultural side road. The Austin turned over. It was catapulted into a wheat field. The milk truck disappeared without a trace. It was a hit and run."

"You are trying to tell me it was the Andersons, aren't you? The Andersons drive a black Austin."

"Yes, it was them. And the child was in the car with them."

"What happened to the Andersons? Where are they now?"

The police chief looked around with an eerie expression. He really did not want to say anything. But then he got a hold of his official voice. "Both the Andersons are dead. They are in the morgue," he said.

Stynfeldt let out the air of his lungs with a whistle of despair. His face turned white. His body slumped down in his chair, as if a heavy blow had knocked the life out of him. He looked at the police chief. His voice was toneless. "What happened to the baby?"

"The child was found in a wheat field nearby. There was not a scratch on her. We called the child's grandmother. She picked her up at the hospital."

2.

DEATH IN ROME

THIRTY YEARS LATER

In the pink light of ages, the Eternal City in the misty, blue distance looked more like a mirage.

In the countryside near Rome, a gentle breeze came up from the blue lake Albano cooling the green hills crowned with the old buildings of the town of Castel Gandolfo and the ancient pink castle, which was the Pope's summer residence. It was a place closer to heaven than to earth.

High in the hills, a sun-filled meadow, deep with weeds and grass, brimmed with the wild flowers of late summer. On the far side of the meadow was an old farm building which belonged to the estate of the Pope's castle. Near the farm building was a grouping of old trees, thick with green leaves that gently moved in the breeze, casting shadows on the ancient walls.

Maria Magdalena, an easy spirited, young nun from Castel Gandolfo, took an afternoon walk. Her face was full and innocent and her white, speckled skin was slightly pink from walking in the sunshine. She walked, contemplating the lovely countryside, and she decided to pick some flowers for the altar of the Virgin Mary. As she crouched down to pick the flowers, humming a Hail Mary, she felt the air change suddenly. She could not say exactly what it was, an ever so slight atmospheric change, or the cool breeze, which now, it seemed, had turned hot. Her tearing blue eyes were drawn to the grey wall of the old farm building, where she saw light reflections that looked like the headlights of cars projected on the wall. The lights seemed to form the twelve points of an even-sided inverted configuration, which reminded her of a cross. This was strange, she thought, and she felt a little frightened. She could suddenly feel her heart beat. There were no cars or even bicycles around. Where did the light reflections come from? "Probably sun rays dancing through the branches of the trees which look like light spots on the wall," she told herself. She felt hot now, and the yellow sunlight suddenly looked strange. She was not sure of what she saw. Now it seemed dark shadows were cast onto the same wall. She stared at the wall, thinking of past miracles, apparitions and the like. But this was different, this dark shadow was projected from behind her. Maria Magdalena turned around.

In the contrasting light, the silhouette of the cross looked like an ominous black scarecrow in front of the bright, blue background. The cross was erected on the hillside in the middle of the meadow. The pitiful figure clinging to the cross looked like a bundle of black rags.

Maria Magdalena's first instinct was to run, but she stood very still, not wanting to move. She felt the cross drawing her in like a magnet. Coming closer, she could first smell the nauseating stench of death. Then she saw it clearly. A priest had been crucified. Just the thought of seeing a priest crucified was about the most repugnant thing she could ever imagine. It was as if they had killed the innocent lamb of God all over again.

Stepping closer, she forced herself to look at it. She tried to open her eyes wide, which took an effort because her eyelids wanted to stay closed. Her hands dropped the flowers she had just picked. She reached deep in the pocket of her habit for the small, hand-embroidered handkerchief she always carried with her. Finding the handkerchief, she pulled it out and held it to her nose. Feeling weak in the knees, she forced herself to look straight at the object in front of her. She tried to be analytical and cool like the detectives she had read about in her mystery stories.

The priest, in his black robe, was bound to the cross. His head was pulled up and back by the garrote that strangled him. The wire had cut deep into his throat. His black tongue protruded from his narrow mouth. The heat of summer had already taken its toll. Flies buzzed about the priest's blue-green, swollen face, which looked grotesque. Maria Magdalena looked at the thin, twisted body of the priest. She looked down at his hairy, skinny legs in his worn down, lace-up boots that dangled from under his robe, which was pulled up in the process of the hanging,

Maria Magdalena swallowed deep. She tried to keep herself from throwing up. The grass around the cross was growing tall and undisturbed. It should have been trampled on or pushed down, she thought. There were no footprints or paths through the grass, or any other signs that anyone had been there. There was just this ghastly thing in the middle of the meadow.

Maria Magdalena looked at the distant walls of Castel Gandolfo looming high up on the hill. Coming down the hill had been easy. Trying to get back up there, in a hurry, was like trying to climb Mount Everest. She looked at the dead priest one more time and crossed herself. She then turned around and forced her feet to run uphill through scratching thorns and stinging nettle as fast as she could. As the back entrance to Castel Gandolfo came in sight, she threw her arms up in the air and she screamed breathless. "Help! Help!"

The Swiss Guards, in their historic uniforms, guarding the castle's entrance, at first did not understand what the screaming, red-faced nun, running toward them, meant.

When she reached the Swiss Guards, Maria Magdalena fell to her knees. Her wavering arm pointed down the hillside. "It's the priest," she screamed." The priest is crucified!"

One of the Swiss Guards quickly passed his old-fashioned pick to the other guard to hold. He reached into the narrow guardhouse and pulled out a semiautomatic gun.

He pointed the semiautomatic at the sunny hillside Maria Magdalena had just come up. "Is there anyone coming up behind you?" he yelled.

"No! No!" Maria Magdalena yelled back. "The priest is dead."

The Swiss Guard, still holding the semiautomatic in one hand, fetched Maria Magdalena. "Calm yourself," he said as he lifted her up. "Call the *Vigilanza* and call Swiss Guard backup," he said to the other guard, who quickly disappeared into the guardhouse to make the calls.

"Let's go inside," he said to Maria Magdalena, walking her across the courtyard into the castle.

Castel Gandolfo, filled with breezes from Lake Albano below, was one of the Pope's favorite places. It was his vacation home, where he stayed during the long, hot Roman summer. Even though, this was not a real vacation, and he still had to follow a harrowing schedule. Here in the countryside he could relax a bit, walk in the lovely gardens and look down at the lake, which, on clear days, was so blue it rivaled the sky. Maybe some night, he would put on a business suit, go out to one of the local restaurants, and talk to every-day people.

Maria Magdalena was just a kitchen helper in the castle's kitchens, which was feeding over a hundred people most of the time. She was not supposed to approach the Pope, or to talk to him without an intermediate. However, this time, the Swiss Guard took her right into the antechamber of the Pope's quarters, which was guarded by the Spanish Cardinal Alvaro de Castaneda.

The Cardinal sat behind a large, antique rose wood desk. "What is the matter, child?" he asked.

Maria Magdalena told her story, teary-eyed. As soon as she finished she sensed a rustle of fabric, a whiff of incense, and then the Pope himself appeared in the antechamber.

"What is the matter, child?" The Pope repeated the words of the Cardinal.

Maria Magdalena fell to her knees. She had seen the Pope many times from afar and in the castle's church on Sunday. Seeing him, this close and in the same room, was like seeing the face of God. Sobbing, she told her story again.

The Pope, with kind eyes, took her hand and lifted her up. "We must pray," he said. "Please go to your chamber and pray."

Maria Magdalena wiped away her tears and straightened herself up. She looked directly into the Pope's sky blue eyes. "Yes, your Holiness," she said, "we must pray."

The Cardinal picked up the receiver of a purple colored phone on his desk. The connection clicked, "Ormani—Security," a voice answered.

"You know who this is?" the Cardinal spoke into the purple phone.

"Yes."

"Okay. I think we might have some trouble here."

A gendarme of the Vatican *Vigilanza*, with a piece of paper in his hand, appeared at the open door. He bowed deeply. "Excuse me for interrupting—your Excellency—your Holiness. We found this on the priest. We think it could be important."

"Excuse me," the Cardinal spoke into the phone again, "we do have some trouble here, indeed. I will call you right back."

The Cardinal hung up the purple phone and stretched his arm out toward the gendarme. "Give it to me!" He grabbed the paper, dismissed the gendarme, and went back behind his desk to study the paper.

"What is it, Alvaro?" The Pope asked.

"I don't know, Papa, it is too early to tell. It seems one of our priests has been murdered in a very gruesome manner and there is some kind of ransom note."

The Pope's blue eyes grew wide. "Who would want to murder an innocent priest?"

"We don't know, but we might have to consider interrupting your vacation and moving the papacy back to Rome."

The Pope shook his head. "But you know this would be very complicated and it could draw a lot of attention. Whatever it is, I think, we should ride it out here at Gandolfo. The castle is like a fortress, easy to defend."

"With due respect, Papa, we only have one dead priest and some sort of blackmail. We must analyze everything before we decide what we should do next."

The Pope smiled his caring smile. "You are right as always, Alvaro. I leave it all in your capable hands. In the meantime, I will go and pray for the priest. Do we know his name?"

"It is all still under investigation. I will let you know his name as soon as we find out."

The Pope expressed gentle concern. "Thank you, Alvaro, you are a true pillar."

The Cardinal picked up the purple phone again...

3.

REVELATION

ROME AND THE VATICAN, 30 YEARS LATER.

Laura d'Andres was not a secretary, but the assistant to Count
Ormani, who was a nuncio to the Vatican and the head of Vatican
security. Laura's job in a high level, trusted, and vital position
in the Vatican was most unusual for a woman and it was not
honorary but it paid handsomely. Laura was grateful for her
position and the work she was able to do. She did her very best
to meet her responsibilities knowing her job was unique in this
world.

Count Ormani, a high-ranking Maltese knight, came from
one of Rome's oldest families. As such, his job at the Vatican was
entirely on an honor basis.

As a young orphan, Laura was adopted by Amanda Ormani,
the Count's sister, who changed Laura's family name to d'Andres.
Laura grew up in the Ormani family castle in the Toscana.

At age thirty-four, she was a lovely, slim woman with porcelain
skin, dark curly hair, and green-blue eyes. At first sight, she seemed

delicate, but she could show that she possessed great strength and that she could defend herself if necessary. This was due to police training she had received by the Roman police after she finished her studies at the University of Florence, and she had obtained a masters degree in anthropology and a Ph.D. in religious science. She began to work for the Count at a time the Count was in charge of the Bank of Rome.

Laura's life in Rome was simple and complicated at the same time. Her job at the Vatican and her connection to the Ormani family put her in a somewhat rarefied position. Her work consumed her. There was not much time for friends or lovers. She regarded many of the nuns and priests, who were so plentiful in Rome, as her friends and family. In addition, the Ormani's castle in the Tocsana was always open to her during vacations or holidays. The eternal city itself was the home she loved. Other than that, in her mind, she remained a grown-up version of the orphaned child for all the time she ever remembered. Vague shadows of her parents and things they had taught her remained in her thoughts and dreams. She sometimes looked at the statue of the wolverine suckling the founders of Rome—Romulus and Remus. She was like them. The city of Rome was her mother and the Vatican was her father.

At the end of a long day, Laura felt overwhelmed and tired. The thought that she was all alone in this world was depressing her and she knew she needed a break.

She decided to take a short walk to one of her favorite places. It was a place that combined incredible beauty with incredible spirituality, a place where she felt like a little girl looking at the wonders of the world. It was a place that gave her the feeling that she was in touch with her parents, who died long ago.

The Sistine Chapel was gloriously serene. Subdued rays of

light streamed through the clerestory windows. The misty twilight painted dots of color in mysterious places.

Laura felt like an angel, in between heaven and earth. It was not clear if she imagined or actually heard bell-like voices of Gregorian chanters sounding as if they were coming through mystic channels from centuries past.

Standing at the chapel's back entrance, she saw a priest holding a tall cross made of ebony and silver. The priest walked down the center of the chapel toward her. Laura thought she was seeing a vision. This was unusual, because most of the time the chapel was either full of tourists or, as it was in the early evening hours, empty. The priest was accompanied by two altar boys wearing red cassocks and white surplices. The boys gently swung their holy incense kettles. This was even more unusual because incense of any kind was seldom allowed in the chapel for fear it might damage the magnificent frescoes and paintings covering every inch of the walls and ceiling.

Laura loved the scent of incense. Her eyes followed a thin stream of holy smoke going up to Michelangelo's frescoes depicting the creation of Adam. As the priest and the boys passed by her, the priest, murmuring prayers, blessed her with the sign of the cross. *"In nominee Patrii, et Filii, et Spiritus Sancti*—In the name of the Father, the Son, and the Holy Spirit."

The last rays of sunlight came through the clerestory windows of the chapel, illuminating the interior, so densely covered with priceless art, it looked like one huge mosaic made of glowing jewels.

As she walked down the center of the chapel her thoughts drifted back. She tried to remember her parents. What was the message they had tried to instill in her. She heard her father's voice sounding in her mind again. "Can you tell me what this is all about?"

Maybe it was the feeling of being in the chapel, which, like a temple, combined art, religion, and culture in the highest sense. Laura suddenly knew the answer to the question, "what is this all about?" It was a simple question, to which the answer was more complicated than obvious.

She could barely make out the ceiling in the falling darkness when a small dot of light briefly touched the center painting to the left. It was "The Creation of Adam". The painting depicted God in heaven, surrounded by heavenly beings. God reached down to a man on Earth, touching his finger. The touch of God, like a spark, ignited Adam with the spirit that made him human. Laura stared at the image and she remembered that the gift of the spirit was not only to be human, but beyond this, to be enlightened. It was men's responsibility to use the godly spark to light the fire of enlightenment within so that the full meaning of God could be understood and man himself could live in the image of God.

She had wondered about the Holy Spirit, which was sometimes called the Holy Ghost, since her childhood and she tried to imagine it. She vaguely remembered her mother telling her that the Holy Spirit was a substance, like stardust, that was brought from heaven to Earth to change monkeys into humans. This was hard to understand, but it seemed to make more sense now. As such, the Holy Spirit was the most wonderful thing that had ever come into the world, the spirit of humankind, creating art, music, poetry, science, and progress. Above all, it had accomplished more than one could ever imagine in the fields of science, technology and the welfare of human beings. She remembered her parents saying the human spirit was a gift that, like a seed, was planted in us, and we should cherish and nourish so that we could progress toward enlightenment.

Laura began to see it all with clarity. It was so obvious. The human condition had become worse. The spiritual seed was not growing, it was drying out, and it was in danger of dying. The human spirit was not going forward but backward. Humans were becoming worse than animals, much worse than the monkeys they were supposed to have come from. It was as if the spiritual seed, before dying out completely, had grown one last bitter root that, almost unnoticeable, had become grounded in the Devil's black fields of hell.

What was it Michelangelo tried to express in the frescoes he painted while lying painfully on his back on a scaffolding close to the chapel's ceiling?

Laura's eyes filled with tears, as reality occurred to her. For centuries, the Church had painted and sculpted, expressed in music and in elaborate scriptures, the word of God as they pleased. The world's greatest artists, architects, composers, and poets, hired to do the work in the name of the glory of God, expressed the interpretation of the Church. Religious storytellers told a story about the divine truth, which became distorted and infused with the evil spirit of the Devil, planted subconsciously in the human mind, until it had nothing more to do with the truth. This lead to centuries of the Church's, sometimes, unholy conduct which was more often influenced by the devilish politics of ignorance, cruelty, and greed. Many great artists had known the truth and had tried to express it in forms not readily apparent to the clergy who fed them. They understood the universal truth and wanted to convey the message with clarity. The truth could be seen in great museums all over the world, depicted in paintings, and expressed in sculpture. It could be understood by listening to some of the great works of classical music and it could be experienced in the world's greatest architectural monuments.

From the beginning, there had been a devilish rift between the truth and some of the dogmas of the Church. How could they allow it? How could they let it happen? The thought of it made Laura's heart suddenly beat faster and she felt like she was going to pass out. She was overwhelmed knowing some of the clergy had been taken by the Devil and misinterpreted the truth for centuries.

Laura took a deep breath of the chapel's musty air to compose herself. She loved what she called the cathedral smell, a mixture of frankincense and myrrh married with the scent of the century old building and the scent of the artist's paint and sweat, which, of course, she imagined. Michelangelo's "The Creation of Adam" was barely visible right above her. Artists like Michelangelo and Leonardo da Vinci had known the truth she thought.

The chapel now had fallen into darkness. The coolness exuded by the old walls was soothing. The elaborate breath of ages permeated Laura's mind. It was as if she just had a vision of the divine, as if she had experienced a moment of enlightenment.

Laura exited the walls of the Vatican through a side entry not many knew about. Her apartment was in an old, quiet part of Rome, not far from the Vatican.

The castle of St. Angelo loomed ominous in the shadows. Laura wondered why it was not lit up for the tourists as usual. She walked on a narrow walkway above the river Tiber next to a small park. The buildings on either side of the river were purple silhouettes in front of a red and golden sky dipping into darkness. The ancient river below looked like it was flowing slowly.

She briefly stopped and looked up at the sky. The stars were out. Their sparkle was dimmed by reflections from the city lights. Her favorite constellation was visible in a very dark patch of sky, over a bridge down-river—Orion, the greatest constellation in the Northern sky, was hanging there at a strange angle. Why was this constellation so prominent among others, which represented the signs of the zodiac or were named after animals or pagan gods? Was it because Orion's symbolism should not be disregarded? Connecting the stars with lines, one could see in Orion a sort of stick figure with a head, two arms, and middle, girded with a belt from which hung a hunter's sword. Laura remembered her father telling her about the constellation of Orion, which was also called the Heavenly Hunter, or the Master of the Beasts. Orion was the subject of mythological stories and ancient sagas. Her father thought that what they called the Holy Ghost or the enlightened spirit of humanity came from a planet somewhere among the stars of Orion. The constellation itself was the symbol of a crucified man. The top star was the head, bent to the left, and the other stars were like the nails in the cross. Two through the hands, two through the feet, and a belt or loincloth at the middle. Her father never said it was Jesus. To him, it was a symbol reminding us of a man who had mastered the beast within and who had overcome his beastly instincts by enduring the ultimate suffering.

Laura looked down at the water from above, the river Tiber, a Roman thoroughfare through the ages. In the reflection of the city lights, the slow moving water looked like it was covered with a thin film of gold. Yet, she knew that under the surface the flow of the ancient river could be quite rapid, the waters were highly polluted, and big and small rats burrowed in the riverbanks that had not been cemented over. They lived in the waters and in the ancient drain and sewer systems.

Her eyes became drawn to a black mass in the distance on the embankment below. It was something that seemed to have been dumped on the cement next to the water's edge. First, she thought it was a dead nutria rat, which could get as big as a dog. But this was much bigger than a dog. Probably just a bag of garbage someone had left along the river, she told herself. Coming closer, she could see the black pile was crawling with hundreds of skirmishing rats. Standing on the promenade above the riverbank, she could see it better now. It seemed to be a cadaver shrouded in black cloth. Her heart pounded in her ears. Her eyes strained to see exactly what it was. She looked for stairs leading down from the promenade to the river, when she saw a cement embedded staircase, a short distance up-river near a bridge. She ran to the staircase and then stopped dead right on top of it. A large nutria rat sat in the middle of the stairs right below her. It seemed to be chewing on a human bone. For a moment, Laura stood frozen. Then she took a deep breath. "Nutria rats are not flesh eaters," she told herself. She picked up a rock and threw it at the rat. The rat scrambled downward and disappeared into a black drainage ditch.

Laura ran down the steep and narrow stairs, along the cemented riverbank, to the black mass. Her feet ran in a hurry now. She was stomping down on the soft bodies of hundreds of rats. Some rats were squashed right under her feet, some tried to bite her feet and ankles covered with the rat's blood and guts, some scrambled away to the river's edge. Her feet crushing the warm bodied rats to a pulp, sent a horrific message to her brain. She was living the most atrocious nightmare. Squash. Squash. She tried to avoid the rats, but there were too many of them. Her feet squashed them like ripe fruit filled with blood when she slipped and fell down on the cement next to a black clad body. The rats scrambled and scurried away.

Laura knew what she had found as soon as she saw the small silver cross dangling from the ivory colored beads of a rosary chain, which lay on top of the plain, black cloth of a nun's habit. She tumbled down and landed sitting on the blood stained cement. When she smelled the stench of decay, which had already set in, she held her breath desperately trying not to throw up.

The nun's pudgy, white face was grotesque. Her black, swollen tongue protruded from her mouth. The garrote, with which she was strangled from behind, had almost cut her head off. The nun's veil had been pulled off her head, revealing thin, white hair. Her robes were intact and dry. She had not been in the water. It seemed the Sister was strangled at the very spot Laura found her. Despite the distortion of death Laura recognized who she was. Sister Rosemary had worked in the Vatican kitchens. Laura remembered seeing her not long ago behind the cafeteria line. Sister Rosemary was making breakfast, serving coffee and warm pastries. She was vividly talking to as many people as she possibly could.

Even though, Laura was in a fog of pain and confusion, one lucid question came to her mind: "What was Sister Rosemary doing on the Tiber's riverbank in the middle of the night?"

Laura looked up and around herself. Nausea wrenched her stomach again and again, ice-cold terror gripped her pounding heart, and tears streamed down her cheeks. Trying to keep herself from screaming, she sat there sobbing until she got a hold of herself.

Kneeling on the cement in the tacky blood of the dead nun, Laura looked up. She could see a small part of the walls of the Vatican looming in the distance. From deep within, she wanted to say a prayer for the nun. She looked up at the sky. The sparkling stars of the constellation of Orion were still there. It occurred to her that the spreading outline of Orion now looked even more like a crucified man than a warrior or hunter. She thought of the priest who had been crucified and strangled the same horrible way as the nun. "The lambs of God," she whispered. "They are killing the innocent lambs of God."

Laura eyes wandered from Orion back to the nun and she prayed,

"The lord is my shepherd, I shall not want. He makes me lie down in green pastures, he leads me beside the still waters. He restores my

soul, he leads me in the paths of righteousness for his name's sake. Even, though I walk through the valley of the shadow of death, I will fear no evil for he is with me.

Saying the prayer had a great, calming effect on her. She thought saying prayers or chanting in any language or creed was like appealing to the forces of the Universe, which represented God. God was far too high above to be prayed to directly. But he could hear the hum of all prayer combined, which slowly melted the hardened ice of evil.

Laura knew she had done the right thing. Now all that was left to do was to call the police. But she was painfully rigid, and her knees hurt from kneeling on the cement. She tried to get up, when she saw a dim, yellow light on the promenade above. The light approached steadily. She stared at the light with a strange feeling, not being able to decide if what was coming was friendly or dangerous.

Clearer now, she could see what it was, and she sighed with relief. It was a person on a motor scooter. "What could be more harmless than that?"

The motor scooter purred closer and closer and then stopped dead on the promenade right above.

Laura tried to get up. She waved her arms. "Help! Help!" But the nun's unbending arm had fallen across her lap. It kept her down.

The cyclist got off the motor scooter. His figure stood tall and menacing right above her. He just stood there very still. It was as if time stood still too.

Laura felt as if, she was suddenly in a déjà vu of a nightmare. She could feel her heart pounding. She strained her eyes to see the man, but he was like a blurred shadow, barely visible in the contrasting light. Then, in the instant flicker of a passing light, she could see him.

The cyclist held a large rifle. He pointed it directly at her.

Laura almost stopped breathing. She saw the gunfire but she did not hear the sound of the shot. She let herself fall and tumble downward on the cement of the river embankment. Sliding down, she could feel the roughness of the cement scraping the skin of her face, hands, and legs. When she landed at the river's edge, she just let herself roll over and into the water.

The water was pitch black and cool. It carried her downriver fast. Knowing the river was more like a sewer, she kept her eyes shut and she tried not to get water into her mouth and nose. She kept below as long as she could. When she saw red circles in front of her eyes, and her lungs shriveled inward, her body clenched and then burst into one great gasp for air, blasting her upward. Sucking in the night air, panting, heaving, breathless, she drifted faster now, but thanks to the grace of God, she thought, she floated right into a dilapidated old rowboat, which was moored in the water dead ahead of her.

The boat's rusted metal stern hit her hard in the chest and almost knocked her out. Squirming with pain, Laura tried to grip the metal stern of the boat, but her slim hands could not hold on to it. She was going under, drifting right past the boat when her foot became entangled in a sort of line or rope arresting her tumbling body. She somehow found the slippery rim of the boat again. Her slithering hands grappled on and she lifted her head out of the water. Trying to catch a breath with heaving lungs, she managed to look up-river. She could not see anything clearly, but it seemed the shooter had disappeared.

Mustering up the last bit of strength, she pulled herself up. Her feet found the bottom of the shallow part of the riverbed. Staggering, she waded ashore.

A couple of young lovers on the river bank thought they were seeing a ghost or a scene from a horror movie when they saw

Laura's terrible, black silhouette emerging from the river. Her hair and clothes clung to her body and she was covered with blood, mud, and sand.

Laura's voice came out faint and hoarse, "get the police!" she cried out, before she crumbled to the ground.

4.

NEW YORK

On one of those warm, lingering summer days, the air in mid-town Manhattan was sweet and clear. The usual crazy Manhattan boogie went on in the streets.

A pigeon looked down the sun-filled steeples of St. Patrick's Cathedral to the cool concrete of the streets, where the small figure of a priest was seen. The priest wore a charcoal grey suit, accented by his black bib and white, starched collar. He walked quickly from the Archdiocese's office, across Fifth Avenue, up to Rockefeller center. He was deeply caught up in his thoughts. As he walked across the plaza, he briefly looked up at the sculpture of Atlas holding up the world.

Entering one of the tall buildings that formed Rockefeller Center, the priest headed straight for the elevators. The elevator stopped at the eighteenth floor. He got out. He walked down the corridor to suite number 1813, the offices of the private investigator firm of Mauser and Cordes.

The receptionist looked at the slim, Spartan-looking man

who had previously been announced by New York's Archdiocese of Saint Patrick. She buzzed the intercom, "Mr. Cordes, Father Renquist is here."

The room was bright and filled with sunshine. John Cordes was a cosmopolitan, medium tall, man in his late thirties. His easygoing good manners and looks defied the fact that under his light unstructured suit was a well-trained, muscular body with alert reflexes. As a former CIA agent he was not only in top notch condition but he also had in-depth experience and knowledge of international crime and terrorism.

John took his feet off his large desk. scattered with files and stacks of paper. He jumped up to shake hands with the priest. "Please, sit down," he said, pointing at a visitor's chair.

Father Renquist sat in the chair. He briefly glanced around, noticing a silver frame with a color photograph on John's desk. It was a snap shot of happy looking, pretty, young woman, tossing a delightful looking, young boy up into the air.

John Cordes eyes met the priest's. "My wife and son.—What can I do for you?"

The priest cleared his throat and winced. "I don't know how to say this. I am here not as an emissary from the Archdiocese of Saint Patrick but as an envoy of the Vatican. You see—it is not easy to convey this—but the Vatican is being terrorized."

The look in John's cool, grey eyes intensified. He could not hide a nuance of sarcasm. "So you are here to tell me, the Holy Church is in trouble?"

The priest got up and went over to the water cooler. He took one of the small paper cups out of the holder. "May I?"

John's voice was slightly impatient. "Of course you may! And please, call me John."

"Okay, John." The priest sat down. He sipped the water like

a nervous little bird. "Can I trust you to keep what I am going to tell you confidential?"

"I am a professional, I have handled hundreds of cases with discretion."

"I know, John. We checked your background. I have personally seen your dossier, your work in the drug and terrorism world. With your former CIA connection, it seems you have a very good grasp of what is going on in the underground in many parts of the world. And though, you are not a member of the Church any longer, we know you are trustworthy—" The priest took another sip of water, uneasy. "You see, John, someone has gained access to the Vatican Secret Archives. They have taken controversial documents and other evidence, which, if made public, could become very embarrassing and potentially explosive for the Church."

John nodded, "I see."

"The Vatican Secret Archives are not accessible without a special permit. In order to gain access, scholars and clergy must present a case for what they are looking for, before they are admitted. It is almost impossible to penetrate our security system. Whoever took this evidence from the archives and delivered it to the enemy was an insider. You probably know how dense the Vatican security is. And our intelligence is even better—a worldwide network."

John's thoughts drifted back. The priest was right. John had come upon secret agents of the Vatican and their work several times during his career. He had encountered their feelers connected to the CIA and other intelligence agencies around the globe. John recalled a paramilitary with a killer instinct who went by the name of Raphael. He was supposedly an ex-Vatican soldier, before he became a world-class terrorist. This was years ago, when John had ties to the CIA.

John's mind wandered forward to the present. "You are telling me, they didn't get this evidence just by walking in, or breaking in, because both scenarios are impossible?"

"Correct, John. It was an inside job. And they are threatening to publish whatever they have, unless we pay them five hundred million dollars."

"Is that all?" John said. Do you know in what form the money is to be paid?"

The priest's Adam's apple moved as he swallowed. I do not know the details. The message we got from Rome was that this is beyond the ordinary scope of what Vatican security is used to handle. They need help from someone who has international experience. We know what kind of work you do, John. You are one of the best terrorism profilers in the world. Count Ormani, the head of Vatican security, is asking for your help in this precarious situation. And believe me it is very unusual for the Vatican to call on an outsider instead of relying on their own security and intelligence network."

"That's right. They have plenty intelligence of their own. Why would they need me?"

"A case of extraordinary proportion, John. Your expertise is needed, and you know the Church pays well."

John looked at the picture on his desk. "I don't doubt the Church pays well. But money has no meaning. As a former Catholic, I would be willing to help the Vatican. As I told you on the phone before, I am in no position to travel to Rome. I'm afraid I can't help you at this time."

The priest's kind and knowing eyes looked at the picture in the silver frame. "I heard about the accident," he said. "I am truly sorry John."

John's grey eyes blinked. "It has been almost two years now since the crash. My wife died instantly. My little son Eric was in a coma for three months. When he woke up, he would not, or could not, speak. He has been undergoing treatments in a psychiatric hospital ever since."

The priest cleared his throat, "I understand, John. You must pray for courage, acceptance, and wisdom."

John tried to hide his despair and emotional emptiness. "Courage and wisdom I can understand, but acceptance would be hard."

"I know. I know. I understand your grief, but I also have to insist you must help us. They killed a nun and a priest in a horrible way. Imagine—crucifying a priest. It is sheer terror. They are sick. If we do not meet their demands, they are threatening to kill every nun and priest in Rome, bomb the Vatican, and kill the Pope. They are attacking the world's holiest shrine. We cannot allow this to go on. What if they attack other religious symbols around the world, temples mosques, and synagogues? Don't you see we are at the brink of cultural and religious anarchy?"

John nodded. "I admit this is not an ordinary case, but I can't leave New York at the moment."

The priest did not want to hear it. "What prompted you to leave the Church?" he asked, evading the subject. "You are not a Free Mason or part of any lodges are you?"

John frowned. "If I had a connection with any such groups you would know it. Wouldn't you? I am not against the Church. I just think the Roman Catholic Church is supposed to spread the gospel of Jesus, who died to save the spirit of humanity, but they are so self-serving they do a very bad job. The Church does not lead its followers into enlightenment—it leads its followers into confusion. And they do nothing about their ties to unsavory crime organizations and certain Masonic lodges who will commit any crime, pretending they are protecting the faith."

"Well, John, I am sorry to hear this, because I think that

deep in your heart, you are still a believer. I think your point of view is very interesting. I hope and pray that one day you will understand the ways of the Church again and you will see us in a different light. But right now, I am not here to convert you back to our faith. At this point, I would say, as far as this business is concerned, your personal beliefs don't matter, and I am only here to ask for help from someone who is qualified to help—and that's you, John."

The priest insisted. "You must help us. As you know, miracles do happen, especially to those who—"

John picked up the thought. "Like celestial brownie points, you mean?"

The priest nodded with a kind expression. "Something like that."

John could not help but sense the priest's compassion. He liked him. He thought the priest's arguments made sense. "It's not the Church. It's my son, Eric."

"What about Eric?"

"They say he could be coming around soon. It is important, I be here with him when he comes out of his autistic state."

"What if I promised that if you went to Rome, I would visit your son every day? I am very good with children. I have seen some cases like this. I think, maybe I could help a little."

John was still undecided. "Maybe. I don't know. I am going to visit Eric in the hospital this afternoon. Would you like to come with me and see him?"

"I would be delighted." The priest smiled reassuringly.

"My secretary will give you the address. Say, can you meet me there at four-thirty?"

After the Father left, John tried to collect his thoughts. "No phone calls for the next ten minutes," he told his secretary. He was tempted to go over to the liquor cabinet and pour himself a drink. Talking about his wife's death and Eric always did this to him. It left him wanting to take a drink, and another, and then one more, and so on. He remembered Diana who had kept him from drinking too much. "Just be drunk with life," she would say, "and not with whiskey." He thought of Eric, their son, who had been dealt such a tragic blow so early in life he could not handle it. But, at least, there was hope that with special care and the healing gift of youth, he could come around.

Father Renquist seemed to be at ease visiting Eric in the rehabilitation hospital. "I told you I have been in this hospital before, and I have helped with similar cases. I know what to do to some degree." He looked toward heaven. "The rest is up to modern medicine and the Almighty."

That afternoon, Father Renquist taught Eric how to play chess, winning the child's trust and affection. From then on, the Father visited the handsome nine-year old every day, rain or shine. And John found some reassurance seeing that Eric visibly enjoyed the Father's attention.

When John saw, how content Eric seemed in the father's company, he felt easier. Finally, he changed his mind, and let the father convince him, it was all right to leave for Rome, where he was urgently expected.

Father Renquist had one more request, before John left for Rome. He wanted to get Eric a dog. "Eric has been asking me in his own special way with drawings and descriptions by hand. He wants to have a dog. I have made the necessary arrangements with the hospital. They said it was O.K. for Eric to have the dog if certain rules where met. What is most important, Eric remembers you had a boxer when he was little. You know that kind of dog with soft lips. Eric drew the dog and wrote the word Satchmo next to it. Was that his name Satchmo?"

"Of course! Why didn't I think of it? Our boxer Satchmo! He is still lives at the house. Most of the time he is alone with the housekeeper. I am sure, he misses Eric just as Eric misses him. And there is that old record that Diana always played for Eric, telling him the singer's name was Satchmo too."

On his way to the airport, John stopped at Eric's hospital one more time, where he saw a scene he would not forget too soon. Father Renquist and Eric were in the hospital's lounge room. They were deeply involved in a game of chess. Eric had his arm around his large, brindle boxer dog, who too was watching the game, absorbed, just like Eric. Satchmo-Louis Armstrong's old song was playing on Diana's old record player.

"I see trees of green, red roses too.
I see them bloom, for me and you.
And I think to myself what a wonderful world..."

Standing in the doorframe of the room, John did not want to interrupt the scene. He felt Eric was content, and it made him feel content too. Father Renquist looked briefly at him. John signaled him. "Good bye. Give my love to Eric. I am off to Rome."

5.

THE VATICAN

They did not meet in the Vatican's assembly building which was a large, modern building that could seat over 6000 souls. They met in one of the inner assembly rooms, reserved for high council. The air in the room felt dense and hot. The Holy Father himself was present. He had interrupted his vacation unofficially and had come to Rome for the day.

Vatican security had skipped all routine measures it would usually take to bring the Pope back to Rome officially. They had just driven him back in a bulletproof, black limousine which was followed by several heavily armed utility vehicles.

Il papa was seated in an elevated chair on a stage framed by red velvet curtains. His white robe and scull cap underlined his pink complexion. His face reflected the learned innocence that is only mastered by high spiritual achievement of mind and soul. His hands moved gracefully, from time to time touching the bejeweled, golden cross he wore on his chest.

The room's silken red walls were adorned with precious paintings and mirrors resplendent. The ceilings were covered with magnificent frescoes. The room was filled to capacity with high-ranking church officials.

Nuncios, Bishops and Cardinals from all over the world talked to each other under their breaths, murmuring with subdued voices, trying to find out why they were brought to Rome for this emergency meeting. They wore their red cassocks and scull caps which was thought to enhance the beauty of the priest in his external behavior, but which also symbolized that they would defend the Pope to the point where they would spill their own blood if necessary.

At each of the flanking walls were four fierce looking Maltese knights, the defenders of the faith, in their black hooded mantles embroidered with the typical white, eight-pointed crosses. It was not common knowledge, but most of the clergy in the room knew the Church knights belonged to the militant order of the Knights of St. John, and the Militia Christi. They were SWAT teams on high alert, armed to their teeth, and carrying such modern weapons as MPK 2000 submachine guns, pistols, and bayonets under their decorative cloaks. They had been called to come to the aid of their supreme commander, the Pope, by Count Ormani, a top ranking master in the hierarchy of the Maltese order and the head of Vatican security.

The Swiss Guards, in their fifteenth-century blue, red, and yellow striped uniforms and their funny looking plumed helmets, guarded the closed doors at the far side of the room. Despite their outwardly clumsy and old-fashioned appearance, they were fully trained, armed soldiers.

Below the Pope's staged chair was a podium with a microphone. Count Ormani, an aristocratic looking Romanesque man in a black business suit with a small platinum Maltese cross pinned to his lapel, was in the process of addressing the assembly.

Laura d'Andres was the only woman in the room. She sat at a

desk, which had been set up unobtrusively to the side of the Pope's stage. Her hands briefly touched a sizeable folder placed on top of the desk. The black folder was marked with the insignia of a white Maltese Cross and the words TOP SECRET. In her pinstriped designer suit and white silk blouse, she looked thin and elegant. Her dark curly hair and bright blue-green eyes accented her white complexion. Working a stenographic reporting machine, she looked up at the Count attentively from time to time.

The uneasy hum filling the room suddenly quieted. The Count was ready to speak. A tall, imposing looking Cardinal of the African contingent, seated in the rows toward the middle of the room, stood up impatiently. All eyes followed him. His husky, deep voice resounded clearly. He simply said. "Can you tell us what this is all about?"

The Count looked at him indignantly. "Sit down, please!" He waived his hand with a perturbed gesture. "I will explain it, as far as I understand it."

Laura relished the poignancy of the African Cardinal's question, but she was still not certain she knew the answer, even after the Count had described and explained the precarious situation the Church was in.

First, a priest had been found in the countryside near Castel Gandolfo. And then, a nun was found dead, strangled on the banks of the river Tiber. The priest had been murdered similar to the nun. More precisely, he had been strangled with a wire garrote, and he had been bound to a cross. It was not known if the priest was strangled before or after he was crucified. A note was found on the priest. It said the priest was chosen to die by an organization for the advancement of science who called themselves A.P.S. If their demands were not met, more priests and nuns would be killed, the Vatican would be bombed, and the Pope would be assassinated The Count did not really know who or what

A.P.S. was or what the letters stood for. He conducted a search throughout the Church's international intelligence network, but it turned out no one knew anything about A.P.S. or an organization for the advancement of science.

The note also said that A.P.S. was able to retrieve scientific evidence from the Secret Archives of the Vatican, which proved that most off the Vatican's centuries old dogmas were wrong to the point of being ridiculous. The complete Catholic doctrine was a hoax, built on a gathering of fairy tales, and there was strong evidence that life on other planets existed. They demanded to be paid five hundred million dollars, or they would publish the evidence and continue killing priests and nuns, wherever they found them, until their demands were met. Instructions on how to conduct the payment of five hundred million dollars were given—

"A fine mess this is," the Count concluded his address of the assembly. "And it all sounds like the lunacy of a crazy man. However, we cannot underestimate the threat, because it is real. That is why we had to bring all of you to Rome. So you can help us find and fight this unknown enemy of the Church—an enemy who is devilish, brutal and dangerous—an enemy who does not understand what our dogmas are all about. Someone who is against everything the Church stands for. Someone whose strength or deliberation we do not know. And what is worse—we do not know what they potentially could do to us because we all know the limitations of our defense mechanisms. Meaning, if they want to blow up the Holy See tomorrow and kill the Holy Father, we really do not have much to put up against them. The Roman police are already involved, in conjunction with the Italian secret service agency. We have also contacted the government of Italy, trying to get protection of the air space of the city of Rome, including the Vatican.

6.

UNHOLY TERROR

John arrived in Rome during the early morning hours. He was pleased the Vatican had made his travel arrangements first class. In the plane's front compartment, he was hugged comfortably by his sleeper seat and the sound of the jet's engines felt like a lulling hum. For the first time, in years, John had relaxed as if he was sleeping in a cradle.

After he checked through customs John took a taxi to one of Rome's older luxury hotels, the Excelsior. He showered and dressed in a light grey business suit anticipating the first meeting with an envoy of the Vatican around noontime. John did not think he would come to Rome and be allowed to just walk right into the Vatican. However, the Vatican's prerequisite that he had to meet their representative at the hotel first, seemed like a waste of precious time.

The Hotel Excelsior was not too far from one of Rome's liveliest piazzas, the piazza Navona. John decided to take a walk there and have breakfast in one of the sidewalk cafes.

It was the perfect Roman morning. Church bells were

ringing, pigeons were purring, and the typical tourists were taking pictures. The eternal city seemed to be rewarding its citizens and tourists alike with its spectacular sights. John breathed the light air. It made him feel at ease. He felt fit to deal with the heavy task that loomed dangerously close.

As usual, Laura d' Andres enjoyed her morning cappuccino in one of the most popular sidewalk cafes at the Piazza Navona. In her yellow linen suit and white silk blouse, she looked fresh and relaxed.

However, Laura's outwardly relaxed look was pretended. Ever since the horrifying murders of the priest, the nun, and the threat to the world of the Vatican, the center of her life, Laura was in an agitated state. It was not just that some usurpers who had found a weakness in the Vatican's thousand-year-old dogmas were blackmailing the Vatican. It was a threat against everything spiritual. She nervously tried to sense the menacing enemy, fearing that bombs could explode in an instant. However, the familiar Roman morning scene was somewhat calming her nerves. It seemed the world she knew was going on in its usual way. And the sight of an extremely attractive looking American in a light grey business suit, who was sipping an espresso, was even more reassuring.

John looked at Laura from behind an Italian newspaper he held upside down. He smiled at her with a boyish smile and he said, "sorry for staring, but do I know you? I think, I have seen you before—in a museum maybe—have you ever been to New York?"

"I was in New York a long time ago as a student, but now I live in Rome, the greatest city in the world. I love Rome, don't you? I am sure you have never seen me before. But, I believe I know who you are."

John dropped the paper. "Is that right?"

Laura nodded smiling faintly. She took a sip of her cappuccino. Her eyes wandered across the sunny piazza. Japanese tourists with cameras took pictures of one of Bernini's great fountains. A group of seven nuns in white habits and winged hats walked across the piazza in file murmuring prayers of the rosary as they walked.

The sound of screeching tires struck the scene like lightening. The car, a black Maserati with tinted windows, came slamming around a corner heading toward a pedestrian zone.

On the crosswalk was a pretty, young woman who was holding the hand of a girl about eight years old. In the flash of a moment, they were hit by the Maserati, which came roaring at them like a huge black meteor striking a flock of small birds. Mother and child evaporated from sight under the racing car.

The car raced on and, with a loud screech, stopped in front of the nuns. Three men, wearing black ski masks, jumped out. Two of them wielded guns they fired wildly into the air. A stray bullet hit one of the nuns in the center of her forehead. Another nun was shot directly in the heart.

Laura's vision, with sudden shock, became overexposed. She could see the bullet hole gushing and blood staining the nun's white robe. For a moment, Laura stood paralyzed with fear. Then, electrified in panic, she focused on helping the nuns—the dear Sisters she knew so well.

People around her cried, screamed, and scrambled. Some tried to hide under cars and the marble topped café-tables.

Laura's first instinct, too, was to hide under one of the tables. But then, she desperately wanted to help. As if in slow motion Laura got up from the table. She pushed through the crowd toward the nuns. She reached the first nun, who had fallen to the ground, and tried to lift her up. Looking at her Laura knew the Sister was dead. She gently let the limp body glide out of her hands.

One of the gunmen grabbed the Mother Superior. He held a gun to her head. He pushed a packet into her hands and he yelled into her ear. "Make sure you deliver this to your pappy-pope and no one else!"

He pointed the gun directly at her face. "If you try anything, we will kill every nun and priest we can lay our hands on," he screamed.

As fast as they had appeared the gunmen reverted into the Maserati which took off flying.

Laura was among the sobbing and crying nuns. She knelt down at the side of one of the fallen nuns and tried to lift her up. Holding her in her arms, she searched for the nun's pulse knowing it was in vain. The nun had died instantly.

Blood was everywhere. Laura looked up. The intermittent silence was interrupted by muffled cries coming from the staring crowd and the distant sounds of police sirens coming closer. Laura felt an enormous panic rising up her spine and hot tears streaming down her cheeks. She looked at the crowd. Extremely distressed she screamed. "Is there a doctor? Please call a doctor!"

The onlookers stared back at her like a silent wall. It was as if they were watching an action scene in a movie or TV show.

Laura dropped the light body of the nun she still held in her arms. She got up. Her suit was soaked with blood. Looking at the unresponsive crowd who stood watching the scene, Laura screamed again. "Help! Someone help!"

The Mother Superior, still in shock, looked at Laura in a daze. As she suddenly recognized Laura, she looked down at the package she held in her blood stained hands. She gingerly handed the package to Laura and she said, "*Signorina* d'Andres—what happened?"

Laura, close to hysteria, took the package. She was fighting a feeling of panic. She shook her head in despair. "I don't know! I don't know!"

In an instant, John had leaped over the cafe's balustrade. As he ran across the piazza, he pulled out the gun he wore in a holster under his left arm.

At the side of the piazza was a row of taxicabs. Some of the drivers, who were waiting for clients, had abandoned their cabs at the first indication of trouble. They had run to the scene of the incident to see what was going on. The first car in the row of empty taxis was a small Fiat. The Fiat's door stood open. The car's radio played a popular song: *Volare*.

John stopped in front of the cab like a bolt of lightning. Throwing his gun on the passenger's seat, he jumped into the taxi and took off after the Maserati.

Racing through the streets of Rome at a nauseating speed was an exhilarating experience. Buildings, fountains, statues, and all the familiar sites flashed by. This is one hellish way to see Rome John thought as he raced around the Coliseum.

Across a larger piazza full of people John could see the Maserati slowing down. He tried to make out who was in the car, but could not see behind the tinted windows. He had a hunch the car was full. Probably there were four of them, the two gunmen, one reservist, and the driver. For a moment, he thought of using his gun. Then he decided this was not a good idea in these streets filled with people.

The Maserati went on, speeding and slamming through crowds of pedestrians who jumped aside like fleeing deer.

At one point John almost caught up with the Maserati. He stuck the hand with his gun out the side window trying to fire at the car's tires. However, the road was bumpy. The little Fiat rocked up and down like crazy. The chase was on at maximum speed when a slim figure holding a semi-automatic appeared hanging out of the Maserati's right rear-window. The man fired wildly at the Fiat. John ducked behind the steering wheel. He tried to aim at the man and he fired three shots in a row. Bang, bang, bang. It seemed the man was hit, because his gun fell to the cement of the street racing by. The man disappeared back inside the car.

John, in full pursuit, had gained so much distance he was ready to ram the Maserati in front of him when the Fiat suddenly slowed down and sputtered. John, seeing the Maserati was getting away, shifted the creaking gears. "Come on, *bambino*, we have to make it faster," he yelled under his breath. The Fiat gained speed again. The he radio still played *Volare*. John tore around a corner into a narrow street leading down to another piazza.

The girl appeared before the windshield like an apparition. In a microsecond, John noticed she wore stiletto pumps and a short, tight dress. She seemed to be limping. John's foot hit the brake. For a moment, the Fiat swerved dangerously. It hit a curb and a cornerstone before John managed to bring it to a halt. John cranked the window down. "*Mama mia*, do you want to kill us both?" he yelled. The girl was voluptuous and beautiful, with olive skin. She smiled at John with a sweet smile. She then turned around and limped away. One of her stiletto heels was broken.

John spotted the Maserati in the distance below in the middle of a traffic circle. His foot pushed the gas pedal to the floor.

The chase continued into the hills when the Maserati, racing down a narrow, pebbled street at high speed, suddenly hit a drainage ditch in the road. The car was catapulted up through mid air by a great jolt and then thrown down into an even narrower street where it got wedged between the old walls with an awful noise.

Stuck between two buildings in mid-air, the Maserati briefly seemed to exhale. Oil and gas dripped from its bottom and sparks flew from under its hood. The intermittent silence was disrupted as the car exploded with a loud thump.

John was still going fast when he saw a wall of flames and black smoke directly in front of him. As he slammed the brakes down, the Fiat swerved, skidded, and then finally came to a halt.

John let out a wheezing breath. He got out of the car. He approached the scene cautiously. Through the smoke, he could see the burned-out hulk of the Maserati stuck between the buildings. The car's frame already seemed to be cooling. Residual flames licked up a two story building on the left. A woman screamed in one of the second floor apartments.

John got closer, trying to look inside the car. The car was so high up, John had to stand on his toes to get a good look. When he saw what the flames had left inside of the Maserati, he gasped for air. He knew he should not have looked. He should have just left it up to the police. What he saw was probably going to imprint the back of his mind forever. Three of them were unrecognizable. Their blackened skeletal bones were clinging with pieces of burned flesh. The fourth one was fused like a burned straw doll. He still showed a flicker of life coming from a blackened eye under a burned lid. John knew he had no choice. He drew his gun, and aimed at the middle of the thing he thought could still have some excruciating life in it. He ended it.

"The forensic guys will have a field day," he thought as he drove the Fiat slowly down the street, trying to find the direction he had come from. He could hear the sirens of fire engines and police.

It took John about an hour to explain to the chief of police who he was and why he had hijacked a taxi. At the end of this process, the police chief of Rome, a staunch man with black hair and a white complexion, became friendlier. He rubbed his thin, black mustache and he managed a faint smile. He pushed some papers across his desk for John to sign.

John signed the papers.

"I can tell you this, Mr. Cordes," the police chief said in broken English. "Here in Rome, it does not matter if you are a guest, or you are working for the Vatican. The Vatican is an autonomic state with its own government, which consists of the hierarchy of the clergy. It has its own police and intelligence service, the Swiss Guards, the Church agents who usually are knights belonging to different orders, and the Militia Christi. It has a radio station which broadcasts in thirty-eight languages all over the world. The radio station also happens to be a sophisticated surveillance operation, equipped to detect movements of international governments. The Vatican also has its own bank, which is internationally tied with large corporations and financial institutions. It also has a small railway, a post office, a heliport, and its own head of state that, naturally, is the Pope. The Pope commands the Swiss Guard, a troop of only a hundred and fifty, and Vatican security, a troop of many. The Vatican security headquarters are in the catacombs below the fortress of Saint Angelo and the Tower of St. John. They are connected to the Vatican by underground tunnels. Extremely well trained and well-informed militant Church agents operate the security headquarters. The militant Church agents, or the Militia Christi, as they call them, are some times trained in African countries like Ethiopia. The Church agents who are the most trusted and the closest to the Pope are the Knights of Saint John. There is also a division who are spies—"

"Who exactly are the militant Church agents?"

"As I just told you, they are a highly trained, superbly outfitted, elite troop on high alert."

"Why are you giving me all this information?"

"Because, I know Americans are naive and I want you to

know the fabric you are dealing with. I also know, the Church will never disclose these facts to you even when you are working for them. And there is one more thing. All the Church agents and special forces of the Vatican can only act in the state of the Vatican and not in Rome without special request or permission. This goes for you too. No matter how important they think your mission is, they cannot protect you as long as you are in Roman territory. I must warn you Mr. Cordes do not pull out your gun in public, chase any more cars, or steal any more cabs. I could arrest you right now for these offenses. However, Rome is Rome, and the Vatican probably is the heart of Rome. I know Count Ormani very well, and I am willing to work with him as long as what happens in Rome is taken care of by the Roman police. You understand?"

"I understand." John gathered up the papers. He watched the police chief probingly. "Does the Roman police have any idea who is behind the terror attacks? I mean, they have terrorized your city for some time now. What have you found out?"

"We looked at a lot of film from the security cameras at the airport. We checked all incoming flights for the past two weeks. It was a long shot. They could have arrived on trains or cars or who knows what. I think we were lucky though, because there was a group of six suspicious looking Asians, all dressed in business suits, arriving from Hong Kong about ten days ago. Naturally, we combed the city, but the men had simply vanished."

"Well," John said. "There are a lot of tourists from all over the world in Rome. A group of Asian businessmen should not look too suspicious. Do you have any data regarding their identity?"

"Customs control is still going through their computer data. So far, they have found only two matches. Both are Chinese nationals born in Peking. Names and birthplaces—that is what customs control can give us. It is going to take a long time to find these men, especially in China. It's like looking through the proverbial haystack."

"I have a hunch there are a few ways to find out."

"Good luck Mr. Cordes. And if and when you do find out, be sure to let us know immediately."

The great front entrance to the hotel Excelsior was in itself a neo classic landmark. It was busy as usual. Bellmen and door attendants helped hotel guests who were coming and going.

A famous Italian movie star, carrying a toy poodle signed last minute autographs. *"Ciao, bambinos!"* She waved and smiling a wide smile, she disappeared into the waiting car.

The black limousine with the Vatican's standard pulled up under the spacious carport in front of the hotel. A chauffeur in a charcoal grey uniform held the door open for Laura d'Andres who got out of the limousine. Wearing a chic but subdued suit, she carried a business-type attaché tote on her right shoulder.

The doorman held open the revolving glass and brass door through which Laura entered the hotel. She walked through the foyer up to reception. "How can I help you?" the chef de reception, a small, maniacal man in a black suit, wearing the golden keys of his profession on both his lapels, asked.

"I am Laura d' Andres. Here to see Mr. John Cordes from New York."

"Of course, *Signorina*. I believe Mr. Cordes is waiting in the Bellini room." He motioned a bellhop. "Amadeo, please show Ms. d'Andres to the Bellini room."

Amadeo clicked his heels and bowed. "Follow me, *Signorina*."

Even though, the Bellini room was more luxurious than comfortable, it was still one of Rome's favorite meeting spots.

John sat awkwardly on a settee at one of the low, antique tables, waiting for the envoy of the Vatican he was supposed to meet in neutral territory around noontime. Of course, it was no longer noontime. He had to reschedule the meeting after the morning's terrifying events had rattled the city of Rome to the core.

The room in its neo-classic pomposity was something he was not used to. Near the entrance stood an old man in a black tuxedo. He played a viola with abandonment. On a card table nearby four aristocratic looking women in their forties sipped white anise liquor, enjoying small cakes and whispers of gossip. An older Italian man sat comfortably in an easy chair reading a paper. Next to him, upright and perfectly still, sat a beautifully groomed *Magyar Wislar* dog, wearing a platinum collar. A young American couple laughed and giggled. They were obviously honeymooning.

As John's eyes wandered around the room, they came to focus at the entrance door, held open by a door attendant. The lovely woman he had seen earlier at the café at the Piazza Navona came through that door. John was surprised to see her. He got up from his seat. He was even more surprised to see that she walked straight to him. He got up from his seat, "I was hoping we would somehow meet again, after our last encounter was so blatantly interrupted," he managed to say.

Laura looked pale, but she held her head up high. She looked at John with a sly smile. "I am still trying to get over this morning's terror and I still feel a little shaky. Can you tell me, how you disappeared so fast?"

"Please—I am John Cordes from New York City."

"I know who you are. I made your travel arrangements. I am Laura d'Andres, assistant to Count Ormani, the head of the Vatican's security. How was your trip?"

John was intrigued. "Oh, it was fine, just fine. But this is even more of a pleasant surprise. I was expecting a priest or church official as the Vatican's envoy—and not someone so lovely—"

"Thank you for the compliment. Let us sit down and get to the point. I want to fill you in about some things. First, I would like to tell you I am very glad you could come. Father Renquist told me about your son. How is he?"

"Well—thanks, he's fine. I think he is making progress. Strangely enough, a little old priest has gotten a lot of his attention lately."

"Father Renquist is a real sweetheart. He stayed with us in Rome for a while. He is a Jesuit priest who is actually part of the Vatican's undercover security agency. Your son is in good hands with him."

"You mean to tell me little Father Renquist is a spy? I didn't know something like that existed."

Laura nodded and tried to smile again. "And he recommended you as someone who can be trusted because the last thing we want is a scandal."

John took in her lovely, esoteric face. "You can trust me. I have handled hundreds of cases, all in strict confidence. How about a drink, a Campari-Soda maybe?"

"Thank you. But tea will be fine." Laura's eyes looked intense. "I need to fill you in on the strange and horrifying things that have happened while you were in the air, Mr. Cordes."

John touched her hand lightly. "Please, call me John."

"Okay, John. I think I changed my mind. I should take that drink after all. A Campari-Orange, please!"

John signaled a waiter, "Campari-Orange for the *Signorina!*"

Laura looked around with a frantic expression.

John could feel her tension. "Just relax," he said. "It's safe around here."

Laura swallowed. She tried to control her anxiety. "Don't worry, I am fine. It is just the nuns—I knew them personally—and the rest, I have to tell you, it is even worse. It is like the whole world is suddenly going insane."

The waiter brought Laura's drink on a silver tray with a glass of water.

"Thank you," she said to the waiter. She took a long drink of water and then put a manila folder on the table. She opened the manila folder and took out some enlarged photographs she handed to John. "They found this near Castel Gandolfo. That is the Pope's summer residence." Laura took a sip of Campari.

John looked at the photographs. They looked like ordinary police shots. However, when he saw what they depicted he swallowed hard and he shook his head in disbelief. It was a pathetic looking little priest who was strangled with a garrote. The priest was crucified.

John put the pictures down and he looked around. He took in the refined coolness of the Bellini room full of decadent Roman society. It was a stark contrast to the nauseating pictures of death.

Laura's hand trembled as she took more pictures out of the manila envelope. "And this is what I found while you were in the air."

John looked at the pictures. This time it was an elderly, heavy-set nun. She was strangled the same way as the priest. The nun looked like a bloody, dead rat, John thought.

Laura took another sip of the Campari. She explained the circumstances of the priest's and the nun's deaths and she handed John the police reports so he could study them. "Unfortunately, that's not all of it. Two nuns were killed in this morning's attack and two of them are in the hospital. One of them is in intensive care. She is not expected to live. Two pedestrians were also killed." Laura's voice trembled again—"a young woman in her twenties, a wife and a mother of three, and one of her daughters—she was eight. The car, a large, black Maserati did not even try to stop. It just ran them over without stopping."

John shook his head. "Murdering bastards!"

Laura pointed at the pictures of the priest. "Why was the priest crucified? I mean, they could just have strangled him or killed him otherwise," she said with a weak voice." Does this have anything to do with the crucifixion of Christ?"

"I can't tell. But I think that by using sensational, disgusting methods they want to spook you and terrorize you—Does any one have any clue who is behind this? I mean we have seen bombings attributed to the red brigades, the murder of Italian bankers, and of officials in high office—What about the Mafia?"

"Don't act naïve, John. You are not supposed to say these things aloud. You know best that the red brigades are cowards. The will bomb a train station or a car but they will never dare to attack the Vatican directly. In addition, the members of the other club, you mentioned, are holier than thou. They are so holy, in fact, they will commit any crime including murder and extortion to protect their own holiness. I cannot tell you more than this. You know the facts yourself."

Laura sipped her drink. "What I can tell you, the priest had a rather lengthy extortion note pinned to him. The Mother Superior was handed another note, during the shooting this morning, which she handed over to me. We are still analyzing that second note. There is some evidence, it is a group of terrorists who claim the Church has a history of negating technology, science, and progress ever since the times of Galileo. For example—the Church is hiding scientific evidence of any kind that suggests there could be intelligent life on other planets. It seems the terrorists managed to obtain some documents and objects from the Secret Archives of the Vatican which could damage the credibility of the Church forever because it proofs that there is intelligent life on other planets."

John looked stern. "Okay and where do I come into the picture?"

"I believe there are many sources of good intent in what the Church stands for and in what we believe. In simple terms, I should say that in the ongoing battle of good versus evil, good must win or all will be lost."

"And you would like me to be the hero who helps you, the good guys, just like in the movies, nice and simple."

"It is neither simple nor nice." Laura was emphatic. "For God's sake, they are killing innocent people and innocent nuns and priests. It is like killing little lambs. Who is next? The Pope himself?"

John looked around the room and then focused on Laura again. "It's hard—isn't it?"

Laura's blue-green eyes turned to fire. Not many people can imagine something like this. I mean they are not just attacking political and social-issue targets. They are attacking religious and cultural symbols. Where does it end? It takes a special person to deal with something like this. You are this person, John, especially as a former Catholic. My job is to work with you in liaison—"

John smiled impishly. "I wouldn't mind a liaison."

"You know I didn't mean anything like that." Laura was cool and restrained.

"Of course not, Laura. I apologize. I could not help it—a game of words."

"Well, I think this is not the time for games or smart jokes."

"You are right. Just help me see the whole picture and tell me why you think the Catholic Church are the good guys. After all, they have a wretched history of distorting the truth and corruption, and killing people, all in the name of Jesus. Don't you know your Holy Church has conducted more wars and killed more people in the name of Jesus Christ than all the rest of them combined?"

Laura was exasperated. She stared at John, speechless. "Don't ever say anything like this ever again around here John, someone could hear you. If they found out I was even listening to something like this, they would kill me, and then they would probably kill you too." She lowered her voice. "I can tell you, my faith has been challenged many times because I really know too much. But no matter what the Church has gone through in its history and what it is going through now, they ultimately are the good guys because they are teaching and maintaining the word of Jesus who died in the name of the spirit of humanity."

"What kind of spirit do you mean the alcoholic or the self-serving kind?"

"No, John. Stop it! I mean the little bit of substance that distinguishes us from the animals, the "missing link." if you will. The spirit that is in more primitive terms referred to as the Holy Ghost which is maintained and furthered progressively in the Church by the Illuminati."

"I can see you know your religious science. You sound very believable."

"I am believable because I believe in the spirit. And I believe that the Church, even though it has had a tortured history, still wants to further the spirit of humanity— *spiritu tuo*—and they want to do no evil."

John shook his head. "I think you should rather say they want to see no evil."

This made Laura chuckle. "The things you say are really somewhat funny, John. But stop acting smart. Let's not talk about this any more. Let's just say we just want to exist in peace here and now, and we want you to find these terrorists, wherever they are, and turn our world back to what it was before they started up with us."

John returned her intense stare. "Okay, I promise I'll do my best to help you. By the way, you can stop trying to convince me. I have already committed with Father Renquist."

"Good." Laura said. "Then, let's not waste anymore time." She looked at her watch. "Six thirty, already. I must go back to the office to confirm you will be working for us. I know the Count wanted to see you today, but it is too late now, and besides, we are bringing in an expert on the stolen items, from Cambridge, England. He is arriving tomorrow afternoon."

John followed Laura out of the hotel while she kept talking. "I am afraid you are on your own for tonight, John, which is not bad considering you are in Rome."

They stood under the carport in front of the hotel, waiting for Laura's limousine to pull up. John tried to hold on to her. "Would you have dinner with me tonight? I would like to invite you. I am sure we have many more things to discuss."

The limousine pulled up. The chauffeur held the car door open.

Laura looked at John with slight regret. "I would enjoy going out to dinner with you very much, but I can't—a pressing engagement."

"You mean, a date?"

"No nothing like that. I very seldom date, and if you care to know, I am not married. It is strictly business—and holy business as such. I will see you tomorrow morning bright and early."

Laura suddenly turned around and looked directly at him. "You are good and strong John, that's why I want to warn you before you get in with us. All of this must be kept in strict confidence. There cannot be any breaches or leaks to the press.

The curia is very sensitive to something like this. People have been known to be killed—."

"Are you trying to tell me the Church kills people who are in their way or who betray them?"

"No, not really, but they have been known to have some ties with unsavory people, and there are some secret organizations which will protect the interests of the Church no matter what."

"I know—the Mafia—"John said in a way that made Laura chuckle again.

"John looked at her determined. I don't mean to be funny and I don't want you to think I am a naïve American. I have worked in this field all my life. I have been in the CIA, which I cannot regret, because I learned most of what I know there. I have connections to secret services and spy agencies all over the world and I know more about the machinations of the Vatican than you think."

"Shut your mouth, John. What ever you think, or you know about the so-called machinations of the Vatican are half-truths and lies. We know you are one of the best-connected agents in your field. That's why we hired you." Laura turned toward the car. "I will see you tomorrow." She slipped into the depth of the limousine that swallowed her.

John stared after the car that quickly disappeared into the heavy traffic. Laura had just left him hanging there without any real information or insight.

Later that night, John had a simple plate of pasta somewhere in a dimly lit tavern. Despite the place was one of those typical tourist rip-off places, the wine and cheese tasted good.

He was wide-awake from jet lag. Laura had stirred something in him. He could not pinpoint what it was, and he did not know if he could trust her or if she even understood what his work was all about. He was used to solving cases efficiently and quickly. Here, it seemed, they had a *manjana* attitude. It was a good thing he liked her. They were probing his intelligence and patience. Laura would be the key that would eventually open the whole case for him.

For the rest of the night he had nothing to do, and he did not feel like sleeping. Therefore, he kept visiting nightclubs and bars, combing through Rome's underground. He was trying to find anything leading to the terrorists. He almost hoped they would rise up and strike again, giving him a chance to pursue them. But all remained quiet that night—almost too quiet—as if the exploding Maserati had taken all of them to hell. Maybe this was it, John thought. There was evidence of four bodies, or what remained of them, in the burned out car. Maybe there were only four of them. Perhaps the nightmare had ended.

7.

THE COUNT

Distant voices of a jubilant chorus praised the glory of heaven, while the usual crowds admired the greatest architectural monument to God on Earth. Guided groups of tourists, common people, priests, monks, and nuns swarmed like ants. Their presence could not diminish the exalting beauty of one of the world's greatest edifices ever built by human hands because Saint Peter was built to accommodate thousands of worshipers.

Laura and John stepped out of the bright sunlight into the grandiose coolness of the great basilica. Laura quickly pulled a pastel colored scarf, she wore around her neck, over her head. John looked around the basilica in amazement. He took Laura's arm. She looked at him with a reassuring smile. They walked toward the center of Saint Peter. Arriving at what seemed the center point, they made a right turn and walked out into the walled city-state of the Vatican.

Laura let the scarf glide down to her shoulders. It seemed she liked being on John's arm. "Just hold on to me," she said. "As you know, this is the Vatican—a small state in itself. They call it the Holy See or the State of God."

John looked at the well-kept park like grounds and buildings that were interconnected by asphalt streets and walkways. "This place is not very big. Is it?"

"It is only about a mile long and a mile wide but it is very old and very special."

They walked past administrative buildings through gardens with fountains and statuary to an older renaissance style building, which was elevated on a small hill. John looked at the graceful woman on his arm. He was not sure if he was accompanying her or she was guarding him.

Laura caught his thought. "You didn't think you would walk into the Vatican just like that?"

"That's why we had to meet at the hotel first, right?"

"Correct."

"By, the way—I thought women were not allowed to hold any jobs in the Vatican, unless they were nuns. You are not a nun, are you?" he asked brazenly.

Laura was amused. "I am not a nun."

John let out a sigh of relief, "Thank God for that. Not that I don't like nuns. It's just that it would be such a waste."

Laura looked at him. "I am the assistant to the Vatican's head of security, his Excellency Count Ormani, who is not only from a very old Roman family but who is also a Maltese Knight. It is a great honor for the Count to serve the Vatican. When he took this honorary post, he brought his own personal things to his office—artworks, furnishings, anything to make him enjoy his surroundings. I already was his assistant then. The Count's sister adopted me when I was a baby. The Ormani family was very good to me. I grew up in one of their castles in the Toscana. It was a wonderful place. I had the best food and the best education. After

I finished my studies at the University of Florence, I began to work for the Count full time. At that time, he was in charge of the Bank of Rome. He insisted in bringing me with him to the Vatican. It took the clergy three months to finally decide I could work here. I am still not allowed to enter certain areas of the Vatican without special permission."

They now walked up an open staircase toward the doors of the Count's office. As they stood on top of the stairs, they had a good overview of the tiny state of the Vatican and the city of Rome which encroached at the walls. They paused briefly to take in the sights of the surroundings. John dropped Laura's arm. They looked at the ancient buildings, lush gardens, and the tiled roofs of Rome right beyond the wall. The scene seemed to be bathed in an age-old light. "This beats working in an office in thirty Rock any time."

"What's that?" Laura asked.

"Oh, it just means my office is at Rockefeller Center. They call it Thirty Rock because it is on 30th Street. New York it is really a fine city but it is nothing like this."

Laura looked around. "Rather impressive, isn't it? From the outside, it looks just like an assembly of old buildings. But some of them hold some of the world's greatest treasures inside. Saint Peter to me is a rock also, the rock the Catholic Church is built on."

John took her arm again as they walked on. "I know it's called the rock of ages. I know a few things about the Vatican, how it is structured. It is a world in itself. You must be very religious with all this holiness around you."

"Well, if you really want to know it, I am not so religious. But I believe the father, the son, and the holy ghost make up the wholeness of God which is the good force that holds this world together. And that without religion the world would surely fall into the devil's hands. But my work here has not much to do with religion. The Vatican is run like a small country or big business. No one will ever question my religious beliefs as long as I work well with the Count."

John pointed at tall radio towers in the Vatican gardens, which looked out of place in the serene surroundings.

"What's that?"

"Oh, those are just the Vatican radio towers. The main broadcast center is outside Rome in Santa Maria di Galeria. Vatican radio broadcasts all over the world."

"Isn't it also the place where Vatican intelligence monitors the activities of major governments along with individuals suspected of demonic affiliations?"

"I don't' know what you are talking about. I have never seen anything like this. But then I am not allowed in all areas of the Vatican."

John was not sure if Laura just wanted to avoid talking about the Vatican's radio set up and monitoring systems or if she really did not know very much about it. It seemed in her position she would know everything but she had orders from the Count not to disclose it to him. It did not matter. He had a very good idea of how the set-up worked even before the Roman Chief of Police had tried to explain it to him. He changed the subject. "You are pretty amazing. I am glad you are here."

Laura's face blushed slightly. Her smile told John she liked him too. She looked away quickly.

They had reached the top of the staircase and they stood in front of a large mahogany door, which swung open quietly as soon as Laura touched a buzzer to her right.

The Count's male secretary, an eccentric looking figure in a black suit, starched shirt, and red tie greeted them. He quickly pushed a buzzer, which opened the door to the main office. "The Count is expecting you," he said.

The Count's office was a great room with silk covered walls and deep, precious rugs. The walls were adorned with the Count's ancestor's portraits in gilded frames, Maltese Knights painted by famous artists. The wall on the right side of the room was glowing with a different sort of life, television screens, and built-in monitors, which currently were soundless. It was as if the Count could monitor the world from his office in the Vatican as he pleased.

At a large inlaid conference table, which could seat twenty-four, were count Ormani and his Eminency the Cardinal Aristide de Montaigne, a taut, tanned, white-haired French aristocrat with sharp blue eyes.

A good-looking nun rolled in a bar-table covered with white linens. On it was a fine silver tray with small silver cordial cups, a silver bowl containing smoked almonds, a bottle of fine old Amontillado, and a white peony in a small crystal vase. The nun served the Count and the Cardinal at the table. She looked briefly at Laura and the stranger standing in the doorframe. She then curtsied and bowed back out, brushing slightly against Laura as she left.

The secretary ushered them in. The Count's deep voice filled the room, introducing John to the Cardinal. "Your Eminency, may I present John Cordes of the firm Mauser and Cordes, New York."

John simply bowed.

The Count's voice sounded out again. "Mr. Cordes—his Eminency the Cardinal Aristide de Montaigne."

John smiled and bowed again.

Laura walked up to the Cardinal. She curtsied and took his extended hand, feigning to kiss his ring.

"Sit down, sit down!" The Count ordered them. "Would you like some refreshments?"

They both declined.

John pulled one of the heavy carved chairs from under the table, helping Laura to be seated. He then sat down himself.

On the polished surface of the conference table was a bloodstained plain-paper package cut open through the center. The contents of the package were spilled out on the table, three paper pages of a ransom note and a roll of 8-mm film.

The Count did not smile as he said. "Welcome to the Vatican, Mr. Cordes. We are certain we can trust you to keep all this in confidence and you will help us to determine who stole certain items from the archives using them for blackmail. We believe it could have only been an inside job." He pointed at the wall full of monitors and television screens. "We have state-of-the-art security. Someone who had knowledge, this evidence was in the Deep Archives is the link to the terrorists. There is no conceivable way they could have gained access otherwise." He pointed at the electronic wall again. "Our security is tight, as you probably know, and as you can see. We have already started our own investigation. However, at this point we feel we should bring in someone of your reputation and experience, even though you are an outsider."

John cleared his voice. "I am grateful for your trust. I might be an outsider but I know how to conduct my business."

The Count stared at him probingly. "No doubt! No doubt! And, by the way, your fee payment arrangements will be handled directly by the Bank of Rome."

John looked straight back into the Count's jet black eyes. "I am not worried about payments—after all the word of the Church is better than gold."

The Count managed a cool smile. "That's true. Anyway, my trusted assistant here, Miss Laura d'Andres, will arrange all the details. She speaks several languages and holds degrees

in anthropology and religious science. She will work with you
directly."

John looked at Laura. The fact, he had liked her from the
beginning, had to be set apart. He had never worked with a
woman before but he knew whatever happened, she would be a
fine working partner. He smiled. "I will enjoy the opportunity to
work with Miss Andres."

John pointed at the electronic wall. "It would be very helpful
if you could show me how the security systems work. I would like
to check some of the collected data."

The Count's eyes were like slits. It was obvious he was not
ready to expose the Vatican's security systems to a stranger. "We
will think about it, Mr. Cordes. In the meantime Miss d'Andres
can explain other things to you."

The Cardinal took a delicate sip of Amontillado. His steel
blue, eagle eyes scanned them. He spoke with a French accent. "If
I may interrupt, ladies and gentlemen, I must be going. *Il Papa*
himself is conducting a meeting."

He looked at John. "Mr. Cordes, I want you to know
something about us, in strict confidence. You see, at times, the
Church seems eternally conservative and old-fashioned, and many
of its doctrines are very old and have never been updated. For
example, when it comes to suggesting a date for the creation of
the Earth, the Church still maintains that Darwin's theories were
erroneous and that the creation of humans on Earth happened
exactly as it is told in Genesis. This was researched and proven
by a Bishop of the Anglican Church by the name of James Usher
who was one of the most learned capacities in his field, in the year
1650? After many intense studies, Bishop Usher came up with
the conclusion that Adam and Eve were created by God around
4500 B.C. More precisely, he proved that the creation of Adam
and Eve occurred on October 23, 4004 BC, a Friday. He even

included the apple of temptation, the devilish snake, and all the rest. What should we think about this? Bishop Usher was not a wise man, a charlatan, or just naive. Usher was commissioned to conduct these studies, proving that humankind did not evolve but that God, as written in the gospel, created man on Earth. This is what we still maintain today."

The Cardinal interrupted his thoughts and took another relishing sip of Amontillado. "Ah, our Spanish brothers really know how to make good sherry wine. I think this is where the real rift between the Church and science occurs. It is all in the interpretation. Of course, we are at fault here too because we have never updated many of our doctrines, some of which are ancient. It is, like saying, the Earth is flat. It makes no sense. However, in theory, it is still the Church's official version of the Creation today because this doctrine was never revoked or changed. How can we explain modern science, space travel, and the possible existence of life on other planets? How can we deny these things? We don't have to deny them because it is all here in the holy book."

His elegant, long-fingered hand pointed at a leather bound bible, resting on a bookstand next to the table.

"The Book says God created heaven and earth, the sun, the moon, and the stars. It says, God rules not only on earth but also in heaven. This means, God is the creator of the Universe, of all the galaxies, solar systems, suns, stars and planets, and billions of them. How presumptuous of us to think we are alone here on Earth—God's only creatures. He created light from darkness—meaning progress, evolution, and science on many of the planets, not just ours. God is the power and the glory that holds the Universe together. Why would God create man in his image on one small planet alone and forget about the rest of this magnificent Universe, which is unimaginably vast in our view or which could be unimaginably small in a different view, all depending on relativity."

"I truly appreciate your input, Cardinal—I mean your eminency." John said. He had the distinct feeling the Cardinal was leading him on. "Ring around the roses—" John thought.

"Just don't ever say where you heard this!" the Count interjected.

The Cardinal got up, and walked toward the doors. He stopped, and turned around. "Good bye, Mr. Cordes. I am sure you can handle these terrorists." His hand performed the blessing of the cross, "*Dominus vobiscum. Et cum spiritu tuo.* Do you know what this means Mr. Cordes?"

John jumped to his feet. "I am afraid I don't know exactly, your Eminency."

Cardinal de Montaigne smiled coolly. "Just ask Ms. Laura, she knows all about it."

John bowed. "Thank you, Cardinal—your Eminency."

Count Ormani shook his head. "Cardinal de Montaigne has very liberal and somewhat dangerous views, bordering on heresy. I guess it is a prerequisite of the French to think this way ever since Voltaire and the French revolution. Which does not mean the Cardinal's point of view always coincides with the doctrines of the Catholic Church?"

"Don't worry, Count. We all know the Cardinal is somewhat eccentric." Laura said with an appeasing voice.

"You are right, Laura." The Count poured himself a small glass of Amontillado and downed it with one gulp. "Knowing the Cardinal, I should have avoided having him come to this meeting but he insisted. And the Cardinal is my superior." The Count shook his head and he sighed with embarrassment. "I guess it's time for a break. Let's break for lunch."

Pink sunlight played with blue-green shadows. Somewhere from an open window came the music of Vivaldi. Encased by a trimmed hedge, the Count, Laura, and John were in one of the Vatican's private outdoor restaurants. The table was laid out with fine linen, silver, and crystal.

A roly-poly monk removed empty plates, half-empty glasses and a cheese and fruit tray from the table, after they had finished their lunch. The monk's fat cheeks puffed up with a subservient smile. He poured strong, hot espresso from a fine china jug into exquisite small cups.

Laura looked as if she was in an old master painting. She smiled a Mona Lisa smile. "You know this is a very special place, John. I feel almost like I am part of eternity."

John smiled back at her. "The background becomes you. You fit in like a jewel in a crown. Or like a great work of art in a beautiful room."

The Count glanced at them with his pensive, Roman eyes. "Fancy words, Mr. Cordes—so much unlike you. I suggest, we come back to reality and remember what we all are here for," he said slightly sarcastic.

"Yes, Count." Laura said. "Sorry—too much enjoyment is not good for us."

"Correct, Laura." The Count picked up a twist of lemon peel from a small plate and tossed it into his espresso. He then picked up a lump of sugar and dropped it into his cup. After briefly stirring with a tiny silver spoon, he sipped the black, strong coffee. "Do you like Vivaldi, Mr. Cordes?"

John listened to the music coming from the open window. "Well, I think that's very pretty. But frankly, I am more a fan of Dave Brubeck or of Gershwin maybe."

Laura smiled amused.

The Count looked at them, sobered. "And upon this rock I

will build my church and the gates of hell shall not prevail against it. Do you know what this means?"

"The Rock is Saint Peter, and it shall never be disturbed or put at risk, John said. I know Saint Peter is the Rock of Ages, the greatest testimony to God on Earth. Frankly, I do not like the Church doctrines in particular. But I believe in the teachings of Jesus. I also think that once they attack religious shrines like the Vatican, it could be more destructive than a nuclear war."

Laura turned pale. She caught John's thought. "You mean cultural and religious wars?"

"I tried to tell you this before, when we talked about criminal minds."

"This is unimaginable—religious wars that would destroy the spiritual achievements of men, turning us back to the state where we began two hundred thousand years ago—a thought that is terribly frightening."

"I don't know Laura. I am educated to some degree but not educated enough. I do not know what would happen if they tried to wipe out religion and culture. Anarchists and dictators have tried it. They all failed. Basically, I think humanity is ahead of itself when it comes to the belief in the spiritual in one form or another and the spiritual people will carry on, providing us with a future."

Laura sighed. "Thank you John, for saying this."

John looked serious. He felt no matter how hard he tried he could not get any real information from them. He tried again. "Can you tell me, thinking of all possibilities, who do you think would attack the Vatican?—Maybe splinter groups of Church agents, Free Masons, Corpus Dei, or organizations that practice Devil worship—Or fanatic, religious Muslim terrorist groups. There are also political groups like communists and free thinkers who hate the Church."

"I hate to tell you this," the Count said. "You are wrong with all of this. There are many religious groups and sects that are distant from the Church—black sheep so to speak. But how ever crazy their interpretations might be they all believe the Pope is still their father, the holy Church is still their mother, and Saint Peter is the church that was built in the name of Jesus. They would never go against members of their own family in Jesus however, radical or nonconformist they might be. Unless, of course, they are in it for purposes of their own gain. On the other hand, there are some real fanatics who want the world to view God from one angle only—theirs. I agree with you, orthodox fanatics are the greatest threat to humanity. Greater then wars and weaponry and all of the rest combined. There could be some crazies out there, fanatic about their crazed believes."

"And the Catholic Church is not fanatic about its beliefs?"

"No John. We are not fanatics. Far from it. Jesus preached love and tolerance and that is our credo. That is what makes us so vulnerable against those militant crazies. Why do you think Maltese knights are called the defenders of the faith? We have highly trained elite troops like the Swiss Guard and the Militia Christi. And we have spies and security agents all over the world, most of them don't even belong to the clergy, they are just civilians like you and me."

John could not help himself. He swallowed a chortle when he heard the Count comparing himself to "you and me." He said, "like the Mafia and Cosa Nostra—brothers in crime?"

The Count swallowed hard. His pallid face suddenly caught a trace of pink. Ignoring John's statement, he went on smoothly. Be very careful about what you say aloud, John, especially when you do not know what you are talking about. The Vatican and the Pope are most vulnerable, preaching love your neighbor and your enemy. The love of Christ is the most vulnerable thing on Earth someone must defend it. And the Church provides a pasture for all its sheep, white or black. We do not sit in judgment over criminals. We leave that up to the civil courts and to God's final judgment. Jesus forgave the thief who was crucified with him as soon as the thief found the love of God. We will not judge any of our most fervent believers, even though they might be members of the Mafia or other organizations whether they are deemed criminal or not. On the contrary, we will embrace them as true believers who have the means and want to help protect the Holy See."

Laura was wide-eyed. "Thank you Count, for making us understand."

"You know this better than I, Laura. You are the one, who has a PhD in religious science. Excuse me, I must attend to some business at hand. Laura, we will continue our meeting in my office in about an hour."

"Yes, your Excellency," Laura acknowledged the Count as he left. She turned to John. "Let's walk. I want to show you something."

Inside the Vatican-Museum galleries, the usual crowds admired the priceless art.

Again, John found himself amazed by the rich surroundings.

"This is beautiful, isn't it?" Laura whispered, pointing at a large painting in a gilded frame. She then pointed at a simple steel door in the far corner of the elaborate room. "Beyond that door is the Vatican's official library. But the explosive stuff is kept in the Secret or Deep Archives, a large, modern, museum-like library that is fully air conditioned. It contains many papers, documents, and books, written with the countenance of faith and religion and centuries of writings for and against the Church. These materials can only be accessed by researchers with a stated purpose and with special permission from the Pope himself. The Secret Archives are in the necropolis below the basilica, called the City of the Dead because it is the place where all the dead popes and the highest-ranking church officials are buried."

John stopped Laura in her tracks. "How did they get into the Secret Archives? Can you show the place to me now?"

Laura was evasive. "I don't know—I have to ask the Count. Later, I can possibly show you the archives and all our security procedures and codes. All those are kept in the Count's office, in the fortress of St. Angelo, and in the Tower of St. John. Maybe they will let you check the security cameras. But first, let me show you this." Laura led John to another large painting in a gilded frame. "Tell me what you see," she said pointing at the painting.

John again felt Laura was clearly evasive. He looked at the painting. "I don't know. Funny looking people aren't they?"

"They are not funny, they are simple. I love the old paintings, their interpretation of the culture of the day and of thought and religion. It is like looking at fairy tales that really happened."

John thought Laura was leading him on because he had insisted seeing the Vatican's security set-up and the Secret Archives and she was not prepared or allowed to show him anything. He played along with her game now. He bent down and read the inscription on the label below the painting, "Adam and Eve, driven out of Eden by God after having partaken in the forbidden fruit."

Laura pointed at the picture. "Do you think they were driven out of paradise because they ate the forbidden fruit?"

John looked puzzled. "I really don't know that much about religion. I was raised Catholic. Then I became a Harvard fellow—law-school, that is. I became more interested in Eastern philosophy and martial arts. I think Adam and Eve, if they existed, probably were in love with each other. I think that unconditional love between couples and their children is what keeps this world going."

"That's a really nice thought. You must have loved your wife very much to say something like this. I know all about what happened to your family. What I am trying to say is, I am sorry, John."

John straightened his back. "Don't! I was married very happily but then my wife died. Things happen. My son Eric is a terrific kid." John's overwhelming pain lingered like a dense, grey cloud. It was as if suddenly they were alone in the room, as if all the tourists around them had disappeared. They just looked at each other in silent amazement, probing the strong current, drawing them irrevocably together.

"I am sorry," Laura said. "I shouldn't have brought you here or brought up the subject of your family. Let's go back to the office. I'll get permission to take you through the archives."

They stepped out of the museum's doors and saw a priest in a black, silk-belted frock, running toward them. "Miss Andres, Miss Andres," he yelled waving his hands in the air. He was very young and handsome with dark hair and bright, blue eyes. "Miss Andres! Miss Laura!" He stammered, out of breath. "The Count sent me to tell you—it's Father Francis—you know, the Chaplain of Saint John Lateran. He was gunned down not even an hour ago while reading a mass."

In a dense moment, Laura observed the tears welling from the priest's pretty eyes streaming down his cheeks. She tried to control her own feelings of ice-cold panic.

"Count Ormani wants you both to come to his office right away," the priest said, hysterical.

Laura hugged the priest. "I am so sorry."

The priest looked into Laura's weary eyes. "Why are they doing this to us?" he sobbed.

8.

THE RIFT

After the drapes were drawn, the Count's office seemed musty and cool. Count Ormani, like a big black crow, sat at the head of the conference table. As soon as Laura and John stepped into the room, his voice came out of the dark like a fencing sword.

"Mr. Cordes," he said in a mocking tone, which made Laura shiver. "We brought you here to deal with this evil that has befallen us. But what do you do? You are being wined, dined, and entertained by one of Rome's most beautiful women while the infidels are killing more priests."

John straightened his back, his reflexes on alert. "I do not like what you are saying, Sir, and I do not feel even obliged in any way to try to understand what you are insinuating. This situation was entirely created by you, and if you think you know more than anyone else does, I will be more than happy to leave it all up to you. Why are you refusing to let me see your security and surveillance data? Do you think I am some kind of naïve fool? I probably know more about your security programs than you do.

I just want to get to the point of it. I cannot get to the bottom of this case without your cooperation."

Laura was agitated. "Please John, we will cooperate. We all are just so upset. Let's go on with our work, let's find them, and put an end to all of this."

The Count seemed to have been calmed by her words. He cleared his throat. "Right. Let us sit down and come to the point. We have asked Professor, Dr. Frederico Stynfeldt from Cambridge to pay us a visit. He is the foremost authority on DNA and bio-anthropology in the world today."

The Count pushed a button on a speaker box on the table. near him.

The male secretary's voice came through, sinuous. "Yes, your Excellency."

"Bring in Professor Stynfeldt."

Stynfeldt, carrying an attaché case, entered. Though he was in his seventies, with a salt and pepper beard and greying temples, he did not show his age. He was tanned, fit, and well preserved.

Stynfeldt briefly acknowledged the people in the room and then went behind a projector set near the conference table. He turned the projector on.

An old black and white film was projected on a small bright screen. On screen, in a vast and arid valley somewhere in Africa, the sun began its descent. Stynfeldt's educated voice sounded tense as he explained the images. "This was taken in Tanzania, Africa, circa 1939, so please excuse the quality of the film. Here you can see a part of the Valley of the Rift, the Olduvai Gorge, which is the world's most famous anthropological site. In prehistoric times, there was a large, primeval lake in this region, which gave habitat to lush vegetation and to many species. It was like the original Garden of Eden." The film showed a silvery band of water to the north of a valley. "This is the lake today. A saline lake left over from the original, much bigger lake. As we know now, the Olduvai Gorge is the original cradle of mankind—the place where humanity began."

On film, a handsome young explorer couple, wearing desert gear and carrying rucksacks, halt at a ravine. Two local guides accompany them. They all look dusty and tired. The camera closes in on the explorer couple. The woman is slim. She wears beige britches, an open collared shirt, and lace-up boots. Due to the quality of the film, sharp details of her features are dim—a flicker of bright eyes, a light complexion and dark curled hair. The husband with his beard is handsome wearing his khakis and tropical helmet.

"These are my old colleagues Leo and Marthie Anderson. They died a long time ago. But they are still today considered the most accomplished paleontologists ever. The Andersons spent many years digging at the Gorge and they found hundreds of bones, fossils, and fragments now kept in museums. What they found that day, however, was very different from your normal digs. It was profound and sensational.

On film, the explorer couple descends into the ravine then walks up a hillside. A ray of sunlight hits a spot on the hillside. They walk toward that spot. They suddenly they stop as they see the entrance to a cave down in the shadows. Eerie, diffused light comes from the cave. Marthie and Leo look at each other. They enter the cave slowly and carefully.

In a shallow ditch filled with white beach sand, they discover an intact male and female human skeleton. Their hands are entwined, as if they were holding hands in death. The female's head rests near the male's shoulder. The camera zooms in on the grave, which is outlined by twelve fist-size rocks or minerals—the sources of the eerie light.

The projection froze. The film stopped rolling. The image of the skeletons and rocks remained on screen.

"Please turn on the light," Stynfeldt said.

Laura obliged by turning on a desk lamp, close to her on the conference table.

Stynfeldt pointed at the fading images remaining on screen. "Marthie and Leo didn't ship their discovery to their lab at Cambridge. Their discovery was far too important to be subjected to loss or error. They did something un-orthodox. They packed their find in a piece of luggage—a carpetbag. They carried or smuggled, if you will, the bag with them to England, without registering their "export" with the governor of Tanzania, who required all fossil finds to be recorded and approved to leave the country."

"The lab in Cambridge was, and still is today, one of the most sophisticated bio-paleo labs in the world. Maybe you can guess. I was in charge of the Cambridge lab at the time the Andersons arrived with the carpetbag and I am still today—after a short hiatus in the sixties."

Stynfeldt moved closer to the screen, waving his hand across it. "Not having determined exactly what it was they had found, but suspecting it was a very significant discovery, perhaps the most significant ever, Marthie and Leo swore me to secrecy. After conducting many intensive tests, we discovered that the skeletons and especially the skulls reaffirmed their expectations. — These specimens were obviously Homo sapiens that were in between thirty-five thousand to two hundred thousand years old. Which is not old considering the history of our planet? However, what is puzzling and significant, the humans made the leap from hominid or homo erectus to human or Homo sapiens not in a matter of millions of years but in a matter of days or months. The theory

Homo sapiens evolved from homo erectus that evolved from the chimpanzee is wrong, and the fossil records prove this.

Stynfeldt paused and continued. We know that there is no consecutive link between homo erectus and Homo sapiens. Homo erectus simply disappeared from this Earth at the same time Homo sapiens appeared. The "missing link" is not missing—because it never existed. All those anthropologists and scientists looking for a connection between the last of the hominids and the new Homo sapiens search forever and ever. They will never find "the missing link" because homo erectus was transformed into Homo sapiens by a form of DNA change or a change of chromosomes of a small amount of mitochondrial DNA. Human DNA is almost 98.5% identical to that of the chimpanzee and only 1.5% makes up the DNA the difference between ape and human. When it comes to the evolution of humans, Darwin was wrong. Humans did not evolve. they were created. They were created by a sudden DNA change, which was induced into a small group of hominids by an outside source. This is the greatness and importance of the Andersons discovery."

Stynfeldt was exasperated. He paused and then continued. "DNA science, however, was not discovered until 1953, by one of my flamboyant colleague at Cambridge, Francis Crick, and his American counter-part, James Watson. DNA science revolutionized the way we look at biological genealogy forever. Now we can trace back the genealogical make-up and ancestry of all species. In addition, with this new science we are able to prove beyond any doubt what the Andersons discovered is true.

And because of DNA science we now know that all of us humans on this Earth today came from only one fertile female who lived at the Olduvai Gorge between two hundred thousand to thirty five thousand years ago—the mitochondrial Eve or the human Earth Mother. You see, the mitochondrial DNA is only passed on by a female. With DNA sequencing and lengthy mathematical projections, which now can be done by computers, we are able to determine the existence of the mitochondrial Eve and the Y-chromosome Adam."

"The most amazing thing about all of this is that the DNA which makes up the difference between hominids and humans is very small—only 1.55%. How can such an insignificant amount of genetic information make such a big difference? A difference so profound it made up a whole, superlative new species—intelligent human beings."

"It is unfortunate that intelligence is not used by the majority of people living on Earth today. Most humans go through life clueless and without comprehension of the fantastic achievements of some of their fellow men in medicine, space travel, and computer technology. There is only a small elite of scientists, great thinkers, and artists that were able to make a quantum leap in developing human intelligence and reaching a state of the art of science and technology beyond anything ever thought possible. Which actually lead to humans landing on the moon.

"But enough said about the subject of DNA," Stynfeldt continued. "Look at these rocks or minerals. I took a small scraping from one of the rocks at the time, which we later tested at NASA by X-ray-diffraction mass-spectroscopy, confirming what the Andersons suspected. It looks like whatever is contained in the rocks came from a planet in the constellation of Orion. After further testing, we found the rocks emitted frequencies like microwaves. They seemed to contain a message. We could only guess the meaning of all this and we arrived at this conclusion, whatever transformed this particular group of only about two dozen hominids into humans and whatever brought these rocks to Earth, must have come from out there." Stynfeldt looked up at the ceiling as if he was looking into space.

"Actually, a fascinating story," John said.

"Let me tell you, there is more—The Andersons knew they had found something very unique, but in 1939, fourteen years before the advent of DNA science, they could only guess. They knew the change in the hominids had occurred very quickly. What ever it was that changed them significantly gave them the gift of speech and laughter, changed the size of their brains and their very brain structure, as well as the structure of their bones and skulls and the appearance of their hair and skin. You see, the Andersons did not know about DNA and the linkage of DNA and viruses. However, they knew about viruses. They thought the transformation could have been caused by a form of virus—they were pretty smart, I should add."

"I understand what you are trying to tell us, Professor Stynfeldt. But again, all of these findings are mere speculation," the Count said.

Ignoring the Count John said, "But what is the significance of the rocks?"

Stynfeldt pointed at the rocks. "You see, these rocks were somehow deliberately placed in the grave at the Olduvai Gorge, by someone who wanted to convey a message. The rocks represent the cores of twelve beings or entities that existed on the planet Sigma Ori in the constellation of Orion. These entities gave up their existence, so to speak, so that they could be here with us. They traveled to Earth and decided to stay. Their cores or souls or some of their substance, if you will, are contained in the rocks."

Stynfeldt got up from the table and went over to a black board, which was set up next to the movie screen. He picked up a piece of chalk and drew a configuration on the board. "Who knows what this is?"

"It looks like an even-sided cross but I don't think it has the same meaning," John said.

Laura pointed at the brooch on her lapel, a small diamond pin in the shape of an even-sided cross, marked by twelve small diamonds. "I inherited this pin from my mother. I thought it was a cross but someone once pointed out to me that it could also be the shape of a chemical ring."

"That's right," Stynfeldt said. He pointed at the cross, "one, two, three, four, five, six, seven, eight, nine, ten, eleven, twelve points to be connected. This is a dodecahedron, a geometric figure." He drew another twelve-pointed configuration. "You see the formation can be drawn this way more like a cross, or that way more like a chemical ring. This is definitely the chemical ring for a form of carbon."

Stynfeldt drew on the blackboard again. He drew a small circle at each connecting point of the dodecahedron and then drew a rough configuration of the stars of Orion above it. "Who knows what this is?"

"It looks like the constellation of Orion," Laura answered.

"That's right. Let's say each of these little circles represents a rock." He drew lines from the rocks, connecting them with the stars of Orion. "When you arrange the rocks in a certain way, so that they align with the stars in Orion and you bombard them with a source of energy, let's say with radio waves, the rocks will come alive, so to speak, meaning the message they contain will come across to us."

"Really? That is amazing. You mean these rocks are the souls of aliens who gave up their existence to be here with us and teach us a lesson?" John said.

"Something like this is what the Andersons figured after deciphering the message of the rocks. The Entities inhabit a planet in Orion, which we think might be Sigma Ori. They are made of light and plasma, with a diamond like core of carbon. They contain an organic substance, which contains their soul or their nuclear DNA, which contains the third genome. This substance did not originate in Sigma Ori but it came from a planet near the star Sirius, which is one of the brightest stars in the sky and is linked to Orion. The substance was transferred at some point in time to other planets in the Milky Way system or in our case the Earth, as an experiment to better the Universe."

Stynfeldt went on. "What is the significance of the twelve rocks? First, they are telling us there definitely is life on other planets, and secondly, they are telling us that they are from a carbon planet and that they are a higher form of carbon. If arranged in the form of a dodecahedron or twelve pointed carbon ring and aligned with certain stars in Orion, their inherent power could be released."

The Count shook his head and turned the light one notch higher. "Let's see if we can shed some light on this nonsense. How do you know this all came from the constellation of Orion? And the rocks are a higher form of carbon, like diamonds?"

"Well, first of all, this story is told in the ancient sagas about Orion, who is called the Heavenly Hunter or Master of the Beasts. Watch the words, Master of the Beasts. It is a master who has mastered the beast within. It is a master who has achieved a higher degree of understanding or what we call enlightenment. Secondly, in laymen's terms, we now have scientific means, electro spectroscopy. With this, we pretty much can determine from where in the Universe a substance comes. These rocks definitely come from a carbon planet, somewhat similar to our own Earth but much more advanced. You see, carbon is the only element forming life, as we know it, including animal and plant life. Only, the creation of the carbon-based human is not perfect. Humans tend to have tremendous flaws. Why is it we cannot function with respect to the incredible complexity, which keeps us living? The Earth is made of marvelous bio-chemical systems, which are constantly abused by us as we are abused by our fellow humans. Why?"

"I think you are getting a little ahead of yourself, Professor Stynfeldt. You know very well that most humans do not understand the complexity of life on Earth. If they did, the studies of the mysteries of the Universe would become accessible to anyone. And anyway, you can't prove any of it," the Count quickly added.

"But it was proven by the Andersons," Laura said.

"The Andersons, the Andersons." The Count looked at Laura intense. "You and I know why you are defending the Andersons," he said gravely.

Laura turned pale.

"Tell us what happened to the Andersons and their great discovery."

"You know as well as me, what happened."

"Let's hear it, Professor Stynfeldt."

Stynfeldt was clearly reluctant to talk about some of the painful experiences of the past, but he went on anyway. "It all happened in one single day, September 8th, 1940. The day after the beginning of the *Blitz,* which eventually killed twenty thousand Londoners. This has nothing to do with the Andersons, only with my own state of mind."

"You see, during the night of September 7th to September 8th, 1940, the Andersons had finished their work in the lab. The paper was complete. Their findings were ready to be published. I was very nervous that night because of the bombings. All kinds of thoughts went through my head. What if a stray bomb fell on Cambridge and wiped out the lab? I urged the Andersons to pack up all the evidence and take it to the bunker. I mean the cellar-vault. That is what they did. They packed everything into the same old carpetbag they used to bring those things from Africa in the first place. Only the bunker was already closed that night. The carpetbag was left locked up in the lab instead."

"At midnight, all of us met at Great Saint Mary's Church, because of the bombings. That was the last time I saw the Andersons alive—the next day, September 8, 1940, the Andersons died in a horrible car crash, and the carpetbag was stolen from their lab."

Stynfeldt was visibly upset. "Can I have a glass of water, please?"

Laura poured a glass of water from a pitcher and handed it to Stynfeldt.

John had followed Stynfeldt's discourse with great interest. "Excuse me, lady, and gentlemen but is this what we are looking for—a carpetbag?"

"That's right. A carpetbag, containing two skulls, some skeletal bones, twelve fist-size rocks or minerals that look like dark-red diamonds, handwritten books, and a one hundred and twenty page dissertation ready for publishing," Stynfeldt replied.

"And the bastards that raid our city and kill our nuns and priests," the Count was quick to add. The Count looked at Laura. "I am sorry, Laura, but unfortunately I think what the Andersons came up with makes no sense."

The Count paused and changed the subject. "I also think it is time to tell the truth. The images of the scientists Marthie and Leo Anderson, you have just seen projected, are very special to someone in this room. Marthie and Leo Anderson were Laura's parents. My sister changed Laura's name from Anderson to d'Andres when she adopted her."

Saying this, he stared at Laura. She glanced back at him, painfully, with tears in her eyes.

After the Count had made his blunt statement, the room fell

silent. It was as if they all had to come to grips with what the Count had just said semi-casually.

The first one to react was John. "I am so sorry to hear this Laura."

"That's all right. I have known it all along, John. I am used to it."

Stynfeldt, however, was flabbergasted. He looked at Laura, trying to find his composure. His hand slid across the shiny surface of the table trying to reach hers. His voice trembled and his eyes seemed to look back inside his mind reeling back thirty years.

"Is it you, baby?" he said.

Though she had known it for some time, Laura too, was moved to the core. "Yes, uncle Fred. It is me."

"I should have known it. You look just like her, the same dark hair, the same complexion, and the blue-green eyes."

"What happened?" John interrupted their consternation.

"I told you what happened. The Andersons were both killed. However, their four-year old daughter, who was in the car with them, survived with not a scratch on her. The last thing I knew, she was taken care of by her grandmother. I tried to stay in touch with her but during the perilous times of war I lost track."

Laura swallowed. She pulled out a tissue to dry her tears and blow her nose.

"I am so sorry, Laura," John said. He then turned to the Professor. "But tell me what happened to the rest of the evidence that was left in the lab?"

"There was not much left. Only some of the test results recorded earlier and some papers I found in the waste basket."

"Lost or found, the significance of these findings is not so great," the Count said coolly. "None of it was ever proven."

Stynfeldt shook his head. "You keep saying that. But you do

not understand. Marthie and Leo Anderson operated in 1940. Their instruments were not sophisticated and DNA science did not exist. Their discovery was questionable then. Today, with modern equipment and modern techniques, it can all be proven with certainty. The theories of evolution are fine as long as humankind is excluded. Your belief in a living God is fine when one sees God as the creator of the entire Universe. Only one thing is dramatically different. The human DNA or the enlightened human spirit, as Marthie Anderson called it, was brought here from another planet. Now that would change your petty, little belief systems wouldn't it?"

The Count's voice was deep and strong. "Professor Stynfeldt, I can assure you the belief systems of this world are neither little nor petty, as you put it. Even if it were true humans were created by changing the make-up of some ape's chromosomes or DNA by some abstract carbon people, it still would not explain man's eternal soul, which we believe came from the breath of the almighty God."

"You can believe as you wish," Stynfeldt said. "It is true. The pace of science is a rapid one. Not too long ago, men believed the Earth was flat and if you sailed to the end of the ocean, your ship would fall off into the abyss. Even the most learned scientists of today cannot explain it all. For example, we know what a black hole is like and how it sucks in matter. However, we do not know if it is the beginning of the formation of a new star or the end of a dying star that is becoming a white dwarf disappearing into a black hole. We do not know what lies beyond—call it God or the power that holds the Universe together. But to make us believe we came from Adam and Eve about four thousand years ago, as Bishop Usher suggests, or that we are the only intelligent civilization in the Universe, is utterly absurd. We are not alone, and not the highest-developed civilization, either. This was the earth-shattering discovery made by the Andersons. But the powers that be in this world, like the Church and other large governments, which I do not want to mention, do not want their people to know this because they are afraid of losing their magnetic power over the masses."

"Professor Stynfeldt," John said. "Please tell us what happened after the Andersons deaths and the loss of the carpetbag. Did you ever find out who stole the carpetbag and what happened to it?"

"Not at first. You see that terrible war business, the Andersons senseless fate, and the loss of the most significant anthropological find ever, was a little too much for me. For a while, I was abusing some substances, which are neither good for the mind nor for the soul. I became addicted to alcohol and drugs. But that was a long time ago."

"Only a few years later, after the advent of computers, I was hacking around on my computer one day, and I found it. It sobered me up in an instant. A Jesuit monk at the observatory of Castel Gandolfo by the name of Gonzalo published a paper, 'The Pope's Little Space Aliens'. It was about a collection of more than 200 meteorite space-rocks, which are kept at Castel Gandolfo, some of them containing evidence of extra-terrestrial life. Gonzalo had studied twelve rocks, he found in a carpetbag, which was kept in the Secret Archives of the Vatican, which definitely confirmed the existence of extra-terrestrial life. Right there and then, I knew I had found the carpetbag and I was elated knowing the evidence was safe. I tried to contact the Jesuit monk, Gonzalo, and I applied for special permission to access the archives. But as many times as I tried, I was told there was no monk named Gonzalo and they had no knowledge of the existence of a controversial carpetbag, space rocks, or what I was even talking about."

The Count's voice was sharp. "You know this is all nonsense, Professor Stynfeldt."

Stynfeldt felt the blood rushing to his head. He sneered at the Count. "That's just the point the Church has maintained throughout all this time, isn't it? You cannot prove it. Therefore, it does not exist. But you know, Count, the times are changing and the Church cannot much longer maintain the theory of the three monkeys."

The Count looked surprised. "And what might that be?" "You know the old foil, see no evil, hear no evil, and speak no evil."

The Count just looked at Stynfeldt with wide-open eyes—he was speechless.

John looked at his watch. "Excuse me, Professor Stynfeldt, I think rather than discussing the religious and scientific aspects of the circumstance, we should try to figure out how to deal with the terrorists."

"That's right, Mr. Cordes." The Count had regained his composure. He buzzed the receptionist on the intercom. "Can you send in someone to open up these drapes and bring us some coffee? I feel like my brain is fried."

After the marathon, meeting everyone was grateful for the coffee break and the soft air coming through the open windows. However, they were not finished yet. The Count looked at Laura, who looked pale and drawn.

"Laura, you haven't said anything. What do you make of all of this? What should we do in this thorny situation?"

Laura was evasive. "I don't know. I have to think about this for a while to come up with something." She picked up the extortion notes from the table, and read:

"You have chosen to ignore us. We have the carpetbag. We have the evidence. We know how to decode the message of the space rocks. We have proof, that humanity is only an experiment. This evidence will create anarchy. If you do not meet our demands, we will set your world on fire. We will continue to kill nuns and priests. You have

three days to make payment arrangements at the Bank of Zurich according to further instructions. Et cetera—"

Laura looked up. "It's like they are raving at us, like they are really angry with us."

John turned to Stynfeldt. "Professor, have you ever talked about this in public? I mean, how did they learn these findings were hidden in the Vatican?"

"Without the physical evidence I couldn't prove anything. However, I lectured about the findings of the Andersons all the time. It was not an easy task because the scientific community, including most of my colleagues at Cambridge, questioned the veracity of the story and tried to ridicule it. In 1965, I published an article about the Andersons in the *Journal of Astrophysical Science.* You can find this journal in every university library worldwide. Later, I also published a book about the subject. I had to comment on the mighty Church a little, about their doctrine of the Creation, and how they kept the truth about the origin of humanity in the Secret Archives of the Vatican. I was critiqued and brandished as someone who tells fantastic stories about extra-terrestrials and little Martians. But eventually, I developed a small following of believers."

"You are insane!" The Count screamed. "We brought you here to help us understand why they are attacking us and not to accuse us of all this unfounded nonsense."

The Professor reacted cool. "I beg your pardon, Sir, but you know the truth better than I."

John had become impatient. He was ready for action. "Please gentlemen, let's act, and not react. I think so far I have heard enough. I believe I should go to Zurich. The terrorists have made a big mistake involving the bank of Zurich, a prominent bank. The bank has nothing to hide and they cannot hide anything. The bank of Zurich, I think, is a good lead. Come on, Professor

Stynfeldt, I will give you a ride to the airport." He turned to Laura, "*Signorina* d'Andres maybe you can accompany us to the airport? We can talk more about strategy in the car."

"But there are no more flights from Rome to Zurich today. I have already made reservations for you on *Alitalia* for tomorrow at ten-thirty."

Laura looked at Stynfeldt, business-like. "And you, Professor Stynfeldt, are on the same flight tomorrow to Zurich, from where you have a flight home to England."

The Count looked at Laura and smiled a thin smile. It was obvious he wanted to get rid of Stynfeldt as soon as possible. He then turned to John. I am afraid, Mr. Cordes, you will have the pleasure to stay in Rome for another night. I am sure, Laura will be happy to show you around. But first, Laura, we must send out bulletins to all monasteries and churches in and around Rome, warning every nun and priest of the imminent danger."

Laura looked directly at the Count. "Excuse me, your Excellency, but this was already done immediately after the first priest was murdered. Also the chief of police of Rome has promised to increase police forces around the churches and monasteries."

The Count smiled. "That's my lady Laura."

Laura did not smile back.

John dreaded spending another night in Rome. He was not getting anywhere with the case. The explanations and lectures that Professor Stynfeldt gave them had been interesting. But they were not helping much to detect who was behind the terror imposed on the eternal city of Rome, the Vatican, and the large numbers of nuns and priests, present as much as the pigeons and as vulnerable. It was as if the Vatican had buried itself behind impenetrable barriers and they treated John, as was their custom, as the outsider he was.

Laura had kept most of her composure throughout the ordeal of the terrorist attacks. She was surprised to find she possessed more strength than she ever thought possible. To discover that Stynfeldt was still alive, telling the story of her parents, was the best thing that had ever happened to her. It was as if she had suddenly come across a long-lost relative. She could not help feeling great affection and admiration for Stynfeldt, her "Uncle Fred," the only connection to her past she had left in this world.

Laura, John, and Stynfeldt had dinner that night in one of the low-key Roman restaurants known by serious insiders. A small place with food that would make the angels sing opera. Consuming copious amounts of a lovely Italian red, they sat there until the morning hours.

Stynfeldt told never-ending stories about Cambridge, his long lost friends the Andersons, and their marvelous discovery, he trusted John would be able to reclaim soon. Finding the carpetbag and publishing the story of the Andersons, he had taken on as his mission in life and he was going to see it through, no matter what. With this task, Stynfeldt was no longer alone. He now had two more accomplices, Laura and John, helping him to fulfill his lifetime's ambition, which was bringing the incredible, world-shattering discovery of the Andersons to light. A discovery which would change the perception of humanity on Earth once and forever and which would help project the planet into a future where love and spirituality reigned, just like the best of them had envisioned.

9.

TERROR AT DA VINCI

The next morning, at first, turned out windy and cool. Later, the sun, trying to break through the thick, low-hanging clouds, did not heat the moist air but the exhaust of cars, trucks, and motor scooters that caused a cloud of smog covering Rome.

A black limousine with the Vatican's standard pulled up curbside at Rome's busy Leonardo-Da-Vinci-Fiumicino airport. The chauffeur got out first. He opened the car doors for John and Professor Stynfeldt who were getting out with their carry-on briefcases. They both came around to Laura who was in the front passenger seat of the limo. Laura rolled down the window and extended her hand through it.

Stynfeldt took her hand first with a light grip, no more than a slight touch. "Good bye, lovely Laura baby. I will see you in Cambridge soon. Please come as soon as you can—we'll write the book."

Laura looked at him with admiration. She swallowed the

glint of a tear. "Yes, uncle Fred. Take care of yourself." She smiled through the open window.

John took Laura's hand. "Goodbye, Laura. I will return as soon as I find out what is going on with the thugs and the bank of Zurich. The bank will be able to tell me who is behind this. They gave this valuable lead away foolishly. I'll let you know what I find out."

Laura smiled bitter-sweetly. "I hate to see you go, John. I felt safer while you were around." All of a sudden Laura's smile froze.

The sound of machine gunfire abruptly rattled through the air. Two masked gunmen appeared out of nowhere, firing wildly in their direction.

"Down! Down!" John yelled at Laura before he dropped to the floor and rolled halfway under the limousine. Glancing behind him, he saw one of the gunmen igniting a large grenade and throwing it at the limo. The grenade bounced off the side of the car with a clank. John tried to catch it with his bare hand as it rolled under the car to the opposite side of the lane.

Frozen in terror, with the paralyzing feeling, there was no time to do anything. John watched a transit bus full of people coming down the bus lane. The grenade exploded the bus, which immediately became engulfed in a ball of fire.

To John, the next moments were like watching the rerun of a nightmarish movie. He was held to ground besides the limo incapacitated by a barrage of bullets. He could see that within minutes the burning bus, turned into a casing of molten metal. Inside the bus, behind a sick, dense cloud of smoke, he could see incinerated people burning. Their black silhouettes were turning to ashes. With a shot like sound, the bus windows blew out, sucking in oxygen, which fed the flames inside the bus even more.

A screaming man covered in flames jumped through one of the windows. He fell to the blackened cement. John could hear weakening cries coming from inside the bus. He tried to get up and he tried to get around the car to the bus lane. He desperately wanted to help the burning man or any one left on the bus. But the limo was again hit by a staccato of machine gun fire, which nailed him to the ground.

In the same instant, Stynfeldt, who stood frozen at the curb, was hit. His body was briefly jerked back and forth and then crumpled to the ground.

Trying to avoid the bullets, John crawled over to Stynfeldt. He lifted him up with both hands and he checked his vitals. Stynfeldt looked like he was dead. His face was waxen and there was a clean, neat bullet hole on his left temple.

"Professor Stynfeldt! What's with Professor Stynfeldt?" Laura yelled.

"Get down Laura!" John pulled out his gun. "Get down Laura!"

John now took cover behind the limo, firing his gun in the direction of the gunmen. One of the men was hit. He fell down with his head hacked backwards. As if this was a sign, the other man disappeared toward the airfield where planes took off into the hazy blue sky.

John stayed low, taking cover. He crawled to the wounded gunman on the ground. Rolling over, he sat up, lifting the man up with him by his shirt's collar. Ignoring the man's terrorized expression he pointed the barrel of his gun directly at one of the man's eyes, touching the eyeball. "You murdering creep. Who are you?"

The Chinese man shook his head in defiance. John dropped him like an empty bag. He could see the man was dying. A trickle of blood came out of his mouth and his pupils rolled back. John reached into the pockets of the man's overalls. Still aiming the gun at the man's head with one hand, he let the wallet unfold with

FREDERICA PRATTER

his other hand. "I didn't think terrorists would carry I.D." John said under his breath. He looked at some kind of plastic access card with the man's picture smiling sheepishly back at him. Under the picture, written in Chinese, was a name, Ming Chew, and a company logo, A.P.S.-Kuei-Lin. John smiled grimly. "Got you, you son of a bitch. I know exactly where Kuei Lin is."

He dropped the man. Just as he huddled back toward the limo, his eyes checked Stynfeldt again. Looking closer, he noticed Stynfeldt's hand moved ever so slightly. Could he still be alive? John crawled over to him. Stynfeldt still looked dead. John did not want to take any chances. He picked him up under the armpits and dragged him to the limousine.

The driver's body blocked the front seat. Laura could see he was badly wounded. He was unconscious and covered with blood. Laura managed to check his vitals. She knew they had to get him to a hospital fast. She got out on her side of the car and ran around it. Laura strained trying to get the driver out of the driver's seat into the front passenger seat. She dragged and pulled the unresponsive body, tacky with thick dried blood. John saw Laura's struggle. He dropped Stynfeldt and came to help her. Pushing and dragging they managed to get the driver into the passenger's seat. John then went back to Stynfeldt. He picked up Stynfeldt's light, limp body and carried him closer to the limo.

Laura held the back door open. She looked at Stynfeldt. It was as if she watched her own father die. At this point Laura became hysterical. She sobbed and cried aloud. Then she got hold of herself. "Put him in there," she said, pointing at the limo's back seat.

John somehow managed to lay Stynfeldt down on the car's back seat.

Laura got into the driver's seat. "Come on! Come on! They both are in bad shape. We must get them to a hospital. Fast!"

John jumped into the back seat behind Laura. He pushed Stynfeldt's limp body to the side trying to make room for himself. Stynfeldt's body slumped halfway to the limo's floor. John slammed the door shut.

Laura took off with smoking tires. She was fully hysterical now. As the long car swerved dangerously, hitting curbs and sidewalks with people jumping and trying to get out of the way, Laura managed to gain control over herself and the car. She raced the limo out of the airport and headed for the nearest hospital. Going at a blood-raising speed, she skillfully avoided obstacles and oncoming traffic. "God! Oh God! What are they going to do next?" Laura screamed, breathless.

John tried to hold on in the swerving car. "Insidious, murdering bastards! I know who they are! And, Laura dear, I hope you know your way around here because I don't know where we are going!" he yelled."

"Trust me—I know Rome like the palm of my hand!" Laura yelled back.

Beyond ancient buildings, the outline of a whitewashed, modern hospital building came in sight.

Laura stopped the limo in front of the emergency entrance at a weird angle.

There was nothing more they could do. Laura and John just stood there and watched as they wheeled both men away.

Laura looked down at her bloodstained hands and clothes. "Do you think they are going to make it? The driver's name is Bruno. He has driven me many times. His wife is pregnant. Professor Stynfeldt is my only connection to the past. He is the only one left who knew my parents." Laura was shaking out of control. "Take me home, John," she said.

John gave her a fatherly hug. "They are both going to be okay." Looking over her shoulder at the limo John doubted his own words. The right side of the car was riddled with bullet holes and there was a lot of blood on the front seat.

People coming in and out of the hospital had formed a small circle around them. They stared at them in silence.

Suddenly three police cars with lights and sirens came sweeping around the corner of the parking lot. The people around them rushed back, as police officers poured out of the cars, pointing their guns at John and Laura. "Don't move!" one of the officers yelled. "You are under arrest. And we are taking this!" He pointed at the limo.

Two of the officers quickly seized the limo.

With their hands cuffed behind them, John and Laura arrived at the police station in separate cars. Several paparazzi, who had appeared out of nowhere, took their pictures as they were getting out of the police cars. Passing the cordons of curious by-standers, they were quickly ushered into the Police Inspector's office.

When he saw Laura in hand cuffs, John became flushed with anger. He could hardly compose himself. He shook his own handcuffs in front of the Inspector's face. "Lovely methods you have here! Don't you know we are the good guys?"

The Inspector smoothed his moustache and smiled slyly. "I'll know the good guys, when I see them. But right now, I am blinded."

"Take off their shackles!" he commanded. He bowed toward Laura. "Miss d'Andres, I apologize. Please sit down. I must ask you some questions. A glass of water for Miss d'Andres, please!"

Laura was visibly shaken, but she tried to regain her composure. "You have no right whatsoever to arrest us."

The Inspector looked serious. "As I told John before, I know you both work for Vatican security. However, these attacks occur on Roman territory, and both of you are witnesses. We are going to need signed statements from both of you about what happened at the airport. We must ask you to tell us how you are involved and what you know. This is for your own protection."

White faced, Laura hissed at him. "What do you mean— involved? Do you think we are involved with the terrorists?"

"I didn't say there is a connection between you and the terrorists. I just know you know more than we do and we need to know everything. For example, we know very little, why they are terrorizing the city of Rome and why they are targeting nuns and priests. And what is it they stole from the archives that would enable them to hold the Vatican hostage?"

Self-restrained John sat down next to Laura. He exhaled. "This doesn't mean you have to arrest us every time you want to talk to us."

"Okay," the Inspector said, less agitated, "let's have it out. I will tell you what we know, before you fill us in on what you know. Originally, six assassins of Chinese origin came to Rome approximately two weeks ago. Four of them burned when the Maserati exploded. After that, there were only two of them left. One of them, I believe, was shot at the airport by your hands, John. The last man escaped, but we have very good trail on him. However, they are all linked with a small sleeper cell of Italian nationals here in Rome. How many of them there are is hard to say because they keep coming in and out of the woodwork."

The Inspector sounded concerned. "One thing we know, Laura d'Andres is definitely a target. It seems they know who she is. We are offering you police protection, Miss d'Andres."

Laura looked at the Inspector and then at John. "It seems they know who I am? Are you saying, you think I know who they are?"

"No, Miss Laura! But we want to protect you as a witness."

"Does this mean I will be followed by your men everywhere?" Laura asked. "I like my privacy."

"You will barely notice it," the Inspector answered. "Please believe me. You are in great danger. You could be kidnapped or killed like the nuns. We cannot let anything happen to you. Our job is to protect you, Laura."

"Take it. Take the police protection," John said. "Okay," Laura said.

The Inspector turned to John. "Now to you, Mr. Cordes. What can you tell me about all of this?"

"Well, Inspector, we are certainly willing to sign statements. But neither I, nor Laura can give you any information about what is going on. It is privileged information, something you can try to find out yourself or from Count Ormani. But I doubt the Vatican will disclose any of it to anyone. You can root out the evil, but not the cause. I have a very good idea who is behind this. It is something we might be able to talk about in the future—but not now. Because if they find out what I am up to, or if my hunch is wrong, I will be cooked either by the Vatican or by the perpetrators."

John continued. "I am leaving this country for a short time, hoping I can resolve the situation. When I return, I am willing to fill you in about everything. But first I want to make sure my suspicions are real."

"That's all fine. But what if you don't return of your own free will or if anything should happen to you? After all you are conducting a risky business."

"That's a risk we must take. Neither Laura nor I can tell you anything at this moment. We are sworn to secrecy. You won't get anything out of us not even if you torture us."

The Inspector smiled bitter. "I am very used to the Vatican's methods of secrecy. This goes on all the time. They will not cooperate, even when it is in their own, damning best interest. It's like they are guarding the Holy Grail or something."

Laura looked at him. She was pensive—you do not know how close you are to the truth, she thought.

10.

NIGHT OF ORION

They took a taxi to Laura's apartment, which was on the third floor of a renovated, old building on a narrow street not far from the Vatican. A few pedestrians stopped and looked at Laura and John as they got out of the taxi in front of the building.

"Do you want me to stay with you?" John asked.

Laura shook her head. "No—Not here. I need to get out of Rome tonight. I am going upstairs to clean up. You should go to your hotel and do the same. And change your clothes—dress nice but relaxed. And pick me up when you are ready. I would like to show you my favorite place in the country. It is peaceful there."

Back in his hotel room, John showered and shaved. He felt physically strong. That always counted when he was involved in a case like this. It was the most important part—Do not let death and terror get to you. Because if you do—let them get to you—they will surely kick your feet away from under you in a flash. He put on light tan pants, a white shirt, and a light, charcoal grey jacket. He was confident he could solve the case—the lead was real.

The phone in the room rang. It was Father Renquist from New York telling him his son Eric was fine. He was having a good time and he seemed to be making progress.

John missed Eric terribly. He felt brief guilt about leaving him. For an instant, he thought of heading straight back to New York. Then he thought of the Father's kindness, his own deep involvement in this case of international proportion, and Laura. He thanked the priest, and he told him he expected to be away for another ten days. He was going to China on the first connection out of Rome.

After he hung up the phone, he walked over to the windows and lifted the curtains, which kept the afternoon heat out. The roofs of Rome were colored a golden hue by the setting sun. He stared at the tiled roofs and distant cupolas, unable to get over a queasy feeling—something was not as he thought it should be—something was wrong. He remembered Laura growing tense and pale in the Count's office, any time the work of her parents was mentioned, and the Count telling them it must have been an inside job. He thought about Laura's reaction when the Police Chief suggested she should be watched for her own protection. Did they want to watch her because she was a target or because she knew more than she admitted? Or both? Whatever it was, John knew Laura was one of the loveliest women he had ever met. It was hard to believe she could be involved in any wrongdoing.

Count Ormani, on the other hand, was a dark enigma. John had never met a more complex personality and he hedged the strangest feelings against him, he could only describe as deep distrust. John was aware that it was rumored the Vatican had many extended orders and affiliates within Rome and around the world who interpreted the doctrines of the Church in ways, which were sometimes absurd and cruel. Some even had turned to witch craft and worship of the devil. The Count, it seemed to John, was not above any of it. As an official of the bank of Rome, he could be involved in all kinds of financial machinations, with or without the knowledge of the papacy. Whatever it was, John probably would find out soon enough.

Later, when John approached Laura's apartment, he saw a character leaning on a wall not far from the building's entrance. He was almost certain it was a plain-clothes policeman. The Police Chief works fast, John thought. He walked up the three floors to ring Laura's doorbell.

Laura looked beautiful as she stepped out of her door, which she quickly locked behind her. "You look very handsome, John," she said with a slight smile.

"I can only return the compliment," John smiled back at her.

Laura's face turned serious. "You know, I really want my privacy tonight. Could you make sure we are not followed?"

"Well, I saw a fellow downstairs. He seemed to be looking up and down the street. We better go out the back door."

"But there is no back door, only the front entrance. What can we do?"

"Don't worry, I have an idea," John said.

They walked down the stairs.

"Wait here and watch me." John went out the front door and walked up to the police officer. "*Mi scusi*," he said, asking the man directions how to get to the Via Apia.

The man pointed and gesticulated vividly as he described the road through the seven hills.

Behind the man's back, John saw Laura sneak out of the building. She disappeared around a corner.

"*Gracie, gracie*," John said to the policeman. He walked in the opposite direction and turned left into the next side street.

Laura had already hailed a taxi. She sat in the back seat of the taxi car waiting for John in the quiet street. The taxi soon was at the outskirts of Rome following the picturesque road into the sunset.

John watched the road behind them in the rearview mirror. A pale yellow nondescript car, which looked like an old Opel, seemed to follow in the distance behind them. John caught the taxi driver's glance in the mirror, knowing that the driver also was aware of the car following them. "Driver! I think we have some company, but we want to remain incognito. Do you know what I mean? Do you think you could lose him?"

The driver's eyes in the mirror acknowledged. "Not a problem, *Signore*." He swerved the car around and took a quick detour.

The road soon lead through hills and vineyards that were dotted with pines and outlined with cypress. They could see the white houses and the pink summer villas of Rome's old families. Sometimes they came so close to the shore they could see a small band of the blue Tyrrhenian Sea in the distance. Then the blue of the sea was replaced with the blue of a lake, which reflected the sky. A hillside, with impeccably maintained park-like gardens, rose near the lake. On top of the hill was a pink castle, centuries old.

"We are as close to heaven as it gets," Laura said.

John looked at the castle. "What do you mean?"

"That's Castel Gandolfo, the Pope's summer residence. Over there, below the castle, you can see the small town of Castel Gandolfo. We are in the papal domain again, meaning the entire area belongs to the state of the Vatican."

John looked at the castle. It was a well-structured sixteenth century building. Its beauty lay in the simplicity of its architecture. Oddly enough, on top of the building were two tall protruding domes. John's eyes widened. "What's that?"

"That's the Vatican observatory. It is one of the most modern observatories in the world. It has a seventy-three inch telescope. Jesuit priests run it. It ties in with an observatory near Tucson, Arizona, which gives them even more range. The Jesuits run back and forth between Castel Gandolfo and Arizona all the time. Coincidentally, the space rocks, Professor Stynfeldt was talking about—they are called "the Pope's little space aliens". They are keeping a collection of hundreds of them in the observatory. Some of them are similar to the rocks my parents found in Africa. They know some of the rocks contain matter which proves there is life on other planets."

"But they will never admit it. Will they?"

"Never!"

John pondered the ominous domes that overshadowed the castle. "You mean the Church is looking to the heavens for an answer?"

"Well, it is not as simple as that. Astronomy is one of the oldest sciences in the world. This observatory was established in the sixteenth century. The castle once was the residence of Pope Urban VIII, the same Pope who condemned Galileo. The Church still maintains the doctrine today, trying Galileo was wrong, nothing more and nothing less. And Galileo's findings are acceptable as a hypothesis."

"You mean they haven't admitted yet that Galileo was right?"

"That's right. Only that the trial against him was wrong, nothing else, and that his findings were acceptable as a hypothesis. It's a little crazy isn't it?"

John looked at the shining domes again. He was pensive. "You mean to tell me that they are conducting the most advanced studies of astronomy and maintain state-of-the-art observatories, but they have not admitted yet Galileo was right?"

"Yes. You see, you have to understand what the Church is all about. It is not about what men can learn through science, it is about faith and believing. Either you believe or you don't. Both science and religion are abstract concepts. Most of the scientific evidence around us, like the movement of atoms or the speed of light, we cannot see, even though we know it is there. This is also the case with religion. We cannot see God even though we know he is there."

John put his arm around Laura and pulled her close to him. "You are amazing," he said.

The taxi followed a narrow road up into the courtyard of a quaint country inn. It was a place known by insiders for its relaxing atmosphere, good wine, and excellent food—a sanctuary for the weary.

"Under what names are we checking in?" John asked the delicate question. "We can check in as Mr. and Mrs. or as individuals."

"They don't care. Half of Rome is here under false names anyway. Just check in under Mr. and Mrs. Smith or whatever name you like. Get a suite of two adjoining rooms. It is not the weekend they should have rooms available. Some people here might recognize me, I should not check in under my own name."

"Okay, Mr. And Mrs. Smith it is."

Sometime later, John waited for Laura at the inn's open bar, on the roof terrace that overlooked the lovely grounds. Maybe it was just a hunch, but he could not rid himself of the feeling they had been followed. He sipped his Bourbon and soda slowly. He was in a pensive mood and he reminded himself to remain as alert as possible.

John watched Laura's sleek figure in her white bathing suit as she crossed the tropically landscaped pool area below the terrace. She dove into the dark blue water like a dolphin. As he watched her doing laps he could feel her enjoyment of the water.

He looked beyond the pool area, down the hillside at the blue lake. The countryside looked like a scene from a romantic movie. Swallows flew up from the vineyards where earthy looking people harvested grapes while singing old love songs. It was an unreal scene to good to be true.

John could see part of the road winding up to the inn and into the courtyard below. Not many people were arriving or checking in. But then, the pale yellow car, that he thought had followed them all along, came slowly up the driveway. It pulled into the inn's courtyard. John looked down at the two men in dark, shiny suits who emerged from the car. "Sons of bitches," he murmured to himself. "What do you want?" He began to feel a little edgy. He admitted to himself that he wanted Laura very much at his side.

When she appeared on the terrace like a vision, shortly after he had his second Bourbon and soda, he felt relieved.

In the restaurant, that overlooked the countryside and lake, the mood was subdued. It was as if the warm, romantic scenery had absorbed the thoughts and conversations of the few couples, at the restaurant's tables, who were enjoying the evening.

There was a three-man band, but even they played low. A waiter in a white jacket came over to their table and poured them two large glasses of perfectly tempered red wine.

Laura raised her glass. She looked through the ruby red liquid straight at John. "Thank you for rescuing me."

John too raised his glass. "If you want to know the truth, I don't think I rescued you. I rather think you rescued me."

"Well, maybe we rescued each other." Laura looked around. "Thank God, for a place like this. Far away from the crazies of this world. Everything is perfectly beautiful. It seems life goes on here eternally without any trouble."

John took another big gulp of the velvety wine. "To you, Laura, and to eternal beauty. This is lovely and you are just as lovely. I think your driving saved the driver's life and maybe the Professor also. You are quite something."

"Let's hope and pray—" Laura's blue-green eyes sparkled. "You should know people in Rome are very special. We adore life and beautiful things. Why should we have to deal with violence and the murder of the innocent, when everything could be so perfect?"

John touched her hand lightly. "You really have been through a lot in a short time, haven't you?"

She nodded. "True, but I am beginning to feel a little better now."

"Do you think what the Professor said about the discovery of your parents is true?"

"I am convinced it is true. It does make sense, doesn't it? I studied anthropology, paleontology, and religious sciences. Many learned scholars say similar things. Evolution went on according to Darwin. Then, all at once, something unexpected happened. I think this unexpected event really happened and my parents knew it, and proved it to a point. Now, that we have new DNA science and improved analytical science, it is even more real."

John took Laura's hand. "I believe you. But tell me, what do you think will happen to the perception of the world we know if the truth comes out?"

Laura was suddenly overwhelmed with love and pain—love for John and the pain she felt thinking of the world they lived in.

"I don't know. I think the followers of the devil are trying to take over the world and destroy the human spirit. As it stands now—it looks like they are winning. The followers of the antichrist are terrorizing and killing people in the name of God. The devilish, perverted people are spreading unspeakable evil. I am afraid, they would not care too much about the origin of humanity and the human spirit, anyway. The holy Church could probably be convinced eventually by scientific evidence but it would take them at least three hundred years to admit the truth or the possibility of the truth."

"True Laura, but tell me one more thing. I have had the strangest feelings about the Count. Tell me what side you think the Count is on. What is his game? Financial gain, devil worship, or both?"

"Laura let out a constrained laugh. You are crazy, John. I think all the complicated rules of the Vatican are driving you crazy, dear."

"I am sorry, Laura."

"I admit the Count acts a bit flamboyant and mysterious. However, he is very dedicated to the faith and to the Church. All his dealings through the bank of Rome are completely honest and integer. He is a grandmaster of the Knights of St. John, which is the order that is the closest protector of his Holiness the Pope himself. I have worked close enough with the Count to know him well and to know there is nothing wrong or suspicious about him."

John was smitten by Laura's beauty and honesty which he thought came from within the depth of her soul. "Well, I don't know. I think you are right. I admire you, Laura. I have never met anyone with so much passion and understanding of the human condition. You have a brilliant brain in that beautiful head of yours and a lot of compassion. And, I think it is time to calm down and relax. I am feeling as hungry as a wolf. Let us just enjoy the evening. No more political or religious discussions. Let's just try to forget it all, for now." John lifted his glass. "Come on drink up, it will make you feel better."

Their food finally arrived. A six-course meal, which could have made anyone sing arias of Italian opera. They washed it all down with the fine-bodied red wine they were drinking before.

"By the way," Laura said. Considerably calmer now, she raised her glass again. "This is my most favorite wine. I hate to tell you this. It is not from here from the Romagna, but actually from, the Toscana. It is called Santa Christina. It's from an estate in the Toscana, near the castle where I was raised."

John looked at the ruby liquid in his glass. "Personally, I like Bourbon or Scotch whiskey but this is something I could get used to. You are right this wine is especially good. I can taste in it the land and the spirit of the people inhabiting it," he said dreamily.

Laura looked at John. She began to see him as he was. "You are quite a poet, John."

John looked at her. He took her hand and kissed it. He smiled a wicked little smile. That's because you make me feel like dancing."

His mentioning the disco song made them both chuckle. After they finished their last bit of bread, cheese, and grapes, John noticed the small band played a more upbeat tune, *Volare*, a favorite among popular Italian songs. "Would you like to dance? Or are you still supposed to be in mourning over the nuns and priests?"

"And, don't forget the mother and her young daughter, the people in the bus, and the driver and Professor Stynfeldt," Laura said with a pained expression. "The body-count is rising. I do not think anyone would mind if we danced, especially not the nuns or the two little priests, who were killed so horribly. I am still hoping the driver and Professor Stynfeldt are alive. Our hospitals are very good—I am praying for a miracle—and I do not think dancing is bad or could be harmful to any one. So let's dance. It won't make a difference to any of them now."

"Good, Laura. Just hold on to me. Most people experience tragedy in their lives one way or another. Life itself just makes us go on. It seems as long as we have a spark of life in us we will go on, no matter what happens."

"Yes, John. We must do it all, no matter what."

"No, Laura. We must not do it. We want to do it."

"Whatever you say, John."

John held Laura in his arms. They danced a slow, romantic dance.

"We deserve this," Laura whispered. She looked up at John. "I feel like I am being carried off by tiny, tiny birds."

John held her firm. "You know how it is with Italian music and wine. It's guaranteed to make you float to heaven—*nel blu di pinto di blu*—."

"I think it's your dancing John. You are very good."

"You know how it was with Ginger and Fred."

Laura chuckled. "I know."

They looked at each other, knowing they were falling in love.

Laura looked up at the night sky, where she could see the twinkling stars of the constellation of Orion. "The Heavenly Hunter looks like he is on the warpath tonight, but never the less he is our witness."

John did not really understand what she meant, but he was too content to find out.

Looking over John's shoulder, Laura suddenly froze in his arms.

"What is it?" he asked.

"Just go on normally," she whispered. Church agents!"

"What do you mean?"

"Two Vatican under cover agents. We call them Church agents. They are armed and very dangerous. I hope they are not looking for us."

John managed a glimpse in the direction Laura had indicated. He saw two handsomely groomed types in dark, button-up suits near the bar. The only thing strange about them, they looked like twins, or clones of each other.

John danced Laura unobtrusively into a corner of the terrace.

There was an ancient, travertine staircase leading down into the dark gardens. The midnight air smelled of fresh earth, orange blossoms, and jasmine. Neither John nor Laura ever forgot what the air smelled like that night, because it was their first passionate night together.

The constellation of Orion was slowly paling, as the promise of a new morning washed out the sky.

At Laura's and John's balcony, the French doors were open. Sheer drapes billowed in the breeze. Around four o'clock in the morning, the breeze discontinued blowing, and a soft mist settled in.

Set against gold and beige silken walls, a four-poster bed was large and luxurious with cream-colored bedding. John slowly woke up, immediately thinking of Laura. He reached for her. His hands searched the bed. "Laura," he whispered, "where are you?" He thought she was probably in the bathroom, but when she did not return, he turned on the light. The room looked less enchanting in the early morning hours. One thing he knew immediately. Laura was not there. She was gone.

John got up and went into the bathroom. He peed as quickly as he could, and he grabbed a towel, which he tied around his waist. Extremely troubled by the disappearance of Laura, he looked everywhere, the adjoining room, the bathroom, the closets, and out the windows and balconies. Finally, he opened the suite's door and looked out.

The thick, old walls of the corridor wound around to a wooden staircase, leading down. He noticed a large, wooden cross on the wall next to a candelabra with a flickering torch. He looked up and down the corridor and decided there was no one. The inn looked like it was deserted.

A gigantic shadow was suddenly projected on the whitewashed

wall. In a moment, John noticed it was a man's shadow, raising a muscular arm. He got a glimpse of the arm. It was covered tightly with some kind of shiny black cloth.

Strong hands took the cross from the wall.

As John turned around, the cross came down on his head. John felt himself falling into twirling darkness.

It was almost noon when John slowly came around. He noticed the warm sunshine and the soft, earthy air in the room. The room had been picked up. It was shiny and bright. John was lying in the bed, which had been made meticulously. He was wearing his pajamas. The delicious smell of fresh coffee taunted him pleasantly. Next to the bed, on a side table was a silver tray with coffee in a silver can, croissants, jam, butter, and the neatly folded morning paper.

The last thing he remembered was walking down a corridor with a towel around his waist. He looked at the pajamas, the neat room, and the breakfast. How did I get like this? he thought. Are they trying to play tricks with my mind? He shook his head, immediately feeling a slight headache, a little dizziness. He dropped the impulse of wanting to jump out of bed quickly, and he reached for the paper instead. He unfolded the paper.

Laura's and his picture were on the front page next to the images of the burning bus, "Nineteen killed and many wounded in terror attack at Da-Vinci-Airport. Two suspects were arrested."

"Two suspects were arrested?" John jumped out of bed in a hurry, feeling the slight headache again. "Thanks Inspector for breaking our cover," he said with clenched teeth. "And thanks for arresting us. I forgot we were photographed in front of the police station."

Fully dressed and ready to go, John discreetly talked to the inn's morning receptionist. He asked him if he had seen Laura d'Andres leave earlier that morning by herself.

The receptionist gave him a strange look, then told him he had not seen her, nor did he have any idea who she was or what John was even talking about.

Laura had disappeared from the room without a trace. For a moment, John thought Laura just might have left him after a one-night stand, going on to her normal life. But when he thought of the intimacy of their lovemaking and their happiness, he knew this could not be. Laura would never have left him just like that. Something must have happened to her.

While he was waiting for the taxi to pick him up and take him back to Rome he tried to make several calls from the reception hall's phone booth. First, he called Laura's private number. There was no answer. The phone just kept ringing. Then he dialed Count Ormani's office in the Vatican.

"Count Ormani is out of town," the secretary informed him.

"Can I speak with his assistant?"

"Sorry, but Miss d'Andres has not yet come in this morning."

"Are there any messages for John Cordes?" He tried his last shot.

"Sorry, no messages," was the answer.

The taxi took John straight back to Rome to Laura's apartment building. John walked up the three stories, taking two steps at a time. He rang the doorbell several times. No one was at home. On the floor in front of the door was a bottle of fresh milk and the morning's paper. On the front page was the ominous picture the paparazzi had snapped when John and Laura were taken into the police station in handcuffs. "Scandalous." John thought. "The paper is actually saying Laura and I are the suspects arrested in this case. It's insanity!"

No one stopped John from entering the Vatican. He walked briskly up the stairs to the Count's office. It took about three minutes after he rang the buzzer several times. The door quietly swung open.

The Count's secretary, in his black suit, white shirt, and red tie, jumped up from behind his desk. "I am sorry, but the Count is not here, and neither is Laura d'Andres," he said with weasel eyes."

"I was working with the Count and Laura just yesterday. Where have they disappeared to in such a hurry?"

John knew the secretary was lying when he said, "a pressing engagement, out of town."

John walked right past him. "I don't believe you." He opened the door to the Count's inner sanctum.

The secretary went after him, trying to stop him. "Don't! Don't!" he screamed. "You have no right—"

Through the door opening, John could see four men sitting around the conference table. He noticed they were all handsomely groomed and they wore the same black suits made out of shiny, jute-like material and black ties. They men looked more like clones of each other.

John remembered seeing two of the men at the inn. Church agents, Laura had called them.

One of them quietly rose to his feet, and picked up a submachine gun, which lay in full view on the conference table. He pointed the gun at John. "I must ask you to leave," he said.

"But I was working with the Count and Laura only yesterday," John tried to protest. "They are not here. Please leave!" the man said.

In the back seat of the taxi, John sorted out his thoughts. He was not much concerned about the Count's disappearance. But he was deeply concerned about Laura. He knew, he should leave for China as soon as possible, and he knew he could not leave without knowing Laura was safe. The taxi was driving around Rome aimlessly, when a tall, white building came into sight.

"Stop right here," John said to the driver. He paid the cabby, and went straight into the hospital.

11.

SALVATION

John briefly talked to the hospital's receptionist at the front desk. He then took the elevator up to the second floor.

Stynfeldt was in a private room on the second floor. He was propped up in a raised bed. He was pale but happy and alert. He managed a smile. "I am glad to see you, John. And thanks for rescuing me."

John nodded. "You are welcome."

"It's a miracle I am here," Stynfeldt said.

John noticed the fresh bandage on Stynfeldt's temple. "What happened?" he asked.

"This is unbelievable. The bullet went right into my head, right in here." Stynfeldt pointed at the bandage. "I was not unconscious for long—woke up when they wheeled me into the hospital. I did not even realize I had been shot. I mean, it did not hurt. Now it hurts a little, but they gave me some pills. The bullet was stuck in my head between the brain and the skull bone. It did not even scratch the brain. They pulled the damn thing right back out.

Sheer luck I would say, especially at my age. It's like it was not meant to be—not yet—like I still have things to do in this world."

John sat down on a visitor's chair. "Congratulations, Professor."

Stynfeldt could not hide his emotions. "I heard the Vatican driver was hurt too. He is right here in this hospital. Do you know how he is doing?"

"They operated on him for almost six hours. He is still in critical condition."

"A lucky duck am I." Stynfeldt sighed.

"Professor, how do you feel? I mean, is it all right if I ask you a few questions?"

"Just go ahead, John, ask. I am fine. But first, for God's sake, can you tell me who attacked us and why?"

"Let me answer your question with a question, Professor," John said, sliding his chair closer to the bed. "Have you ever heard of Kuei-Lin?"

"Isn't that a town in Southern China?"

"Correct. Kuei-Lin or Guilin is a town in Southern China. The outfit I am interested in calls itself A.P.S.-Kuei-Lin—ever heard of them?"

Stynfeldt's mouth fell open. "You mean Advanced Plasma Studies?"

"Is that what the letters stand for?"

"Son of a—are they behind this?"

"It looks like it."

"I know that company. They have been around for some time. At first, the Chinese government funded them. Their main purpose was to develop an alternative energy source, so that China would not have to depend on oil. They were developing fuel cells using plasma technology. They were also trying to make hydrogen fuel from seawater. Imagine splitting water—H_2O—and getting hydrogen as an abundant source of clean energy and oxygen, to enrich our atmosphere?"

Stynfeldt tried a faint smile. "Whatever they tried to do, was truly laudable because this entire absurd oil business would be out of commission if they had succeeded. Using oil as an energy source was one of the greatest mistakes humankind ever made throughout its history. Imagine, pumping the precious substance made from the bodies of prehistoric animals out of the ground, as a source of energy to propel metal boxes like cars and planes, running all over, polluting the atmosphere, and causing global warming. Who knows, disrupting the tectonic structure, because oil serves as a hydraulic fluid for the tectonic plates. And have you ever thought that global warming could not only come from carbon pollution, but from within. From within the Earth, I mean. After they suck out all the oil that insulates us from the great heat within the core of this planet—Just think of the terror and the misery mammoth oil has brought this world."

John nodded. "I can see your point. But what about A.P.S., the company?"

"I am sorry, but all that oil business is just one of my pet beefs, which has nothing to do with your question. I think the pills are making me edgy."

Stynfeldt went on. "Anyway, a few years ago, China went nuclear. The government of China withdrew their funds from A.P.S. The company was taken over by a private party no one knows much about. They went underground. About two years ago, they contacted me. They asked me to consult with them. I told them I was only a bio-anthropologist doing research in the field of linking DNA and anthropology. They wrote me back, they were expanding their research to include space and plasma studies, which makes sense because the entire damn Universe is made out of plasma."

Stynfeldt continued. "Then they wrote me, they had read my book, and they were interested in the work of the Andersons. I told them, the work of the Andersons was probably buried in the Secret Archives of the Vatican, with access denied. Anything known about it was in my books and papers, which could be found in the open literature at several university libraries. I've not heard from them since." Stynfeldt reached for a glass of water on the side table.

John helped him get the water, "I wonder why, all of a sudden, they were interested in the findings of the Andersons and why they would attack the Vatican?"

"I don't know, but I heard the company was run by a real mad-man, mad as a gorilla and power crazy. That's all I know."

"Well, Professor, I think you know plenty. This is very helpful. Believe it or not, I have once or twice been to Guilin before. It is one of the most beautiful places but also one of the most dangerous ones. I am going there to find out what's going on at that A.P.S. outfit. But first I must find Laura." John told Stynfeldt about the disappearance of Laura. He carefully avoided the subject of their romance and that they had fallen in love.

Stynfeldt, who was visibly upset upon hearing the story of Laura's disappearance, had guessed it. "You and Laura like each other," he said. "You can't deny it. It is obvious."

John hesitated. "It probably is obvious. After my wife died, I never thought I would look at another woman again. Laura is so different—I liked her from the first moment on, and when I got to know her, I could not help but to love her.

"That's understandable, John." Stynfeldt gave his blessing. "You are a good man. Laura deserves someone like you—please find her, John!"

12.

CATACOMBS

After John left Stynfeldt in the hospital, he wandered around the old cobblestone streets near Laura's apartment. He thought of Laura and agonized about what could have happened to her, imagining all kinds of things. Then he knew he probably would not find the answer walking around the streets, which, in the afternoon siesta hours, were nearly empty. He did not know where to begin his search for her and he tried to regroup his thinking. What could have happened? Was there a connection between Laura's disappearance and the absence of the Count? There probably was.

John heard the chime of a church bell. It reminded him of the insignificance of perceived time. Then suddenly he saw him. It was one of the Church secret agents wearing the typical black suit and tie.

The man came around a corner, slow at first, scanning the sleepy streets with slanted eyes. Then walking quickly, he disappeared into the shady entrance of a small church. He had not seen John. This was a good sign, John thought. He followed the man into the church. The church was small with a narrow nave, and very old. Diffused light came through the stained-glass windows. He saw the man disappear behind the high altar, shadow-like. Carefully avoiding any noise his shoes would make on the polished stone floor, John followed him behind the main altar. The man had disappeared. There was an opening in the wall, a rough-hewn staircase winding down. John smelled a musty smell, like the breath of ages, coming from below.

On his way down the stairs, John's hand held on to a narrow, wrought iron handrail leading him through the darkness. Through the hollow of the catacombs, he could hear the footsteps of the man running down below him. Suddenly the footsteps stopped. John strained his ears listening trying to see through the darkness. Nothing. The sound of the footsteps suddenly stopped. John stopped in his tracks. He listened hard. The caved walls of the dugout staircase were visible now in a warm glow of orange light. He smelled smoke. Was there a fire deep in the catacombs? John sensed it more than he heard it. Accompanied by grunts and heavy breathing, the footsteps ran back up, fast now, toward John.

The man let out a blood-curdling roar, a war cry of proportion, as he came back up from below, wielding a long thin knife at John.

Taking advantage of being in the high position, John catapulted himself downward, trying to avoid the shiny knife.

As John's body-weight smashed into the man like a ton of bricks, the man bellowed, keeled over, and crashed against the porous wall behind him.

John's hand snatched forward, grabbing the man's arm like a vice, slamming it against the wall. John could hear the knife's metallic sound as it hit the floor. His foot booted the knife away. He could feel the crush of breaking bones as his fist landed one of his famous punches right into the man's face. The man collapsed in an obscure corner. Catching his breath, John pulled himself together and continued downward.

Flickering firelight now illuminated the ancient sepulchral vaults with mounds of skulls and heaps of bones. A musty old tunnel, built of rough-hewn stones, lead to a large, circular torture chamber, illuminated by a fire glowing in a blacksmith's fire pit. The room was distinguished by primitive instruments of torture, casting shadows on the walls. A spiked ball, held up by a chain, was connected to some kind of a release switch.

Laura was in the middle of the torture chamber. She was sitting in an old-fashioned torture chair with a guillotine above her. Her hands were bound behind her back. Her blouse was ripped. The spiked ball was aimed directly at her face.

Count Ormani stood near Laura who looked distressed but defiant. His hand reached for the release switch of the spiked ball.

John briefly thought the scene looked like it was out of a cheap horror movie, and he wished it were not real. But as soon as he heard their voices, he knew it was very real.

The Count was raving. "It was you, Laura. You, yourself delivered the carpetbag to the terrorists. You know who they are, don't you? A filthy Chinese crime organization. They hate Western religion and culture. Their only purpose is to make China predominant, so that they can take over the world and destroy it."

Laura sounded frightened. "I am not a traitor. And the medieval torture methods you are trying out on me, do not frighten me either. They haven't been used since the inquisition."

The Count was still raving. "It was easy for you to steal the carpetbag and hand it to these criminals. Tell me the truth, Laura—the complete truth. Or the ball will come down. This is unbelievable! After all we have done for you!"

Laura's voice trembled. "I didn't know who was behind this. The woman who called me said she represented a group of scientists at the University of Hong Kong who wanted to use the findings of my parents for a peaceful purpose. They offered me money, which I refused to take. I just wanted to bring the evidence that was discovered by my parents back to the light, so it could be useful to help better the world."

"You are naïve, Laura. You are worthless to us now, a traitor in the highest sense. It would be a pleasure for me to kill you, to see that beautiful face smashed to a pulp. The Council of the Knights of the Inquisition might decide you will have to be executed, anyhow."

Laura's voice came out pitched. "You know I would never even dream of doing anything against you. I didn't even know my parent's discovery was right here in the Vatican, until these so called scientists told me, to my surprise, it was right here in the Vatican Secret Archives. You know best—I was just a baby when my parents died."

"That's cute, Laura. I am just wondering if you still have other things left from your parents, some papers, books, or other evidence. You better tell me right now, Laura, or I am afraid—"

Laura saw John from the corner of her eyes. Her frown turned into a faint smile.

John motioned her not to give him away. He appeared behind the Count, swiftly ramming the barrel of his revolver against the Count's neck. "Slowly, Count, take your hand off the switch—very slowly—and step back."

Letting out a screech of surprise, the Count crept away from the release switch.

Keeping the gun aimed at the Count at close range, not letting the Count out of his sight, John managed to step up to the torture chair and to free Laura.

Laura was even more weakened by the sudden feeling of relief.

Her legs wanted to buckle, but she propped herself up. She got up slowly.

John motioned her toward the door opening.

Laura inched along the wall toward the door opening, when out of the shadows, the Count suddenly attacked, wielding a huge sword.

Laura, in a daze, noticed the Count looked like an avenging Samurai.

The sword came down almost cutting off John's hand, which held the gun. With a loud clank, the sword became stuck on the rough surface of an ancient wooden table.

The Count grabbed John's arm, jamming John's hand on the table, flinging John's gun out of his hand. He came straight at John like a charging bull.

John threw himself against the Count and engaged him in a wrestling fight.

The Count, being older and having lived far too well, was no match for John who knocked the teeth out of the Count's jaw. Collapsing like a worm-eaten, old monument, the Count fell into the torture chair.

Laura, still in a daze, inched along the wall toward the door opening. Set on her escape, she did not realize that her shoulder touched the spiked ball's release.

The ball came down, smashing the Count's head to a pulp. At the same time, the guillotine was released by the impact. It cut off one of the Count's arms. The Count's brains and hot blood splattered about the room.

In an instant, John was next to Laura, leading her out of the torture chamber. Laura tried to turn around, to see what had happened to the Count. But John put his arm around her, pushing her gently through the door. "Don't look back! Don't look back!"

On their way up through the catacombs, John noticed the Church Knight was gone or he was hiding in the shadows.

As they came out of the darkness of the catacombs into the dim light of the Church, John could see Laura's face was as white as marble. She trembled. "Let's sit down here for a moment," he said, leading Laura to a church bench.

They sat close together. Laura was leaning heavily against John. John put his arm around her.

She looked at him, holding back overflowing tears and hysteria. "The Count is dead! Isn't he?" she said, feigning calmness.

"Yes, Laura. The Count is very, very dead."

Laura's eyes stared into space. After a long silence, she came back. Her vision focused on the main altar. Floating above the main altar was a triangle with a large eye painted on it. The eye seemed to be staring at them. Laura looked up. "This is the All-Seeing-Eye, the symbol of the Illuminati, the Masons, and the Maltese Knights. I am scared, John. The Eye looks at me as if it knows I killed a Maltese Knight. I am guilty having caused all of this."

"Don't be silly Laura. You did not kill the Count and you did not cause any of this. They would have attacked the Vatican with or without your help. The Count's death was an accident. And God only knows what the Count would have done to you."

"But the Church agents don't know it was an accident. They will think I killed the Count on purpose because he found out about my dealings with the terrorists. I am sure, the Count told them all about it. You do not know how dangerous they are. They will come after me, just like the Count, thinking I am a traitor in the highest sense. The punishment for this is torture and death."

"Tell me about your dealings with the terrorists. Was it really you, Laura?"

"I am afraid so—I was, at first, contacted by a woman who

said she was with the University of Hong Kong. She said the University of Hong Kong studied the work of my parents and they wanted to complete the work and publish it. I did not think anything was wrong with that. I thought the Vatican did not care one way or another, and the carpetbag had been forgotten in the Deep Archives. What was strange though. Two men from mainland China, not from Hong Kong, came to get the carpetbag. They offered me money—fifty thousand dollars. I told them I did not want money, only recognition for my parents. Two weeks later, the terror began. I am guilty, John. I think I have committed a terrible sin!"

Suddenly, the entrance door, at the far end of the church flew open with a loud bang. The menacing silhouettes of four of the Church agents were set against the bright sunlight streaming into the obscurity of the old church. Stalwart, with their semi-automatics pointing at John and Laura, their voices hollered loud, disturbing the sanctity of the church. "Don't make a move! Come with us! Let's go!"

John's eyes squinted. "Don't you know this is a house of worship?" he yelled at the top of his lungs. He grabbed Laura's arm They ran toward the front of the church, to the altar. They could see the All-Seeing-Eye above the altar. It was hit with a salve of machine gun fire. They dove around the altar and hurried back down the stairs into the catacombs.

It got pitch dark very quickly as they ran down the worn-out stairs. The way down seemed longer than before. At some point, they took a different turn. This time the stairs ended in another part of the catacombs. They stumbled through a maze of vaults and tunnels Laura tried to hold on to John. "Please, please, don't go so fast."

John pulled her into a side chamber. They both caught their breaths.

"I am scared."

"Shah, don't say anything—just listen." Through the porous walls, they could hear the Church Knight's footsteps. Only it seemed the steps were running away from them, like little pounding feet of mice—diminishing. John's voice echoed clearly through the caves. "Where are we?"

Laura's voice was more like a trembling surge. "We must be in the oldest part of the Christian catacombs, somewhere in between the river Tiber and the Vatican. These catacombs are three stories deep and two thousand years old. The early Christians were not allowed to bury their dead within the confines of Rome, so they went underground and they dug out and built this puzzling maze of catacombs. We will never find a way out of here. We'll starve to death."

John tried to calm Laura by joking. "I am not planning to become one of the skeletons yet. How can you think about food in a situation like this? We can always catch rats and lick the moisture off the walls, pretending we are drinking catacomb branch-water."

Laura's chortle was constrained. "This is not funny, John."

"I know, Laura—not too funny—but I have seen worse." John searched his pockets. He found the small flashlight he usually carried with him. He turned it on. The chamber was filled to the top with bones and skulls.

"Nice," John said.

Following the thin stream of light through the tunnels, they passed many other rooms and caves full of human bones that were lit up temporarily and then fell back again into two thousand year-old darkness.

After they had stumbled about for some time, which felt endless, they finally found a tunnel leading upward. As they moved upward, it got lighter. The dugout merged into a structured corridor. The stamped down earth became polished marble. The structure became familiar.

Laura was excited. "I know exactly where we are. I recognize these walls. We are in the necropolis under Saint Peter."

"Is that good or bad?"

"I think it's good. We are within the borders of the Vatican. If we somehow can reach the Cardinal and explain everything before the Church agents find us, I think, they won't kill us."

"Oh no!"

Coming around a bend, they suddenly found themselves in front of a huge, solid-oak door, spanning the entire space of the vaulted dug-out. John tried the heavy cast iron door handle. It was locked, as expected.

"Of course, the Vatican's security is—"

"Very tight, as we know. John finished Laura's sentence.

Laura tried to act calm but she was frightened.

"We never get through here and if we turn back we never find a way out. The catacombs will swallow us. People have gotten lost down here before. Wandering through the black maze, crazed—their skeletons were found years later.

"Don't worry, Laura. I have an idea. I am going to shoot the lock. We have to do it carefully though because if the bullet ricochets in this narrow corridor, it could kill us both."

John led Laura behind the first bend in the corridor. Standing in front of her, he took cover behind the bend. "Put your hands over your ears! Are you ready?"

"Ready!"

John planted his feet firmly on the ground. He held the gun with two outstretched arms. He aimed and fired. They both felt the impact of the blast numbing their ears, a big round hole marked the door where the lock had been. In the silence following the blast, the door creaked. It gently swung open.

"We are underneath the basilica of Saint Peter," Laura explained excited as they walked in the hollow corridors of marble mausoleums. The tombs of the City of the Dead were bathed in dimmed, artificial light.

"Many popes and saints are buried here, and many more are still to come."

"May bee you could show me the Secret Archives now?" John said in a sarcastic mood.

"You never give up, do you?" Laura answered.

They came out of the necropolis near the main altar of Saint Peter.

"Hold it right here." John took Laura's arm and pulled her behind the base of a huge, twisted column. From behind the column, they peered into the main nave of the basilica populated by a never-ending stream of tourists and clergy.

"I could have told you so." John whispered. Among the crowds of tourists, they could see the Church agents who had entered Saint Peter from the other side of the necropolis.

Laura sighed. "Don't worry, they won't use their weapons in this church."

"No—Laura? I would not depend on it. They are defending against a threat to blow up their world. They are on a knife's edge. I think they will shoot, if necessary, even if it means shooting up the holiest church in the world."

Hiding behind columns, statues, and altars, John and Laura finally managed to walk out of the basilica and into the Vatican, without being seen by the Church agents.

The Count's secretary almost fell from his chair when Laura and John entered the Count's offices. His pink nostrils sniffed them over. "Ms. d'Andres, I thought you were gone—

"You thought I was dead, didn't you? I am not. The Count is dead instead."

The secretary turned ashen. "Oh God Almighty!"

John pulled his gun from the holster under his arm and pointed it at the secretary. "Thou shall not call God's name in vain! Don't you remember?"

"Yes. Yes. I remember."

"Call the Count's superior!" John insisted.

The secretary, with eyes bulging, trembled like a wet dog. "You mean, call Cardinal de Montaigne?"

Laura's voice cut through the room. "That's right. And hurry. We have not much time. The Church agents are after us."

"I don't know if the Cardinal is available. It is not like I can just call him any time."

"Just call!" John motioned his gun, pointing at the phone on the desk.

"Okay." The secretary picked up the phone and dialed.

At this moment the Church agents, with their semi-automatics readied, came storming through the door.

"Please don't shoot!" The secretary screamed in pitched panic.

John's revolver touched the secretary's temple. "He is right. Please don't."

The Church agents stopped in their tracks.

During the momentary stand off, Cardinal de Montaigne, in his purple scull cap and purple trimmed black frock, was a welcomed sight as he came sailing through the door. He waved his hand with a gentle gesture. The golden cross he wore on his chest gleamed, and his blue eyes shone. "Not so hasty, gentlemen. Do not act hasty. We all must know what is happening here before we act," he said with his French accent.

Laura sighed, relieved.

The Cardinal went straight into the Count's main office and

sat down at the head of the conference table. "Everybody, please join me. Gentlemen, please put your guns away and secure them. And, please, calm down."

The Cardinal, Laura, John, and the secretary sat around the table, while the Church agents remained standing. The Cardinal's piercing eyes looked at Laura inquisitively. "Now Laura, tell us all, what is going on? Tell us the truth, my child."

Laura was glad to talk. She told the story from the onset. She talked about her parents, the explorer couple, and their discovery they placed in a carpetbag. And the woman with a Chinese accent, who called from Hong Kong, asking if she knew the carpetbag was kept in the archives. How she told her she thought the carpetbag was lost. However, the woman insisted the carpetbag was in the archives and asked Laura to retrieve it. Somehow, the Count had found out it was Laura who handed the carpetbag to the enemy. That is when the Count sent the Church agents after her. They kidnapped her from the inn near Castel Gandolfo, and took her to the torture chamber in the catacombs. The Count threatened to kill her, but John found them. Thank God. During the ensuing fight between the Count and John, the Count was unfortunately killed by accident.

When Laura finished telling her story, she was near tears. "I never imagined giving the carpetbag to the wrong people would cause such a furor. *Mea culpa, mea maxima culpa*," she said.

The Cardinal understood what she meant. It was all her fault.

"I am begging your forgiveness," Laura said. "All of this horror was caused by me. It is my fault. I will never get over it, causing the deaths of the nuns and the priests and all the others—"

The Cardinal shook his head. "God's ways are strange. Given the circumstances and having John as a witness to most of this I am inclined to believe you, Laura." His eyes intensified. "Just don't be so presumptuous to think you caused all of this. You are just a minute little part in enormous, big clockwork. They would have attacked us with or without your help. I want you to come to my quarters for confession, tomorrow. Just make an appointment with my secretary. So I can absolve you of the sins, you may have committed, unwillingly."

Laura nodded with tears in her eyes. "Thank you, your eminency."

The Cardinal addressed the Church agents. He told them to find the Count and prepare him for a funeral. "That's all!"

The Church agents heeled, bowed, and left as fast as they came.

The Cardinal now turned to Laura and the secretary. "Your job is to cook up a plausible story about how and why the Count died so suddenly. Laura, you will be in charge of this office, until we can find a successor for the Count."

Laura was grateful and relieved. "Your Eminency, I thank you for your generosity and kindness."

"That's all right, child. Just make sure you come to confession tomorrow."

The Cardinal turned to John. "Mr. Cordes, I heard you will be going to China?"

"That's right, your Eminency. I'm going to Guilin, in Southern China, on the first connection I can get out of Rome."

"Let me know when you are ready. I want to bless your journey. Laura, will you take care of John's travel arrangements?"

"Yes, Eminency." Laura paused for a moment and then said with a strong, composed voice. "Since I have caused a lot of harm, I want to help and make it better. And since I know all about our missions and connections in China and Hong Kong, I am respectfully requesting to be allowed to go to China with John Cordes."

The Cardinal shook his head. His sharp eyes looked straight at Laura. "I don't know if this would be wise, child?"

"That's out of the question," John interjected. "It is far too dangerous. Besides, I always work alone."

"I am the one who hired you, John, and this is my case. You promised you would work with me in liaison—you remember. I had police training, not with the Militia Christi—they would not let a woman in—but with the Roman police. I am very familiar with the far East. Just last year, the Count sent me on a mission to Tibet. Imagine, a woman in Tibet, an oligarchy, similar to the Vatican but even more constrictive. I could be very helpful to you, John. Anyway—you have no choice in the matter. I am coming with you, whether you like it or not."

Laura turned to the Cardinal. "Please your Eminency, you were willing to put me in charge of the security department. I must have a chance to help end the terror. Someone will have to accompany John Cordes to China and there is no one else better qualified than me."

"Well, maybe you are right, someone representing the Vatican should accompany John. I can see, logically, it would be you, Laura. And it probably is not such a bad idea, considering we will have a lot explaining to do about what happened to Count Ormani and how?"

The Cardinal cleared his throat. "The Count was a Maltese Knight in a high position in the Vatican. There could be an inquisition into the circumstances of his death by the College of Bishop's or by different orders of the Maltese Knights, the Militia Christi, and others over which I don't have much control. If Laura became the subject of an inquisition, it could become very unpleasant for her. I am not sure I could protect her as much as I wanted to. If the press somehow found out, how and why the Count died, we could have a major scandal on our hands. Your role, Laura, in the matter and the circumstances of the Count's death could become a major issue. You could be investigated and dragged through the mud, so to speak. There could even be a trial. The media would have a field day with you. They would love nothing more than a witch-hunt involving a woman in a trusted position in the Vatican."

The Cardinal turned to John. "Considering these circumstances, I think it wouldn't be such a bad idea to send Laura with you to China. A nice, long trip away from here could probably save her many unpleasant experiences and heart aches."

Laura took the Cardinal's indecisiveness for a positive answer. You know your Eminency, I am not afraid to face anything that could come up concerning the Count's death. Because I know now, it was an accident. John explained it all to me. The real reason I want to go with John is that I need a chance to help find the killers, and to vindicate myself that way.

The Cardinal took a long hard look at Laura. "I know child. I know. You are a good and honest person, in addition, your are very strong. So go with God—go with God and John to China."

Laura beamed with gratitude. "Thank you for everything, your Eminency." She turned to John. "It will take me about an hour to make our travel arrangements."

John knew he could not fight Laura, not now or ever. She just did something to him he could not easily explain. But that was not all. John had a very uneasy feeling about the Cardinal's remarks about an investigation in to the Counts sensational death. It made sense. If the media found out about this, their pursuit of Laura could be relentless. If the Church agents decided to make her the subject of an inquisition, it could get worse. In that case, Laura's life would be in danger.

John looked at Laura. "Okay, Laura, you are coming with me. But do you know where we are going?"

Laura was excited. "I certainly do. You told me yourself, John."

"And do you know about my contact in China? An old friend from my CIA days."

"You can tell me all about it on the plane, John.

13.

CONFESSIONS

It took Laura only a short time to make her and John's travel arrangements to China.

However, before they left, there was one more important issue Laura had to resolve. Cardinal de Montaigne had insisted she come for an audience-confessional to his offices. This was most important for many reasons involving Laura's well being and sanity, which had been badly damaged by the acts of death and terror she had witnessed. Self-doubt of her own role concerning her job as the assistant to the Vatican head of security, Count Ormani, whose death in the dungeon still hounded her with feelings of guilt, caused her never-ending nightmares.

Laura, at this point, was not sure of her own beliefs and convictions any longer. She felt more like a leaf shaking in the wind, an ice-cold wind, which chilled her soul to the core. It all was unbearably confusing and she needed the Cardinal's fatherly advice more than ever. She also could not shed a deep fear that the Church agents could come after her again, avenging the Count's death, and accusing her of heresy, especially, if they found out more of the details about the evidence contained in the carpetbag and their significance. They were known to use the old inquisition methods of torture and death. She knew that the torture room in the catacombs had been used by them several times in the recent past and that it would be used again if they deemed it necessary to purge her soul from "the temptations of the devil." In some instances, tortured victims had been found hanging under bridges or smashed to a pulp by falling from high monuments. There also were rumors that some of the women had been burned as witches at the stake in some old abandoned quarry outside Rome.

Laura waited in the Cardinal's reception room. She wore a lightweight, plum colored linen suit and a small black lace mantilla, which covered her hair. She shivered when she thought of all the things they could do to her. Worse, since Count Ormani had shown his true face to her in the dungeon, she was not sure about the Count's integrity any longer and she began to wonder if he had been involved in serving the more sinister elements in the Vatican, that everyone was aware of but no one ever talked about.

Cardinal de Montaigne's office, which was on the second floor of one of the Vatican's administrative buildings, was unexpectedly unpretentious, unlike the lavish space that Count Ormani had occupied in the older part of the Vatican. Laura remembered that the Cardinal, Aristide de Montaigne, though he was from a family of old French aristocracy, who owned several castles and had holdings in France, was originally a Franciscan-Jesuit monk, sworn to austerity and poverty.

A young Friar with a fresh, joyful smile served as the Cardinal's receptionist. "Just relax Ms. Andres," he said, "the Cardinal is waiting for you." The Cardinal's inner office was a pleasant large room. Sunshine and sweet, warm air mixed with traces of Rome's smog came through the tall, half-open windows.

As long as she had worked in the Vatican, Laura had always admired the cleanliness of the windows in the administrative buildings, which were always kept shiny and spotless in their painted white frames. She could hear church bells ring outside the windows in the Roman distance, and the tic-tac of a wall clock inside the stillness of the room. It was one of those moments she could almost feel eternity. Laura looked around herself. The walls were covered with bookcases full of precious books and bundled documents. The room was furnished functionally with contemporary furniture, a large shiny mahogany desk with a leather chair, some visitor's chairs, a settee consisting of a rigid, red sofa, high-back chair, and a marble coffee table. An impressive but simple wooden cross hung above the travertine fireplace. The only other embellishment in the room was a painting of Saint Francis of Assisi, which took up almost one half of the East wall.

Laura admired the painting, which showed the Saint surrounded by animals depicted as God's gentle creatures, when the white haired Cardinal, wearing his purple scull cap, purple rimmed and belted cassock, and golden pectoral cross, came out of his study.

"That's a Tintoretto," he said with his French accent. Don't worry I don't own it. It is a loan from the Vatican museum."

"It is peace on Earth," Laura said, still looking at the painting. "It is wonderful. I feel privileged to see it." She turned around and looked into the Cardinal's sharp, blue eagle eyes framed by his taut, tanned face. The Cardinal was all about strength and clarity of mind she thought.

Laura's fingers touched the Cardinal's out stretched hand. She curtsied, remaining respectfully distant.

"It's good to see you came, Laura. We should talk about some very important things."

"My confession. I'm ready for it."

"Yes, your confession, we do that later but first we must talk."

An older nun in a black habit came in from the Cardinal's study room. She placed a tray with a bottle of Amontillado-sherry and two sherry glasses on the coffee table.

"Thank you, Maria-Lourdes," the Cardinal said. The nun bowed her head slightly and then disappeared through the front door.

"Sit down, let's talk, have a sherry. There is nothing better than a glass of sherry to relax your mind and sharpen your thoughts."

Laura sat on the sofa. The Cardinal sat on the chair close to her. Tasting the sherry, Laura thought of lovely fountains in Spanish gardens and she began to feel less anxious.

"As you well know, there are several reasons I asked you to come to my office."

"Thank you for seeing me. This is a great honor."

"As a Cardinal I can make decisions and recommendations whether or not someone should be excommunicated or become subject of an inquisition. I know your soul is pure. I will recommend you highly and I will protect you as much as I can. But as you well know, even the powers of a Cardinal can be limited, especially in cases that could slip into the wrong hands, the hands of persons that could secretly be affiliated with the forces of the Devil."

"I always doubted they existed," Laura said quietly.

The Cardinal nodded gravely. "But they do exist—even here in the Vatican. There are some who believe in the existence of the Devil almost as much as we believe in the existence of God. In addition, there were hushed rumors for a long time that Count Ormani had some questionable affiliations. The Count was under investigation for the past three years, not as much as for demonic associations but more for financial machinations concerning the bank of Rome."

Hearing this Laura suddenly felt sick. She almost fainted. "It can't be true!" She took the glass of sherry and emptied it. "I swear to you, I don't know anything about this," she said with a toneless voice. Nothing like this ever occurred with my knowledge during all those years I worked for the Count."

"I didn't think it did. Let me ask you this. You are a learned woman, a theologian, and an anthropologist. You do understand that before I can absolve you from your sins I need to see you clearly. I need to know exactly were you are standing. I am convinced you know nothing about the Count's secret dealings. It is clear to me, you did not kill the Count but that it was an accident. I only need to hear one thing from you Laura, loud and clear, You do believe in the Holy Trinity of the Father, the Son, and the Holy Ghost, and you do believe that Jesus is the son of God who took away the sins of the world through his own suffering on the cross—Amen!"

Laura's eyes filled with tears of righteous anger. Her voice came out strong. "I don't understand how you could even ask me such a question. Of course, I believe Jesus is the son of God, and everyone knows that I am especially partial about the Holy Ghost, which represents all that is good about the human spirit. And I believe that Christ died on the cross not only to redeem us from our sins but to save the human spirit for all mankind."

"Please calm yourself, Laura. You know, I had to ask you these questions. Now that the cat is out of the bag, so to speak—"

"Are you referring to my parents and the carpetbag?"

"Well, think of it, Laura. A lovely young orphaned woman works for an eccentric Roman aristocrat in the Vatican. All is fine for years. But all of a sudden, it turns out the lovely young woman is not an orphan but the daughter of well known paleontologists who more than thirty years ago discovered the "missing link" is not missing. No one had paid much attention to that discovery. They treated it like some loony curiosity, which was buried in the Deep Archives. Now, whoops, the cat is out of the bag. And this earth-shattering discovery is used to upset the world's believe systems, and to rain terror upon us. And not only is it affecting us here in Rome, but all of us—Christians, Jews, Muslims, and alike—anyone who wants to believe in an old-fashioned version of God is affected by this. How do you combine your belief in God and in the son of God, Jesus Christ, with the belief that men were created by some aliens as an experiment to better the world?"

Laura dried her tears. She sat up straight. "May I remind you, your Eminency, that you yourself gave us a speech how God was not, as Bishop Usher described him and as he is depicted in so many paintings, a bearded old man who sits in judgment somewhere in heaven above the clouds. But God is the creator of heaven and earth, the entire universe, the planets, the stars, the moons and the suns. And that Jesus Christ was the human child of a universal God, just as we are human children of a universal God. Jesus was the essence of humanity in its highest form, so pure and so much like God, he could perform miracles, which were meant to show us that the glory of God was ready to be understood by humans. But among us measly earth-worms only a few ever get to the state where they can see and understand the godliness of Jesus as the savior who tried to save the human spirit."

The Cardinal followed Laura's words, approvingly. "Well, the picture is not as dark as you paint it, Laura. Christians on this Earth today are many billions strong."

Laura continued. "But there is a difference. The Church believes that man was created by God approximately four thousand years ago. My parents were scientists who found proof that man was created by someone introducing the godly DNA to a selected few humanoids, our African ancestors. Both thought-trains believe that we were part of evolution, the same as animals, until we were made human by the touch of God, just like in Michelangelo's painting of the Creation. The difference is only in the science. A very small difference, that leaves plenty of room for the evolution of species as discovered by Darwin. It also leaves room for God as the Creator, if one believes that God is the Universe or the creator of it and that there could be life on other planets, all under the same God. Only that some of these extraterrestrial societies could be closer to him then us. And the Holy Ghost or the Holy Spirit is the substance of life of all beings on earth and in heaven. And God could exist in a much more refined form somewhere in heaven—heaven being the Universe." Laura let out a deep sigh. She felt physically and mentally drained. "This is my confession, Cardinal, there is nothing more I want to say."

"Please calm yourself," the Cardinal said. You have just given me a beautiful confession. He got up and picked up a purple stole that had a cross insignia embroidered at each end. He put the stole around his neck and he held one end of it against Laura's forehead.

Laura who had been to confession before was not confused or startled by this gesture. It meant the Cardinal represented Jesus Christ who wiped away all her sins, committed knowingly or unknowingly, with the end of the stole from her forehead. *"In nominee Jesus Christi te absolvo."*

Laura bent her head and folded her hands in prayer. "Thank you Lord, Amen."

The Cardinal sat down in the chair again. "Thank you Laura for sharing your mind. Your view of the world very much coincides with my own."

"That's because I followed and studied many of your teachings, your Eminency."

"That's very good, Laura. It is always so uplifting to find brothers or sisters with a good mind. However, there is one more subject, dear to my heart, which is often overlooked. He pointed at the painting of the Saint Francis of Assisi. Would you allow me to share a few moments talking to you about Saint Francis?"

"I couldn't think of anything that would be more rewarding, your Eminency."

Laura got up from the sofa. She stood directly in front of the painting. It was an ideal scene. It showed Saint Francis in the lovely Tuscan countryside, surrounded by gentle looking animals that shared the love and peacefulness of the moment with him. A sweet, little lamb was hanging over the Saint's shoulder.

The Cardinal had come up behind Laura. He began to explain the painting. "You see, Saint Francis actually believed that animals have souls similar to us humans. He understood their role as a part of God's magnificent creation, which does not coincide with Darwin's theory of evolution, but with the idea that animals are creatures of God, as wondrous as any thing. That's why cruelty to animals is a deadly sin—"

Laura suddenly felt ill. The room began to spin around her. Saint Francis' sweet little lamb was going the slaughterhouse. She had a vision of tortured animals and slaughter so massive she was sick with repulsion. She could hear the cries of the innocent creatures and smell their blood. In her mind, she saw streams and oceans flowing with blood. A whirlwind of repulsion broke her and took her down. Laura crumbled within herself and she fainted, sinking to the floor.

"Water! Water!" Someone yelled.

Laura drifted into consciousness. She was lying on the Cardinal's rigid, red sofa.

The young Friar held smelling salts under her nose. The Cardinal, sprinkled drops of holy water over her.

Laura sat up. "What happened?"

"I don't know." The Cardinal pointed at the picture of Saint Francis. "You were standing there, looking at the picture of Saint Francis and then you fainted. Is there anything wrong with this picture?"

Laura too looked at the picture. "Is there anything wrong with this picture?" She repeated the Cardinal's words thinking for a moment. "I can tell you what's wrong with this picture. It is too nice. Like all religious pictures, they are just too nice. They do not reflect what is really happening in this world. What is real in this world could make your hair stand up straight. The world is sliding into the abyss of hell and nothing can stop it. Especially not the holy Vatican who is trying to stop the Devil by showing the world pretty pictures of Christ and of Saints, preaching love and harmony in God."

The Cardinal's face turned pale. "I am sorry to hear this coming out of your mouth, Laura. I think the events of the past few weeks and the knowledge of the discovery of your parents have had a confusing effect on you. I really think it is best for you to go away for a while. Go with John to China. When you come back, maybe you will see it all in a different light."

The situation suddenly was tense. There was nothing more to say.

Laura felt awkward. She straightened her spine and she nodded and curtsied. "Thank you, your Eminency. May I have permission to leave now?"

The Cardinal performed the blessing of the cross over her. "Yes, child, go with God."

As soon as Laura had left the Cardinal's offices, the Cardinal went into the reception room. "Do you have Laura d'Andres dossier?" he asked the Friar.

"Yes, yes. Here it is, your Eminency."

The Cardinal opened the folder. He looked at Laura's picture smiling faithfully into the camera. "It's a shame," he said, "such a lovely child."

He took a red marking pen from the Friar's desk. He wrote something in large, red letters across the first page of the dossier.

The Friar dutifully applied a blotter over the Cardinal's writing. When he read the words that were written all over Laura's dossier his face turned white. *Persona non grata*—he knew what that meant.

"Should I file this, Eminency?"

"No, no," was the Cardinal's response. Leave it on my desk. We will have to work with this."

14.

GUILIN

The long flight to China was not as strenuous as John and Laura had anticipated. The service in the first-class cabin took up part of the time, pleasantly.

Laura was a little quiet, John thought. Perhaps she was pensive, thinking she had attracted the terrorists in the first place and then she had pushed herself on this trip with him. Although John was used to work alone, he had to admit he liked the fact that Laura was at his side. On the other hand, business and pleasure did not mix. Laura was just that, a mixture of a straight, intelligent partner and a lovely, vulnerable woman. He did not want to jeopardize her safety or his own. His was a hard-core business. Distractions could be dangerous.

In the window seat next to him, Laura took a tiny sip of a cordial they had just served them after a six-course meal with champagne and wine. She was a little drowsy. She smiled at John. "You don't mind I insisted coming with you, do you?"

John took her hand and placed a light kiss on her fingertips.

"I am used to work alone you know that. I never mix up my professional life with my private life. I know how to keep the two apart and I think you do too. We're not on a honeymoon and you better realize that."

Laura straightened herself up. "I know we're not on a honeymoon, even though it would be nice. Believe me, after what happened in Rome to all these people, you can trust me. I am fully focused on the job. I have had training, and I want to help you to get them."

"It's just—you know how to get to my weak side." Holding her hand firmly, John pulled her to him and kissed her hard and longingly.

Laura came out of the trance of the kiss. "I like your answers," she said. "I admit, I have been mixed-up by you from the beginning but what ever there is between us has to wait at least until we have accomplished our mission."

John kissed her fingertips again. "I love you, Laura. I loved you from the first moment on, but I have to agree with you— regretfully and respectfully. We will handle this one in the most professional way possible."

John had seen Kuei-Lin or Guilin before. It was one of the highlights of Southern China. They were on their final approach to Guilin airport. John woke up Laura, whose head rested on his shoulder. He pointed to the window. "Look down Laura—you must see this." The plane came in over the wide basin of the Li Jiang River, the ancient River Li, known as the magic soul of Guilin scenery. From the air, they could see almost the entire expanse of the river basin from Guilin to Yangzhou. The mirror-like waters looked like liquid, green jade, reflecting the myriad of grotesque pinnacles of the region's cone-shaped calcite hills and mountains.

"This place looks like it is closer to heaven than to earth."

John felt a little stab of pain. Laura's words reminded him of Diana, who had said the same thing about Guilin, when he brought her here on their honeymoon.

Before then, John had done some work as a consultant for the CIA. They had asked him to help them explore drug trafficking in Southern Asia. After spending close to three months in the region, John found out, and lined out to the CIA, that the source of the widespread drug network in South Asia was Hong Kong. And that the entire drug trafficking operation in Southern Asia could be traced to one man in Hong Kong, as evasive as a fly. His name was Tan Chee Hong. It had come to fighting in South Vietnam between the locals and the troops of Tan Chee Hong. These territorial brawls were called the Drug Wars. John had followed one of his leads to South Vietnam. He was almost caught and killed near the border between South Vietnam and China but he escaped along the route of the river Zuojiang into the province of Guangxi, an autonomous region in Southern China, from where he made it to the city of Nanning. There, he was able to contact a CIA operative, a young man called Jimmy Lu. Jimmy picked John up in Nanning and brought him to his hometown Guilin, from where he helped John to get back to the United States.

Guilin, a 2000 year-old city on the River Li, was named after the local Cassia trees which bloomed in late summer, when their intoxicating scent filled the air. John was so impressed with the beauty of the place, he later brought his bride here for their honeymoon. Diana was half-English and half Chinese. As a child, she had traveled the world with her journalist parents and she had seen many beautiful and interesting places. She fell in love with the sights of Guilin, and to her the place was closer to heaven than to earth.

Looking down at the area of Guilin from the plane, images and thoughts crept into John's mind. He tried to control his emotions with a sort of mental exercise he always used when he was in danger of drifting back too much. The thoughts of Diana and Eric were treasures buried deep in his heart. He knew he could not let them come to the surface now. He had a job to do, a dangerous, tedious job. He had to avoid giving in to his personal feelings. Any thoughts of his wife or the honeymoon they had spent here in Guilin had to be set aside. Concentrating on the job ahead helped to avoid painful memories of the past. This time John was in Guilin not as a tourist, but for one reason only, to follow the lead to A.P.S.

The badge on the Chinese man, he had shot and killed at the Rome airport, had clearly shown the town of his origin—Kuei-Lin, or Guilin, and the name of a company—A.P.S. John needed to find out everything he could about the connection between the gunman at the Rome airport and the Chinese company called A.P.S.

Not knowing it would come in handy one day, John had kept his relationship with his good friend Jimmy Lu over the years. When John informed Jimmy Lu that he was coming back to Guilin, Jimmy Lu was delighted and excited to see his old friend again.

John and Laura had traveled for almost twenty-eight hours from Rome to Guilin. They were exhausted. John knew it was not wise to show their faces in town where he, with his tall American looks, and Laura with her Italian accent, style, and grace, would stick out among the tourists.

John was pleased to see his old friend Jimmy Lu among the expecting crowd at Guilin airport. Good old Jimmy Lu, he thought, seeing Jimmy Lu, in a black T-shirt and Jeans, looked still well trained, and fit.

Jimmy Lu, at this point, had given up all his CIA connections. As a graduate of the Columbia School of Journalism in New York, he was now a journalist at the Guilin newspaper, reporting local news and translating culture West to East.

Jimmy Lu walked toward John with a big smile on his face. "It's good to see you old friend."

Seeing his friend made John feel glad and at ease. "Like-wise, like-wise," he smiled. They briefly hugged.

John introduced Laura. "Meet Laura d'Andres, from the Vatican security."

Jimmy Lu was pleasantly surprised. He shook Laura's hand and bowed. "I didn't know they employed women in the Vatican and especially not such beautiful ones."

"Laura is very different," John said.

Jimmy Lu nodded and smiled. "It is a great pleasure to meet you, Miss Laura."

Laura nodded at Jimmy Lu. "Like wise, like wise."

Jimmy Lu took their suitcases off the belt. "I didn't think it would be good for you to stay in any of the hotels in town. I think it is better you put up with my small place in the country for the time. The house is rather primitive but it is in a beautiful place right on the River Li and it is safe there."

John agreed. "Thank you. We will be very happy to stay at your house."

Jimmy Lu still drove his old yellow Volkswagen bus. The bus rattled along the winding, twisting country road, past the town of Guilin.

Terraced rice paddies, water buffalo, and bamboo groves characterized the crystal-clear waters of the River Li, and of course, the many bizarre calcite hills and mountain cones, which had fired the imagination of artists for centuries. The hills beyond hills, reflected in the water, made the landscape look like a strange fairyland. Along the riverbanks they could see peasants with turn-up trousers and cone-shaped straw hats, cormorant fishermen in narrow bamboo boats, women doing their washing, and bathing children.

During the ride up the river, they tried to talk about old times, but the noise of the rattling bus swallowed their words.

John, in the front seat next to Jimmy Lu, rode quietly, trying not to lose his balance.

Laura, who sat not far behind them, tried to hang on and enjoy the scenery.

Jimmy Lu's small house on the River Li was in a verdant area of tall grass with bamboo and cassia trees. It was built on stilts made of strong wooden logs. It had bamboo walls and a thatched-grass-roof. There were no windowpanes, just window openings covered by roll-up straw mats. A small wooden staircase led up to a lanai overlooking the river.

The inside of the house was scrubbed spotless. There were some bamboo furnishings, a futon-type sofa bed, and a large mahogany desk, which looked out of place. The futon and chair pillows were covered with water-buffalo leather. Modern amenities included a radio, a small television set, and a fifties-style refrigerator. The house had electricity but no indoor plumbing.

Jimmy Lu brought John and Laura's two suitcases from the bus. He showed Laura to a tiny room that was an addition to the small house.

The room contained a single-frame bed, with a white mosquito net, a nightstand with a lamp on it and a chair. "Miss Laura, you'll be comfy here, I hope. I have fired up the hot tub and the outhouse is out there too."

Laura felt like she was on a vacation from the accomplishments of civilization. The trip to China and the ride along the river had impressed her deeply. The primitive but clean nature of Jimmy Lu's place felt incredibly relaxing. She sat down on the bed and sighed.

Jimmy Lu stood in the door and his smiling eyes looked at her. "Do you need anything?"

"Thank you Jimmy, this is very nice, I like it very much. Instead of using your hot tub, I think, I will just go take a swim in the river. The water looked so nice on our way up here. If you have a towel, I would appreciate it. I did not bring a swimsuit. Is it Okay to swim without it?"

"It is quite Okay. Not many people around here. John and I will not look. I promise." Jimmy Lu pointed to a towel laid out on the bed. "Towel for you," he said. "You are right. river is very clean and mild, perfect for bathing."

"Are there any things in the river I should look out for?" Laura asked.

"There is nothing scary in the river, just some fish and sometimes water snakes. But they are harmless."

From the shore, the water's surface looked inviting, promising respite and coolness. Laura took off her clothes and wrapped the towel around her. She walked down to the river and let herself glide into the water. Swimming in the alkaline water of the River Li was most soothing. Laura closed her eyes and let herself go. Floating between heaven and earth, she could see John's face in the clouds. It made her sigh.

After she came up from the river, Laura put on the black Chinese cloth suit Jimmy Lu had laid out for her on the bed. She towel-dried and brushed her hair and then she stepped out of the house onto the lanai.

"How was your swim?" John asked.

"Oh it was just wonderful."

"Welcome to my small paradise," Jimmy Lu said. He served them tiny cups of chilled rice wine.

John and Laura sipped the rice wine. "Thanks again. It is good to be here. John said. How long has it been—?"

"I think it has been about thirteen years since the drug wars and ten years since you brought Diana for your honeymoon."

John nodded. "That's right. Because Eric is nine years old now."

Jimmy Lu looked serious. "I am glad to be able to tell you in person, how sorry I am the accident happened. Diana was such a great person."

"Was that your wife's name, Diana?" Laura asked. "What a pretty name."

John swallowed the stabbing pain the mention of Diana always caused him. "Yes. Diana was her name. She was a great person. Wasn't she? It was a terrible thing—"

Jimmy Lu was solemn. "You mentioned in your mail to me that, at the time, you were not completely convinced it was an accident. Could it have been some kind of hit from one of the hoodlums you crossed?"

"Not hoodlums, Jimmy. I have been very successful as an investigator. My investigations deal more with major corporations, drug cartels, and crime organizations. The thought had occurred to me, Diana's car could have been hit intentionally. But so far I have no proof of it."

"Well John, if you should ever need my help, I would be willing to come to New York and help you investigate. Although I am somewhat out of the loop, I have not forgotten what I was trained to do."

"As you know, all these years, I have worked alone. However, when I think about it, I probably could use some qualified help. And I know you are still sharp, Jimmy."

"Yes, John. Not as sharp as you are, I am sure. Tell me, how is your son? How is Eric?"

John's thoughts of Eric were more gratifying now. "He is doing better, thank God. He is supposed to come out of his autistic state soon. I did not want to leave him, but this little old priest is taking care of him."

John's thoughts wandered. "By the way—did you know the little old priest is from the same profession as you and I—the priest is a Vatican spy? Did you know the Vatican has undercover agents?"

"Isn't it true, Laura?"

"Yes, it's true." The Church has to protect itself. That's nothing new."

"During our CIA days we made connection with Vatican agents quite a bit. Don't you remember?" Jimmy Lu said.

John nodded. "I remember."

Laura finished her rice wine. "I think I need to relax for a while. I am exhausted from the trip. Do you mind if I lie down?"

"Please do," Jimmy Lu said. "I will call you when dinner is ready."

"Sweet dreams." John said.

After Laura went inside Jimmy Lu continued. "Tell me, John, why did you bring Laura? She certainly is an exceptional person, but as you just told us, you always work alone."

"You just said it, Jimmy. Laura is exceptional. I have never met anyone like her."

Jimmy Lu nodded. "Confucius says—this could be a new beginning for you, John. I am happy for you—By the way, I meant to tell you, I am also foreseeing happy times. I am engaged to a wonderful woman by the name of Micha who lives in town. Maybe you can meet her after you conclude your mission here."

"I would be very glad to meet her, Jimmy. And I am happy for you."

They both drank a little more rice wine and continued to talk quietly about the old days.

Drifting back from his thoughts about the past, Jimmy Lu smiled slyly. "Tell me one thing," he said, "would you mind if your contact here is beautiful?"

John was cautious. "If you are trying to tell me my contact is a woman, you can say so. And—no—I don't mind if she is beautiful, as long as she knows what she's doing."

Jimmy Lu grinned. "Chyna knows more about what she's doing then you or me. You can trust her. It is all settled. She will come here tonight. She will be your guide. But before, I want you to relax—take a load off—and take a bath."

"Take a bath how?"

Jimmy Lu handed John towels and a black Chinese pajama suit. He pointed at a wooden, barrel shaped tub under a cassia tree. Below the tub was a cast-iron stove, heating the water. The water itself moved by some swirling action. "We have all amenities of the West here and more. By the way, if you need to relax otherwise, the place is over there." He pointed at a small building, which looked like an outhouse.

Sitting in the hot water up to his neck, John relaxed. He relaxed as much as possible, knowing the relaxation would help him gain the strength necessary to deal with what lay ahead.

From the hot tub, John watched Jimmy Lu prepare their evening meal. The small kitchen set-up was outside on the lanai. It consisted of a cabinet, housing some plates and chopsticks, a wok, a rice steamer, and a two-burner hot plate. There was a tin tub for washing the dishes and laundry. It looked like Jimmy Lu was frying a fish in the wok, and he was preparing rice and vegetables in a steamer.

Jimmy Lu waved his hand. "Come on John, dinner is ready."

John dried himself and then put on the black pajama suit.

Jimmy Lu had set up a small table and three chairs on the lanai. He poured more rice wine. "Here's to friendship and a good mission."

"Let me get Laura."

"I have already told her."

Laura stepped onto the lanai, refreshed. She looked delightful in her black Chinese suit. She could smell the food. Her mouth watered. "I am hungry," she said.

She looked at the food Jimmy Lu had prepared—"Oh, that looks really good."

"Fish is really fresh," Jimmy Lu said.

John and Laura loved Jimmy Lu's food. They ate hungrily, tearing into the fresh fish with their chopsticks.

After they finished their meal, John began asking Jimmy questions again. "Tell me, what you know about A.P.S.?"

"Well, as you know, I have given up all my CIA connections and I have tried to concentrate on my reporting and teaching. I think it is time for me to settle down and get married. I am not as well informed as I used to be. Not much is known about A.P.S. around here. Most people don't even know they exist. The ones who do know don't want to go near the compound. Some of the people who have wandered into the area have disappeared. The plants and compounds up in the mountains are heavily guarded. I was able to find someone who knows one of their engineers. She will be your guide. She will meet you here later."

"What about our notorious friend Tan Chee Hong, China's number-one drug dealer?"

"Tan Chee Hong is still very much around. However, after your last encounter with him, it seems, he settled down a bit. It seems you stepped on his foot too hard. I think he turned the drug dealing over to a group of Vietnamese hoodlums. He has become a legitimate businessman, selling goods and services all over the world. He's made billions and his business in Hong Kong is, at least outwardly, legal."

"Interesting," John said.

"When are we beginning our mission?" Laura asked.

Jimmy Lu turned to Laura. "Since I didn't know you were coming, Laura, the arrangement to go to the A.P.S. compound was made for John only."

Laura was aghast. "It took me over twenty eight hours to get here and you mean to tell me now, I can't go with John on this mission?"

"I am sorry Laura. The trip is going to be very strenuous and there is a woman-guide for John, who knows the territory. She will take him to the compound. No arrangements were made for you. Besides, three people would be just too visible."

John tried to calm Laura. "He's right. It is very dangerous. Most of all, if I go in, someone has to stay here as a back up at base camp. And that's you Laura."

Laura was reluctant but she began to see his point. "Maybe that's true, but Jimmy Lu could be watching base camp. Please, John, take me with you."

"I can't, Laura—not this time. Please understand. It was all pre-arranged and I really need you to stay here as a back-up."

Laura was truly disappointed, but she was inclined to understand John's point. "If you say so, John—okay."

"Okay, then," Jimmy Lu said. "It is settled. Laura will stay here with me. In the meantime I suggest to you, John, you should relax a bit because you are going to need all your strength."

After they finished their meal and licked their chopsticks, Jimmy showed John to a doublewide hammock strung between trees behind the house. "Since you are neither James Bond nor Superman, I think it would be wise for you to rest a bit. You have about an hour before your date gets here. So sweet dreams, old friend."

John did not feel like he was James Bond or Superman, even though he wished he were. He felt no guilt accepting the comforts Jimmy Lu provided.

"Happy dreams," Laura said as John fell asleep in the hammock.

It was pitch dark when John woke up. Beyond the black outlines of the trees along the riverbank, he could see the shining water lit up by silver moonlight. John heard the tak-tak-tak of an outboard motor and he saw the light spot of what seemed to be a lantern floating above the water. He heard a loud whistle, almost like a bird's call.

Jimmy Lu came around the corner of the house. "It's time to go." He handed John a pair of soft, black leather boots. "Take these and put them on."

The boots felt comfortable. The left boot had a shaft for a knife sewn into it.

"Put this in there." Jimmy Lu handed him a long, thin, Samurai-type knife, which John stuck into the boot's shaft.

Laura watched a Chinese program on the small black and white TV set. She gazed at John as he took off his pajama jacket. Her eyes secretly caressed his lean, muscular torso.

John took the leather gun-strap with his gun from the desk. He took the gun out of the holster, and cleaned and loaded it carefully. When he was done with this chore, he put the gun back in the holster and strapped it to his body. "Never leave home without it," he said, putting the pajama top back on.

Laura got up from the sofa. John felt her stare. "I'd like to hug you John, but with the gun and all—"

He embraced Laura firmly and quickly. He kissed her forehead tenderly. "Be good, Laura. Moreover, be safe. I'll see you in the morning."

She knew John's coolness was due to his concentrating on the mission ahead. Still, her heart was ripped apart—she did not want to see him go. She wanted to be in his arms, to love him and hold him. Even the tiniest thought, something could happen to him and he might not return, was driving her to the brink of insanity. However, if John could be cool, so could Laura. She swallowed the notion of wanting to cry hysterically. Instead, she looked at her wristwatch. "If you are not back in ten hours, we are coming after you," she said calmly.

"That's right. Ten hours." Jimmy Lu said. "It's time to go now. Laura do you want to come with us down to the river?"

"No thanks. I am going to wait here." Standing on the lanai, Laura watched the two men walk quietly under an arch of blooming trees down to the boat dock. The river's dark water glistened in the moonlight. The black silhouette of a Chinese junk or sampan glided smoothly toward the shore. It docked at the small wooden pier.

The sampan was approximately thirty-five feet long and ten feet wide. On top of it was a thatched bunk-hut made of straw and bamboo that could sleep four. Outfitted with an outboard engine, the sampan was driven by an old Chinese man in the typical black cotton suit and small black-ribbon hat. The old man's mouth, under a thin, long moustache, managed a smile. One of his front teeth was missing.

Out of the boat's bunk-hut, the slim figure of a woman appeared on deck. She jumped onto the dock, cat-like and helped Jimmy Lu tie up the sampan.

"This is Chyna, your guide," Jimmy Lu said. "You can trust her."

"Pleased to meet you," John said, realizing at the same time, politeness was not necessary.

"Let's go," she said.

John gave Jimmy Lu a quick, manly hug. "Good-bye Jimmy, and thanks for everything."

"Good bye old friend and take care of you."

Neither one of them had the slightest inkling that they had just said their last good byes.

15.

A.P.S.

Ink-blue shadows marked the meandering valleys reaching into the hills. Bright moonlight delineated everything with clarity. The bizarre calcite cones and hills looked surreal in the contrasting light. They were reflected by the waters of the River Li flowing like liquid mercury. The wide river glistened as if in broad daylight. The sampan's black silhouette was gliding up-river.

The old man in the shadows at the sampan's stern smoked a cigarette, which lit up his face periodically. He talked quietly to the obscure figures inside the bunk-hut. "Soon we will be near camp. Secret government installations in these hills. Some people, very afraid, will not go near there. They say dragon lives in these hills. People know dragons don't really exist these days. It is a saying that means place is very dangerous—stay out! My daughter Chyna, she grew up here, she knows way. She very intelligent. Used to work for scientists in lab. She knows no dragon lives here anywhere—only danger."

174

John lifted the flap covering the opening of the sampan's bunk-hut and looked out. "Cut the smoke, old man. They can see that glow from miles away."

Chyna's voice came from behind him. "It does not matter. They know sampan comes up river every night. Come on American relax. I will make some tea." John dove back inside the hut. The flicker of the lantern, bouncing to the boats rhythm, lit up the inside periodically.

John's grey eyes glinted in the darkness. "So a dragon lives in these hills? That's interesting."

Chyna gently shook her head. "No dragon lives here, for sure. But that's what they want everyone to believe—it is just a story to scare people. They have managed to keep people away by instilling fear. It is true—some persons who tried to get too near to the compound have disappeared. So people just stay away from the place and pretend it doesn't exist."

"What do you know about A.P.S.? The old man said you were a scientist in a lab—is that so?"

"I am not a scientist. I am an actress. I met the First Engineer of A.P.S. We were engaged."

"You were engaged to their first engineer?"

"Not to their first engineer. The First Engineer in all of China, Ling Mao."

"I am sorry, I didn't understand. The First Engineer in all of China—that's different."

"It is true. We were engaged, and he told me many things about that company. He even took me up to the compound several times. He explained all about what they are doing. He is very proud."

"You are no longer engaged. Why?"

"The man is a pig."

"Well, that explains it."

Chyna's delicate hands poured tea from a straw-encased earthen wear pot into tiny cups. She handed one to John. "Drink this, American—it will make you feel much better."

John took the tea. "Thanks, and please call me John."

"Okay, John, and please call me Chyna."

"Okay, that's fine. What does it mean—the name Chyna?"

"It means some sort of bird sound or chiming. My mother liked it because Chyna is pronounced like China, which is like Chyna. So, you see—?"

"So I see." John sipped his tea. He looked at Chyna again, and realized how beautiful she really was, with her black silken hair and golden almond eyes. She reminded him of a rare ancestral bird, a raven maybe. However, something about her was odd and he could not pinpoint what it was.

Chyna felt his stare. "I am of the Miao people. My people go back for many generations. We play old instruments. I learned to play the lute. This is how I became to be an actress."

John stared at her face, fascinated. He swallowed his tea. "You mean you are one of those classic trained actresses of the ancient Chinese theater?"

"That's right. I studied many years. The traditional characters and expressions where taught to me by great masters."

"Have you ever heard of Tan Chee Hong?"

"I don't know who you are talking about. Am I supposed to know him?"

"Well, maybe not. But tell me all about A.P.S."

"I don't understand everything about them. I am a graduate of the University of Hong Kong—I can tell you many things, interesting or suspicious. The First Engineer, Ling, tried to explain most of it. It seems he talked about clean, unlimited energy sources and a bomb. A bomb that can wipe out entire countries but will not poison the air."

"You mean a clean bomb?"

"That's right, that's right."

"But why are they attacking the Vatican?"

"I really don't know anything about this. I could not tell. Maybe it has something to do with mind control and their space program."

"You mean to tell me, they have a space program?"

"I am not sure."

"Do you mean they are like communists?"

"Communists? No, they are not like them. I know communists. Many people in this country are communists. They have no choice. They hate them too. They want a new world order or something like that. They want to make the Vatican pay. They think there is a lot of loose money in the Vatican, secret money they keep in secret accounts all over the world. I can only guess."

"Are they anarchists?"

"What do you mean?"

"I mean are they against religion?"

"I know they hate religion of all kind. They hate the Vatican and the Pope."

"What do you know about the Vatican and the Pope?"

"Nothing! They just hate religion."

"Okay, I believe you. How long did you date the First Engineer?"

"Oh, three months maybe."

"That's not very long. Why?"

"I told you before, the man is a pig, and I couldn't stand him."

"But how did you meet him in the first place?"

"I first met him when we were both students in Hong Kong. Then some time, much later, I met him again in Guilin."

"When you were in Hong Kong, did you ever hear of Tan Chee Hong?"

"You have asked me this before. I have not heard that name."
Chyna sat on the bunk across from John. She bent forward so that
her face came close to John's. She breathed a warm breath of tea
onto John's cool skin. "You are very nice, John."

John looked at her. "I can say the same about you but that's
not what we are here for."

Chyna sipped more tea. "And that's a shame John."

Though John knew from experience he was attractive to
most women, he thought Chyna came on to him a little too
fast. Something about her was strange. A small yellow light kept
flashing in his mind—caution.

The sampan had quietly docked at the bank of a side arm of
the river, from where a crooked, stony path, barely visible, led up
into the hills.

Chyna took up a leather backpack, on the bunk beside her,
and rose to her feet. She took out a black knit watch cap and, with
one sweeping move, grabbed the mane of her hair and twisted it
into a knot on top of her head. She pulled the watch cap over it.
She then shouldered the backpack.

John too put on the black watch cap Jimmy Lu had given him.

"Are you ready?" Chyna whispered.

John nodded. "Yes."

The old man smiled his thin, toothless smile and waved his
bony hand as he disappeared in the mist behind them.

Camouflaged by night shadows cast by large rocks, stones,
and occasional fir trees, they quietly tracked up the mountainside
for at least an hour and a half. Below them, they could see the river
valley becoming more distinct the higher they climbed.

John looked down at the mirror-like surface of the river. At
one point the river valley bent at a sharp angle. On the river's
shore, beyond the bend, a sizeable installation of piped-in reactors

and cooling towers came in sight. John knew immediately he was looking at a large chemical plant.

"What's that?"

"That's one of their fuel plants. They are making hydrogen fuel from water. They have done it for years."

"I'll be—you mean they are using the water from the River Li estuary to make hydrogen?"

"Yes, but that's not all. They have another bigger plant further up the valley on the main river." Chyna sat down on one of the rounded rocks. "Let's rest."

"Okay." John sat down on a rock next to her. They both looked down at the hydrogen plant, which had suddenly appeared out of the fog.

John could see it was placed well and built sturdy. Dimly lit by occasional industrial lights, it was enclosed with a fence covered with military camouflage cloth. On top of the fence were large rolls of barbed wire. There was a narrow gun tower at a corner. It was not clear whether the tower was manned or not. John shook his head. "The EPA would have a field day with a plant like this sitting next to a natural river."

Chyna let out a giggle. "You Americans think of the strangest things. First, the thought of protecting nature is unknown to us in China. The most important thing is industrial progress. Second, not many know this plant actually exists. The ones who do know are either scared, they don't care, or they are paid off."

John thought that Chyna was really two faced. At times, she acted feminine and almost child-like. But then, she seemed to know what she was talking about. It occurred to him more and more, Chyna was an enigma.

After tracking up a steep incline, they finally arrived at a narrow plateau on top of the hill. Looking down at the valley beneath, they could make out some buildings and installations barely visible in the mist coming in from the river in patches. As the mist slowly drifted out of sight, they saw the buildings of a sizeable compound on the ground.

The moonlight lit up their plateau like a circus arena. They cowered behind rocks and shrubs in fear they would be detected.

The numerous cone-shaped hills around them, in the diffused light, looked soft like they were made of dark blue velvet.

Suddenly, out of the darkness, a light spectacle began to unfold directly before their eyes.

A blinding light laser beam came from the top of one of the hills, incredibly sharp. Another one followed from another hill. Then one by one, from corresponding hills around them, more laser beams appeared, piercing the night with concerted beams of light until there were twelve in all.

They looked to the bottom of the hill. In the increased light, they could see more installations. On a flat area the size of a football field were twelve polished steel poles arranged in the form of a dodecahedron, the shape of an even-sided twelve-pointed cross, similar to a chemical ring for carbon. Each pole was outfitted with a holding device on the top. In each holding device sat a fist size clump of rock, emitting an eerie glow. The glowing rocks seemed to be connected by beams of phosphorescent light particles, which made the configuration look like a large contemporary sculpture suspended in mid-air. The laser beams came from the hills in certain angles. Each beam hit a corresponding rock, piercing it, going through it, reassembling, and bundling beneath it in a center location.

They looked at the spectacle with strained eyes. Their eyes followed the beams to the point where they bundled. It seemed a thin streak of light connected this point with something in the sky above. They saw the streak going up to the night sky. The sky was now clear. The constellation of Orion was right above. The heavenly hunter looked large and distinct. Its stars were twinkling brightly. It seemed the faint streak of stardust connecting to the laser bundle was aligned with a star in the constellation of Orion.

The spectacle was mesmerizing. Not far beneath the center of the bundled lasers, a sizeable mercury-like bubble formed, hovering and humming. From its underside, a gentle stream of phosphorescent light particles or photons rained down like fluorescent rain, falling into a mirror-lined steel funnel on top of one of the compound's main buildings. The funnel, equipped with a reversed pump, sucked in the photons one by one and in groups.

They looked at the unbelievable phenomena occurring in plain view.

John let out a whiff of amazement.

Chyna tried to keep a straight face, not showing the fear she felt creeping up her spine.

The events the Andersons had written about. The experiment Stynfeldt had talked about. Were they happening right here in front of their eyes?

As if Chyna had read his mind, her words came out as if she was in a trance, answering his question. "I don't know. But it looks like it. I think the First Engineer was talking about DNA and how fluorescent rain could change animals into human beings."

This was it.

The silence was shattered by the loud tak-tak-tak of the rotor blades of a large helicopter. The chopper came up from below and over the hill like a huge insect, cutting the soft night air to pieces, bursting into the wide mellow sky. Blinding the two intruders, it pinned them to the ground. Hovering in mid-air directly above them, it whirled them around in a tornado of dust and light.

Three Chinese men with machine guns, uniformed like green

berets, came up over the hill, pointing their guns point-blank at them.

John and Chyna struggled to their feet. One of the men yelled, "Fold your hands behind your necks!"

Wavering on their feet, they folded their hands behind their necks.

Another one of the men briskly searched them both, but he did not find John's gun or the knife in the boot.

Idiot, John thought with brief relief.

The chopper fell off in a swift maneuver down behind the hill, and then appeared once more, fleeting into the hilly distance.

The men forced their guns on them. "Damned Americans, enemies of the people! Go down! Let's go straight down!"

John and Chyna followed the narrow path leading down to the A.P.S compound. The leader of the troop, following behind them, pointed his gun closely at their necks. He kept hurling insults at them they did not understand.

A cool, contemporary reception area was brightly lit. On the wall behind the reception desk was a polished steel sculpture in the shape of the chemical ring for hydrogen. The logo of A.P.S, the lettering, "ADVANCED PLASMA STUDIES" was made out of thin, polished steel that flashed brightly under the symbol.

It seemed a dutiful, pedantic male receptionist had been waiting for them. He wore a neat, black suit, with a white shirt, and a yellow silk tie with the outline of a black dragon. It quickly became clear he was more than a receptionist and that he was some kind of executive.

The three soldiers motioned John and Chyna into the reception area with their guns.

The receptionist's high-pitched voice sounded artificial. "Welcome to A.P.S, Mr. Cordes, of the New York firm Cordes and Mauser. Your firm has an international reputation. I wish you would work for us."

John smiled grimly. "Let me guess—A.P.S—Advanced Plasma Studies—weren't you sponsored by the government of China?"

"Correct, Mr. Cordes. But now we are not receiving government funds any longer. When China went nuclear, the government lost interest in furthering our technology. Dr. Lee Ho Ming took over the company. That's why we must look for funding all around the world so we can keep developing our science and technology which is superior to any company in the world in terms of providing energy and other related needs."

John shook his head. "And the way you arrange for funding is by blackmailing and killing the innocent? Instead of going to the bank, you just attack institutions you think have money, like the Vatican, and you help yourself?"

The receptionist stared at John, aghast. "Not exactly. I really do not know anything about how our company is funded. I am not in charge of financials. All I know, our technology is the most advanced in the world—the state-of-the-art. We have hydrogen fuel made from water, and we have a plasma bomb."

"You are spilling the beans awfully fast."

"I don't know what you mean—spilling beans?"

"I mean, we haven't been here for more than ten minutes and you are already bragging the story of A.P.S. to us."

"I don't know what you mean by bragging, either, I am just telling you facts. And I can tell you, I am not worried about bragging too much because I know whatever I tell you, whatever you see here, no one will ever know about it too soon."

Chyna was pale. "Does that mean we are not getting out of here alive?"

"Don't worry, Miss. We are not that kind of people."

John found this remark especially aggravating. "You are not that kind of people? But you use terrorist's methods killing nuns and priests?"

The receptionist smiled sarcastically. "People are expendable. China has more people than any other country in the world. If necessary, we can reach the moon by standing on top of each other's shoulders."

"I'd like to see that." John said sarcastically.

Chyna, who knew the receptionist had no intention of joking, interrupted him. "Don't John—"

The receptionist motioned the soldiers. "Dismissed!"

"The soldiers retreated outside the entrance door, where they remained like well-trained dogs.

The receptionist took the backpack from Chyna. "Just a precaution," he said. He looked at John, knowing the guards had frisked him. "No gun, Mr. Cordes? That's a little strange."

John smiled with steely eyes. "Just dropped the damn thing in the river."

"Well yes, if you say so." The receptionist motioned John and Chyna to follow him. But it was actually he who followed them down a hallway to the main laboratory of A.P.S.

The first thing they noticed the place was vast, brightly lit, and highly technical. At numerous lab benches with complex scientific equipment, scientists and technicians worked in shifts. They all wore the same white lab coats stitched with the logo of A.P.S. Across the lab, in a center location, was the outline of a funnel coming through the roof. The funnel ended in a glass-enclosed cloud chamber.

They were attracted to the cloud chamber immediately. Followed by the complaining receptionist who tried to keep pace with them and divert them, they walked to the cloud chamber as if drawn by a magnet. As soon as they stood in front of the chamber, they saw it. Inside the cloud chamber was an aura of light. The aura, made of light particles or photons, was in neither the shape of a human nor an animal. It seemed to be converging from one to the other. In the stream of blue-green light particles, a human figure emerged at first, and then turned into the shape of an ape or primate. In the process, the shape of the ape was transformed from primate back into the shape of a woman.

They stared at the experiment, which faded in and out, trying to comprehend what they saw.

"The Andersons were right," John said under his breath.

"We told you so." The receptionist caught up with them. "We told you we have the technology and the know-how. But the Vatican did not believe us. Instead of paying us, they sent you. They made a mistake they will regret and you will regret too, Mr. Cordes, as you will soon find out."

John's attention shifted. "Don't threaten me. I made no mistake. I know exactly what I am here for."

"Okay. In this case, please follow me. I want to introduce you to the supreme Commander and the First Engineer."

They followed the receptionist through the lab to the bench of the First Engineer who was discussing a project with an older Eurasian man, neatly dressed in a Mao suit.

Chyna tried to get John's attention, indicating the First Engineer with her eyes. "My ex-fiancé," she whispered.

John looked at the pudgy man whose face somehow reminded him of an insect. "No wonder he is your ex-," he whispered back.

The receptionist was perfectly polite. "Please meet Ling, the First Engineer, and Dr. Lee Ho Ming, the supreme Commander."

The all bowed as if this was a business meeting. No one shook hands. They all kept their distance in a barely noticeable stand off. The first engineer showed no sign of recognizing Chyna.

The Commander's eyes squinted. "Welcome to A.P.S." He

recognized Chyna. It was clear he found her very attractive, but he acted stern. "And who do we have here? The fisherman's daughter, who is considered a national treasure, is betraying her own people by bringing spies into her country?"

John's eyes focused on the white tiled lab bench behind the First Engineer. On the bench was a yellow and black carpetbag. The bag was open. Next to it were Marthie and Leo Anderson's handwritten books and two human skulls exhibited on glass stands. There was also a package of some kind of rolled up linen material cut open exposing several fossilized human bones.

"I see you have found the property we are looking for."

The Commander followed John's eyes. "Found and put to good use. This will propel us into the third millennium, fast. All Western belief systems, as they stand now, will be eliminated. Do you have any idea what the Andersons have found?"

"Maybe. But tell us."

The Commander pointed at the First Engineer. "Can you explain it to them, Ling?"

"I am happy to." The First Engineer pointed to the smaller of the skulls. "We believe this is the greatest anthropological find ever discovered. This is the skull of the mitochondrial Eve or the Earth Mother. The other skull could be her male counterpart, the y-chromosomal Adam. However, he is less important, because the DNA or the gene information of all humans is only passed on by the female—by the mother. The mitochondrial Eve is the single woman who is the most recent matrilineal ancestor for all living humans and from whom all mitochondrial DNA in all humans that lived after her is derived."

The First Engineer continued. He pointed at the larger one of the skulls. "This could be Adam, the male counterpart of the mitochondrial Eve who is our patrilineal, most recent, common ancestor. Anthropologists, because of fossil as well as

DNA evidence, theorize that the mitochondrial Eve and the y-chromosome Adam lived around 200,000 years ago in parts of East Africa, which are now called Kenya, or Tanzania. Moreover, as we now know because of the discovery of the Andersons, they actually lived near what today is known as the Olduvai Gorge in Tanzania, the world's most fertile anthropological fossil ground. This is why the mitochondrial Eve is also referred to as the African Eve. The time she lived, is calculated based on the molecular-clock technique of correlating elapsed time including the genetic drift. According to the most recent findings of the mitochondrial DNA data, the title mitochondrial Eve or African Eve belongs to the same original woman. Family trees that were constructed based on mitochondrial DNA, show that the living humans whose mitochondrial lineages branched earliest from the family tree are indigenous African Homo sapiens and the lineages of indigenous peoples or Homo sapiens on other continents all branch off from the African lineage. Anthropologists therefore reason that all living humans descend from the African Homo sapiens who migrated out of Africa to populate the rest of the world."

The First Engineer continued. "If the mitochondrial analysis is correct, then, because the mitochondrial Eve represents the basis of the mitochondrial family tree, she must have predated the exodus of Homo sapiens from Africa and she must have lived in Africa. Therefore, most researchers take the mitochondrial evidence as support for the "single-origin" or "Out-of-Africa" theory, which has been proven now beyond a reasonable doubt, by these findings here."

"Can you explain this in layman's terms?" John asked Ling.

"Yes, I will try. What I am saying is, these two humans whose skeletons we see here, lived in a small group of Homo sapiens near the Olduvai Gorge in West Africa. Only the DNA of one of the females in the group was passed on to her daughters and so on.

We believe that is what we have here. The mitochondrial Eve—or the Earth Mother."

John thought of Stynfeldt, who had explained the science to them before and who had told them the same thing. It was true, John thought. It was complicated but easily understandable at the same time. Looking closer at the small, brown skull, he suddenly felt as if they were touched by the breath of ages.

The Commander interrupted his thoughts. "But this is not all. Let me show you something over here. Ling show us the cloud-chamber."

The First Engineer bowed. "Follow me please." He led their small group back across the lab to the cloud-chamber installation. The experiment was still in progress. The woman in the cloud chamber, showered with blue-green photon particles, was still fading in and out, from human to primate to human.

The Commander was eager to explain. "You see, Mr. Cordes, this experiment, in progress now, will be concluded very soon. The chromosomes making up the monkey will be transformed into the chromosomes making up the woman. The woman will have a human mind and soul." He turned to Ling. "Can you explain it, Ling?"

The First Engineer calmly bowed again and smiled. "Yes supreme Commander. He looked them over, and then pointed at the cloud chamber. "You see the differences between chimpanzee and human are just ten times greater than those between two unrelated people, and ten times less than those between rats and mice. In fact, chimpanzee and human DNA is 98.5% percent identical. Even though the difference in DNA is only about 1.5%, the results are profound, because that small difference makes all the difference in the world—that difference is responsible for creating a brand-new species. We do not know exactly how we arrived at being able to change the monkey's DNA. I am still trying to come up with a formula. We just followed the instructions of the Andersons. We aligned the twelve rocks with certain stars in Orion, and bombarded them with electromagnetic waves. It seems the resulting photon shower, under certain conditions, can produce the results we are seeing here. We think this is what happened originally. The existing hominids in Africa were exposed to this kind of a photo-trans-genetic-electromagnetic shower of fluorescent photons, which transformed them."

"A scientific miracle!" The Commander beamed. And Ling, the First Engineer thinks this process could also be reversed. Meaning a human being could also be transformed back into a monkey, with the mind and sense of an animal. It will take some doing— but you, Mr. Cordes, and little Miss Chyna here, will have the honor of serving as the first specimen used in this experiment. A perfect male and a female of different races—how utterly suitable and exciting."

John smiled grim. "I could see why some ladies would think I am a nice specimen—but I don't think, I would be useful for such an experiment. And who knows—this entire thing could just be one of your magical tricks—a Las Vegas smoke and mirrors show."

John had hit the Commander's nerve. "Believe me, Mr. Cordes, this is no Las Vegas smoke and mirrors show but the real thing and you soon will find out. You see, there is a small catch to this too. An interesting bit of information as a sideline. Using you and Chyna as specimen will also prove the theory that Ling developed. Race is only skin-deep. Where the human DNA structure is concerned there is no difference between races. All humans on this Earth came from one woman out of Africa. The racial differences we see today occurred due to climatic and other environmental influences. Under the skin, we are all the same, Mr. Cordes."

"That's plausible, isn't it?" John admitted.

"Not only is it plausible—we have living proof it is real. This will obliterate Western philosophy and science forever. We will be able to create a deep rift between what religious movements prescribe and what people actually are willing to believe. The religions of the Occident are going to look ridiculous. The collective mind of humanity will not know what to believe anymore. At that moment, we will hit them with a new religion, the religion of annihilation. The ultimate form of equalization. All humans will be created equal, as they say in your constitution so eloquently. Except we mean it. Men will become a swarm of worker bees and we will be their kings."

"Excuse me, but I have never heard of king bees—only queens."

"Nonsense, that's not what I was I meant. You know very well what I meant—bees and bee keepers."

John tried to sound amused—he was not. He briefly thought of Laura and her unfaltering belief in the human spirit. "A very wise young lady told me once the human spirit is invincible. I am not an expert in this field but I think she tried to tell me, the spirit of men is much greater than you think. You will never break the human spirit with your cheesy theories."

It was obvious, the Commander did not want to hear any of what John was trying to say. He was tired of raving. His attention shifted to Chyna. "Could be, could be—but putting this point aside, Mr. Cordes, I just realized that your lovely companion here, Ms. Chyna, is one of our nation's greatest actresses."

John looked at Chyna. "Is that so?"

Chyna somehow acknowledged.

The Commander turned to her. "Won't you entertain us at dinner, Ms. Chyna?"

Chyna was evasive. "Well, I am really very tired—and besides I need my costumes."

"We will provide you with everything necessary. I also should tell you, you really don't have a choice in the matter."

Chyna was hiding her fear under a graceful mask she put on. She smiled and bowed several times. "I will perform for you, supreme Commander, the very best I can."

The compound's commissary and dining room were adjacent to the main labs. The company's personnel and management gathered there for late-night meals, which were not unusual, since the labs operated twenty-four hours a day and food service was provided all the time. An intriguing array of Chinese food was laid out on a buffet table from which male stewards served a group of about thirty men sitting around a large banquet table. They talked, gesticulated, ate, drank, and smoked, all at the same time. The room was filled with the hum of their voices.

John noticed the favorite drink was Scotch whiskey and most of them smoked Marlboroughs. He sat at the table, wedged in between the First Engineer and the Commander. Under different circumstances, he would have enjoyed the meal and the exotic almost cozy atmosphere. Nevertheless, the look of the two guards armed with machine guns, who were at the entrance of the dining room, reminded him very well that he and Chyna were prisoners.

The Commander acted like a polite host. "What are you drinking, John? I am having Crown Royal and branch water. It really goes well with our food. I hate wine. It is very overrated. I mean wine is a symbol of Western culture. The Greeks, the Romans, the wine producing regions, even your stupid little Jesus called wine his blood. Wine is nothing but fermented grape juice."

John swallowed. He certainly was not the zealous type but

hearing Jesus irreverently called stupid somehow cut into his deeply rooted feelings which was a result of his catholic upbringing.

He glanced over the Commander's remark as if he had never heard it. "Crown Royal and branch water is just fine for me too." John tried to think about a way to provoke the Commander, to lift him out of his stereotype act. He knew if he pushed the right buttons, the man would probably start raving again spilling out the information John wanted.

"By the way, we saw a chemical plant on our way up here. What do you make there?"

"Well, if you like to know, it is a pilot plant producing hydrogen fuel from water, which can be used in cars with very little or no conversion and very little outfall. We have had the technology for years. We are ready to take it public, meaning we are ready to kill the entire stupid oil business."

The more he drank, the more talkative the Commander became. "By the way, can I call you John?"

John was amused but he tried to look serious. "Of course you can call me John, but what should I call you?"

"Well, I am the Commander. I command all of A.P.S. They call me supreme Commander. By the way, what do you think of the food service we provide here? Our chef is from Peking—he is a master of Asian cuisine which is unequaled in this world."

John knew the moment had come to goad the Commander, to get him raving again. He took a sip of his drink. Are you talking about your chef cooking domestic animals like cats and dogs?"

"What's wrong with that? What is the difference between slaughtering a cat or a chicken? Dog meat is very tasty and healthy, you know. Most of our domestic animals are raised for food anyway."

John was disgusted. "Personally speaking, I love my dog and I would not consider him dinner. I think the food here is good, except I really do not care much about braised chicken feet and I have had better fare in New York, in Chinatown. I also love wine. There is nothing like a good Italian red. Moreover, calling Jesus little and stupid is like calling Confucius a nerd. And how did you come up with the title of the supreme Commander? It sounds like you are a villain in a movie, like a "James Bond" character or what?"

For a moment, the Commander was speechless. He looked at John with insane eyes. "How can you say anything like this? Are you out of your mind?"

"I didn't say it—you did. I think the one who is out of his mind is not me. It is you, Sir, supreme Commander."

The Commander took a deep drink. His eyes gleamed. "You will regret your words—later—but just let me tell you this, here and now. We are sick and tired of the West's antics. We are sick about your stupid wars over oil and tired of the politics of the American presidents, American politics, and the CIA. They have staged a theater of the absurd."

He ranted on. "We loath your religious wars, the fighting between Muslims, Jews, and Christians, who all seem to believe in the same, basically, but are killing each other, and your stupid Pope, who thinks he is God's voice but cannot make up his mind on how to save the world."

On he went. "Thanks to you, John, we have not been successful in getting money from Rome. The Arab countries are going to be much more fruitful because they are immensely rich. All those intolerant religious zealots, riding high on a wave of oil, thinking they own the world, are going to be reduced to nothing. They are going to be lucky to be sent back to the sixth century where they belong—roaming Bedouin tribes crossing the empty deserts of this world. No longer will they be a threat to humanity. If they try to infest this planet again with their religious insanities, like locusts or some other insect plague, they just will be exterminated like killer bees. I am telling you John. We have a bombshell."

"What do you mean?"

The Commander took a deep draw from his cigarette. "Well, if you are interested I will explain it to you. First of all, your atomic energy and your atomic bombs are stupid."

"I noticed you are using the word stupid again, but go on."

"Yah, it is so. The reason why your atomic energy is stupid is that it is dirty. If you release all your missiles and bombs, you will destroy the planet making it useless for millenniums to come. Who will inherit the Earth after a nuclear war?—No one! We want to inherit the Earth. We want to own it. Why would we want to pollute the real estate we want to own? Why would you have the value of your real estate diminished by stupid bipartisan politics, religious fanatics, wars, and pollution? Why not create eternal stability and eternal peace on Earth? Why not bring everything under one management—ours?"

"It makes sense, Commander. By the way, where did you learn your English?"

"Oxford. And yes, it makes sense. We have a bomb readily available. A clean plasma bomb more devastating than any of your atomic bombs. A bomb that derives its power from the containment of plasma."

"A hydrogen bomb—that's nothing new."

"No, not a hydrogen bomb, a plasma bomb. It is new because our methods are new. It is like nothing anyone has ever seen and more powerful than anything, believe me. We have contained the unbelievable energy of the sun. We have the know-how to contain plasma." His voice became high-pitched. "Do you know what this means? Unlimited energy?"

"Not exactly. But I am sure Ling, who is called the First

Engineer in all of China, can explain it." John knew he had the Commander going strong. The man was high.

"I have now told you about our bomb. What tops it all off, the bombshell I mentioned, are the findings of the Andersons. Military power, bombs, and such can control territories. As it stands now, people are prepared to die defending territories or to die for religious beliefs. Again, how stupid is this, in a society, which is supposed to think universal? They will never learn. They will never think. They only follow their stupid animal instincts. They would rather die for a cause than be controlled. However, we will teach them a lesson. We will control them, we will make them uniform and conform to our new religion of annihilation."

"That sounds very much like a horror movie, or something out of a sci-fi novel. Do you think you are in some kind of a horror show? Do you really think you can succeed with this? Others have tried it before. As we know, this kind of control freakishness has failed miserably. Because the human spirit is strong and the want for freedom is greater than the want for life."

"Nonsense. Humans are worse than animals. Look what they do with their freedom. They kill each other. Humans don't deserve freedom. They must be controlled. With control over the very fabric humans are made of, their chromosomes and DNA, we will reign absolute. As you might suspect, and what the First Engineer has indicated, the Andersons discovery is also a first step to human cloning. We will create them in our image in any shape we want."

"I hate to see this, Commander, because you aren't pretty."

That remark did not faze the commander. He glanced right over it. Either he did not understand it, or he pretended not to understand. He continued his ravings. "We will be able to control each and every human being. We will not only form their physical shape, but most important, we will control their minds—No more fat, ugly people, or homo-sexuals. No more idealism or dying for the fatherland. It only leads to unnecessary killings and war. No more religion, which is the mother of all evil, and no creativity in art or thought. Creativity will be left to us. The ones who resist will be annihilated with our bombs or with other fine methods. Then, finally, there will be peace on Earth."

Again, John tried to taunt the Commander with irreverence. "Excuse me, Mr. Commander, but it seems I have heard this song before. You have not invented human stupor or cloning. That is what they all want. Big governments and religious freaks all want world control. What you are telling me is nothing new. It smells a bit like an old shoe. With due respect, Sir, I think you are out of your mind."

John's remark hit the Commander right between the eyes, which looked like slits.

The Commander, aghast, was silenced. With a hoarse voice, he uttered a few more words. "The dictators of the past were dilettantes. The writers who described them gave them too much power and credit. They were beginners. We are professionals. We know what to do and how to do it, unfailingly."

John thought all of it was just too much. He was glad everyone's attention turned to the small makeshift stage on the wide side of the dining room.

Chyna was on-stage. She was accompanied by a paper dragon and a poetic Chinese clown.

John got a brief glimpse of the bulge of a gun and a knife, on either one of the actors on the stage beside Chyna. He was not sure what he saw but he knew it was there. Chyna, just like himself, was a prisoner threatened by guns and knives. This was somewhat of a surprise because John had initially suspected that Chyna, in some way, was linked with A.P.S. If she ever had been connected with them, it did not seem to be the case now. John tried to think what her role really was, but he could not figure it out. Maybe he was more suspicious of her than he ought to be. Only, his instincts had never failed him yet.

The spotlight was on Chyna, who was on the stage in a beautiful old costume made of fine colorful brocades and silks. Her hair was not confined or lacquered but long and wild. Her light makeup accented the animalistic beauty of her features. Her small, perfect feet, beneath the silks and ankle bracelets, were exquisitely bare. She looked like an ancient princess who had just run home, across miles on high plains, after making love to a far-away princely lover.

On the stage, projected behind Chyna, was a painted image of the bizarre calcite cones of Guilin. The hills were not green but brown, and they were barren and split with deep black crevices.

Chyna was dancing a woman's nightmare, fighting barrenness. As her dancing got faster, her hair flew about her and the colored silks rushed around her. As the light changed from red-hot to cool-blue, a mountain God appeared over the tips of the rounded hills, mysteriously crowned and marble white in his masculinity. Chyna's dance now became purposeful as she seduced the mountain God. And the hills turned green.

In the next scene, Chyna, with her hair still flowing down, was more subdued. She seemed to be older. She played a lute and she sang and recited poetry.

John listened to her singsong. He could not understand any of her words but her gestures and expression seemed to tell a story, of romance and lost love.

Chyna was a remarkable sight. As she played and sang, it became more and more obvious, her attention focused on John. Her eyes searched for him. Her tender gaze and her wild expression captivated him. She sang as if only for him. After she struck the last chord, she bowed and smiled, accepting the applause with lowered eyes. She then left the stage gracefully and walked barefoot across the crowded, smoke-filled room. Again, with lowered eyes, she curtsied in front of John. "Do you like?"

John took her small hand and looked deep into her eyes. "Do I like? Of course, I like. You are very beautiful and very talented."

"And unusually spirited," the Commander said. "Come on, sit down with us." He snipped his fingers. "Will someone bring a chair and some food for Miss Chyna?"

Chyna took off some of the outer, brocaded silk layers of her costume and she handed them to an attendant. She sat down at the table between the Commander and John. She was the only woman in the room and she looked extremely pretty in her silky, cream-colored underclothing. Eating like a starving cat, she seemed to be purring with every bite she took.

John noticed she had skillfully avoided the First Engineer all evening.

The Commander kept pouring whiskey, straight from a bottle into her teacup, which she seemed to drink in an unlikely manner.

John was glad—the Commander stopped raving as Chyna took up his attention.

Chyna was nothing more than polite to the Commander. She tried to give all her attention to John.

John had seen some strange scenarios before, but this was becoming unreal quickly.

One of the stewards set a small silver bowl on ice in front of John. It contained something that looked like a whitish pudding of some sort.

Chyna smiled at him. "Eat, John. Great delicacy. Will make you strong."

John picked up the silver spoon, which accompanied the dish and dipped it in the pudding. "What is it?"

"Flesh, monkey brains—from fleshly killed monkey—almost live."

"Dear God." John dropped the spoon. He felt his stomach wrench part of the evening's meal up in his throat. His trembling hand found a glass full of good old Scotch. He put it to his lips and let the musky liquid run down.

It was long after midnight when John woke up. The first thing he noticed, he was lying on a bed with a straw mattress and he still had his clothes on—the black pajama suit Jimmy Lu had given him. He could feel his old friend, his Walther PK, still under his arm and he still had on the boots with the knife in the shaft. His right wrist, with some kind of rope, was lashed to the bedstead made from bamboo sticks.

Chyna was asleep on the same bed next to him. One of her hands also seemed to be tied or shackled to the bed. She wore her black pajamas again. He could not remember at what point she had changed her colorful stage clothes or how they had come to share the same bed in the cottage. A slight feeling of nausea told him that they probably slipped something into their drinks.

Moonlight came through a narrow window. In the dim light, John could make out the interior of a small one-room cottage, with a thatched roof and bamboo walls. He looked at Chyna, who slept as if she were in nirvana or elsewhere. He remembered seeing the Commander pouring whiskey in her teacup. In her deep sleep, Chyna looked beautiful in a different way. Her even featured face was peaceful. Her long hair looked like midnight blue strands of silk spread across the straw filled, sackcloth pillow.

John pulled on the rope tying up his hand. The loop easily slid up and down the bed frame made of timber bamboo. Idiots— Houdini would laugh at this. He twisted and turned his arm and hand up and around the bed frame. It did not take long before

John freed himself. He lay on the bed perfectly still, when he heard muffled sounds outside the cottage. Trying to determine what was going on outside the cottage, he saw a big, hairy, black spider coming down the wall. The black widow stopped on the pillow near his ear. John saw its protruding little nostrils, trying to smell him. John felt himself sweating a little and he wanted to jump. But then decided it was better to stay calm. It seemed the spider decided it did not care for John's smell. It went back up toward the roof.

John thought he should free Chyna, just in case a sudden departure would become necessary. He rolled over and reached for the other side of the bed frame searching for Chyna's tied up hand. This move woke her up.

She grasped the situation immediately. There she was tied up with the most handsome, desirable man on top of her. John's face was right above her close enough for a kiss and his body touched hers. She wriggled with delight. "John, oh John, come on—I like you so much."

Still just looking to untie her, John became aware of the sensuality of the moment. Being in bed so close with this ravishing young woman was very tempting. He looked down at her.

She was ready for him.

John took a deep breath and then just kissed her lightly on the cheek. "Hush, beauty babe. I am truly sorry. But as it stands, I have a girlfriend in Rome."

Chyna was almost moved to tears with disappointment. "And, Rome is far, so far away."

"That's true. You are really very beautiful, but I think we better find out what's going on around here."

Chyna could not hide her anger any longer. She burst out loud. "No one knows more than me about what is going on around here. I can tell you all about it. I hate these A.P.S. people.

I hate these people of and for the people. They are evil. They are lifeless marionettes. Take me out of here, John!"

"Shah, not so loud—be quiet." John tried to calm her but she moaned hysterical.

"Quiet!"

There were sounds again coming from outside. John motioned Chyna to be calm. He listened closely.

Again, muffled sounds.

He got up. Moving slowly and carefully he looked out the window. He could see the outline of a guard shouldering a semi-automatic. The guard was leaning against the wall of the cottage. Another guard was coming up the path leading to the cottage from below. "That's why we were tied up so sloppily. They are guarding us closely. They think no one can escape the compound." John went back to Chyna's side of the bed. It did not take long for him to untie her.

Chyna sat up on the edge of the bed. She was still trembling with sexual tension. "Let me tell you, not many men have ever turned me down, but you—John Cordes—you are something else."

John briefly wondered how she knew his full name, but then his attention was taken up by something going on outside the walls.

He quickly sat down on the bed beside her. He took her in his arms. He rocked her hard and short. "Be cool," he whispered. "It is not you, babe. It is something else. I cannot explain it to you now." His eyes signaled toward the door. "Besides, we have company, outside." John got up from the bed. "Stay here and don't make a sound." He peered out the front door. Overlooking the situation from his low point, he knew right then they could have just plainly walked out. There was no one. The guards were gone—

The night still felt cool. Further down on the path leading to the main buildings of the compound, John could see a black, crumpled mass in the middle of the road. Taking cover in the low shadows, John slid down to the point where he could see what it was. It was one of the guards sprawled out on the ground. His throat was slit. John crawled closer to the guard. He took a pair of night-vision glasses off the dead man, whose bloodless eyes stared in cold terror, reminding John of the eyes of a dead fish.

John sat up and looked around through the guard's night-vision glasses. The compound seemed deserted. John examined the guard and he found a hand-grenade tied to his belt. "This could be handy to assure we have a future here," John said to himself. He felt his perspiration drying coolly on his skin. Carefully, as if handling a raw egg, he took the hand-grenade off the guard and put it in his breast pocket. John looked up.

Chyna stood in the door of the cottage, trying to see what was going on.

"Come on down," John motioned her to follow him. As she caught up with him he took her hand and led her quietly down the path.

The main lab was deserted. Dim, phosphorescent light pulsated in the space casting overly enhanced shadows on the walls. The source of the pulsating light was the cloud chamber installation they had seen before. They moved with silent caution through the lab. As they approached the cloud chamber, the outline of the woman inside it took shape. The beautiful, iridescent woman stood suspended motionless in her glass cage. It seemed she was without life. They looked at her with reverence. She looked more and more like an icon made of stardust.

Chyna looked at the woman in speechless amazement.

John still had some doubt, what he saw was real and not a vision of his dreams. When suddenly the woman opened her astonishing golden eyes and looked directly at them, they both shrunk back in awe.

Out of the woman's mouth came a singsong in a language, which at first was not clearly understandable. But as their ears became used to the sound of her voice it was as if the ancient Greek words she uttered, translated themselves simultaneously into English. Transcendentally, in their minds, they could understand what she was saying.

The woman said something like this, "Your origins are with us. We created you, so that the spirit could transcend your planet, as it transcends many parts of the Universe. You can feel your origin deep inside of you and know you are not alone. We are in the constellation of Orion, waiting and hoping humans will finally become enlightened." She looked at them intensely. "We all are part of the holy Spirit in God. You must believe. Your ancestors knew what you have forgotten—your spirit came out of Orion. Orion is not the symbol of a beast master it is the symbol of the master of the inner beast. Humans must overcome the inner beast so that they can become fully spiritual. The difference between beast and human is very small. It is easy—so easy—we are waiting—"

At this moment both Chyna and John felt it. The woman was not a mirage. She was real.

Chyna was moved to tears. She was drawn to her. It was like seeing a sister or a relative, a relative from ancient times. Her hand touched the glass enclosure. "Lady, we believe you," she whispered.

John cleared his throat, admitting the scene was touching. He too was moved to the core.

As they both contemplated the woman in the cloud chamber,

Chyna seemed to have a revelation. "Is this the ancestral Earth Mother—the spiritual mother of all human beings on Earth?" she asked.

"I doubt it," John said. As I remember what Professor Stynfeldt explained, I think it is more likely she is the configuration of some entity out of the galaxy of Orion."

All of a sudden, all hell broke loose. Loud thumps of several explosions trembled through the air, hitting the building like shockwaves of an earthquake. John saw Chyna freeze in terror, as an intense, deafening explosion blew half of the roof off, setting the building on fire.

There was no time to loose—but they were both so mesmerized by the woman in the cloud chamber they could not tear themselves away from her. The woman now trembled weaving back and forth. Her likeness ebbed in and out. Her voice flickered. She faded at a fast pace. "Just remember—control the powers you have created—don't kill the spirit." Suddenly she disappeared as if she was switched off.

Large sheets of dense, black smoke filled the room. They could feel the heat of flames. The smoke made them cough. Trying to find a way out, they held their breath.

John knew there was something here he could not leave behind. His eyes caught Chyna's. "Follow me!" Hurdling over debris and chemical equipment, they moved quickly to the First Engineer's lab bench. John stuffed the books, skulls, and bones into the carpetbag and signaled Chyna, "time to take off!"

One of the uniformed guards suddenly popped up in the doorframe. He fired his machine-gun into the air like a mad man. Glass tubes and equipment shattered. Things flew through the room. The guard kept firing at them as they managed to take cover under a lab bench. John took the hand grenade out of his pocket and pulled the release with his teeth. He noticed Chyna was cowering behind him, shaking like a wet cat. He rolled the grenade toward the guard, aiming as if he were on the green of a golf course, trying to land a birdie. The exploding grenade opened the way for them. They ran out of the burning building, which was rocked by more explosions. Running toward the hills, they passed by the metal posts of the outside experiment which was dead now.

John stopped in a flash. He picked up something from the murky ground and stuffed it into the carpetbag.

They ran up the hill as fast as Chyna could make it. Breathless, with heaving lungs, they fell down behind some shrubs and rocks.

John found the night glasses he had taken off the guard. Trying to determine what was going on he took a good look from his high vantage point around the compound. Not far behind the field of the former experiment was a passage between two hills. John's night glasses focused closer on the spot. He saw four Hummers entering the high valley, one by one. The Hummers stopped on a small plateau. Twenty to thirty men in paramilitary uniforms emerged from the vehicles. John's glasses focused on a very large, tough-looking man, uniformed like a Green Beret, who seemed to be the leader. John let out a faint whistle—he immediately recognized the man. It was Raphael, a mercenary soldier, who did dirty work for drug lords and intercontinental criminals. John shook his head and clenched his teeth. "And whom do we have here?—No other than Raphael himself—I know you from the drug wars, you mercenary son of a bitch. What are you doing here attacking A.P.S.?"

Their attention switched suddenly to the main building below, which was rocked by another explosion. It looked like the compound was burning. Men ran around screaming in agony and panic, some were on fire.

Perched behind rocks and shrubs, they looked up at the sky. The image of the constellation of Orion was fading fast. The darkness of night gave way to a red dawn. They looked down at the place where a scientific light spectacle had taken place just a few hours before. With the lights and laser beams switched off, the installation looked stark and less important in the increasing daylight. As the bright flash of another explosion highlighted the site, they could see men climbing up the polished metal poles on which the space rocks still sat suspended. Two of the masts were still live with electricity. The two men climbing the masts like May trees, all at once, let out screams of pain as they were electrocuted by the power still contained in the masts. It seemed they were fried and wrapped around the poles. The other ten men made it to the top of each of the corresponding poles. They dismantled the rocks and put them in jute sacks they had tied around their waists.

As more explosions shook the buildings, John signaled Chyna. "I think it is time to say good bye to A.P.S."

Chyna was beside herself. "Whatever you say. Just get us out of here."

John tried to find the direction to the river, he imagined was not too far below them to the East. They were on a different hill from the one they had climbed initially. But there were just too many hills all around them. It was quite confusing sitting in a maze of mountain cones. It was almost impossible to determine, which was the direction to the river. As far as John knew, they could have been on the backside of one of the cones, not being able to see the river at all. It was a maze within a maze. John knew one thing they had to move downward. "All paths lead to Rome." The old cliché came to mind unexpectedly. It made John smile. "Do you know the way out?" John asked Chyna.

"Not really, I have never been on a hill like this. I only know we must go down."

John looked at her. You know honey that makes sense. Okay, let's just head down."

Climbing down a steep, calcite mountain cone, without a path to follow, was tough and arduous. Their hands and feet were cut by abrasive stones and rocks, and pierced by tree branches they tried to hold onto. When their feet finally touched flat ground, they sighed with relief. Soon they found a path, which seemed to lead back through the burning compound, down to the river. As they headed for the river, they passed by some of the compound's side buildings, which were in rubble.

There was one sight John never forgot, which burned in his mind for a long time. As they passed by the Commander's house, they saw the front wall of the house, like a doll's house, was gone. They could see the rooms of the house in sections, the main room, kitchen, bath, and bedroom. The bedroom was illuminated by the cozy fire of a brazier still burning. The Commander, in blue pajamas, was propped up in bed by pillows. His throat was slit from ear to ear. At his side, in a white nightgown dowsed with the Commander's red blood, sat his wife—she was alive—stunned in panic.

"Don't look back." John put his arm around Chyna, so she would not see the gory scene. For a moment, he saw a flash back of another gory scene, and the woman he tried to protect then. The thought of Laura hit deep and fast. But for some reason, her image turned into a wave of comfort and warmth.

Chyna fought John's protectiveness. She wriggled out of his arm. She wanted to look at the reality of it—hard—and as long as it took. And she did. "I am glad I can be a witness to the end of this coward who is responsible for the deaths of many."

John grabbed her hand firmly. "Come on, let's go."

They ran toward the cool safety of the river, where the sampan waited for them in the dusk.

16.

TRAGIC RIVER

Coming down from the mountains, they reached the boat during the early morning hours.

It seemed the old man had waited patiently for them. "Thanks for waiting," John said. Oddly, the old man did not respond.

"Is there anything wrong?" John asked. The old man just shook his head.

He must have lost his voice, John thought.

Chyna was exhausted. She was pale and shaky. She looked like she was on the edge of a nervous breakdown. She slipped into the dark interior of the boat's bunk-hut and made some tea. She passed the cup to John with trembling hands. Her voice was hoarse. "Here, John. drink tea."

John was grateful for the warmth of the tea. "Thank you, Chyna."

She just stared at him with a forlorn stare and then followed what looked like an old habit. Without saying a word, she pulled out an opium pipe from a straw case under the bunk. She lit the pipe skillfully. As she smoked, her eyes became glassy. "Thank God for relaxation," she said, slurring her tongue. She offered the pipe to John. "You want some opium? Is very good for you."

"No thanks. Nice habits you have around here."

Chyna lay down on the bunk. She snuggled into an old army sleeping bag, which she pulled up around herself. "Good night, John," she said with eyes telling him she wanted him. Soon she was fast asleep.

John could feel his blood pressure rising. His eyes were bleary and his mouth was dry. A small hammer hammered inside his brain. The movement of the sampan made him feel seasick. He went out onto the boat's deck and looked around. They were on a wide part of the River Li. The old man had turned the boat about and headed for the homestead of Jimmy Lu. The bright blue water mirrored the beginning of another day, as the golden ball of the sun rose behind pink and orange veils of fluffy clouds.

As they got closer to the shore, John's eyes searched for Jimmy Lu's small house. He saw nothing. The air was smoky and foul, unusual in this land of effervescent, natural beauty. "What's going on?" John asked the old man at the rudder.

The old man just glared at him with empty eyes. "I don't know—*velly* unusual situation."

John looked inside the boat's bunk-hut. Chyna lay in coma-like opium dreams. Nothing was going to wake her up. "Why do you have to do this just now when I need you?" he said, not expecting an answer.

The closer they got to the shore, the more concerned John became. "What happened to the house?" he asked the old man. "Is this the right spot? Are we near Jimmy Lu's house?"

"Yes—Yes," the old man answered. "I know the River Like a bird—don't know what's going on."

Just before the sampan landed at Jimmy Lu's dock, John saw

it. An empty space, a silent void—the house was burned to the ground—gone.

John did not bother help secure the boat, he just leaped ashore and ran up to the place as fast as he could.

The first thing to do was to look for Laura and Jimmy Lu. There was no trace of them. At least there was no sign they burned to death, John thought. The house was gone. A thin cloud of smoke rose from the smoldering ashes and debris. The hot tub had holes in it. It looked like someone had fired a machine gun at the hot tub. Jimmy Lu's cozy haven, his small paradise, was no more.

"Who could have done this? And why?" John asked the old man, who had quietly come ashore behind him.

The old man just shook his head and grinned his toothless grin.

He probably knows more than he will ever admit, John thought, feeling a hot and quiet anger rising. He spent at least two hours searching the entire area for a sign of Laura and Jimmy Lu.

John saw that Jimmy Lu's yellow Volkswagen bus had stopped short in the middle of the road. The driver's door hung open. John approached the bus with caution thinking a sniper could be lurking in it. It was nothing. The bus was empty. John checked the bus carefully for any clues. He sat in the driver's seat and started the engine, which sounded fine. The bus had enough gas to drive to Guilin and back.

Just as he was ready to give up his search, a ray of sunshine touched the bus moist windshield. Someone had drawn two Chinese symbols in the dust on the windshield. John knew immediately what the symbols meant. The Chinese symbols spelled "Hong Kong" and "China."

Was Jimmy Lu trying to tell him to go to Hong Kong? Why did he use the symbols for Hong Kong and China? Hong Kong at this point was an autonomic region, not belonging to China. Did he mean to tell him that who had done this was in Hong Kong and connected to China? Why China? Did the symbol stand for China—or Chyna?

John remembered things and people he and Jimmy Lu had encountered together during the drug wars. All traces, at that time, lead to only one man in Hong Kong, a man who now, supposedly, was a legal Chinese businessman. Could Jimmy Lu have meant to give him a clue that Tan Chee Hong and possibly even Chyna were behind this? The drug wars had nothing to do with the terror in Rome or with Laura. No one even knew Laura was at Jimmy Lu's house. Whoever attacked Jimmy Lu could have been an enemy encountered during the long past drug wars, who knew about Jimmy Lu's past as a CIA agent. It was possible that someone from A.P.S who did not like the fact that Jimmy Lu had helped John to find them. They could have launched an attack on Jimmy Lu's little haven, right at the time he and Chyna crept up the hills.

Was it Raphael on a revenge trip? This was unlikely, because Raphael would never compromise a mission by attacking two different targets in one night. Who was behind this? What was this all about? What about Laura? The intertwined puzzle got more complex.

Deep in a whirlwind of thoughts, John looked for the old man. He went down to the sampan and jumped aboard. Inside the bunk-hut, Chyna still wallowed in opium dreams. John was concerned about her overdosing.

The old man reassured him. "She is used to it."

This was the point John stopped seeing the beauty in Chyna. He was plainly disgusted. He could not stand being with her inside the bunk-hut, so he just sat outside near the bow of the boat and let the mellow breeze cool his aggravated mind.

John felt he was at his lowest point. He was thousands of miles away from his son, who needed him and he was chasing after abstract ideologies he could not pinpoint. He thought about Laura, a lovely woman, who slipped through his fingers every time he wanted to protect her and he missed his old friend Jimmy Lu.

The beauty of the River Li in the early morning, however, was soothing. It made him feel calmer, more connected to nature, and to the ones he cherished and loved. Thinking what could have happened to them was like trying to solve a complicated, explosive, puzzle. The thought they could have been killed made the hair stand up on John's neck—it was unthinkable. Still, in his professional life, he had seen death many times, and he had many times come close to the end himself. It was a professional hazard he had to consider and live with. However, he had never gotten used to it, and he struggled to understand the sudden deaths of people he knew. It seemed it made his work, his effort to help the forces of law and order, meaningless. Sitting on the bare wood of the forward deck, John took off his pajama top. Exposing his body to the river's misty, healing air, he assumed a yoga position. He breathed deep letting his body and mind absorb the soft, scented river mist. His thoughts drifted. "Where are you, Laura, and Jimmy?—And then, where are you Diana? Which part of heaven is your domain?"

John did not look in on Chyna. At this point, he just did not care for her anymore. He got up and found the old man working on the sampan's outboard engine. Again, he tried to squeeze any sort of information out of him. "Do you know what happened here? Do you know what happened to Jimmy Lu and Laura?" He felt hot anger rising in his chest again. Looking at the old man, John knew it was useless. It was like trying to squeeze juice out of a dried-out old piece of dirt.

The old man just stared back at him with an empty gaze, "I

don't know. The entire time, last night, I was waiting for you at the river. Didn't move from there, so I don't know what happened here."

"But the house burned down! Didn't you see a glow in the sky, or smell smoke?"

"Not able to see fire burn, or smell smoke—too far up river."

John knew he was hitting rock. He could not penetrate the old man's defiance. "Just go home," he said, "wherever you came from."

"Guilin," the old man said.

"Guilin. Okay, go home. Take her with you. I have no more use for either one of you. Go home to Guilin. I will stay here for a while."

"First you got to pay—five hundred dollars."

"That's right, old man—five hundred dollars. That was the agreement. That money was sent to Jimmy Lu in advance, so he could hire the guide, who was Chyna. Do you think I am stupid enough to carry that much money around with me? Chyna got the money some time ago. Ask her for it."

"It's possible she got the money. But I can't ask her now."

"I am telling you! She got the money! Just go back to Guilin now! Leave! I want nothing to do with you anymore!"

John collected his things and jumped off the sampan. He went back up to the rubble of the house, which was beginning to cool. He thoroughly searched the entire area again and again. There was not a trace of Jimmy Lu or Laura. At one point, John found an old, rust-crusted iron safe among the rubble. Knowing about Jimmy Lu's CIA background, John thought the safe could possibly contain sensitive material and papers. The safe was heavy. John picked it up and struggled with it to the bus. He put it down on a grassy ridge near the bus. He then went back and got his own few things, which he stuffed into a soft, black leather bag. He placed the bag in the bus first and then looked around for some tools. He found a neat toolbox near the bus' spare tire compartment.

It took John about ten minutes to open the old safe. Inside it, he found three manila envelopes, which contained material about cases Jimmy Lu had been working on in the old days, Jimmy Lu's college degree and journalist's credentials, his passport, old family pictures, and a small box of family jewelry. John did not know what to with these things. What if Jimmy Lu came back and needed them?

John looked around. The ruins of the house were not smoking any longer. An eerie silence had set in. It seemed no one was around for miles. Even the boat traffic on the river had ceased in the heat of noon that fed the stagnant air. John did not know why he had a distinct feeling Jimmy Lu would not be back too soon. He stuffed all of Jimmy Lu's things into one of the manila envelopes and he took everything with him.

John climbed inside the bus. He sat down in the driver's seat behind the wheel. He wanted to stay. He wanted to see Jimmy Lu come out from somewhere behind the tall grass, the river, the trees. Most of all, he wanted to see Laura's beautiful face looking at him in the sunshine.

Reluctantly, he had to admit to himself, it was time to go on. He started the engine and cranked the gears. He drove slowly, between grassy fields and rice paddies rimmed by a forest of cassia trees, down the small road that soon merged into the main road to Guilin.

John parked the bus in front of the police station. The police headquarter of Guilin was in a run-down, two-story building of faded imperial glory. John walked up the wide staircase made of grey stone, which was adorned with statues of China's demised imperial empire. The office was rather small and dingy. A beat-up fan blew the stagnant air around.

The detective, who was seeing John, was short and pale with thinning hair and a thin moustache. He wore his uniform with boots so shiny they seemed to be lacquered. He had taken his uniform jacket off, displaying a starched, light-blue shirt and a wrinkled gooseneck throat.

For John it was almost impossible to communicate because the officer spoke no English, or he did not care to. He did not seem to understand the few Chinese words John tried to utter.

After what seemed to be an eternity, during which John had to show him his passport and visa three times, the man finally called in another officer who spoke broken English. John tried to explain what had happened at Jimmy Lu's house.

The officers promised him that they would send a contingent up the River Li to look after the situation. John then left Jimmy Lu's personal belongings, including the passport and jewelry, with them. He decided to keep the old papers containing CIA information for himself.

By the time he checked into the nearest hotel, John was dead tired. He fell into bed and he slept for almost fourteen hours. As soon as John woke up his deep worries about the disappearance of Laura and Jimmy Lu were at the forefront of his mind again. He knew the lead was to Hong Kong when he saw the symbol for Hong Kong on the window of the bus. But how, why, and where in Hong Kong?

John found the answer to these nagging questions unexpectedly during breakfast at the small Guilin hotel he stayed at. The hotel was in a quiet area of town. It looked out on lovely park-like gardens with lotus ponds. The hotel had only six small rooms.

The rooms were very clean and had western style feather beds and running toilets, they called water closets, instead of the usual hole in the floor.

It was just before lunchtime. John was the only guest to be served breakfast at a small veranda overlooking the gardens full of bright sunshine.

A young, skinny boy in a white waiter's jacket, who acted as if he was trained in an English country club, served him jasmine tea. Then he wheeled in an aluminum cart with an array of steaming trays and baskets with dim sum.

John thoroughly enjoyed the authentic food and tea, but he could not take his mind of his problems. As he neared the end of his meal, the young boy came back to present the check under a napkin placed over a tray. John lifted the napkin and picked up the check. He took some money out of his wallet and put it on the tray.

The boy disappeared with the money and then reappeared again with the same tray. "Thank you very much, Sir. This is for you." He presented the tray again to John and lifted up the napkin.

On the tray was a white envelope.

"It's for you, Sir, please take it."

John took the envelope. "What's your name, boy?"

"John Lee, Sir."

"And who wanted you to give me this envelope?"

"I don't know, Sir. Someone passed by. Told me—give envelope to the American."

"Okay. I see. Well, thanks, John Lee."

"Thank you, Sir."

John opened the envelope with a chopstick. The first item he saw was an airline ticket from Guilin to Macao. The second item—an invitation to a party. John swallowed twice as he looked at the party invitation. It was from no one other than his old fiend, Tan Chee Hong, the richest, most notorious man in Hong Kong. John looked at the invitation. The note was spelled out in English handwriting. It said, "be sure to attend. You will find missing items!"

"Missing items? Did Tan Chee Hong mean Jimmy Lu and Laura?"

On the backside of the invitation was another message. "At Macao airport, ask for helicopter Nr. 5, it will take you to party in Hong Kong." John tried to think. Why would Tan Chee Hong want to fly him to Macao first, and then bring him into Hong Kong by helicopter?

John decided not to question the message, but to follow the instructions, so typical for Tan Chee Hong. He was ready to go along with it. He was eager to meet his old sparring partner again, hoping that Tan Chee Hong, with his powerful connections and feelers throughout all of Southern Asia, would know or could provide information about what happened to Jimmy Lu and Laura.

Anticipating the party, John had a dinner suit made at the local tailor in Guilin. The tailor, a skinny man, as perfectly mannered as he was dressed, took only four hours to complete the suit.

Later that night, John boarded the plane from Guilin to Macao.

17.

TAN CHEE HONG

The heliport was on top of a cool, green hill on Hong Kong Island. Built into the flank of the hill, connected by a bridge, was Tan Chee Hong's sixteen-story building. It was not considered a tall building, since Hong Kong was a city that boasted some of the tallest high-rise buildings in the world.

Tan Chee Hong's building was a perfectly designed architectural marvel. Round like a drum, the building housed multiple vertical manufacturing facilities on each floor. The upper three floors, called the penthouse, were reserved for Tan Chee Hong's city apartments, offices, and art gallery. On the rooftop of the penthouse was a shining, Olympic-sized, swimming pool surrounded by classic statuary. Walking across the bridge from the penthouse-pool-area onto the hill, one would first find a sizeable garden with tropical plants, and a rose and flower garden. The heliport, separated by cement walls, was further up behind the gardens.

Beyond the heliport, on the highest point of the hill, was an odd-looking new addition to the compound. Only a few of Tan Chee Hong's servants and workers knew it was there. It was a highly guarded area enclosed by a barbed-wire fence. Tan Chee Hong had built some kind of observatory there, half of which was underground.

Tug, Tan Chee Hong's first assistant, was a blond, Nordic man. He wore a black pinstriped suit and white gloves, which looked peculiar on a man who was built like an ox. His thin, rimmed glasses lent a slightly intellectual guise to his otherwise buffed appearance.

Tug had finished gathering a bouquet of fragrant tuberose from the garden on the hill. Holding the bouquet gently in his large hands, he walked back to the penthouse. He did not acknowledge the guards near the pool area. He walked by them along the walkway leading to the penthouse's roof top-entrance. He swiftly sailed into the penthouse's elegant foyer made of stainless steel, white marble, and glass. Next to the gilded doors of a large elevator was a marble staircase, winding down. Tug did not take the stairs—he took the elevator. The elevator's power panel indicated three penthouse floors. Tug, with the flowers in hand, pushed button number two. He exited the elevator on the middle level of the penthouse—the apartments of Tan Chee Hong.

Tug walked from the elevator anteroom to a great, round table in the main living room and arranged the flowers in a crystal vase. He looked around the apartment and sighed. To him, it was the most beautiful place on earth. The interior and furnishings reflected top-of-the-line, contemporary luxury. The cream-colored walls were adorned with a fantastic contemporary art collection. There were cases with collections of minerals and semi-precious as well as precious stones and there were shelves and pedestals with modern sculptures and antique statuary. It all reflected Tan Chee

Hong's grand style and impeccable taste that Tug admired more than anything.

Tug could hear the gentle trickling of water and the hum of a male and a female voice coming from the apartment's dining room. For a moment, he tried to listen to the conversation. Then he just went on busying himself with his chores, knowing listening in would not make a difference to him one way or the other.

Inside Tan Chee Hong's oval dining room, water trickled in a water feature made from semi-precious stones. The shiny table, which could accommodate up to twelve, was elaborately set for only two. The food was arranged on fine china plates and glistening silver platters. It looked like it was prepared by a French chef—and it was. A bottle of vintage Dom Perignon was cooling in a silver cooler.

The roasted duck on Tan Chee Hong's platinum-rimmed plate was barely touched. Tan Chee Hong, a pale, slim Chinese man, dressed in a black Savile Row suit, was at the head of the table. In contrast to his otherwise demure appearance, his eyes sparkled with the coldness of black diamonds, and his white, effeminate hands were heavily bejeweled. His right hand held a burning cigarette in a long, ivory cigarette holder. The hand swiftly touched down like a bird of prey, extinguishing the cigarette in the barely touched duck meat on his plate. Next to him at the table was Chyna. Her hair was pulled up and elegantly groomed. She wore an elaborate dress made of antique Chinese silks and several necklaces, bracelets, and ankle-bracelets, all encrusted with rare jades and jewels. Chyna had barely touched her food. She looked pale and withdrawn.

Tan Chee Hong reached for her hand and kissed the tips of her fingers. "My dearest girl! You are almost as beautiful as some of my art. However, I would like to know why you lead the American to the A.P.S compound when you knew I had a great deal of interest in that facility? This is an unforgivable act of betrayal. Tell me, haven't I been good to you, always?"

Chyna looked down at the food she had not touched. "Most revered Tan Chee Hong, I did everything to please you. Everything you asked me to do and more. I would never dream of betraying you. When you asked me to find out what was going on at the A.P.S. compound, I had to sleep with Ling, the First Engineer, even though I cannot stand the man. He told me all about their experiments, their products, and their technology. I told you everything I learned from him."

Chyna sounded exasperated. "When they asked me to contact the lady in the Vatican, I told you. When I found out what they wanted from the Vatican, I told you all about it too—the carpetbag, the experiments with the twelve space rocks— I told you everything. Revered Tan Chee Hong, I work only for you and I tell you everything. Please believe me, I would never betray you."

Tan Chee Hong stared at her with a cold stare. "You remind me of a mynah bird."

"I hate A.P.S.—you know what they did to my brother."

"Yeah, it's too bad about your brother, a brilliant young scientist like that. Industrial espionage, they called it. All he did was spilling some information about their projects. They put him on trial and executed him."

A single tear ran down Chyna's cheek, making a trace in her powdered make-up. She could not hide her deep distain for Tan Chee Hong any longer. A faint, bird like cry came through her rouged lips. "Why did you have us involved in your spy ring?"

"But child, that's easy to see. I heard about A.P.S. The most advanced company in Southern China. I wanted to acquire them. They could have been a gem in my collection. You and your brother both were there with just the right degree of beauty and intelligence, the perfect pawns in my little game of chess. Coming to think of it, they could have accused you of spying too. They could have executed you just like your brother. But I saved you. Didn't I? And this is how you thank me."

"And, by the way, you have not told me yet. Why did you lead the American to the compound?"

"I just told you so—I hate them." Chyna sobbed.

Tan Chee Hong shook his head. "I don't believe you. Your old man was probably greedy for the money. What I give you is never enough."

Chyna's voice continued pleading. "I was going to tell you all about the American too."

Tan Chee Hong pondered her face briefly. "But you didn't. I had to find out for myself what you were up to." He got up from the table. "I will deal with you later."

Chyna stared at the cold food on her plate. An overwhelming feeling of fear crept up her spine.

Tan Chee Hong walked up and down with nervous little steps, talking to himself. "But first I will have to deal with that pseudo-militarist, Raphael. I paid an enormous amount of money to that psycho to retrieve the twelve rocks. You know best, I must have all of them. But what does the idiot do? He loses two of them."

Raphael, a tall, brawny man in a paramilitary uniform was ushered into the apartment's living room by Tug.

Tan Chee Hong, coming out of the dining room, greeted him sarcastically. "Raphael, I think you have met Tug, my art consultant, haven't you?"

Raphael bowed stiffly toward Tan Chee Hong "I remember making his acquaintance."

Tan Chee Hong winced. "Sit down, Raphael. I must talk to you."

Raphael raised his hand to his temple, trying a faint salute. "At your orders, Mr. Tan Chee Hong." He then let himself fall into the low, soft leather sofa.

Tan Chee Hong remained standing. He took another cigarette from a golden case on a nearby table and put it in his ivory cigarette holder.

Raphael jumped up from the sofa and stood to attention. He pulled out a cigarette lighter. His hand trembled slightly as he lit Tan Chee Hong's cigarette. Tan Chee Hong stepped back. "I said sit down. And cut the military crap. You are a lame excuse for a soldier."

Raphael fell back into the sofa Tan Chee Hong took a puff from the cigarette. His eyes watched Raphael closely. He then turned to Tug. "I think I want to show our guest something."

Tug understood what Tan Chee Hong meant. "Okay, follow me please."

Chyna, who had quietly come into the room, joined the small group that followed Tug to the elevator.

The elevator took the group up to the penthouse rooftop. From there they walked across the path next to the swimming pool, up through the gardens on the hill, to the heliport. Beyond the heliport, carved into the mountainside, was Tan Chee Hong's state-of-the-art observatory.

Tan Chee Hong, carefully, unlocked a vault door leading into the cave-like space. The observatory anteroom housed rows of control panels. The main observatory room was a vault chamber crowned by a retractable cupola with a sizeable telescope.

To everyone's surprise, Ling, the First Engineer greeted them in the anteroom. Tan Chee Hong was gloating. "Let me introduce to you—the First Engineer, Ling, formerly from A.P.S., a company I have tried to acquire for a long time."

They all looked at Ling, somewhat startled.

"You changed jobs awfully fast," Raphael said.

Ling tried a polite nod and a smile. "One must follow opportunity when it presents itself."

"That's right," Tan Chee Hong said. "I gave him the opportunity and he followed. Besides, his laboratory was destroyed and so was A.P.S. due to our resident military genius the great Raphael. Ling, the very first engineer in all of China can now prove his talent to us."

"I have seen stranger things," Chyna said. She remained standing next to Ling, who busied himself at the control panels, while Tan Chee Hong, Raphael, and Tug stepped into the vault chamber.

The telescope pointed through an opening in the observatory cupola at a group of sparkling stars far above in the velvet night sky—the Constellation of Orion The ten rocks Raphael had retrieved from the A.P.S. compound, gleamed steadily inside the dark vault. Emitting a fluorescent light, they were placed in a floating installation that seemed to be aligned or connected with the stars of Orion with bright blue laser beams.

Tan Chee Hong, with his eyes, motioned Tug to remain behind Raphael, blocking Raphael's way out. His voice was like thin ice. "I want you to understand, Raphael. I paid you and your men ten million dollars to get these space rocks for me. They are the rarest of rare. I was told they are composed of compounds not found on this Earth. They are beyond the scope of monetary value. What is even better, the head engineer from A.P.S. is on my payroll now. He knows what to do with them. I could have owned the experiment entirely, which would have given me tremendous powers."

Tan Chee Hong stared at Raphael like an anaconda snake ready to swallow a rabbit. "You raided A.P.S.—didn't you? You got the space rocks. Except two of them are missing. And, with only ten rocks, the capacity of the rocks is diminished—

Raphael knew what was coming. He looked for a way out, but Tug was right behind him.

"It was a terrible task. Some of my men were killed," Raphael wined.

Tan Chee Hong remained cold-blooded. "That is of no consequence to me. I must have all the rocks, or this work of art is incomplete, like a beautiful woman missing one eye. It is beyond the scope of my understanding how you could lose two of the rocks. You think you are a great military strategist. But you are nothing but a bloody, psycho-dilettante!"

Raphael's voice sounded pitched. "I assure you, I will get the missing rocks. Please let me prove it to you."

Tan Chee Hong shook his head. "It's too late for that now— But let me show you what the rocks can do even in an incomplete state."

Still at the controls outside the vault chamber, Ling looked inside at Tan Chee Hong—attentively.

Tan Chee Hong gave him a sign.

Ling hit a few switches on the control panel. The vault room's twilight was suddenly cut by bundles of piercing lasers, which collided with the rocks. Tan Chee Hong's, Raphael's, and Tug's figures looked like they were performing a weird disco dance in the flickering light.

Handling some of the switches, Ling, at the control panel, was able to direct the lasers in different angles. First they formed a circle, then they bundled together in a bright piercing beam.

At the next moment, Tug grabbed Raphael from behind with

an iron grip. He firmly and inescapably pointed Raphael in the direction of the laser beam.

Raphael tried every trick he had ever learned to shake off Tug. But Tug's grip held him in a steely vice.

Ling, at the controls, directed the laser beam and aimed it directly at Raphael's face.

Raphael broke down, screaming in agony, as the laser hit him directly in the right eye.

While Raphael lay on the vault chamber's floor like a whimpering bundle of rags, Tan Chee Hong's voice cut through the space again. "I am telling you right now, Raphael, you have exactly six days to find the missing rocks or I will give orders to take your other eye. Yes, we will take both your eyes—one for each rock. You know you cannot escape us. We know you too well and you know us. There is no escape!" Tan Chee Hong turned to Tug. "Take this mess out of here."

18.

HONG KONG

Across Hong Kong-bay at Macao the mainland was obscured in darkness. Against the night sky, a helicopter, like a huge, black insect, rose up in a ballistic curve. As the chopper ascended to the red sky, John could see the last bright orange glimmer of the sinking sun lining the bright blue waters of Hong Kong-bay, which rapidly turned to ink.

The lights of Hong Kong were the most colorful of any city John had ever seen. Deep below the towering high-rise buildings, the streets looked like the lava veins of a seething volcano.

John looked sharp in his evening clothes and he was glad for the tailor in Guilin, who had outfitted him in such a short time. He was relieved to feel his old standby, his Walther PK, in the holster under his arm. He sat next to the helicopter pilot, who tried to bring the chopper down onto the heliport of Tan Chee Hong's Hong Kong building, in a smooth but rather hair-raising maneuver.

On their final approach to the heliport, John got a good overview of the building, which hugged a lush green hill. The light coming from the glow of the city below and the residual light of the departed sun diffused the bright lights that marked the building's heliport and the garden and pool area.

John felt his adrenalin pumping at an elevated level as the chopper landed. He slid out of the chopper, ducking under the rotor blades trying to find his bearings. As the rotor slowed down and came to a stop, John could hear wafts of music, the hum of people's voices, and laughter. Festivities were going on.

There were approximately three hundred people from Hong Kong and from all over the world attending Tan Chee Hong's party.

Armed security was placed at strategic points.

John checked in at a security point just below the heliport. He was glad they did not frisk him. The Walther PK remained snug under his arm. He then walked across the bridge from the garden to the rooftop area where he was checked again but not frisked.

The party was in full swing. An international crowd, dressed in the latest designer fashions, dispersed around the roof-top-pool-area and into the penthouse. They were sipping champagne and cocktails while conversing in several languages.

John noticed some faces in the crowd who seemed familiar. However, he was in no mood to socialize.

Near the entrance to the penthouse was a white-skirted table with a large ice sculpture of a leaping Koi. A stunning looking Chinese girl in a tight gold-lame dress was behind the table. She poured French champagne from bottles kept iced in silver coolers. She easily and charmingly conversed with people in three languages. Next to the champagne table was another white-skirted table with large tins that were cradled in beds of ice and brimmed with an assortment of the choicest caviars.

John took a glass of champagne from the Chinese girl. The

girl smiled at him sweetly. "And don't forget lovely caviar, Mr. Cordes—vely, vely yummy."

John was vaguely spooked. "How do you know my name?" He downed the champagne. "Never mind." Behind him he felt a slight, light, movement—the rustle of silk, the scent of a perfume. He turned around—it was Chyna.

Chyna, more beautiful than ever in a dress made from antique Chinese silks, with her raven hair flowing down her back, stood next to the statue of a Roman goddess.

John had a brief mind-flash of Chyna and a Roman goddess, who reminded him of Laura. Was his mind playing tricks with him or was it all very real? He quickly got a hold of himself and tried not to show his surprise. "Why?—What on earth are you doing here?"

Chyna gave him an adoring look. She smiled mysteriously. "I think, I told you, John. Tan Chee Hong is an old acquaintance of mine. I am here to welcome you. I can't begin to tell you how lovely it is to see you again."

John suddenly tasted the bitter taste of bile in his mouth. Chyna's perfume suddenly smelled more like the scent of a rat. He distinctly remembered Chyna telling him she did not know Tan Chee Hong.

"How long have you known Tan Chee Hong?"

"Oh—since I was very young. He paid for my education at the University of Hong Kong."

John shook his head. Hot anger rose from deep in his gut. "But you told me before, you didn't know him. I remember it clearly."

Chyna just smiled at him with a hypnotic stare, not saying anything. Then she said dreamily—"You mistaken, John."

In a way, this reminded John how she had acted in the sampan on the River Li. It seemed to him Chyna could be high again on opium. He had a flashback of seeing the symbols for Hong Kong and China on the window of the yellow bus. Had Jimmy Lu's symbol spelled China or Chyna?

John grabbed Chyna's shoulder. "What do you know about Jimmy Lu and Laura d'Andres?" he said, feeling his anger rising higher.

"I know many things but I can't tell you." Chyna remained in her dream like state.

He squeezed her shoulder harder, shaking her. "If you know many things, you better remember them fast! You better tell me what happened to them—right now! What happened to Laura and Jimmy Lu?—Game's over!" John hissed.

Chyna's eyes were clouded. "I know what happened to Jimmy Lu but I can not tell you now. Let's go inside and join the party. Tan Chee Hong is waiting."

John's anger rose, hot blooded, to his heart. He was losing his composure. "So you know what happened to Jimmy Lu—but you don't want to tell me!" he yelled. He now grabbed her arm and squeezed it hard. "And what about Laura? Tell me what happened to Laura?"

Chyna cried out with pain and fear, trying to wriggle out of his grip. "Let me go! I will tell you! Let me go!"

John squeezed her arm harder.

Chyna felt the fingers of his other hand running down her neck, probing, caressing, finding a vertebra in the delicate bow of her spine and snapping it hard. She felt his clutch around her spine bone and she knew he had her in a grip of death.

"You better tell me now or I kill you." John whispered in her ear.

Chyna cried out again. "Okay, John! I tell you!" She sobbed, trembled, and wriggled out of his loosening grip. "Remember when I danced for you at the A.P.S compound?"

"I remember."

"It was during that exact time, the Commander sent his men down to the river to kill Jimmy Lu and to burn his house. They told me they would kill me too if I told you. They forced my father to show them the way. That's why I got drugged there, on the River Li, because I didn't want to have to tell you."

John's heart turned into a clump of pulsing ice. He dropped Chyna's arm. He raised his fist high wanting to hit her hard but he could not. His fist came down swooshing through thin air. His ashen face looked at her stunned. "You are a disgusting rat!" was all he could say.

"They killed him because he was your friend and he helped you to find them. They would have killed me too," Chyna whimpered.

John felt the old, familiar grief drowning him like a great big wave. He briefly saw flashes of Jimmy Lu's smiling face and the warmth of his welcome in Guilin. He knew he had to use his mind control—there was no time for grief now. His face turned to stone. "What did they do with the body?" he asked with a disembarked voice.

"They sunk it in the river not too far from the shore," Chyna replied.

That was it. The final horrible truth. John stared at her. "I guess there is nothing more to say."

"I am sorry John. I liked Jimmy Lu. He was a nice man."

John shook his head in desperation. "Just do me a favor and never mention his name again. You are not worthy to even say his name."

Now the thought of Laura hit John like a large brick of ice. "What about Laura? Is she alive?"

"She is alive—So to speak."

"What do you mean? So to speak?"

Chyna looked solemn. "If you come with me, I will show

you. Please come with me. I must bring you to Tan Chee Hong. He is waiting."

John had no choice. He followed Chyna into the penthouse foyer and into the elevator full of people. The elevator sank one floor and opened at Tan Chee Hong's pent house apartments. In the crowd of party guests, John followed Chyna out of the elevator with his eyes cast to the floor. He did not immediately see the surprise Tan Chee Hong had in store for him.

Halfway into the room Chyna turned around. "I think our host has prepared a surprise for you."

John stopped in his tracks and looked over Chyna's shoulder right into the large salon. The elegant room was decorated with bouquets of scented fresh flowers. There was a sumptuous buffet and a bar. A small band played discreetly. Tan Chee Hong, in a black silk Mao suit, was receiving his guests. John noticed next to Tan Chee Hong was a lovely looking female figure who was obviously acting as a hostess.

Chyna glanced at John's face, which froze in cold terror.

John looked past her into the room full of people. He focused on the female figure standing next to Tan Chee Hong. The hostess in the reception line—was Laura. John was utterly startled. "What on earth—?" He looked closer at Laura. She was a picture of perfection. Her hair was done up. Her make-up, like a doll's, was perfect. She wore a perfect little black dress with high-heeled shoes. On her neck was a beautiful, golden jewel. Only, the jewel was not held up by a necklace. It just sat there imbedded in her skin—a large emerald cut yellow stone bordered by small, glittering diamonds. John kept staring at Laura.

A waiter came by and offered him a glass of champagne. John just waived the waiter aside without taking his focus off Laura.

"What in the hell, is going on?"

"Oh, just one of Tan Chee Hong's little tricks. But let me

introduce you." Chyna took John's arm and led him to the reception line.

"Honorable Tan Chee Hong, allow me to present John Cordes."

John managed a short bow, which was an unintended reflex. He did not take Tan Chee Hong's extended hand.

Tan Chee Hong looked intensely at John. "You mean the American CIA agent John Cordes?"

"I am not a CIA agent."

"If you are not a CIA agent, what are you? A spy?"

"You know very well who and what I am."

"That's right. I do remember you well, from the drug wars." Tan Chee Hong smiled thin-lipped. "Indeed, Mr. Cordes, you really managed to cause us some considerable damage then. But that was a long time ago. And maybe it was for the better. Because today I am just a reputable business man, engaged in only legal business."

"That's commendable," John said absentmindedly. He looked at Laura.

Laura looked back at him without recognition. It seemed she was in a sort of catatonic state.

Tan Chee Hong followed John's eyes. "I think you know who this is?"

John ignored Tan Chee Hong's remark. He took Laura's hand. Her hand was limp and cold.

"Talk to me, Laura. Why are you here?"

Laura acted like a marionette. "Very pleased—very pleased to meet you," she said mechanically.

Tan Chee Hong looked amused. "The reason you were invited to our little soiree, Mr. Cordes—I believe you have knowledge of the whereabouts of some items missing from my art collection. Some sort of minerals or space rocks. Two pieces, to be exact."

John sounded disinterested. "Could be."

"I am prepared to offer you five million dollars in cash, plus the freedom of this lady here if you can come up with the missing rocks."

"Even if I knew where they were, I could never sell them to you." John nodded toward Laura. "You see, the rocks actually belong to Laura. They are a legacy from her parents."

"Nonsense, what would she do with them? She has no use for minerals like these. I pay the money. I get the rocks. I must have all of them."

He waved his bejeweled hand with a sleek gesture. Trying to sound amicable, he said, "I tell you what, John, let us finish the reception. Enjoy the party. We will meet with you, in let's say— twenty minutes and possibly finalize a deal."

John felt trapped and angry but he said. "I doubt there will be a deal but I will stay around."

He tried to mingle with the crowd but he could not shake off Chyna. She just followed him around like a domestic cat. He could not take his eyes off Laura, who stood next to Tan Chee Hong, acting like a puppet.

Chyna was next to John, pretending she was admiring some of the art displayed throughout the apartment.

John still had not taken his eyes off Laura. She looked beautiful with her white skin, dark hair, and blue-green eyes. The golden, gleaming jewel on her neck enhanced her beauty, even more.

"What is that?" John asked Chyna.

"You mean that stone on her neck? That is one of Tan Chee Hong's specialties. A hollowed-out topaz. It contains a powerful drug, which is slowly released into the bloodstream. It puts her in some kind of state. I mean, your friend Laura may be there in the flesh but she does not know who she is or where she is. It is as if she's there, but nobody is home. Her mind is shut down. If she is exposed to the drug too long, the state she is in could become permanent. She'll never come back."

John sighed in despair and swallowed hard. "And of course, you didn't know anything about this either," he said sarcastically. "Can you tell me how Tan Chee Hong knew about Laura?"

"I don't know. He did not tell me. Maybe someone from A.P.S. told him. Maybe the First Engineer, Ling. I don't know. It seems Tan Chee Hong knows many things."

John shook his head. His anger rose again. Breathless, he said, "are you sure it was not you, who made the connection for him?"

John gripped Chyna hard, again. "You better tell me what you know, or I will make sure you regret ever meeting me, for the rest of your miserable life."

Chyna screamed. This caused some of the party people to look at them. She tried to wriggle out of John's grip. "Let go John! It was not me! Some of Raphael's men found Laura by coincident. She was hiding in Jimmy Lu's bus next to the burning house. They brought her to Hong Kong to please Tan Chee Hong."

Chyna looked at John cat-like. "I know you couldn't do anything bad to me or any woman. You are one of the good guys."

John loosened his grip. "Just don't try me."

Chyna's face shone with the excitement of pain turning into infatuation. "Don't look at me like that, John. I know you could kill me, snuff me out like a weed. But I am not a villain. There is nothing I did or could have done against you. Don't you see I am just a pawn in a game?"

"You are a deadly pawn in a deadly game," John said grim. "Just watch out the game doesn't catch up with you."

John let go of Chyna. He could tell, he was not getting anywhere with her at this point.

Across the room, Tan Chee Hong had finished with the reception. He led Laura out of the room in a courteous manner.

"Excuse me, John," Chyna said. She quickly turned and disappeared in the direction Tan Chee Hong and Laura had taken.

John stared at the point where they all had disappeared. He tried to sort out his thoughts. He took a glass of champagne from a waiter. He sipped the champagne absentmindedly and then put the glass down on a table.

A good-looking woman approached him, she smiled. "Didn't we meet in Bangkok before?"

"That's possible," John said. He did not seem to see the woman, he just watched the party scene aimlessly. "Will you excuse me?" he said. He left the woman standing by herself, and walked over to the elevator in the apartment's foyer.

The elevator door opened in front of him. John stepped in. He looked at the power panel. There were three buttons, indicating three floors. He pushed floor number three, the lowest. Nothing happened. John noticed the cover of what could have been another panel, hidden in the polished steel siding of the elevator below the first panel. This was not obvious. It was just an indication. He tried, and pried around with a key from his key chain and managed to open the secret panel. Before him, in the cubbyhole, was another panel with a key in a turnkey hole. John turned the key and pushed the elevator button again. The elevator descended smoothly to the floor below.

John stepped out of the elevator. The space was light and airy, taking up the entire building's floor. It was Tan Chee Hong's art gallery.

John walked around the gallery, which was as spacious and well designed as any museum of international repute might be. The paintings looked fascinating, a collection of great masterpieces—everything from Da Vinci to Van Gogh. As John looked closer at the paintings, many of them seemed familiar. It was as if he had seen some of the art before.

He stared at one of the paintings, trying to figure out what was going on in Tan Chee Hong's gallery, when he felt a movement behind him.

It was Chyna.

John was not pleased to see her. "Why do you keep creeping up on me? What are you doing? Are you following me around?"

"I am not following you around, John. I just want to warn you. Get out of here, quickly. You are making a big mistake. If Tan Chee Hong finds you in his gallery, he will surely kill you."

"Why, Chyna? Because there is something wrong with this art? I am trying to figure it out. I am looking and looking— aha—I think I know what it is." John pointed at the paintings. "All this art is stolen. Look at this—a painting from the Louvre— the Prado—the Metropolitan Museum—I am not a great art connoisseur, but even I can tell where all of this art came from unless, of course, these are fakes."

"You are perfectly right, John. Tan Chee Hong's art collection is very recognizable, and I can assure you, these are not fakes. This is how Tan Chee Hong collects his art. He steals it from the great museums around the world and he replaces the originals with copies. He employs the best artists to forge the paintings, the best methodical thieves to exchange them."

John looked straight at the *Mona Lisa.* "Look at this. You mean this is the real thing?"

"I am not sure, in her case. Tan Chee Hong insists, it is the original and the one in the Louvre is a copy. But let us get out of here. I am afraid—"

"But this is insane! It reminds me of a movie script. I recently saw the film but I cannot remember the name of it."

"Believe me, this is not a movie, it is real," Chyna said, "and we better hurry out of here."

"But with all that money, why doesn't he just buy art like any other collector?"

"Because this art is priceless—no money in the world could buy it."

"And besides, it would not be much fun to buy the art." Tan Chee Hong's voice reverberated through the room. "Stealing it is so much more exciting."

Tan Chee Hong and Tug, who was leading Laura by the arm, came into in the gallery from a side entrance. They were followed by a man in a white lab coat, it was Ling, the First Engineer.

John immediately focused on Laura. He noticed Laura's eyes and expression were completely blank. She walked like a puppet on a string.

Tug held a large gun in his hand, which he pointed at John and Chyna.

Tan Chee Hong said, "I guess, it's time to begin our negotiations. However, this here is not the right place because I get nervous having strangers in my gallery, and I want to show you something else. He pointed at the First Engineer. "By the way, I want you to meet Ling, the first engineer of A.P.S., who is now working for me. He knows the secret of the rocks and how to conduct the experiment."

The First Engineer bowed and smiled. He looked sheepishly at John and Chyna.

"I think we have met before," John said.

Tan Chee Hong stared at them coolly. "That's right. You met him at A.P.S. That is why I know you have the missing rocks, John. That is why, I must insist, I need all of the rocks. I think you understand."

John just stared at Ling. He did not answer Tan Chee Hong.

Tan Chee Hong motioned Tug. "Let's go!"

Tug knew just what his master meant. He pointed the gun at John and Chyna, motioning them to the elevator.

Holding Laura close to him, Tug followed John and Chyna. He pointed his gun at them unfailingly.

Tan Chee Hong and the first Engineer followed them. The group went up in the elevator, out to the pool area, across the garden, and past the heliport, to Tan Chee Hong's observatory.

The First Engineer, Ling, whose domain the observatory had become, dutifully took a key out of his lab coat pocket and unlocked the door for them.

They stepped into the observatory's entrance room, or antechamber, which was lit by yellow electric light. From the antechamber, they could look through an open door into the main observatory-vault-chamber's dark-blue interior, which was illuminated by a source of phosphorescent light. The ten rocks were suspended in mid-air inside the vault chamber. The glittering constellation of Orion was visible through the open segment of the chamber's cupola, in the night sky above.

Tan Chee Hong led John and Chyna into the artificial darkness of the vault chamber. From there they looked back at the anteroom, visible through the open door.

Tug and Ling stayed in the anteroom. Tug held the gun in one hand, holding on to Laura's arm with the other hand.

Ling went to the control panel.

Inside the vault chamber, Tan Chee Hong waved his hand at the installation of the suspended rocks. "When I first learned of the existence of these rocks, I knew I wanted them—they are like nothing in this world. The finest diamonds, the most precious minerals, nothing can be compared to them. When Ling explained their inherent power to me, I knew, I must have them no matter what. And I mean all of them. And you, John

Cordes, will bring the two missing rocks to me." He pointed at Laura standing outside the chamber in the hall room. "Or the lovely lady Laura will have the mind of a vegetable. Better yet, she will be more like a wilting flower for the rest of her life. Because you must know, the catatonic state she is in right now will soon become irreversible."

John could see it in Laura. Tan Chee Hong was right. Laura was pale and shaky. She looked like she was fading fast.

"How did you get a hold of Laura?" John asked Tan Chee Hong.

Tan Chee Hong smiled thinly. "It was Chyna's idea. Chyna knew all about Laura. Chyna was the woman from Hong Kong who contacted Laura in the first place, and Chyna was engaged to Ling, the First Engineer. I also think Chyna likes you, John. I think she wanted to eliminate a rival. Isn't that right Chyna?"

Chyna stared at them. "It was Raphael who found Laura," she said solemnly.

"That's true, that's true, Tan Chee Hong said. The evil Raphael stumbled upon Laura and brought her to Hong Kong. But it was Chyna who dreamt up the rest of it. I had nothing to do with it. I mean, with what went on in Rome. Chyna told me much later what A.P.S was up to. They attacked the Vatican, not I."

"Maybe you didn't have anything to do with what happened in Rome," John said. "But I am sure you arranged Chyna's engagement to the First Engineer so that you could learn everything about A.P.S."

Tan Chee Hong looked at John with an enigmatic smile. "And why would I do such a thing, John?"

"I don't know your motivations. Money, power, the satisfaction of owning the ultimate work of art? You tell me!"

"Well, money doesn't interest me. I think I have enough of

that stuff, however, owning the ultimate work of art—touché, John."

Tan Chee Hong's focus changed. He pointed outside the chamber at Laura. "I can tell you, by the look of her, there is not much time left."

John too, looked at Laura and he could see that Tan Chee Hong was right. John could feel Laura's desperate state—She was at the verge of dying. He tried to pass by Tan Chee Hong to reach Laura. But Tan Chee Hong stepped in his way letting out a whistle.

At the sound of the whistle, Tug immediately pointed his gun at John.

"I would not make a move, if I were you." Tan Chee Hong said.

"I think you belong to the distinguished, criminally insane," John hissed.

"I don't care what you think. I am ordering you to bring me the rocks. If you don't, Laura will die, and I will deal with you the same way I have dealt with others who chose to go against me. Just watch me, John." Tan Chee Hong whistled again and he signaled Ling who was at the control panel.

Ling knew what he was doing—he had practiced before. As he pushed several buttons on the control panel, ten bright laser beams appeared inside the vault chamber, piercing, blinding. A laser beam pierced each corresponding rock.

Ling, at the control panel, directed the central beam back and forth as if he was driving it. He pointed it directly at Chyna, who stood frozen in fear. The power of the beam seemed to increase. It fizzed red hot. The beam hit Chyna precisely in the center of her forehead, where a neat, penny sized hole appeared as she collapsed to the floor.

John saw what happened to Chyna from the corner of his eye

as he leaped, past Tan Chee Hong, out of the vault chamber's door.

He jumped at Tug so fast, Tug forgot to fire his gun. John knocked the gun out of Tug's hand, and then landed one of his special punches right into the face of the tall Norwegian, who slumped down, unconscious.

Laura just stood there expressionless, helplessly shaking like a leaf in the wind.

John finally got to her. He put his arm around her. "Come on, Laura, let's go," he said, when he saw Ling trying to direct the laser beam at them. John let go of Laura, jumped at Ling, and grabbed him by the neck.

John was well trained in martial arts. However, Ling was a master. He knocked John around like a punching ball. John was hit dangerously, several times. He began to see flashes of purple and red before his eyes, knowing this was a fight to the death, when another big blow sent him cowering on the floor. John awaited Ling's final big blow when suddenly the word "control" flashed before his mind's eye. Gathering his last bit of strength John whirled around like a dervish, projecting his entire body at Ling like a cannonball. This was it. John's outstretched leg and foot hit Ling with the full impact of his body weight knocking him out cold.

John, in a daze, sat on the floor. He felt something strange was happening. The light in the anteroom went out. Feeling dizzy and stunned, John tried to orient himself in the darkness. One thing he noticed was extraordinary, he could not hear a sound. The eerie silence was unsettling and even more disorienting. He tried to collect his thoughts and clear the feeling of dullness in his brain. He still could not get up. I have lost it, he thought, when he saw a fluorescent glimmer of light coming from the vault chamber.

At first, it was only a dim, low, glow. But soon the light source became stronger. He could now see flickering veins of light criss-crossing his face and body. The veins of light then turned into thin beams, a mayhem of flickering light beams. In the eerie incandescent glow, John could see Laura standing next to the wall behind him, weaving back and forth like a leaf. The sight of Laura's helplessness gave John the strength to get up.

John got up from the floor on all fours first, and then he rose to his feet. He struggled over to Laura, who stared at him with empty eyes. John touched her shoulders and hugged her briefly. "Hang in there, Laura-baby—we will be out of here in no time."

Inside the vault chamber, the laser-like beams were now going wildly in every direction, and there was a sound like the drone of an electric high power line.

John's attention switched from Laura to the vault chamber. He guardedly entered the vault chamber and was immediately blinded by the brightness of the laser mayhem. As his eyes became used to the light, he could see the chamber was empty. There was no trace of Tan Chee Hong or Chyna's dead body. It was as if they had been sucked out of the chamber. They had just vanished.

John looked for an exit door but he could not find one. Then he felt a breath of air. He checked the far corner of the chamber, from where the draft was coming. He touched the grey, diffused wall. His hand went right through it. There was an opening, camouflaged by a projection, which looked the same as the vault's wall. So that is how Tan Chee Hong and Chyna disappeared—through the walls.

John looked up through the opening of the chamber's domed roof. He could clearly see a segment of the night sky he recognized as the Milky Way. His eyes focused on the constellation of Orion. The stars in the constellation were blinking brightly. His eyes were drawn to one of the smaller stars It seemed a thin beam of light was projected down from that star. The beam of light quickly extended downward. As it came closer, it marked a blue-green streak of condensation in the night sky. The beam of light was clearly directed toward the observatory in a precise and calculated path. When it came through the opening in the cupola, the light inside the vault chamber became brighter, and the temperature rose slightly.

As soon as the star beam touched parts of the laser mayhem inside Tan Chee Hong's observatory, the lasers became extinguished one by one. As it extinguished the lasers, it seemed the star-beam became stronger and stronger until it resonated at a frequency like a high voltage line. John knew enough to stay out of the star-beam's path, sensing its great inherent power. He knew he was right, as one by one, the star-beam hit each rock. Each rock disintegrated with a soft puff turning into silvery powder like stardust. Against the dark-blue background, fluorescent dots of light became recognizable as words.

SPIRITU TUO

Oblivious, Laura stood in the observatory antechamber with her eyes wide open. John just picked her up and hoisted her over his shoulder holding onto her legs. He somehow found the exit. As he stepped outside the observatory door, with Laura hanging over his shoulder, he looked around. They were almost on top of the hill above Tan Chee Hong's high-rise building. John headed down to the platform of the heliport not far below. In the luminous glow coming from the city far beneath, he could make out the helicopter, standing by in parking mode.

Tug started shooting with a semi-automatic, as John tried to carry Laura to the helicopter.

John, with Laura on his back, was halfway to the helicopter, when the helicopter pilot noticed he was being shot at, as a large, jagged crack suddenly appeared in the chopper's bulletproof glass cockpit. This caused the pilot to react. He pulled in the rudder and started to rise vertically.

John ducked, holding Laura with both arms, trying to avoid the bullets. He shielded Laura with his own body. When the chopper rose, he stumbled. The turbulence almost swept them off the hillside to the seething streets below.

John looked in the direction from where he thought the bullets were coming, and for a moment, he could clearly see Tug aiming at them. John thought of his last desperate way of response. Holding Laura with one arm, he pulled out his old standby, his Walther PK, from the holster under his left arm. He pointed it in the direction where he thought Tug was and fired.

A faint cry was barely audible. It seemed Tug was hit.

John took the opportunity to signal the chopper down again.

The pilot had seen him. He touched down on the platform of the heliport once more.

Ducking under the rotor blades John was able to lift Laura, who was unconscious, with her eyes closed, into the chopper's back seat. He looked up to where he thought heaven might be. "Please don't let her die." He got into the seat next to the pilot.

As the chopper lifted off, more bullets came singeing from Tug's direction.

John pulled out his gun and signaled the pilot "cut throat," pointing down.

The pilot understood what John meant. In a swift maneuver, he directed the chopper right above the spot they thought was the shooter's position. For one short instance, in the diffused light, John could clearly see Tug firing his gun at them again.

John aimed his Walther PK in his old precise way and fired.

The impact of the shot was amazing. The Walther's caliber was not designed to blast someone to pieces. The Walther's pointed bullet was designed for precision. When Tug was hit precisely in the heart, it was not the explosion of the bullet but the spasm of death that sent him over the edge of the penthouse terrace. Tug sailed down to the streets of Hong Kong, swallowed up by a reddish beam of light that in this instant looked more like the fire of hell.

The helicopter rose in an almost vertical curve above the penthouse as John put his gun away. The noise inside the chopper was very loud, and the pilot had on his helmet and radio gear. John communicated with sign language. He pointed at Laura in the back, and formed the words, "v-e-r-y—s-i-c-k—h-o-s-p-i-t-a-l."

The pilot seemed to understand. He nodded and gradually pointed the chopper downward, beginning a direct-landing approach over what looked like a maze of searchlights. Coming closer, the lights turned out to be on top of a group of white buildings that looked like a large hospital.

A little edgy, with the feeling they would crash right into the buildings beneath, John told himself this pilot's flying was not what one would call conventional. John looked at the pilot, who just grinned as he bore the chopper straight down performing another one of his chilling maneuvers. He dropped the chopper right onto the heliport of the Hong Kong Caritas hospital.

John's mouth was dry. "Where did you learn your flying?" he asked, as the rotor blades slowed down, and the pilot took off his helmet.

"Vietnam," he said.

"Makes sense," John nodded.

The pilot jumped out of the chopper. He yelled, "you stay here with her! I get help! I know this place!" He ran toward the roof –top emergency entrance of the hospital.

John got out of the helicopter. He looked at his wristwatch, "two thirty in the morning." Standing on the cement of the heliport, he looked into the chopper. Laura was on the back seat. She was slumped over looking like a rag doll in evening clothes. He could see that she was near death. "Hang in there, Laura. They are on their way," he whispered. But she did not respond. John got into the helicopter to be closer to Laura. He held her hand, which was limp and white. He looked at the yellow topaz implanted in the delicate skin of her throat. The jewel was glowing as if it had life in it. John had a momentary flashback. He thought of the space-rocks, which also had elements of life in them. When he touched the topaz probingly, he knew this was a hollow gem of death. He tried to lift her up. It was no use This was the very moment John clearly knew he loved her. He was overwhelmed with despair. "Please don't die Laura," he whispered.

From the corner of his eye, he could see the pilot, followed by a med-crew pushing a stretcher, rushing toward them.

As they wheeled Laura away, John grabbed the pilot's hand. "Thank you, my friend."

The pilot withdrew. "That's not necessary. It's my job."

"But how did you know we were the good guys? You were hired by Tan Chee Hong, after all. You could just have left us there on the pent house heliport."

"I learned my craft in Vietnam. To me there are no good or bad guys, especially when they pay me. But I can always tell when there is someone in distress."

As soon as John had explained to the hospital's receptionist who Laura was, the triage team in the hospital's emergency room descended on her like a swarm of bees.

John was left standing alone in the reception area outside the emergency room. Anxious, he tried to alarm the nurse at the desk, telling her that the jewel on Laura's neck had to come off right away.

The sleepy-eyed, young Chinese woman did not seem or did not want to understand him. John looked around in desperation. He noticed a clock on a wall. It was almost three o'clock in the morning now.

John had lost all sense of time. The only thing he knew, Laura's life was ticking away. He knew he had to take some action, but he did not know exactly what he should do.

He focused on an older Chinese doctor, in a white lab coat over a suit and tie, who wore a stethoscope around his neck. The doctor threw his empty paper cup into a trashcan. He came up to John who stood forlorn at the reception desk.

"Sorry for interrupting," he said, "but did you say drug is in the jewel?"

"Yes-Yes". John uttered. "That's what I am trying to tell her."

The doctor wrinkled his forehead. "Don't worry, we will take care of her. I have seen this kind before—the work of Tan Chee Hong," he said, as he swiftly transited into the emergency room.

At about five in the morning, John, who had fallen asleep sitting on one of the aluminum framed plastic chairs in the hospital waiting room, woke up. The dingy room looked grey in its unappealing boredom. John noticed the smell of linoleum, mopped for decades with bleached water. At this time in the morning, there was no one else in the waiting room. It was quite a contrast to the languid hours between seven in the morning and eleven at night, when dozens of people crowded the room, waiting endlessly to find cures for their pain and disease.

A male Chinese nurse, in a white uniform, appeared in front of John. "Are you John Cordes?"

John got up from the chair and stretched his legs. "Yes. Who wants to know?"

"Please come with me, Dr. Wang wants to see you."

"Who is Dr. Wang?"

"Head of Caritas hospital, Hong Kong."

"Okay. But first tell me, how is the patient I brought in?"

"She is alive. She is in ICU."

John's voice was emphatic. "She needs to be guarded at all times, do you understand? Some people could be coming after her. They are trying to kill her!"

"Please follow me, and explain to Dr. Wang," the male nurse said coolly.

John followed the nurse, through the dimly lit corridors of the vast hospital, to the office of Dr. Wang, which was located on the third floor.

Dr. Ana Wang was a pretty, middle-aged, Eurasian woman with the intelligence of a CEO of a major corporation and the charisma of Mother Theresa. Only a few people knew she was a nun with a PhD in internal medicine. She wore her white coat over a simple blue dress she wore instead of a nun's habit. Ana Wang was the executive director of the Hong Kong Caritas Hospital, a medical facility with more than one thousand beds, she ran with a compassionate hand. That she had come to her office at five o' clock in the morning seemed unreal to John, who was used to Western work practices.

"Thank you for seeing us at this inconvenient time," he said.

"We don't see important people from the Vatican every day," she replied. We know who Laura d'Andres is, and we will see that she gets the best possible attention."

John liked and trusted Ana Wang immediately. He filled her

in on what had happened. As soon as she heard that none other than Tan Chee Hong was involved, Ana Wang picked up the phone and called hospital security. She called for two guards to be placed at Laura's bedside immediately. After she took this initial step, she listened to John's entire story. She thought it was best not to alarm Hong Kong authorities, but to treat the whole affair as an internal matter of the Vatican. Instead of getting police protection for Laura, she would bring in the Knights of the Hong Kong order of Saint John, in addition to the hospital security that was already in place.

When the Catholic nurses, at the hospital, found out who their patient was, small miracles began to happen for Laura.

John thought the intuition of the helicopter pilot, who landed them at the Caritas hospital, was a miracle in itself. The pilot did not know Laura was associated with the Vatican, but he instinctively landed them on top of one of the few and better Catholic hospital's in Hong Kong that provided not only the best possible medical care but that also was a sanctuary.

Laura immediately received priority treatment as one of the few women working for the Vatican in a position of trust and influence. It was as if she were a high-powered Cardinal or church official. She somehow had become a legend, a charismatic hero of Catholic clergywomen. They treated her like a saint who had come from the holy Vatican, a saint, who was in danger of dying.

The deadly jewel was removed from her neck, and a small skin graft was attached in its place. Laura remained in a coma. To bring her back from the drug overdose was a challenging task that took some of the doctors and nurses best skills.

Laura's response to the doctor's efforts was slow at first. After three days and three nights, her vital signs improved to the point, they took her out of intensive care and placed her in a regular hospital room.

John was given a small room on the same floor as Laura. He kept watching out for surprise packages, or visitors, which might have come from Tan Chee Hong. John thought that with his influence and power, it would be easy for Tan Chee Hong to find them. But everything remained quiet. Maybe he has given up, John thought, knowing at the same time Tan Chee Hong would never give up.

During his vigil near Laura's room John sometimes saw unsavory or out of place characters walking the corridors of the large hospital. He was quick to point them out to security or to the undercover Knights of St. John that were placed strategically around the hospital. The center of security was in a small office suite close to Dr. Wang's own office and they could quickly be alarmed by walky-talky. But as often as John followed his haunches and tried to pin point one person or another, it always turned out to be a false alarm.

Ana Wang invited John to use her office and phones so he could make the necessary phone calls. From her office, John called the Vatican and he described the situation to the Cardinal de Montaigne. He also spoke with Father Renquist in New York, who told him Eric was fine but that he had not uttered a word yet.

The Cardinal de Montaigne expressed his concern about Laura, but told John he was glad she was in the good hands of Hong Kong Caritas and of Dr. Wang. He then asked John if they had accomplished their mission and John briefed him on what had happened. A.P.S, the enemy that had terrorized Rome and the Vatican, had been destroyed. Details would be provided by John upon his return to Rome. It was not a coincidence that John forgot to tell the Cardinal about the carpetbag and its contents, because he had mixed feelings about giving the carpetbag back to the Vatican. As far as he was concerned the basic mission, which was to find and destroy the terrorists, was accomplished. It was unfortunate that the carpetbag, which was the subject of the crisis from the onset, was lost or destroyed.

It seemed the Cardinal de Montaigne was content to hear John's story but he still seemed very anxious to bring John and Laura back to Rome. He told John he would make all necessary arrangements with Dr. Wang to bring them in as soon as possible.

Dr. Ana Wang was something wondrous to John. She certainly was an attractive woman. However, this was not what counted so much. Ana Wang was a woman who stood tall in this world, and as such, she was beyond political or sexual approach. She just was a great personality. John understood her just as he used to understand Jimmy Lu. They became fast friends and allies, and she helped him in every way she could.

"I wonder why we haven't heard from Tan Chee Hong yet. It's awfully quiet on that front," John said to Ana Wang.

Ana Wang just smiled a knowing smile. "I don't think you will hear from Tan Chee Hong too soon. The Knights of Saint John are watching him, and he knows he is being watched. As far as we know, he has pulled this kind of stunt at least twice before. One of the persons, he drugged the same way as Laura, died here in the hospital. At the time, we could not prove, it was him. However, this time we have witnesses. He knows we will get him for murder if he dares to make a move. After you and Laura are gone from Hong Kong, we will call the authorities and turn him in."

John caught her thought. "What do you mean, after Laura and I are gone from Hong Kong? How soon might that be? We just can't hop right onto the next plane—in the state she is in."

Ana smiled again. "Don't worry, John, I know how to make small miracles happen. With the help of the Almighty, I will have you out of here, as soon as Laura is ready for transport."

"I bet you will," he said, not really believing her.

With the good care, Laura was given at the hospital she slowly began to improve. After five days, she was still asleep, but her vital signs were stable, and the brain scan showed no obvious damage to the brain.

Ana Wang called the Cardinal de Montaigne in a conference call in John's presence. They decided it was best to remove Laura from the possible risk of Tan Chee Hong trying one of his sneaky attacks again. Despite Laura's fragile condition, it was better to bring Laura and John back to Rome as soon as possible.

"But how?" John thought.

Ana Wang seemed to have read his mind. She opened her desk drawer and pulled out a photograph. It was a picture of a large, white jet plane with a Red-Cross insignia. She showed the picture to John. "Look at this beauty, John—a Red-Cross hospital plane with all the best equipment, plus a doctor and three nurses. And it is parked right here in Hong Kong."

"You mean you have access to a plane like this?"

Ana Wang now smiled wider. She was gloating like a delighted child. "You bet I do. You bet I do."

Two days later, on a warm and foggy morning, during the early morning hours, Ana Wang called John to her office. "Pack your bags, John, and hurry. You are going home. Your plane is taking off in exactly one-hundred twenty-five minutes from now."

Soon afterwards, Ana Wang accompanied John down to the hospital's loading dock. The first thing he saw, waiting at the dock, was a Red Cross ambulance with red signage. The van was heavily guarded by four security guards that looked more like a SWAT team on high alert. "Would you like to sit next to the driver, or would you like to sit near Laura? She is very comfortable in the back of the ambulance."

"I would rather be in the back with Laura."

"Okay, John. Goodbye. I will miss you. Just be sure you come and see me next time you are in Hong Kong," Ana Wang said. "If I weren't a nun, I would give you a hug."

"But I love nunny hugs," John said. He gave Ana Wang a great big bear hug. "Thank you Dr. Ana. And if you don't get Tan Chee Hong, I will come back to Hong Kong and get him myself, and after that, I'll take you to Macao—disco dancing."

"That would be nice. Glancing over John's remarks, Ana Wang smiled her best smile and changed the subject. Be assured, this time we will get Tan Chee Hong—son-of-a-bitch."

John was surprised, by her using a curse word. "But you are not allowed to curse—"

"No, John. We can curse as much as we want, just as long as we don't use the holy name of God in vain. And cursing Tan Chee Hong is not in vain."

Ana Wang suddenly looked dense and pensive. "You know I like you, and I like Laura d'Andres, even though I have never seen her conscious. Somehow, something tells me you are good people. I know that Laura d' Andres, having been in the position in the Vatican she was, would never do anything to harm the Vatican or the papacy. And you know, I shouldn't say this, but you and I know there are certain elements, not only in the Vatican but all around the world, who will not hesitate to defend their faith with the sword—meaning they will kill you if they think you or Laura are traitors. Or even if they think you know too much."

"Sister Ana, you are telling me nothing new. I understand what you are trying to tell me."

"It's just that the Cardinal acted more than strange when he called me the last time. It sounded more like they wanted to take good care of Laura but not because it was in her best interest but in theirs. It sounded more like she was a suspicious person, they wanted for questioning—inquisition they call that. And it looks like they think you might be holding back some evidence of enormous scientific value—Are you John?"

"Of course not. Search me. I am holding nothing back."

Ana Wang smiled at him. "But I know that John. I trust you."

On their way to one of Hong Kong's utility airports, where the Red Cross plane was waiting, John sat next to Laura in the back of the closed ambulance-van. He could not see the crowded streets, the turbulent traffic, and the highly compressed life that was so characteristic of the city of Hong Kong. He could only see Laura, who looked like she was sleeping peacefully. She was a little pale, but she was breathing normally. "Hang in there, you are not going to heaven. You are just going home," John whispered in her ear.

19.

INTERLUDE

The warm colors of summer intensified. The yellows turned orange and gold and the pinks turned red and purple. The air was as warm and as dry as it could get before becoming cool, thin, and chilling. The Chianti and Sangiovese grapes were ripening at a fast pace. The vintners got ready for the harvest. Soon the North-winds would begin to blow the rain clouds out to sea.

The rehabilitation hospital, just about half an hour's drive from the center of Rome, was in a large, nineteenth century building. The former spa hotel had been transformed into a hospice after the war. Park-like grounds with leafy trees, shrubs, some palms, and well-kept seasonal flowerbeds framed the two story buildings.

Laura dreamt she was laying in a sunny meadow half-sleeping and half-awake. She could sense the wonderful scent of each blade of grass in the meadow, awakened by the warming sun light, the sounds of birds, and the lightness of the mild air. As she drifted into consciousness, she felt the softly scented draft coming from a half-open window and she breathed in deeply.

Her body was clad in an oversized white cotton shirt and she felt better than ever as she stretched comfortably in the bed covered with white linens. Her senses were heightened. Her sense of smell was keen, especially. She could smell a park with trees and flowers and the cleanliness of the room—the laundered sheets, the waxed floor, and the delicious scent of coffee coming from somewhere outside her door.

"Where am I?" She noticed the bed was an army cot. It was painted with cream-colored paint and the bedding was very comfortable. Still, the bed-frame was an army cot. Laura concluded that it was a hospital of some sort, a notion that was disturbing. She also noticed a small bird clinging to the whitewashed ceiling of the room. Its jetty little eyes watched her anxiously. As soon as Laura moved ever so slightly the bird flustered all around the room. Looking for a way out, it chirped fretfully and it thumped its little head painfully against walls and windowpanes. Seeing the bird's plight, her feeling of well-being turned into panic. Her heartbeat was racing and she suddenly felt out of breath. "Help! Help!" she yelled.

An older Sister-nurse, in a blue and white starched uniform with a white winged hat, entered the room. She looked at Laura and crossed herself. She then put a cooling hand on Laura's forehead. "Calm, calm, child!"

Laura anxiously pointed at the erratic little bird.

The Sister immediately went to the window and pushed it open all the way.

Laura could now see that the windows were barred with iron bars. This too was a notion that made her feel uneasy. Sensing the way to freedom, the little bird chirped one more time, and then it found its way through the bars to the outside "If the little bird can escape so can I," Laura thought and she felt better again.

The Sister came over to Laura and checked her pulse and vitals. Laura looked up to her with a blank expression. "What happened?" she asked.

The Sister, whose kind eyes betrayed her stern manner, looked down at Laura. "A miracle," she said. "A miracle has happened." She helped Laura to sit up in bed.

Laura felt ravenous. "Could I have some coffee?"

"What about some breakfast?"

"That sounds wonderful."

Laura questioned the Sister again and again about what had happened to her and why she was in a hospital.

The Sister said she did not really know the details of what had happened to Laura. A visitor would come and explain it to her.

Later that afternoon, after Laura had breakfast, and then some lunch, they took her in a wheel chair out onto a large, sunny terrace overlooking the hospice's gardens. Only a few other patients were on the terrace enjoying the warming sun. Laura smiled at them as the sister wheeled her to the far end of the terrace. Laura was pale but she looked as beautiful as ever. Her dark hair curled down to her hospital robe and her blue-green eyes were alive. Her hand briefly touched a bandage on her throat and she wondered why the bandage was there. Something painful and strange had happened to her, but she was not sure what it was.

"Enjoy the afternoon, Miss Laura," the Sister said. "Your visitor will be here soon."

Laura was excited about the promise of a visitor who could tell her more about what had happened. She did not remember much. Her memory of who she was and of people she knew was patchy. She could not imagine what kind of visitor would come to see her.

She looked down at the lovely gardens below the terrace. There was a fountain surrounded by potted geraniums with full blooms of vibrant purple and red. A white gravel path lead through shrubs and trees to where she thought the main entrance to the hospice's grounds might be.

She noticed someone came up the garden path. And she could feel her heartbeat, as she strained her eyes to see who it was. The man walked quickly under the trees through areas of light and shade. His shoes made a crunching sound on the white gravel. He held a sort of a suite case in one hand, his other hand clutched a white triangular object.

John's cell phone rang as he came up the garden path. Shifting the large bouquet of flowers, wrapped in white paper, from one side to the other, he pulled out the phone and answered.

"Hello, John Cordes—"

A child's voice came through the line loud and clear.

"Hello Daddy?"

John had not heard Eric's voice in years but he immediately knew it was he. It was the sweetest sound he ever wanted to hear.

"Hello Daddy?"

John's knees gave in and he sat down on a near by garden bench.

"My God, Eric. I am here! I am here! How are you, son?"

"I am fine, Daddy. I love you."

"Eric, darling. I love you too."

"I miss you, Daddy."

"I miss you too. I will come home as fast as I can."

Father Renquist's voice came on. "I told you miracles happen to those who—"

The phone cut out. John still held the phone to his ear, trying to listen intensely. "Hello! Hello! I'll call you a little later!" His eyes welled up with tears. "Dear God, Eric," he whispered." His consternation changed to joy.

Up on the terrace, Laura saw that the man walking up the garden path suddenly stopped. He sat down on a bench. It seemed the man was making a phone call. She still tried to figure out who the man was, when she saw him breaking into a strange looking dance or jiggle, waving at her a suitcase and a white object, which now looked like a bouquet of flowers wrapped in white paper. She was not sure what the man's emotional gesticulations meant. However, he certainly seemed very happy.

Laura thought of happiness. "Remember happiness"—She heard her mother's voice in her mind. She began to remember her mother's voice telling her humans did not only have a right to be happy but happiness was part of an enlightened state humans should accomplish. The sound of her mother's voice, which came to her through ages gone by, slowly helped clear the fog in her mind. Suddenly Laura's recognition was back and she knew who the man on the garden path was. It was John, the most wonderful, dear, man she had ever seen.

John, vitally handsome and happy, walked up the stairs taking two steps at a time. He stopped when he saw the Sister in charge coming down the corridor.

Sister Dorothea recognized him too. "Mr. Cordes! Mr. Cordes! As I told you on the phone this morning, Miss d'Andres has come around. Do you believe in miracles?"

John smiled a happy smile. "Sister Dorothea! Do I believe in miracles? Of course, I do. Of course, I do. Miracles happen all the time to those who—"

Sister Dorothea finished his sentence. "That's right, miracles happen all the time to those who believe." She looked at the shiny brown leather suitcase John held in his hand. "May I ask you what's in that suit case you brought?"

"Oh, its nothing. Just some items that belong to Laura."

"As you probably know, Mr. Cordes, We have strict instructions from the Vatican, all deliveries to Ms. d'Andres have to be checked carefully, and we cannot let anything come in or out of here without checking it. In addition, as you know, the Church agents are guarding her and watching her closely. You will barely notice them but I can assure you there are Church agents all over the hospital, watching out for Ms .d'Andres."

"Or maybe they are watching Ms. d'Andres. Have you ever thought of it that way?"

John had seen them too—the Teflon clad Church agents that always seemed to loom in the shadows. Knowing the Vatican had a great interest invested in Laura, John had a strange feeling about them. However, outwardly he smiled a carefree smile. "Sister Dorothea, I can assure you there is nothing in this suit case that could be of any interest to the Vatican—just some personal things like books and clothing, Laura might need."

Sister Dorothea, who was frequently taken by John's handsome looks and charm, smiled back at him. She looked at the suitcase. "Well I guess it's all right to bring in a suit case with some of her daily necessities."

Then, John stood in front of Laura's wheel chair. "Hello—Laura!"

Laura's eyes glistened with tears. "John. Oh John. You don't know how much I love seeing you."

John bent down and kissed her on the cheek.

She turned her head so that their lips met in a kiss.

John put the flower bouquet in her lap. "You have come back, Laura."

She held the flowers with weak hands. "I love flowers more

than anything—thank you John, for the flowers and for coming back. You too have come back."

"Even my son has come back. I just received a phone call from New York. Eric has come out of his autistic state. He is talking normally. Father Renquist is teaching him. How do you like that?"

At first, she did not quite understand what John was saying. But as soon as slices of her memory came back, she shared his joy. "It's a miracle. I am so happy for you and especially for Eric."

John was exuberant. "How would you like to come to New York with me and meet Eric?"

The happiness Laura felt seeing John helped her to remember more and more. Now it all came back in chunks and little pieces. "I would like that very much. But I am afraid, it is not possible. The doctor said it's going to be at least six months until I am back to normal." A tear ran down Laura's cheek. "Besides being in a coma for two weeks, I have had a small stroke and I might never be the same—ever again."

John shook his head. "That's not what they told me. You are back and you will be fine, just fine. That's what I was told." John pulled over an empty chair and sat down next to her.

Sister Dorothea, busying herself, came by. She smiled. "Let me take the flowers, Miss Laura."

Laura looked at the flowers one by one. How beautiful they were roses, lilies, and tuberose. Every little petal, every little leaf, was shaped, and scented like it was from heaven. She handed the bouquet to the Sister, reluctantly. She remembered the Sister's name. "Thank you Sister Dorothea."

John took Laura's hand and kissed it. He looked into her eyes. "How are you feeling—really?"

Laura looked back at him with a bittersweet expression. "Oh, I feel fine. Only, I am a little scared because I can't remember most of what happened to me. The last thing I know, Count Ormani was killed somehow, and Cardinal de Montaigne was hearing my confession. He absolved me of all sins. I was glad, because I thought I had committed a great sin. He told me making a mistake was not a sin. Then there was blood, so much blood. Blood was everywhere. That is the last of my recollection."

John held her hand. "Believe me, there is nothing you should be afraid of any longer. The ghosts and evil-minded people are all gone."

Laura was near tears again. "But tell me, what happened?"

John did not think the time was right to tell her the details of what had really happened. Especially not about the death of Jimmy Lu, or that she was now deemed a suspicious person, a *persona non grata*, by the Vatican. She was traumatized enough. He was glad she could not remember everything, or at least her memory was patchy. He decided to give her time until she became stronger and her memory came back fully by itself.

"It is nothing, Laura. It is just—you have been to Hong-Kong and back. That's all."

"I always wanted to see Hong-Kong—" Laura said dreamily. Realizing the impact of what John said, she was startled. "You are joking—Please tell me what happened. And what's in that suit case you are carrying?"

"That's a very long story. Don't worry about it now. The main thing is you are conscious. We will have plenty of time. I will explain everything, later. In the meantime let's just regain our strength and happiness." John carefully placed the leather suitcase on a nearby garden table. "Maybe this will help you to remember." He opened the suitcase slowly. "Do you remember this Laura?"

Laura wheeled her wheelchair closer to the table.

John held the lid of the suitcase open.

She immediately recognized what was inside—a black and yellow carpetbag. She touched the bag. "Of course—I remember—the carpetbag, the space rocks, the story my parents wrote."

John gently opened the bag in front of her. "This belongs to you, Laura. I brought you this as a personal gift. A legacy from your parents."

Laura lifted the carpetbag's closure and looked at the items inside, two skulls, four hand-written books, somewhat burned, and the two remaining rocks, gleaming like two enormous diamonds. She sighed deeply. "Thank you, for saving this."

"You are welcome."

Laura quickly closed the suitcase over the carpetbag as they saw Sister Dorothea coming across the terrace with a tray.

Ignoring the suitcase, the Sister put two cups of tea and a small plate with two amaretto cookies on the table in front of them. "To me, you are very special people," she said. "Have some refreshments—on the house."

"Thank you," John said.

Laura just smiled and nodded thankfully.

The Sister was gone again.

They sipped the tea and ate the cookies.

"I have another surprise for you," John said. "He should be arriving very soon."

Laura's eyes followed John's, as he looked down the garden path in anticipation.

"As a matter of fact, I think your surprise is here."

Another man came up the garden path. His figure was set against the contrasting light, of the sunset.

The man saw them too. He raised his arm and waved at them.

Laura focused on the slim, bearded man. She could suddenly feel her heart beat. "Dear God, it is Professor Stynfeldt!"

Stynfeldt joined them on the terrace. He planted a fatherly kiss on Laura's temple. "Dear Laura, I am so happy you are back."

"But how do you know where I have been? I am not so sure where I have been myself."

"John told me all about it," Stynfeldt said.

Laura thought she was seeing a ghost. In her mind, the Professor had died at Da Vinci airport. "Professor where did you come from? I thought you were—"

"I thought I was dead too. But some miracle happened. I don't know how. Didn't John tell you, he came to see me in the hospital?"

Laura was dazed. "I guess John never told me. Or my memory lapsed. She turned to John. Why didn't you ever tell me the Professor was alive?"

"I thought I told you—but maybe not. Things just started to unravel so fast."

"That's true. Things were happening fast and I have lost a block of my time. The important thing is, you are here, Professor Stynfeldt—alive and well."

Stynfeldt smiled. He touched Laura's hand. "Thank you. I want to say the same about you. I am very glad to see you—alive and well. You used to call me uncle Fred. Don't you remember?"

"Yes, uncle Fred—Professor, I remember."

"Laura—the baby, they used to call you. I think the reason I survived the shooting—the reason I am still here—I still have a purpose to fulfill in this world."

John pulled over another chair. "Sit down, Professor."

Sister Dorothea came by again. "I brought you a cup of tea, Professor Stynfeld."

"Thank you, Sister, I appreciate it."

"This is wonderful, uncle Fred," Laura said. "And I think I know exactly what purpose you have to fulfill." She pointed at the suitcase. "John has brought us a most valuable gift—proof beyond any doubt."

Stynfeldt got up from his chair. His cool voice could not hide his excitement. "John told me on the phone, he got the carpetbag." He opened the suitcase and looked inside. He shook his head in bewilderment. "At last," he said. "It is amazing. I have waited for this moment for a very long time. May I?" He opened the suitcase fully but did not remove the carpetbag from inside it. His hands trembled slightly as he carefully examined the contents of the carpetbag "This is it," he said. "The very same old carpetbag the Andersons used to bring the evidence from Africa in the first place." Stynfeldt took out a handkerchief from his pocket and lightly dusted the table's surface. Then, as if he was handling raw eggs, with the handkerchief wrapped around his hand, he took the two skulls and the two space rocks out of the carpetbag and placed them carefully on the table. "Look at this," he said. "The most significant anthropological find this world has ever seen."

For a moment's time, they looked at the relics and they felt as if they were part of eternity. The sculls emitted a special, mysterious aura. A ray of light came from the setting sun and briefly touched the rocks, which gleamed with fire from within.

Stynfeldt could not take his eyes off the relics. "Do you know what happened to the rest of the rocks?" he asked John.

John wrinkled his forehead. "I know it sounds strange like a fairy tale. But I saw it with my own eyes. The space rocks self-destructed, or were destroyed by some kind of laser beam coming from the constellation of Orion. At that time, it seemed to me, that because they were used for a violent purpose they were turned into star-dust."

"I understand—Stynfeldt said solemnly. In a way that sounds very strange but it is possible. It is also possible you just saw an illusion and the rocks are still intact. You must give me exact details of what happened so I can document all of it. It would be regrettable if we lost ten of the rocks and the skeletal bones. But we have still more than enough evidence here."

When they saw Sister Dorothea approach again, Stynfeldt, carefully but quickly, put the relics back into the carpetbag. He sat down again on one of the garden chairs. "Laura," he said. "I think you know what I have to do. These items have to go into an anthropological lab as soon as possible, so they can be checked for damage and we can preserve them properly."

Laura smiled. "My parents were anthropologists. Their work is in my blood. I understand it all very well. I cannot just keep these things as souvenirs, even though I would like to have them as part of their memory." She looked at the carpetbag. "I want you take the carpetbag and its contents, uncle Fred, and do what has to be done."

They sat talking on the terrace until dark.

The sky was pale at first, but the colors intensified minute by minute until all faded into dark blue and the stars came out. The constellation of Orion became visible in the night sky beyond the black silhouettes of the distant trees.

Laura pointed at the constellation. "Look—Orion—the Heavenly Hunter. My parents talked about Orion all the time. My father said Orion is the image of a man crucified. He is called the Heavenly Hunter because he hunts for the spirit of the human soul. Uncle Fred, do you know what he meant?"

"I don't think he meant Orion is a religious symbol of the crucified Christ or an image of godliness. The Universe is the image of godliness—I am convinced of it. Your parents believed it too. I think your parents only meant that this prominent star formation is a symbol in the sky meaning to tell us that the godly substance of the human spirit, or the form of DNA that created humanity on Earth, came from somewhere in that constellation."

Stynfeldt looked at the sky. "I know this is complicated. It is like taking concrete science into the metaphysical. I wrote a book explaining not only the scientific but also the philosophical meaning of the findings of Laura's parents. I will send you and John each a copy. Meanwhile, I can tell you what I know, and what your parents knew."

"You see, Marthie and Leo Anderson were not only wonderful scientists but also the closest of friends. We all were in accord. What I am trying to say, Cambridge is one of the greatest bastions of human knowledge in the world and many of their departments like nuclear physics and others are at the cutting edge of science in the highest sense. Do not forget that the DNA structure of all living things was discovered by Watson and Crick there in 1953. I remember that Crick himself walked into the Eagle's Inn pub one day and announced that they had discovered the origins of life. However, you must realize that Cambridge is also based on old tradition and that Darwin, for example, posted his theory of evolution there, at first. So if researchers like the Andersons or me suddenly had come up with theories of extraterrestrials and the mitochondrial Eve we would have at least been ridiculed if not persecuted. Everything had to be done under cover until we could prove everything beyond any scientific doubt."

Stynfeldt took a sip of cold tea and then continued. "I helped with the Andersons lab-work off and on, but most of the work was done by them. When they were not on expedition, they lived in a lovely, small cottage in Burwell, which is a quaint little town only ten kilometers from Cambridge, with you, Laura, their adorable little daughter."

"Is it true, they took me to Africa, as a baby? I have no recollection of it. But I do remember the English cottage."

"Yes, Laura. Your parents took you with them on expedition. Marthie would never leave you behind. You even had a nanny traveling with you, making sure you were cared for at all times. The same nanny took care of you in Burwell during the times the Andersons spent all those long hours in their lab at Cambridge. Don't you remember her? Her name was Margie."

"I think I remember her but very vaguely."

"Anyway, I visited Marthie, Leo, and you—the baby—in Burwell every single weekend. We had endless discussions— sometimes until the morning hours. Unfortunately, it did not last very long. After the Andersons came back from Africa with their volatile find, they only stayed alive for about nine weeks. It is still bothering my mind today—was their demise an accident? Or did the same someone who stole the carpetbag also kill them? The longer I think about it, the more I am convinced that is what happened. Someone deliberately forced them off the road."

"But wouldn't the driver of the van that hit them have been in danger of being killed too?"

"Not necessarily. It turned out later, when they analyzed the accident, the white van did not collide with them directly. It kind of nudged or crammed the Andersons car off the road. In addition, something else happened that makes me believe the Andersons death was not an accident. A short time later, their cottage in Burwell was broken into. The place was ransacked and then someone tried to burn it."

"And did the burglars find or remove anything that would have been of interest?"

"I don't think so. I had been to the cottage before and I sadly took anything and everything that could have been of interest, as you put it. There was not much. Most everything concerning the African findings was kept at the Andersons lab at Cambridge."

John was pensive. "Who would have wanted to prevent them from publishing their discovery?"

"Just answer your own question and don't say any more."

"How would they even know about the findings of the Andersons, Professor? I thought you told me you had set up a tight security screen around them?"

"That's true. I tried to do my best to keep them protected and to keep the story under covers. Don't forget, they were quite a famous explorer couple. The newspapers and magazines were always ready to bring stories about them. When they made their discovery, they were not alone at the Gorge. You saw the members of their expedition in the film I showed you in the Vatican. Moreover, there were others, scientists at the Gorge from all over the world. Not that the Andersons would have cried, "Eureka—here—we found it!" They were far too careful for that. But someone at the Gorge could have picked up on it and leaked it to—who knows who?"

"It all makes sense," John said.

The Professor nodded. "As I told you the walls at Cambridge are like the porous membranes of a brain. What I mean, the news of a new scientific discovery is absorbed there like by a sponge. It is very hard to hold back or to conceal anything of magnitude. Someone at Cambridge could have gotten wind that something earth shattering in the field of anthropology was about to be published and they informed the powers that be. Cambridge is full of religious scientists and clergy of all kind, Anglican, Catholic, Orthodox, Judaic—those are the Creationists. There are the bio-paleontologists and paleontologists for whom the credo is Darwin's theory of evolution and absolutely nothing beyond that point. No little Martians or any form of extraterrestrial life, not even microbes or snails. Whatever is alive on this planet is the one and only life that came from the one and only living God or the one and only Big Bang, depending what side you are on. The rest of the Universe can go to hell. Who cares about stars and galaxies and billions and billions of them? To them a beautiful, scientific miracle that is the Universe is nothing but a chemical wasteland. The Andersons discovery presented an inconvenient truth to all of them. They all would have either something to lose or a lot of explaining to do. None of them understand that if they just would be a little more inclusive in their theories, including for example, that we are part of a Universe, and that their could be forms of life in other parts—all would not be fine but all would definitely be better—maybe. You see there were many elements that would have tried to suppress or eliminate the Andersons discoveries. However, the more I think about it, the more I am inclined to think the Jesuits are probably the most suspicious ones, because the carpetbag wound up where it wound up—in the Vatican."

John understood what the Professor said. "You know, Professor, the Andersons "accident" could be investigated, even today."

"You mean that even after all these years you could find out, who stole the carpetbag in the first place, and possibly could have killed the Andersons?"

"It wouldn't be easy but it is possible. The Brits keep excellent records as you probably know, and I am well connected there."

"I am not so sure I would even want to know," Laura said.

John looked at Laura. I understand, Laura. "My wife died under similar circumstances and I am not so sure I want to investigate the more sinister details either. However, the truth should be known. That's my job, digging for the truth."

Laura turned to Stynfeldt. "I understand. I can see the picture more clearly now. Professor, do you think you could take what is in the carpetbag and finish the work of my parents, so that humanity can learn the truth about its origins? Maybe if the truth becomes known, humans will stop killing each other. And maybe in times of peace the spirit will become enlighten and they will find the elusive enigma they call God?"

"I promise I will finish the work, Laura. We will publish it no matter what. This is why I am still here. To conclude this magnum opus and let the truth be known. However, I cannot promise you that it will influence or change the minds of humans. You see the creation of the carbon-based human on this planet was not perfect. Humans tend to have tremendous flaws. Yes, we seem to have our own moral compass pointing toward the spiritual, but no matter how great the intelligence, we succumb to temptation. Killing, warfare, murder, racism, genocide, religious fanaticism, cruelty to animals, a fierce disregard for nature, killing for sport, and polluting the environment—the atrocities go on and on. I hate to be pessimistic. However, when humanity was created on Earth, something went wrong with the experiment. Not enough of the good DNA was transferred. Too many of the animalistic genes remained. Somehow, in the chemical process a new side product was created, a form of evil that goes far beyond the animalistic instinct. Animals, though naturally ferocious, cannot conceive evil. Evil never occurred on this Earth before the event of humanity. Neither the chimpanzees nor the humanoids, even though they had to kill for their survival, knew the concept of evil. The evil on this Earth is exclusively human. Yes, the wonderful human spirit was created in the hominids but at the same time, some of the persistent animal genes were transformed into pure strands of evil. I call it "the Frankenstein Gene," and believe me, there is nothing humorous about it. Though outwardly we have made great scientific and industrious progress, whatever is inside us, call it the soul or the human spirit, has regressed terribly.

Stynfeldt paused and then continued. "You see most every thing on this Earth including animal and plant life is made from linkages of carbon atoms, crystalline carbons, the highest form of which is the diamond, or hydro-carbons like oils or gases. The rocks the Andersons discovered are a much higher form of carbon than what exists on Earth. The rocks are telling us there is a carbon-based form of civilization out there similar to ours but in a much higher form of being. Now, with electro-spectroscopy, we can determine from where in the Milky Way a substance might come from. So part of my work is to find that planet. Circling the one star in the constellation of Orion from whence the rocks came.

It is the source of the human spirit. But even if I find that planet and the living entities on it, we still don't know if our world will be ready to accept this. I mean, we are out there everyday, warning them, lecturing them, trying to make them understand. They just will never learn. Why are humans, who are the godliest creatures on Earth, acting so stupid?"

Stynfeldt had become aggravated. "The Andersons theory should be celebrated as the credo of a new world. The Andersons themselves should be celebrated as great discoverers, like the first astronauts or the first men who walked on the moon. However, I am afraid humanity is not ready to accept the truth. You both know as well as I do, the world does not care. Natural or scientific occurrences count very little unless they are threatening to destroy us. That is the only time they pay attention—when disaster almost strikes. Whatever happens to this planet is of no concern, as long as they are able to go on with their petty, nonsensical way of living."

"You are painting a pretty bleak picture, Professor. Do you think there is any hope for us? What if the entities, who created us in the first place came back to teach us a lesson?" Laura said.

"You mean like a re-visit, resurrection, or the second coming of the Messiah?"

"Something like that."

Stynfeldt was getting impatient. "I don't know that much about religion, but I admit the religious fables often can be interpreted scientifically. But what I meant to say is, once the DNA transfer had occurred, that was it. You cannot just come back later and add a little more salt to the soup."

"What is going to happen to humanity?"

"Unfortunately, I have to think, they have given us up already, or they will give us up very soon. They will just find another planet and try to better the experiment this time. And then, when evil reigns on Earth complete, we will just self destruct."

Laura was resigned. "I think what the Professor is trying to say, John, even if Jesus came back to die on the cross all over again, he still could not wipe away all the horrible deeds that humans have done. The world is too far gone for that. It has slipped into the abyss of hell. Like what the painter Hieronymus Bosch predicted in his paintings in the 16th century. Jesus could die for us a hundred times again and he still could not save us."

Laura continued. "Of course, that's a very negative view. My parents, knowing all of this, were never negative. On the contrary, they were always positive and cautiously optimistic. Look at the accomplishments of humanity in science, art, philosophy and more. Look at the-state-of-the art of technology, medicine, physics, and chemistry. I think it is mind boggling what we have accomplished." Laura was exhausted. Her eyes filled with tears. In her mind, she heard her mother's voice, "Don't forget love!" Laura lifted herself up. "There are many forms of love, beauty, innocence, and hope that still exist here on this planet." Laura looked up, toward Orion. "At least they should give us credit for that."

They all paused and looked up at the beautiful night sky, pondering what Laura had said.

Stynfeldt spoke quietly. "That's true. But don't you think if they outweighed the greater picture, the accomplishments of humanity would be dwarfed by the insanity that's going on in our world?"

Laura took a breath of the night air. "I don't know. I have two degrees and I still cannot understand it all. What should we do, Professor? Is it possible to save humanity from self-destruction?"

"I don't know. I am getting old. The older I get the more pessimistic I become. When your parents first made the discovery, I was convinced it would change the world forever. Even during the sixties, when they preached love all around, I was still optimistic. However, with all that has happened recently, the river of hope is drying up. The river of blood is swelling to new levels. It soon will run over. But you, Laura and John, are young and strong and full of optimism—it's easy for you to believe you can make the world better."

"Don't forget I have a son," John said. "When you have children you must do everything to see they have a future."

Stynfeldt paused, nodded, sighed, and turned to Laura. "I tell you what Laura, you are highly educated and you have more passion and commitment than any one I know. You unfalteringly believe there is no limit to the human spirit, *spiritu tuo*, as it is termed in the Latin liturgy of the Church. You are perfectly qualified to help me write the book about your parent's discovery. A book that will create a loud and sudden bang, which everyone around the globe can hear all at once."

"What do you think about that John?" Laura asked.

"I think it could be a good thing but it also could be very dangerous for both of you," John said, with contention.

"Laura ignored John's warning. She was flushed with sudden excitement about the idea. Her voice was high-pitched. "Do you think we could actually convince them?"

Stynfeldt looked at Laura. Her mother's blue-green eyes, sparkled, expressing compassion, and unrelenting faith in the human spirit. "I think it's possible," he said.

Then Sister Dorothea was upon them, again. "My, oh my, what's that?" she asked when she saw the carpetbag laying in the half-opened suitcase.

"Just something that will shake up this world from here to eternity," Stynfeldt answered.

"Is that so," Sister Dorothea said without an inkling of understanding. "I thought these are some of Miss Laura's personal things. I came to tell you, it's far beyond Miss Laura's bed time. Miss Laura, I am sorry but I have to take you to your room, doctor's orders."

"That will be fine. I feel very tired, anyway. I think it all was enough for me for one day." Laura extended both hands toward John and Stynfeldt. "Good night gentlemen. Will I see you in the morning?"

Both Stynfeldt and John placed kisses on Laura's extended hands. "You can be sure you will see me in the morning, darling," John said. "But Professor Stynfeldt is scheduled to travel back to England."

That's right, the Professor said I am bound for old England. He kissed Laura's hand again and then gave her a hug. "Be well Laura. I hope to see you soon."

Laura's eyes brimmed with sudden emotion. "Yes, uncle Fred. I promise I will see you soon."

She turned to John. "Oh, I just remembered—my apartment—you know where that is, in the old part of Rome near the Vatican. Could you do me a favor, John? Could you go there and see that everything is in order? The concierge has a passkey. She can let you in."

John's lie came out cool. "Don't worry Laura, I will do that. I am sure everything is fine."

Sister Dorothea was impatient. "It's time for Miss Laura to go now. I will send an attendant to pick up her suit case and bring it to her room," she said as she wheeled Laura back towards the entrance of the hospital.

After Laura left, John's voice quietly intensified. "Listen to me Professor. I did not want to say anything before, not anything that could scare Laura or aggravate her condition. She must be kept thinking all is fine.

"I know, I know. All is not fine."

"Just listen to me now, and let me say this quick before the Sister comes back to fetch us. After I brought Laura back from Hong Kong, they brought her here to this hospice. I was at the Vatican only once for debriefing. They thanked me for accomplishing the mission against the terrorists. They are going to send me a check after I send them a written report from New York, in strict confidentiality of course. I am sure, I myself am out of the loop. of suspicion, they trust me because they pay me money. That's how things work. I told them the story about A.P.S. and Tan Chee Hong, which they seemed to believe. However, the one thing that no one really seemed to comprehend. is that it was Tan Chee Hong who used Raphael to take over A.P.S. and that even though A.P.S. was destroyed, Tan Chee Hong and Raphael are still out there scheming evil. I told them the carpetbag and all its contents were lost when A.P.S. was destroyed. I am not sure they believed that part of the story. But they don't know otherwise. Only something still frightens me. I already checked out Laura's apartment in Rome. I did not have to get the passkey from the concierge. I know how to get into a place like this without a key."

"I can imagine John, you can."

"Yes, but here is the bad part. The apartment underwent a severe search. I mean, there was nothing unturned or left out, even the wallpaper was torn off the walls, and the floorboards were removed. It was a complete and a professional job. As soon as Laura regains full consciousness, she will be in great danger. They are going to try to get every bit of information they can out of her. They call that an "inquisition," you know. I think we should consider Laura a prisoner rather than a patient in this hospital."

"I know, John. I have heard of their medieval methods."

"We must figure out a way of getting the carpetbag out of here and out of Rome, or Italy, to a safe place. Do you know such a place, Professor?"

"Yes, I suppose I know such a place and it is not Cambridge. I promise I will take the evidence to where it is safe. Leave that up to me."

John nodded. "We have to take Laura away from here as soon as possible too. It is not going to be easy because the Church agents are watching her like hawks."

Stynfeldt and John looked at each other. Stynfeldt sighed, "I think I could use a long, cold drink. But since I don't drink hard liquor it would probably have to be one of those virgin Bellinis they serve in some bars in Rome. Why don't we meet at a bar later? Remember the Tivoli? And we can talk it all over. Meanwhile, I think I know how to take one of our two little puppies out of here. Concerning Laura, I have no choice, but to leave it up to you, lad. You are the pro when it comes to that. Just make sure she is safe at all times. You know Laura is the only one in this world, which is close to my heart."

Styfeldt looked around himself." I think I'm going to commit a departure, John."

"But how?"

"Not a problem!" Stynfeldt closed the suitcase carefully and then took it off the table. "It's very light, isn't it?" He put the suitcase down in a dark corner next to the balustrade of the terrace. "See you later, John." With an agility that defied his age, he climbed over the balustrade and then down the ivy covered trellis below.

John looked around. The terrace seemed deserted. The only light came from a door and from some of the windows in the hospital wall adjoining the terrace.

John heard a brief whistle and then Stynfeldt's voice came from below. "C'mon, John, the coast is clear."

John almost fell off the terrace as he carefully lowered the suitcase over the balustrade and dropped it into Stynfeldt's outstretched arms.

"See you at the Tivoli," Stynfeldt said as he disappeared into the shadows of the garden towards the walls of the compound.

John turned around.

A Church Knight dressed like a hospital attendant stood behind him. "What are you looking for down in the gardens?"

"Oh, nothing, nothing. I thought I had dropped my keys but here they are." John dangled a bunch of keys in front of the man's face.

"Sister Dorothea sent me to bring in a suit case for one of the lady patients."

"Oh, that! Sister Dorothea already took care of it. *Bella Serra, Signore,*" John said. He walked past the attendant across the terrace into the hospital, then down the stairs, through the entrance hall, and on and out the front door, without any one trying to stop him.

The Roman night air was warm and balmy. It was a blend of many smells. Some traces of sweet rosemary and jasmine mixed with residual smells of petrol and of ancient sewers. The day's riotous traffic was a mere trickle now. Somewhere a sports car revved its engine. The tinge of church bells faded in the quiet streets and the moon appeared orange among silver lined clouds.

'The Tivoli', a small storefront bar with dark, tinted windows, was in a side street near the hotel Excelsior. The low glow of candle lamps lit an interior of contemporary chrome and glass. Due to the late hour, the bar tender took a nap behind a glass case, which displayed assorted drinks and pastries.

Stynfeldt sat at a small marble-top table in a dark corner. He sipped a virgin Bellini. "Has any one followed you?" He asked nervously.

John put a coin in the jukebox. The popular song *Volare*, one of Rome's favorites, woke up the bar tender. A young couple appeared out of a dark corner and made dancing movements to the song.

John ordered a double Bourbon and Soda with a slice of lemon in a tall glass. "I don't think so. The church mice are all sleeping."

"It's funny you should call them church mice," the Professor said. Not too long ago the Vatican was so poor not even the church mice had enough to eat. That was when they coined the expression, "as poor as a church mouse."

"I know. I heard that. It must have been more than seventy years ago. But now, with a little help from their friends, which we shall call the unmentionables, and some very smart investments, they are like gilded angels."

"Do you think they are still that rich or have they lost a lot of wealth, as they claim. I mean, could they have paid the ransom money?"

John shook his head. "You know, Professor, you worry about the strangest things. Of course they could have paid the ransom money, and with the stroke of a pen. Their investments today, are as solid as platinum."

"So you saved them a lot of money, John. That's recommendable, maybe heaven will reward you?"

John took a long drink. "Let's hope so. By the way, where is the puppy?"

"The puppy is at the station all checked in and ready to go. We are taking the train—Roma, Milan, Zurich. From there we are flying home to old England." Stynfeldt looked at his watch. The taxi will pick me up in about 15 minutes."

"Good." John nodded. But what about Laura? How do we get her out of the clutches of the Church?"

"Well, John. My official residence is an apartment at Cambridge. However, I have this secret place outside of Burwell, which is no more then ten kilometers from Cambridge. It is a cozy little cottage. No one knows about it, not even my colleagues at Cambridge. It would be the perfect place for Laura to recuperate. Laura herself told me she would love to come to England and help me finish the book about her parents."

Stynfeldt paused. "I guess this isn't easy for neither one of you, because I know you are fond of each other. But you cannot take Laura to New York and make her a housewife. You cannot keep Laura to yourself. She is far too unique and precious and she must fulfill her purpose."

"John sighed. Unfortunately you are right, Professor. But the final decision is up to her."

"Promise me you will bring her back to England where she belongs."

John's face was pale. The thought of Laura made him feel uneasy. "I promise it, if that's what Laura really wants."

Through the tinted windows, they saw a cab pull up outside the restaurant.

Styfeldt got up. "He's come for me—"

John walked Stynfeldt out to the cab.

Stynfeldt turned around abruptly. He looked straight into John's eyes. "I guess it's all right, all that business—science versus religion. As a scientist, I often toil in between scientific reality and the mystical, in a place, I call the antechamber of God. If anything should happen to me do you think they would let me into heaven pretty easily?"

John was surprised to see the glint of a tear in Stynfeldt's eye. "I don't see why not," he said, clearing his throat.

Stynfeldt nodded self-assured. "That's right. Good bye, John."

"Good bye, Professor. I'll catch up with you soon."

The taxi turned around and disappeared into a fog bank rising from the river Tiber.

John stared after the taxi. He suddenly felt a chill. It seemed as if the Professor had disappeared into the occult.

John went back into the bar and ordered another drink. He sat down at a table near the entrance and stared out the tinted window. It seemed all of Rome was veiled in black. "I wish I could smoke a cigarette," he thought. But since he was a nonsmoker that thought seemed absurd. Or like in the song *Volare,* maybe he could paint his hands and his face blue so he would suddenly be swept up by the wind and start to fly in the infinite sky. He thought of Laura, he imagined was peacefully sleeping in her hospital room. He also thought of his son Eric, who was patiently waiting for his return to New York. And he knew the Professor was right. His feelings for Laura had to be set aside for a long time to come, maybe forever.

John walked up a quiet, tree-lined street in the direction of his hotel when a strange sight brought him back into harsh reality.

On the other side of the street was a monk wearing a helmet

instead of a hood. The man wore a motorcycle helmet and the brown cloth robe of a Franciscan monk, which looked too small on him. Over all he looked funny, like an elephant on a motor scooter. The only thing that was not funny about him was a high-tech, semi-automatic hunting rifle, which was strapped, to his back. A traffic light lit up the man's face under the helmet— yellow, red, green. John did not recognize him in the distorting light.

The scooter moved on.

John continued to walk when suddenly the scooter stopped at a red light down the street. As if in slow motion, the man got off the scooter, then turned around, and pointed the hunting rifle straight at John.

John knew the man could see him clearly through the rifles target-lens. He tried to pull his revolver in the flicker of a moment but the gunshot came instantly with a loud, short bang. The bullet ricochet and was stuck in a wall behind him.

John's gun appeared in his hand. His first instinct was to shoot the man like a poisonous snake that suddenly had raised its venomous head. But firing at a monk on a motor scooter in the middle of the Roman night was not a good idea.

John took off like a sprinter, running after the motor scooter, which slowly gained distance rolling unhurriedly through a red light down the street. John was still running when he saw a loose cobblestone at the curb. He picked up the rock and threw it at the scooter. The impact of the rock on the man's helmet was not great but it caused him to stop the scooter and to look around. Dumfounded he tried to see from where the rock had come.

John had already caught up with him. He flung his entire body weight at him trying to dislocate him from the motor scooter.

The man was unmovable. He let John run into one of his great big fists and knocked him to the ground. John back skidded on the cobblestones and tried to pull himself up.

That instant the man pointed his rifle at John on the ground.

John probed the teeth in his mouth. They were still there. He pointed his Walther PK, directly at the man. Spitting out a little blood he said," who ever you are—I don't think they allow deer-hunting monks in the city of Rome."

"You are right the man grumbled under the helmet. He turned the rifle around and used it like a baseball bat knocking the gun out of John's hand. With his second strike, he whipped the rifle's handle across John's face.

John crumbled into the gutter. "Yank, go home," he heard the man say. His last thoughts before he passed out were about that voice. It seemed he had heard that voice before. It certainly was not a local voice. Who would use the word Yank as in Yankee?

The man on the motor scooter disappeared somewhere toward the Spanish Stairs. From there he dawdled across one of the bridges over the river Tiber.

It was not long John came to and he got up from the gutter. He found his gun and put it into its holster. Then he stumbled along on the right side of the cool, dark street toward a lighted area. As soon as he stepped into the light, he knew where he was. He was at the footsteps of the Spanish Stairs, one of Rome's most popular baroque monuments, where young lovers and people gathered at all times day or night. The few people that where still around shrunk back from John who was a terrible sight with his bashed-in face, his left eye swollen like a balloon, and thick blood coagulating on his suit and sleeve.

John could hear the trickle of clear water and he sensed the fountain before he saw it. He trailed over to the fountain and he felt the coolness of the stone and the lavishness of the sculpture.

He dunked his head into the water remaining under water as long as he could hold his breath. Coming up, out of the water, he looked up letting a soothing stream of the fountain's cool water run over his head and face.

The thought of Laura burned deep in his mind. "If this could happen to him, what could happen to her?" Reality set in. He had a clear hunch that Laura was in immediate danger, more so, than he liked to admit to himself. He grew increasingly concerned and worried about her, thinking he should never have left her all alone at the hospice.

Like an apparition, a young woman came up to John and handed him a white silk scarf she pulled off her shoulders. "Watch out for the *carabinieri*," she whispered, indicating a police officer who came across the plaza toward them. John took the scarf and wrapped it around his head and face. He looked at the young woman, a natural Roman beauty with olive skin and velvet eyes. The thought of her sweet charity, trying to help a stranger, almost moved him to tears. "Thank you, Madonna." He turned and quickly walked across the plaza toward a row of taxicabs.

"But that's ten kilometers outside of Rome," the driver complained as John gave him the address of Laura's hospice.

John waved a large dollar bill in front of the driver's face. "You get me there—and make it speedy!"

When they finally pulled up to the hospice's entrance, the driver turned off the car's headlights. The hospice was locked down and dark.

John tore the dollar bill in half, handing one-half to the driver. "You wait here," he said.

With the white scarf still wrapped around his face, he walked up to the elliptic shaped, glass paneled entrance. Through the doublewide entrance doors, he could see the dimly lit hall of the hospice with its black and white marble flooring and the wide neo classic staircase leading upstairs. The receptionist desk to the right looked abandoned. He rang the night bell at the right side of the entrance door again and again, urgent. He could hear the bell ringing inside but no one came.

After what seemed a long time, a sleepy night attendant finally appeared and came to the door. He looked at John, "I guess you need help, but the hospice is closed. What do you want?" he said grumpy.

"I came to see a friend of mine, Miss Laura d' Andres. It is urgent."

"Are you drunk or crazy, man? You cannot see her now. Visiting hours have been over long ago. Go home. Leave! Or I call security!"

"I wish you would call security because I am very much concerned about Laura's security. I need to see her right now!"

At this moment, two attendants and a doctor in a scrub suit came down the stairs. The doctor, with weasel eyes, was small in stature. He came up to the glass door and spoke through one of the communication windows. "What do you want?"

"I am John Cordes. I want to see Laura d'Andres right now." Pulling out his gun, he pointed it at the door. "Or I shoot the lock."

The doctor made a calming gesture. "Don't be crazy, Mr. Cordes." He signaled the night attendant to open the door.

John went straight through the door and to the stair case leading up to the patient's rooms.

The attendants stopped him, stepping in front of him.

"Wow, stop right here," the doctor said in broken English, "and put that gun away." He looked at John's face, pulling the white scarf off John's head. "Wow!" the doctor said again. He quickly examined John's injury. "You know, you should let us take care of that."

"Wow! Wow!" John could not help himself imitating the doctor who reminded him of a dachshund. He smiled painfully, realizing the situation did not lack a certain kind of humor. "You are right, I should take care of that, but first I must see Laura."

The doctor pulled John to the side. "Laura d' Andres is not here any longer."

John stared at the doctor, "I don't belief you."

"It is true. She was prepared for an operation and transported to the main Caritas hospital in Rome not even 30 minutes ago."

"What do you mean—she was prepared for an operation?"

"Well, the consensus of the doctors decided she should undergo an operation which could be very beneficial in her case."

"What kind of operation?"

"Electroshock therapy."

"Are you insane?" John yelled aloud. "I was with Laura only last night. She was perfectly fine. She was recuperating from her drug overdose. The last thing she needs is electroshock therapy. Everyone knows that it is a barbaric, ancient method which could destroy her brain for ever!"

"I am sorry Mr. Cordes. The operation was ordered by the consensus of doctors and the Vatican."

John was beside himself. "The Vatican has no right to decide what medical treatment Laura should receive. She is an adult who can fully make the decision herself. They are trying to kill her or at least wipe all memory from her brain because she knows too much. And when they are finished with her, and she is reduced to a babbling child, they are going to bury her in some convent where she will not see the time of day again!"

The doctor quickly looked at his wristwatch. "I am sorry Mr.

Cordes but the operation should be in progress as we speak. There is nothing anyone can do."

"There is nothing anyone can do—can do—can do." The words kept hollering in John's mind. He turned around and walked outside through the hospice's front door.

At that moment, a very large object crashed down the staircase behind John. He turned around to see what caused the commotion. It was a fully equipped, fully made-up hospital bed on wheels, which came rolling around the corner of the staircase. It then skipped and hopped down the stairs in weird angles. The bed came to a halt crashing into the glass panels of the entrance, which as if shaken by an earthquake, shattered into small pieces. It rained glass shards all over.

The doctor and the hospital attendants jumped aside trying to avoid the crashing bed and the shattering glass.

John thought it was time to make a run for the taxi. But he briefly hesitated and looked at the havoc the out of control bed had caused. Broken glass was everywhere. He could not believe his eyes when he saw a slim young man on top of the stairs wearing only a surgical gown. The young man ran down the stairs to John. Two men, who wore white lab coats over their dark suits, ran after the young man down the stairs, pointing their semi-automatics at him.

John immediately knew the young man who flung himself into his arms was not a man. It was Laura. Preparing her for the operation, they had cut her hair off.

The two gunmen, who obviously were Church agents, pointed their semi-automatics at John and Laura. "Let her go! Or you are both dead!" One of them yelled.

John held Laura with one hand and his gun in the other. He knew this was a stand off he could not win.

The doctor, brushing glass shards off his suit with his bare hand, came in between them. "Don't shoot," he told the Church agents. "We could never explain this. Let them go!"

John managed a grim smile. He did not put his gun away yet. Slowly backing up he tried to walk Laura out to the taxi. But Laura was bare footed. She had stepped on some of the glass. Seeing that her feet were bleeding, John picked her up and carried her out to the waiting taxi.

"You put on quite a show," the cab driver said as he took off with screeching tires. I thought the rain of glass would turn into a rain of bullets. Better you give me my money now, or I throw you both out of my cab."

John handed the driver the other half of the 100-dollar bill. "Just calm yourself and drive as fast as the old clunker can make it. I'll have another bill for you when we get there."

"But do we know where we are going?"

"Back to Rome, *imbecilio!*"

Laura's hair was short as a quire boy's and she was not wearing much under her hospital gown. She snuggled into John's arms and she lightly touched his face. "What happened to you?"

John looked briefly into the car's back view mirror. The water of the fountain and the cooling night air had a healing effect, he thought. His face looked almost normal. "Don't worry, I'll be fine," he said, "but tell me what happened to you?"

"I don't want to say anything. I just want to stay with you forever, just like this."

John kissed her gently on the forehead. "You look very cute with your new hairdo." He took off his jacket and wrapped it around Laura. "Here, put this on. How are your feet?"

Laura examined her feet picking some glass splinters from her soles. "My feet are all right—I think. It doesn't hurt that much."

John turned to the taxi driver. "The train, Rome, Milan, Zurich—do you know when it is leaving?"

The driver looked at his wristwatch. "It should have left half an hour ago. But that train is always late. Sometimes, it is up to two hours late. If you want to go to the station, there is a chance you might still catch it."

Laura caught John's idea. She sighed and moved away from him. She sat up straight. "You want me to leave with the Professor for England right now, don't you? She said with tears in her eyes. That's all right. I gladly go. But can we stop at my apartment for five minutes? I want to get some shoes, clothes, and things I need. If I miss the train I can always go into hiding and then take another train tomorrow."

Thinking of Laura's ransacked apartment, John thought an immediate get-away would be better. "I don't know," he said. "They could be watching your apartment."

He turned to the driver. "Let's try the station."

Seeing that they were already at the outskirts of Rome, the driver said, "We'll be there in five minutes."

John held Laura close again. "Tell me quickly what happened. How did you escape?"

"I overheard them talking—the night nurse and one of the doctors. The Sister thought I took the sedative she gave me. But I spit it out. I pretended I was asleep. I heard the doctor telling the Sister to get me ready for electro shock therapy. They cut off my hair and put this surgical gown on me. Then they wheeled my bed out of the room to the operating room. God only knows how I did it, but when we were on top of the stairs, I jumped out of the bed and I somehow managed to push the bed down the stairs."

John kissed Laura's forehead again. "That was brilliant, Laura-baby."

They arrived at the station. The driver held his hand up. "*Soldi!*"

"You are a greedy—" John said, swallowing his words he handed the driver more money. He did not say son of a bitch, because he remembered this kind of curse, in Italy, could be taken as an insult to the mother, something that could possibly trigger escalated feelings of revenge.

The driver pointed at a row of taxicabs near the station. "I will be waiting in that line in case you missed the train."

John pulled Laura out of the taxi. He looked at her. She was pale and shivering. He could feel her pain looking at the bleeding soles of her swollen feet. "Do you think you can make it?"

Laura hesitated. She looked at herself. With her stubble hair, barefoot and naked under the surgical gown, which was barely covered with John's jacket, she thought she looked like a scarecrow. "I think I can walk, my feet are not hurting too much, but I don't know if I really want to leave Rome looking like this."

"Come on! Come on! You look fine. Looks don't count in a moment like this. You know what will happen if they catch us."

"Okay," Laura said, "let me try."

At this time of night, there were not many travelers at the station, just the usual bums sleeping on benches and a few railroad and cleaning crews.

The loudspeakers sounded hollow as they announced the train Roma-Milan was leaving.

Styfeldt had spent some time settling himself in his comfortable *Wagon Lit* sleeper compartment. Sleepy and bored out of his mind he was glad the train was finally moving on.

Looking out the compartment's window, he was suddenly electrified when he saw John and Laura on the platform along the long train. They both looked terrible. Laura was hobbling behind

John, whose face seemed to be injured. John half carried and half dragged her along.

Styfeldt hung himself half way out the train's window waving, and signaling them. "Come on," he yelled. "This train is leaving!" He quickly moved back along the narrow corridor to the railroad car's door. He strained to open the heavy door.

Breathless, John lifted Laura up into Stynfeldt's arms. The door slammed shut behind her. Stynfeldt dragged Laura to his sleeper compartment.

The train was ready to move out of the station Laura held herself up at the compartment's open window. She looked at John who looked pitiful standing motionless on the platform, with his injured face.

As if he had forgotten something, John nervously searched his pockets. He pulled out a post card of some kind, he handed up to Laura. He then just stood on the platform looking at her with a painful expression.

Their eyes locked. Suddenly nothing existed around them, only their eyes looking into each other, trying to hold on to the connection between them. The train moved on, pulling them apart, and soon John's figure standing alone, dissolved to black.

Laura never forgot the look of John's eyes, that night, and she knew that she would see his face in the sky among the clouds and the stars. She looked at the postcard in her hands. It was a rather corny picture of the popular Italian singer Domenico Modungo and the words of his song *Volare*—

"Penso che un sogno così non ritorni mai più. Mi dipingevo le mani e la faccia di blu, poi d'improviso venivo dal vento rapito, e incominciavo a volare nel cielo infinito..."

"*I think that a dream like this will never return. I painted my hands and my face blue, then I was suddenly swept up by the wind and I started to fly in the infinite sky...*"

Laura suddenly remembered how to smile.

20.

RETURN

The prominent constellation of Orion ascended to the North.

Laura dreamt she was an indigenous princess. She was in a special place, somewhere in the warm, dark shadows of a high plane circled by dark silhouettes of round mountain peaks. Dressed in a sheet of pure, white silk she was lying on a bed of fragrant flowers looking up at the luminous night sky where she could see a myriad of stars. Though her hair was very short, it was studded with flowers and frosted with stardust.

Superimposed in the sky, among the stars of Orion, she could see the images of her mother and father. They were radiant and they looked serene and happy. Her parents were the first in a very long line of incandescent people that looked like they were shapes made of multicolored blooms and plants. The people queued up, forming an enormous wreath in the sky, a great intricate circle that was the circle of life. In the very center of the circle was the small figure of the African Eve, the Earth Mother. Draped in an iridescent blue wrap, she was ageless and race less—a brown skinned, diminutive woman with intense and dazzling golden eyes.

The impression of the scene was so beautiful it moved Laura to tears. She felt she had come home to her origins. Laura wanted to stay in this place save and warm, when an eerie feeling that some thing was wrong interrupted her lovely dream.

Out of the blue, someone pointed a long pointed icicle at her heart trying to pierce it. She sat up in bed wanting to scream. A thin breeze of cold air came through the pale blue square of the open window. With her sweat turning cold on her skin, Laura slid her bandaged feet into her slippers and walked to the window. Her feet were heeling but the scars were still scratchy and ruff.

Orion faded in the North. Its twinkling stars waved good-bye—show over, at least for tonight. Feeling a little calmer Laura sent a quick prayer to her parents, as she always did when she looked at the constellation. She believed their spirits lived on, somewhere in Orion, on the star from where the human spirit came from.

Shivering, in her white flannel pajamas, she quickly closed the window. She longed to go back to her dreams in her cozy bed with its flowery pillows and down covers. But she distinctly felt something in the house was amiss. She looked at the alarm clock, "three in the morning." She knew, without checking, what was disturbing her. Stynfeldt had not come home from Cambridge last night, again. She was alone in the house. The cottage, which usually was a nest of coziness and warmth, was cold and empty.

In the twilight of the early morning, Laura looked through the house. There was the main room with its ample sofas, Stynfeldt's chair, and a low coffee table grouped in front of a large fireplace. This was the central point of the house. The walls were covered with bookshelves and a small library led to a good size country kitchen. An adjoining bathroom, besides other amenities, featured a great old-fashioned clubfoot tub. Stynfeldt's own bedroom was on the other side of the living room. That bedroom was larger than Laura's. It had a great chocolate brown leather bed and it was decorated with African art and finds. It also had a glassed-in sunny porch that Stynfeldt had converted into a home office.

Laura had been at Stynfeldt's cottage in Burwell not even for two weeks. She had asked Stynfeldt several times, if this was the original cottage, where her parents had lived in. The answer was always no. Her parent's cottage was further up the road. It had been abandoned after someone had tried to burn it. Stynfeldt promised Laura that as soon as she was fit and able to come out of hiding they would go for long walks. He would take her up into the woods, past her parent's old cottage, and to the cemetery on the hill where her parents were buried.

Laura looked forward to be able to go for walks with Stynfeldt. She imagined that was what they did in the English countryside. They would go for long, refreshing walks during all seasons come rain or shine. She also was excitedly looking forward to see her parents gravesite, which she had imagined many times before, but never did.

Laura and Stynfeldt got along well and they quickly established a great friendship. Stynfeld, who thought the world of Laura, treated her better than he would have treated his own kin. In addition, Laura loved and admired Stynfeldt like a long lost relative. They were clinging to each other knowing that they could live and work close to each other and that neither one of them would ever have to be alone again.

Stynfeldt had taken the carpetbag to his lab at Cambridge. Commuting between Burwell and Cambridge in his small black Austin on a daily basis, he had immediately picked up work on Marthie and Leo Anderson's findings.

Laura's dark hair remained short. It stuck out around her

head one inch in length like the soft shield of a porcupine. She liked her easy new hair do and planned to keep it that way. After a few days of adjustment, learning to take care of Stynfeldt and the cottage, she would be ready to ease her mind to the point where she could actually work again. Moreover, work would be fascinating and all consuming, it would take her mind off all the things that happened, and off John who had become a distant good friend. Laura knew it would not be easy to forget about her past but with the help of friends like John and Stynfeldt, she knew her wounds would heel in time and the rest of her life would be dedicated to the great purpose of assisting Stynfeldt in the tedious task to prove to the world that what they knew was the truth about the origins of humanity. With her degrees in religious sciences and anthropology and the work she had done in the Vatican her new line of work would be rewarding. Eventually she could get her things from Rome and move into her own place nearby Stynfeldt's.

John had called several times from New York telling Laura and Stynfeldt he had established Eric in his house in New Jersey and that Eric was going to be enrolled in a normal school. He and Eric were the happiest troopers anyone could imagine. The Vatican had already sent a check for John's services. But they had not asked about Laura. It was as if Laura did not exist for them any longer. Or as if, she had never existed in Rome. John also warned them that Laura should still stay under cover because the possibility that someone could come looking for her or the carpetbag was still great.

Laura quickly checked Stynfeldt's bedroom. Her hunch turned out to be right. Stynfeldt was not home again. The bed was untouched. He had not been home in two days. This was so unlike Stynfeldt who was always glad to come home to Burwell and to Laura. He, normally, called her at least once or twice during his workday at Cambridge to see that she was safe, asking her if she needed anything he could bring her.

Stynfeldt's unexplained absence was highly disturbing. Laura felt that with her already frayed nerves she was helplessly going to slide into a panic. Her legs and feet felt like they were made of wet clay and she could feel her heart race and tighten in her chest. Weak and out of breath, she decided to go into the kitchen to make some tea to calm her nerves. She was about to strike a match when she first heard the hissing of gas and then she smelled it. Her trembling hands immediately dropped the matches when she realized all the gas burners on the stove were on without having been lit. She stared at the stove in cold terror waiting for an explosion that could come at any instant. She wondered who could have turned the gas on during the night without lighting it.

The nauseating smell of gas filled up the house quickly. Laura knew she had to act immediately. Mustering up all her strength, she picked up a chair and threw it at the kitchen window, framed by white curtains. The window burst into pieces and fresh, cool air came in. She then quickly turned off all the gas dials on the stove. Coughing and inhaling gas, she felt nauseous. She tore a kitchen towel off the wall and covered her mouth and nose. She then ran out of the kitchen and opened the front door, wide. Running through the house, she tried to open every window in reach.

Cool ghost-like fog flowed through the open door and windows. Laura felt more scared and alone than ever. She fell into one of the sofas trying to catch her breath. A migraine headache was coming on. Her hand reached for the phone. Frantic she tried to ring Stynfeldt's number at Cambridge. There was no answer, of course. It was far too early in the morning. The college was still asleep. She then dialed John Cordes office in New York. To her immense surprise, Laura was told by an answering service that John Cordes was in transit from New York to London.

"Why? What happened? Why was John on his way to England without calling her first?" Something must have happened that Laura was not aware of.

She got up from the sofa and she walked up and down nervously. She then closed the windows and the front door. The thought that an intruder was in the house while she was sleeping, scared her to death. What if he was still in the house waiting to kill her? She went into the kitchen and armed herself with a large butcher knife. Holding the knife in front of her chest, she checked every nook and cranny where someone could possibly be hiding. She knew the house had a small attic and she climbed up the narrow stairs to the attic door. The door was locked tight. Laura was satisfied that no one could possibly be up there unless they got in somehow over the steep, shingled roof, which was unlikely.

Trying her phone calls several times, she always received the same answer, the Professor is not in, and John Cordes is on his way to England.

The thought of John coming to England helped Laura to calm down. She tidied up her bedroom and the cottage and she made herself a cup of tea. She washed, brushed her teeth, and put on a light blue jogging suit and tennis shoes. She would call the airlines to find out on which plane John would be coming in.

The shrill sound of the doorbell resounded through the quiet house. It startled Laura. She looked at the wall clock, "eight in the morning." Who could it be? Not Stynfeldt. He had a key. He never rang the doorbell. Laura picked up the large butcher knife she had carelessly thrown on the coffee table in front of the sofa. She held the knife close to her chest and tippy toed to the entrance. She looked through the spy hole.

Not all of the fog had lifted yet. On the street beyond the front yard's white picket fence stood a white milk van. Blood rushing to her brain Laura suddenly felt hot. In her mind, she saw a milk van just like this, driving fast along a utility road near Burwell. Like a bullet, the van was going to hit its target without fail.

The driver of the milk van was a freckled young man. He was not sure any one was home at the cottage but he delivered his goods anyway—a bottle of milk, some warm rolls, and the morning's paper. A ray of sunshine came through the clouds touching his carrot colored hair. He still could not tell whether someone was home or not. He waved his hand just in case and he smiled his sunny smile before he drove off.

Laura opened the door.

The fog was giving way to warming sunshine. She looked left and right. No one was in sight. She quickly went out to retrieve the morning's delivery. Then she shut the front door and double locked it.

She was not in the mood to read the paper but the headline caught her eye. Laura sat down on the sofa and unfolded the paper. Front-page news—"Has the Vatican done it again?" A man wearing nothing except a monk's robe was found hanging from the Tower Bridge. The man was tortured before he was shot through the head execution style. The police have not identified the man yet. Nor did they have a clue who could have committed the ghastly crime. The only clue they had was that the man obviously was dead before he was hung from the bridge and that because he wore a monk's robe the murder could somehow be connected to the Vatican. Especially since this resembled the murder of the Vatican banker, Roberto Calvi, "The banker of God," who was also found hanging from a London bridge, the Black Friar's Bridge, a few years ago. That murder was attributed to the Mafia, who was at the time deeply connected to the Vatican. It turned out later that "The banker of God" was not only connected to the Mafia, but also to certain Masonic lodges, whose members were Church agents. The case was never solved and remained a subject of speculations.

Laura looked and looked at the black and white photograph. It was an obscured shot of a ghastly figure in monk's clothing that was hanging by the neck from the framework of the bridge. It was hard to tell anything about the man or who the man was. It all just looked like a distorted mess, reminding Laura of the dead priest, they found crucified near Castel Gandolfo. Though the picture was unclear, it still stirred Laura's emotions. She was drawn to it again and again. A deep chill froze her inside, and she admitted to herself why she could not put the paper down. There was something characteristic about the poor, tortured figure of this man, something that told her it could be Stynfeldt. The thought it could be Stynfeldt was so incomprehensible it did not strike Laura—not at first.

Feeling numbness in her heart and brain, Laura went into the kitchen. She heated some of the milk on the stove and she spread plenty of butter on one of the fresh rolls the milk van had delivered. Laura was famished. She gulped down the milk and bread like it was her last meal. She then went into the living room again and she looked at the paper again. If they had come after Stynfeldt in this gruesome manner, she could be next, she thought. There were several ways they could try to come after her and kill her. It probably was best, to give into them and let them finish their awful business since there was nothing left for her to do or say if Stynfeldt was dead. She found the butcher knife again and holding it close to her chest, she went back into the living room.

Stynfeldt never drank much. Nevertheless, he had a lovely

small bar set-up with crystal bottles and glasses and some bottles of rare, old whiskey and malt. Laura poured some whiskey into one of the glasses and drank it down taking sip after sip. She first coughed a little but then a feeling of warmth relaxed her body and mind.

Calmer now, Laura sat on the sofa. Clutching the butcher knife in her hand, she probed its pointed dip and sharpness. She pointed the knife at her heart and pushed it against her rip cage. "Don't be silly Laura," Stynfeldt's voice sounded in her head. The voice resounded, "silly—silly—silly." Drunk as Laura was, the knife stabbing her heart would not cause her too much pain. Thinking about pain, she realized that she did not feel any pain at all. So why would she stab herself? It was silly. Deep in her thoughts, she picked up the phone again. There was no dial tone.

John arrived at Heathrow airport on time. He tried to call Stynfeldt's number in Burwell. It seemed the connection was interrupted.

An old friend and colleague greeted John at the gate. Lord Charlton Carey, an impeccably dressed, corpulent man with thinning white hair. He was a top senior agent of the British intelligence service SIS, also referred to as M16, of which John had been an honorary member for many years.

"How are you Charley?"

"It is good to see you, John. May I have your ticket, please? He handed John's ticket to a younger agent who accompanied him. Take Mr. Cordes luggage to the hotel," Carey said. He turned to John. "It is all taken care of, John. Please come with me, M16 is waiting for us. However, we first must stop at the morgue at Scotland yard. I will explain everything to you in the car."

"Hold it right there," John said. He pointed at his carry-on case. This is the only luggage I have and I cannot stay in London tonight. I am urgently expected in Burwell.

A chauffeur driven nondescript black car with bulletproof windows waited curbside outside the airport. Carey's accomplice loaded John's carry-on case in the trunk. He held open the car's doors for John and Carey, who sat in the back seat. He then took the front seat next to the driver. He carefully closed the glass partition between the front and the back seats.

Carey also made sure the partition was closed so that he could talk to John in privacy.

As the car made its way through London's busy traffic, Carey talked to John. "When we called you, John, your office said you were already en route. What brought you here so fast? Was it the news about the man hanging from the bridge?"

"You guessed it, Charley."

"What do you know about him?"

"I don't know. I had a haunch. I thought I saw him less than three weeks ago in Rome. He was very much alive at the time."

Carey nodded. "That's right. We called you because we want your input. We have heard some stories about your involvement with the Vatican that lead you to Hong Kong and the infamous Tan Chee Hong, who, as you know, is no new comer to M16."

"Whatever you heard is true. I just hope the man hanging from the bridge is not who I think it is."

"He is not hanging from the bridge any longer. He is now in the morgue at Scotland Yard. As you well know, we often work with the Yard. They have this mess on their hands. The murder of whom we think is a controversial Cambridge professor involved in some controversy about the creation of humanity, which was discovered by a famous British explorer couple, thirty years ago. The Professor was apparently called to Rome as an expert by the Vatican. You must have met him."

John hesitated. "Well, yes if it is the Professor—he became a friend of mine."

Carey shook his head. "Don't tell me you have some feelings invested here, John. We want to see if you can identify him."

"Don't worry Charley. After all this time in the business, don't you think I can set my feelings apart?"

"I don't know. It is not easy for any of us, especially, since in the end, we are all only human."

Carey and John got out of the car at 10 Broadway, precisely in front of the cement-enclosed entrance to New Scotland Yard. The Yard was not new it was just newly located in a listed block of old buildings.

"Let's go, John!" Carey took his badge in his hand and waved it in front of him as if it was the key to the kingdom. The security guards shrank back in awe. Followed by John, Carey walked quickly and without further a do into the building and to a special elevator. The elevator took them directly down to the basement floors. Coming out of the elevator below ground level, they walked down another murky flight of stairs.

Carey quickly aimed his finger at the doorbell. The iron door opened in front of them as if touched by a secret wand even before his finger touched the bell. They stepped into the artificially lit, cold rooms of the morgue, which were always characterized by the distinct smell of formaldehyde and bleached death.

The corpse lay on a slab under bright neon light. It was covered with a white sheet. It reminded John of a small mummy he had once seen.

John stepped up to the slab. The attending forensic doctor lifted the sheet.

The bearded man, who seemed to have shrunken in death, was cut and bruised almost beyond recognition. The hanging-noose had left a deep purple mark around his neck. Exposed on his right temple was a bullet hole.

After examining the body in more detail, John stared at the man's face. It seemed one of his eyes looked at him from under a heavy, swollen lid. Touched by intense neon light the eye seemed to glimmer as if it had still life in it.

"Sorry, not this time, Professor," John murmured to himself. He had seen enough. He waved his hand at the forensic doctor who pulled the sheet back over Stynfeldt. John stepped away saying a quick prayer for Stynfeldt, promising him he would get who ever did this to him.

They went out of the autopsy room into the forensic doctor's office.

"It is him," John said. "It is Professor Frederico Stynfeldt from Cambridge. I guess he did not go to heaven as easily as he hoped to. I saw him in Rome about three weeks ago. He was on his way back to England, to Cambridge, and to his cottage in Burwell. I spoke to him over the phone from New York several times. The last time I spoke to him was about three days ago. He was in Burwell and he seemed perfectly fine. I mean he had no fear or any indication that someone could come after him and do this to him. Although, he made some comments back in Rome that made me think he could have had a premonition."

John paused. "Coming to think of it, he told me on the phone not even a week ago, that he had drawn up a testament, leaving all his possessions and all his intellectual property to Laura d' Andres, his adopted niece and his only living relative."

John thought about the Professor and the upbeat, positive mood he had been in, last time they spoke. "One more thing I need to tell you. It is about the bullet hole in his head. That bullet hole is from an old wound, which was inflicted on him in Rome during a terrorist attack, which he survived. I am a witness to this. This is why you have the bullet hole but not the bullet. The bullet was removed from his head in the hospital in Rome. You can easily check this with the hospital. It seems to me Professor Stynfeldt was bludgeoned to death. He was not shot to death before he was stripped and hung from under the bridge."

The forensic doctor took notes of everything John said.

Carey nodded. "That makes some sense." He looked probingly at John. "It seems you knew him well."

"Yes, I can say that. We became acquainted when we both were called in as consultants to the terrorist attacks on the Vatican."

"Why was he dressed in a monk's robe?" Carey asked.

"John thought about Rome and the man on the motor scooter, who had almost killed him. He was disguised under a monk's robe, an easy disguise that blended in well with all the priests and monks present in Rome. "The monk's robe was just a way to indicate the Vatican," John said.

"Do you think whoever did this was connected to the Vatican?"

"I don't know. It seems unlikely. You and I know the Vatican really does not kill people."

"That's true but they have many over zealous associates, who gladly will do the job for them, like the Mafia and some Masonic fractions.

John shook his head. Not likely. They did not give that much importance to the Professor. If they wanted to kill him, they would have done it in a less spectacular way. Not in a way that immediately makes you think, they did it. I think the Professor was killed by someone who was highly motivated and who wanted to make it look like it was someone connected to the Vatican."

"Well, then tell me what is the motive."

"The motive is a very strong one. If it is who I suspect it is."

The black car with John and Carey was now close to the

headquarters of M16, which was located in a large, modern building in Vauxhall.

"Can you talk to us John?" Carey asked.

"Well, yes Charley. You know I consider myself an honorary associate of M16. I don't see why I would not want to tell you the whole story, signed and delivered. But I want certain guarantees from you."

"What kind of guarantees do you have in mind?"

"I want protection for Laura d'Andres."

"Who is Laura d' Andres?"

"Laura d'Andres was born in London as Laura Anderson and therefore she is a British subject. She is the daughter of the Andersons, a famous British explorer couple who was killed outside Burwell by a milk truck, more than thirty years ago. She is also Professor Stynfeldt's adopted niece and heir of her parents and Stynfeldt's controversial, intellectual property, which is considerable and which could turn out to be sensational after it is published—the perfect motive for Stynfeldt's murder. I will tell you everything I know, if you promise to put Laura Anderson under the protection of M16."

It got dark around five o'clock in the afternoon. Light fog shrouded the few street lamps that came on in Burwell. Covered with a cozy wool blanket, Laura had fallen asleep on the sofa blissfully drunk from Stynfeldt's good whiskey. The butcher knife that had slipped her hand lay cold and shiny on the rug in front of the sofa.

A teakettle whistled. Laura woke up. The cottage was warm and dark. The fireplace was lit and light came from the kitchen. It seemed someone was busy in the kitchen making tea.

"Stynfeldt is home," Laura thought and a feeling of gratitude and happiness overcame her. She sat up straight on the sofa and looked for her shoes. Her foot pushed the nasty knife under the sofa table. "No need for that. Stynfeldt was home—Thank God."

Laura called out. "Thank God, uncle Fred, you are home!"

"A muffled voice came from the kitchen—I am coming, Laura."

A tall figure, silhouetted by the fire light came out from the kitchen, carrying a tray with two cups of tea.

In the dark room, Laura could not make out the man against the light, but she instantly knew it was not Stynfeldt.

"Is it you John?" Laura said with a glimmer of hope in her voice. This is no time for silly disguises."

The man stood in front of the coffee table. His large frame was covered with a hooded monk's robe, belted with a rope, and he wore an eye patch over his left eye. "If you make a move, I kill you," he said, and he flung the tray with the hot tea into Laura's lap.

Laura who could feel the hot liquid scalding her crotch and thighs, screamed on top of her lungs. With tears streaming from her eyes, she instinctively bent down searching for the knife. Then with the gleaming knife in hand, she catapulted herself up and she jumped at him. Aiming the knife at his face, she went for his only good eye.

He grabbed both of her wrists and shook her off like a mad cat. The knife fell out of her hand. "Aren't we a spirited kitten," he said, tossing her back onto the sofa.

Laura crouched on the sofa in a fetal position.

The man shook off the monk's robe. He sat down in Stynfeldt's chair opposite Laura. "Do you know who I am?"

"I don't know," she stammered. It seems I have seen you in my worst nightmare. Laura focused on him. He was a muscular, brutal looking man wearing a Para-military-jump-suit and lace-up army boots. His head was shaven only showing a hint of a marine's crew cut and he wore a black patch over his left eye.

"Let me introduce myself. My name is Raphael, I am a former marine colonel, and I work for the honorable Tan Chee Hong of Hong Kong. Does this mean anything to you?"

Laura was defiant. I may have heard of Tan Chee Hong but your name means nothing to me. What do you want?"

"That's right, Laura, dear. You probably saw me in a nightmare. Do you remember Guilin or Hong Kong? Do you remember Tan Chee Hong? Do you remember Jimmy Lu and Chyna?"

"I remember Jimmy Lu and the house on the River Li. I think I met Chyna once but I don't remember what she looked like."

"Well she was very beautiful, but she also was a traitor. That is why Tan Chee Hong killed her. I did not kill Jimmy Lu or burn his house, it was one of my crews. I was busy attacking A.P.S. that night, orders of Tan Chee Hong. My crew found you at the burning house, and to Tan Chee Hong's delight, they brought you to Hong Kong. You were quite a prize for Tan Chee Hong."

"It is all a patchy, foggy nightmare!" Laura yelled frustrated that the sheer presence of the man had an almost hypnotic power over her that seemed to pin her to the sofa.

"Shah. Not so loud. The neighbors could hear us."

"But there are no neighbors."

"How convenient. So, let's not waste any more time."

Raphael pulled out an expandable rubber covered steel police baton, which was hanging from his black rubber belt. With a loud sickening noise, the baton hit the sofa table almost breaking it in half. "You see this, Laura, the police are looking for it. It is the murder weapon that killed your good friend the Professor. I wiped it clean as well as I could but I think a little of his blood and brain is still on there. It is a shame but the Professor would not talk. He protected you to the end."

Laura was in pain and sickened to the core. "How did you find the cottage?"

"Let us just say I have my ways."

Laura could feel her stomach cramp. She wanted to throw up. "What do you want from me, she said with a weakening voice."

Raphael pointed at his eye patch. "You see this. Tan Chee Hong took my left eye. He will take my other eye if I do not bring him the last two space rocks." With a dizzying bang, the baton hit the sofa table again, this time splitting it in half.

"My parent's carpetbag with the rocks and skulls was given to the Professor for further research. I do not know what he did with it. It is probably somewhere in Cambridge. I would have gladly given it to you if that would have saved his life, Laura stammered."

The baton came down again in a flash. It missed Laura's head but it hit her collarbone.

Laura screamed again as she could feel her collarbone fracture. Num with pain, she looked up. Raphael stood over her ready to hit her again. "Are you sure the space rocks are not here in this house. If you do not tell me where they are I will kill you just like I killed the Professor."

Laura's tried to get control over her faltering voice.

"The rocks are in the carpetbag either in the lab or in the vault at Cambridge. I will take you there tomorrow morning if you want."

"It's too late for that. They are after me fierce for killing the Professor. However, they will not suspect you. You can go there and check out the rocks for me. In fact, we can go there right now. You can shield me Laura-dear, in case anyone tries to stop us."

"I can't do that," Laura said painfully. I have never even been to Stynfeldt's lab. I couldn't find the carpetbag even if I wanted to." Her hands found the silver tea tray. She slammed the tray upwards right in between Raphael's teeth.

For a moment, Raphael stood stunned biting on the silver tray sticking out of his mouth.

Laura flung herself over the back seat of the sofa and ran for the door.

For some crazy miracle, the door was not locked. Laura ran out and down the street. Annoying, cold rain and mist had settled in. She ran as fast as she could, ignoring the pain. First, she wanted to take the turn down to Burwell but when she saw Raphael coming after her from that direction, she decided to take the high road through the woods and up the hill. She knew it was her parent's cottage when she saw it. A spooky looking place surrounded by big old trees. Shortly after passing the cottage, Laura stopped in front of a big white wall and a wrought iron gate, which stood open. It was the Burwell cemetery.

Now, Raphael almost caught up with her. She ran through rows of graves trying to find a place to hide when her instinct told her more than her eyes could see—She stood in front of her parent's grave. It was an old grave with an old head stone under a hedge-rose bush. Laura briefly saw the inscription on the headstone—Martha and Leopold Anderson—explorer-scientists. Next to their grave was a freshly dug-up grave with a big mound of earth beside it. The grave was almost 6 feet deep. Laura wanted to jump down into it and hide but the grave was too deep. She could hear Raphael closing in. She got down on her behind and let herself slide down over the wet loam. Crouching deep in a corner of the grave, she tried to be invisible.

Raphael spotted her right then. He pulled out a light, extendable semi-automatic gun from the armament he wore under his jump suit. He pointed the gun at Laura. "Good by Laura."

Laura screamed. "Don't shoot I am the only one who can lead you to the carpetbag and to the space rocks."

Raphael let out a loud, scary laugh that hollered through

the cemetery. "Is that so, my dear? You just told me you do not even know the way to Cambridge. You are a big disappointment, Laura. I am afraid you are a liability more than an asset. You are right. I should not just shoot you. That is not very creative. I can think of something much better."

He put the gun down and began to shovel the dug-up dirt over her.

"Ashes to ashes—Ashes to ashes," he repeated over and over again as he shoveled the wet dirt over Laura. He let out a chilling laugh. "This is a first. I have never had the pleasure of burying someone alive. I'm really enjoying this."

Laura cried and pleaded with Raphael but he paid no attention to her.

"Ashes to ashes," he repeated as he shoveled the wet, cold loam over her.

They both heard the church bell ring down in Burwell. Raphael was even happier. "Ashes to ashes and the church bells ring what a wonderful, fitting scene."

"You are insane," Laura screamed spitting out wet loam.

"Ashes to ashes," Raphael was a very strong man, it did not take him much time to shovel the dirt into the grave.

Laura tried to escape. Digging her hands in, she tried to crawl up the slippery sides of the grave, but he just kept throwing large shovels full of heavy dirt at her with incredible speed.

Falling down repeatedly, she now was almost buried. She spit and coughed up dirt. Almost completely covered she tried to plead with Raphael again, but Raphael refused to hear her.

Laura kept pleading desperately as much as she could. "Please, please do not bury me alive. I have not done anything to disserve this."

For some inexplicable reason, Raphael suddenly stopped shuffling dirt. "Ashes to ashes," he said like an old broken record.

"You are right. This is far too time consuming. In addition, who knows someone could still find you and dig you out again. Don't worry I wont bury you alive. You are a nice lady. I must make sure you die nicely and you will never talk. I will finish you off with this first. He grabbed his gun and pointed it at Laura's head, which was barely sticking out of the dirt.

"The *coup de grace*," Laura thought waiting for the bullet to hit her and she regretted that she would not even have enough time to say a prayer. She tried to look at the sky. There was only rain and darkness.

As Raphael pulled the trigger, a bullet from John's Walther hit him. Astonished he turned around trying to point the gun at whoever shot him. That moment a second shot hit him again. Raphael crumbled like a mortally wounded elephant. He dropped the gun and fell into the grave on top of Laura.

John looked down into the grave. He saw the heap of a large man in a camouflage jump suit lying in the mud face down. He was almost certain it was Raphael. However, he wanted to be sure. He let himself slide into the grave and turned the man so he could see his face. It seemed one of the bullets had entered his head from behind and it had come out through Raphael's right eye. The eye patch had come off from his other eye. The two black holes of his eyes stared into space. Rain filled the eyes cavities. It looked like the man was crying bloody tears. Only John knew, Raphael was not crying. He was not sorry about anything. Shooting him was far too nice a death for him. He deserved to be tortured just like many of his victims.

John had no time to think about the irony of fate. He heard Laura whimpering and coughing in the mud. He tried to dig her out with his bare hands.

She was very quiet now, pale, and breathing shallow.

The mist had turned to rain and the grave filled up with mud and water. Laura seemed to be slipping from John's hands sinking deeper. John looked around for something to hold onto. He found a scraggly vine hanging from a tree behind a rosebush. The vine was strong enough. Holding on to the vine John was able to pull himself up to the rim of the grave and never letting go of her hand, he pulled Laura out with him.

Rain washed over Laura's face washing the mud away. Like a newborn babe, she took a deep breath. She opened her eyes and looked at John. She laughed and cried at the same time. "John oh John, I am so glad you found me."

EPILOGUE

It was a lovely fall day, unusual for this time of year. Sunshine quickly tried the muddy puddles. The last of the residual leaves, unhurried, drifted from the branches of the trees adding to the gold and purple carpet on the ground.

Stynfeldt's sensational death had caused quite a stir. It seemed he had found fame and recognition in death more than he had found during his life.

Most of them really did not know or understand what it was the Professor had discovered but the rumors were enough to make him a martyr who was tortured and who died for his convictions.

Hundreds and hundreds turned out at Stynfeld's funeral. More than the small cemetery at Burwell had ever seen. There were faculty and scholars of Cambridge's intellectual community as well as clergy of all kind, including scholars of all faiths. The anthropology department and bio-paleontology department, headed by Lord Cavendish himself turned out in numbers.

The small contingent of Burwell's police tried to hold back the masses, stirred by the press, who relentlessly brought news reports about the controversial professor and his space aliens, in the papers and on TV. There was talk Professor Stynfeldt was the winner of the Nobel Price for science.

Among the ones who seemed to know, there was hushed talk about the Professor's merits and accomplishments and that he had not only found the "missing link" but the link that put humans in touch with space and the Universe. Some said that his discovery was greater than what humankind ever could expect to see. Others said that he had seen the face of God. And less spiritual people said that he had to die because he had seen the face of God.

Stynfeldt, who was still traveling through the Earth's atmosphere to the galaxy of Orion, looked down at it all and he smiled a sunny smiled that warmed the scene like sunshine. By now, he was beginning to know it all. He was about to enter the realms of the Spirit of Enlightenment otherwise know as the Holy Ghost, where he was to find completion and happiness. He looked down at the funeral scene swallowing a warm and bitter tear. Knowing that he would never be a human being again was incredibly sad. However, all those feelings would soon be gone too.

The Professor's poor, tortured, remains were laid to rest in the grave next to Laura's parents. As the sun slowly disappeared beyond the trees, the cemetery began to empty.

Laura, who wore a tailored, black suit and a small veiled hat, had found a bench under a willow tree not too far from the graves. Glad to get off her feet, in her narrow black shoes, she sat down. She had a good overview of both her parents and Stynfeldt's graves. Stynfeldt's grave was covered with a mound of flowers and wreaths, so many in fact, the fragrant loot had spilled over and it covered her parent's grave right next to Stynfeldt's.

It was gratifying to see both graves covered with a wonderful thick blanket of flowers. Laura wanted to take a picture. But lacking a camera she just took a picture in her mind, which she filed in the files of precious memories.

As she sat there, looking over the graves and the cemetery, she felt not alone. Even though John was in the air somewhere over the Atlantic, she knew he would be back to visit her. Their friendship would never end. And the dead were there with her. She found solace, knowing that when her time came, her human bones would be resting in the grave with her parents next to Stynfeldt and her spiritual being would be reunited with them in a place somewhere in the sublime realms of Orion. And what a reunion that would be.

As Laura pondered her thoughts about life and death, she could see from her vantage point, a tall good-looking man stepping out of a black Rolls Royce limousine, which had pulled up near the cemetery entrance. The man wore a light, black overcoat over a pin striped suit. As he came closer, Laura saw he was very handsome with his medium length snow-white hair, which framed a rectangular, tanned face with bright blue eyes looking at her through silver-rimmed glasses.

"Are you Dr. Laura Anderson?" he asked.

Laura, who was not used to be addressed by her parent's name or her academic titles, looked at him and nodded. "I suppose I am."

"I am William Cavendish, he said. He pointed at the small bench. Do you think I could sit down there next to you?"

Laura moved a bit to make room for him. She thought it was a little odd she should be sitting informally on a park bench with this high and mighty man. But then thinking about her time at the Vatican, she was used to stranger things.

Lord Cavendish took her hand. He looked at both graves. "I guess condolences are in order."

Laura nodded. "Yes, thank you."

"I came here, of course, for Professor Stynfeldt's funeral, but also to talk to you, Dr. Anderson. You see, when we went through all the work and papers the Professor left behind, we found amazing things. Especially the findings of your parents which are sensational and which could be of such great impact that the world would never be the same. And that maybe, with all this knowledge about the origins of the Spirit of Enlightenment, humanity could finally change for the better. I guess no one paid enough attention to what the Professor was up to all those years. Now we know it is something very big. The work is near completion. It just needs someone to pull it all together. I do not know if the Professor had inklings that he would meet his fate so suddenly, but he left everything to you. And, of course, you are the heir of your parent's intellectual property. Even though, technically, Cambridge could be an owner too. However, we get all that straightened out by our legal department. Moreover, by a coincident of fate, you have the right background to continue the work. Your two degrees and your work experience highly qualify you."

Lord Cavendish cleared his throat. "Therefore, I am pleased to tell you, Cambridge is offering you a position as a science-research-fellow and a monetary grant to complete and publish the work of your parents and of Professor Stynfeldt. You will have the full back up of all members of the scientific community at Cambridge as well as the NASA space exploration agency. We have contacted them already. We work with them sometimes on projects of universal importance."

Laura stared at him wide-eyed as his words began to sink in.

"And that's not all," Lord Cavendish said. "We think that this project also deserves national priority as part of the exploration of space and the Universe. But because of its sensitive nature it must be kept at top-secret level."

"I understand," Laura said.

"Well, yes. I am sure you understand. And that is why you

also are to remain under the protection of the British intelligence service, we call MI6."

Laura sat up straight. She was composed and ready to take on the challenge. "I will be honored to take on what ever you are proposing."

Lord Cavendish smiled his captivating smile. I knew you would. Please call me at Cambridge first thing Monday morning. I will personally guide you through all the necessary arrangements that will have to be made."

Laura took Lord Cavendish's hand. "My parents, Professor Stynfeldt, and I thank you, with all our hearts."

"Very good," Lord Cavendish said. He got up from the bench and pointed at the limo. "Dr. Anderson, could I give you a ride home?"

"I appreciate your offer but I would rather walk. My new home is not very far from here. Just down the hill in walking distance."

Night had come quickly. Laura walked slowly down the road, passing her parent's former cottage, to Stynfeldt's place, which now was her own. Many thoughts turned in her head,—*like the windmills of my mind— Dr. Anderson, you are qualified—humanity was created on Earth by DNA change—we are the direct predecessors of the African Eve—The human spirit is invincible—invincible—invincible—*

Laura looked up at the clear night sky. Orion's stars twinkled above. "Come home, come home to us," they seemed to tell her.

Laura smiled. Twenty, forty, fifty years meant nothing out there. Only here on Earth, given time, she could possibly make a difference.

***